The Once and Future Queen

The Once and Future Queen

PAULA LAFFERTY

First published in Great Britain in 2026 by Hodderscape
An imprint of Hodder & Stoughton Limited
An Hachette UK company

The authorised representative in the EEA is Hachette Ireland,
8 Castlecourt Centre, Dublin 15, D15 XTP3, Ireland (email: info@hbgi.ie)

1

Copyright © Avalon Books LLC 2026

The right of Paula Lafferty to be identified as the Author of the
Work has been asserted by Choose an item in accordance with
the Copyright, Designs and Patents Act 1988.

Edited by Mackenzie Walton
Cover Design by Dauphine Dopamine (Trade) or CatrinaPaints (Deluxe)
Typography & Cover Formatting by Rachel St Clair
Interior Formatting by Alexia E. Pereira
Illustrations by Joe Requeza and Rise+Wander (Aftyn Shah)
Maps by Chaim Holtjer and Paige Dainty

All rights reserved. No part of this publication may be reproduced, stored in a retrieval system, or transmitted, in any form or by any means without the prior written permission of the publisher, nor be otherwise circulated in any form of binding or cover other than that in which it is published and without a similar condition being imposed on the subsequent purchaser.

All characters in this publication are fictitious and any resemblance to real persons, living or dead, is purely coincidental.

A CIP catalogue record for this title is available from the British Library

Hardback ISBN 978 1 399 74599 4
Trade Paperback ISBN 978 1 399 74602 1
ebook ISBN 978 1 399 74600 7

Typeset in Myriad Pro

Printed and bound in Great Britain by Clays Ltd, Elcograf S.p.A.

Hodder & Stoughton policy is to use papers that are natural, renewable and recyclable products and made from wood grown in sustainable forests. The logging and manufacturing processes are expected to conform to the environmental regulations of the country of origin.

Hodder & Stoughton Limited
Carmelite House
50 Victoria Embankment
London EC4Y 0DZ

www.hodderscape.co.uk

To my mom and dad, who never cracked open the countless notebooks of story snippets I left strewn all over the house. Who always bought me new notebooks even though I never finished a single story in one of them in all my childhood. While I believed this moment an impossibility, you believed it was an inevitability. And to Erin, who read every notebook she came across and shamelessly came to me demanding to know what came next. You are the reader I write for.

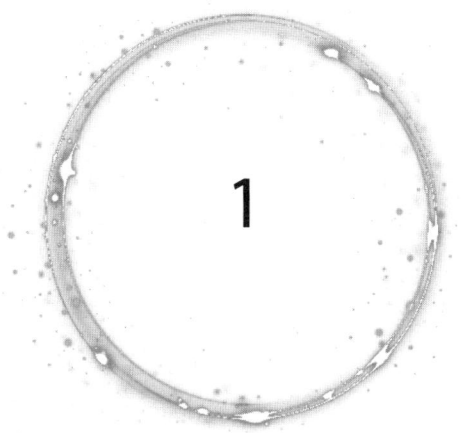

1

To the best of her knowledge, Vera was twenty-two years old. And by the time she finished tying the laces of her running trainers on this early October morning, she had ten hours and fourteen minutes remaining of the life she knew in a little town called Glastonbury in the southwest of England.

Glastonbury's highest buildings topped out at three stories. And still, when the air was just right, wind whipped down the High Street as if in a tunnel. You could almost smell that something there was not simply ancient but sacred. Many tourists have driven near to Glastonbury with the aim of passing by, but were drawn in. All it took was coming close enough to town to see the Tor, the mystical hill that rises above the landscape with its singular stone tower (just ruins, really) perched at the peak.

A passerby aims to pass by, sees the Tor, is drawn in, goes home, and says to the people they love the most, "You have to come and see it, too." And so, pilgrimages to this place began some 10,000 years ago. To even the slightly attuned spirit, Glastonbury positively hums with sacred energy, a mystery never to be solved and always held like a breath of anticipation.

The only poor soul who would say in skeptical disbelief, "A hill? You want me to come see . . . a hill?" simply hasn't seen it yet or, bless them, they have a disposition entirely the opposite of curious. Boring, even, one might say.

The Tor draws a soul in, the wind whips up some untapped and wildly alive place, and the whispers of pilgrims who've walked these grounds echo up through the feet with every step. You drink the waters of the well, and the work is done. Transformation—and something else, too, is ripe for the picking.

Pick a legend: pagan gods and goddesses, King Arthur, even Jesus himself. Their stories all have some home here, along with ordinary, everyday people. Some who live in Glastonbury sell supplies for the household witch, artifacts and gems said to contain deep magic. Others craft handmade goods or brew spectacular coffees. Some sell carpet or repair automobiles. Whether they deal in what might be called mundane goods or not, it can't be helped. Wherever you live, whatever air you breathe, whatever oddball people might pass through, it all becomes ordinary.

And the extraordinary existence of living in Glastonbury amongst the Tor and the legends and the mystical air is all but forgotten in the business of living a life.

Alas, the price we pay for proximity to wonder: it gets cheap.

It was for precisely this reason that as often as she could manage it, Vera would set her alarm before sunrise and jog up the steep path leading to the top of the Tor. She craved the wonder and was willing to pay for it with her footfalls and sweat. She wasn't particularly fast, and sometimes the steeper stretches were more of a trudge, but she loved the predictable race against the sun's morning appearance. Vera woke with just enough time to dress and scurry downstairs from the innkeeper's quarters at the George and Pilgrims Hotel before bolting out the front door.

She carried only a torch for guidance—no phone, no music, no distractions. Just the noise of her feet on the pavement until she turned off the road and onto the narrow gravel path that curved back and forth along the spine of the Tor.

Vera used to grin in the darkness when the wind pushed at her back, feeling like some greater force carried her onward. She didn't believe that anymore. It was only wind, whining in her ears as it whipped by, no longer an omen of good to come. Indeed, its mere sound was a harbinger of remembering what she had lost.

She inhaled a ragged breath, powerless to stifle the rising memory. That sound. It was like the day two years ago when she'd rushed into the university library. Only then, the whistling wind came with flashing lightning in its wake.

It had stormed mightily. She'd scarcely heard thunder like it before or since. There hadn't been many other people there, so Vera weaved through the halls and bookshelves, quietly singing to herself while she waited for the rain to slow.

She hadn't even seen the young man sitting on the floor with his back against the wall (probably because she was so used to no one ever noticing her) until he called out as she passed by, "Do you take song requests?"

She'd stumbled to a stop and spun around to face him. It was the first time Vera met him, though she would come to know him so intimately: Vincent. He smiled without glancing up from the sketch pad on his knees. Over the next two years, Vera delighted in calling him Vincent-not-Van Gogh, the artist who had both ears. His hair even had a shine of red to it under the brightest sunlight.

As she urged her feet up the Tor's steepest section, Vera saw that whole day play out in her mind, like the memory was in fast-forward or like time didn't exist at all. How she'd stopped to talk to Vincent, then spent hours poring over his sketches. It was late evening before either realized that the storm had long since ceased. When they left, they went for a pint (which became three) before he walked her home. Vincent kissed her cheek as he bid her goodnight.

They didn't go many days without seeing one another after that. She'd loved Vincent fast, and he loved her well in return.

He had now been dead for four months.

The taste of love lost was cruel, and the permanence of Vincent's death left her shattered.

These days, her run was less pursuit of wonder and more fleeing from feeling; a desperate attempt to escape the pain of his loss and her own guilt at how she could have stopped it.

It was a fifteen-minute jog on her slowest days. St Michael's Tower, the marker of her destination and the lone structure on the Tor, loomed as a vague dark mass in the pre-dawn light. The tower was nothing more than four stone walls with no roof overhead. If she'd kept jogging when she reached the Tor's level top, she would have continued straight through an open arch doorway on one side of the tower and out another opposite, where it opened to a terrace the size of a back garden with a geographical compass right in the middle. It looked like a round stone bench, but on closer inspection, the silver disk at its center had fine arrows etched into it, pointing in all directions. They marked the bearings for what an observer would see if they could look far enough: twenty-five miles north to Bristol (where Vera had gone to university), eleven miles southeast to Camelot (yes, the one of legend), seven miles southwest to Somerton . . . and on.

More days than not, there were others in town who craved to shake the shackles of mundanity on the Tor at daybreak. Today, there was no one else.

Vera walked past the tower, thoughtlessly trailing her fingers along the stones as she always did out of a visceral pull to connect with the ancient things around her. She looked westward toward the ruins of the Glastonbury Abbey, remembering the time during a school trip there when her primary school teacher scolded her for touching every ruin within reach. It wasn't light enough to make out the town a mile or so down the lane. She couldn't see the abbey ruins from here anyway. The impressive stone columns of a once grand cathedral were tucked away right off the High Street, nestled so tightly that it was another spot of astonishment for visitors. One moment a traveler had their eyes glued to their phone for directions, and the next they rounded a corner, looked up, and had their breath taken away by the scope of the ruins.

When Vera's fingers found the corner of the tower, they lingered there for a breath longer. With minutes to spare before the sun's daily miracle, she took off her shoes and socks and tucked them next to the tower's base while she ventured out onto the grass and wiggled her bare toes on the cool, dew damp ground.

It was barely a stone's throw to her favorite seat in the house. Almost exactly between St. Michael's Tower on one end of the Tor and the large stone compass on the other, there was a perfectly smooth patch of grass for sitting and watching the day begin. According to the compass, she faced legendary Camelot, included in the list for tourists, yes; but locals believed the legends more fervently than anybody else.

It was clear by now with only one, maybe two minutes left before daybreak, where the sun would first appear. Vera trained her eyes on the glowing spot, hardly daring to blink. It was a perfect sunrise day. No clouds to block the view, yet thick mists had gathered low, surrounding the Tor. They would burn away within hours, but when the mist packed in densely, it was like a blanket laid over the valley that held the moment suspended, containing it for an extra second. She held her breath, knowing the first eyelash of sun was on the edge of fluttering into view.

And there it was.

There were taller mountains and more stunning landscapes, but Vera would be hard pressed to believe there was another sunrise quite like this one anywhere in the world.

She stayed for the whole thing until the sun had cleared the horizon, and it worked to buoy her soul. At least for a moment. Then she gathered her shoes, touched the tower one last time, and jogged back the way she came.

If she'd turned to look as she passed the old White Spring temple at the foot of the hill, she might have seen the cloaked man standing in its doorway. He'd arrived inside the temple the moment the sun crested the horizon, and he would be gone, Vera with him, by the time night fell.

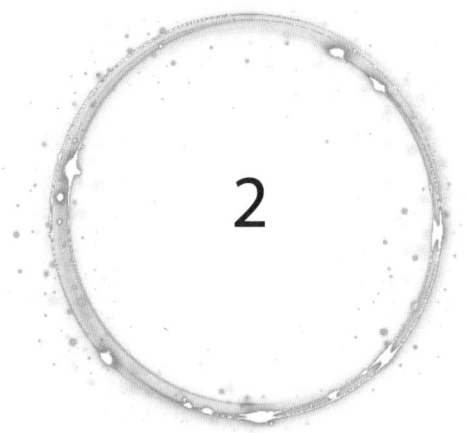

2

Vera never intended to work at the hotel. Her parents had been the George and Pilgrims' proprietors all her life, and she'd practically lived there even before she actually moved into the innkeeper's quarters after graduating from university last spring.

While her mother Allison tended to guests, six-year-old Vera had colored by the fireplace in the pub. When her father Martin swept through the guest rooms, perpetually racing to change linens in a record time, nine-year-old Vera searched for hideouts and hidden passageways. In lodgings built in the sixteenth century, a wandering child was bound to find all sorts of secret spots tucked away.

Vera returned to the hotel with just enough time to shower and get dressed for her many daily roles. She pulled her hair into a low ponytail and decided that was good enough. Tidy and nice. Her features were attractive and even, nothing markedly off-center or unconventional: average-sized nose, standard lips, normal-length eyelashes, unevenly wavy brown hair. Pretty, but not extraordinary.

She was embarrassed to admit it, but there'd been a time when being unnoticeable had bothered her. Now, after losing Vincent, moving through life without drawing attention was a relief. The sphere of her world had gotten very small, and it was the simplest way to press on in the space of loss. And her little innkeeper's quarters, so outside what she'd planned for herself, brought comfort. If she could keep her mind from drifting to him, she'd be fine.

There'd only been six rooms occupied at the George the night prior. Vera got word that one family of lodgers was headed to Stonehenge today, so she carefully built a replica of the standing stones out of butter pats on their table. They were delighted to be greeted by a piping hot breakfast and a preview of their day that they could spread on their toast.

Guests filtered in while Vera served tea and coffee and took their orders. They spoke politely to her but looked right past her. When they left and she wished them a good day, all of them, including the family who'd enjoyed Vera's butter art, said goodbye as if they'd never spoken to her before.

As if she were a stranger.

It would have been jarring if she hadn't spent her whole life this way, with everyone around her treating her as a forgettable background player. There had been a few notable exceptions over the years. Vera's parents, of course. And once, when she was twelve, Vera became inexplicably interesting to her classmates. Girls wanted to be her friends; boys wanted to be her boyfriend. She was invited to special celebrations, even an overnight birthday trip to London. Then, they all simultaneously seemed to decide they didn't want to be around her anymore. She hadn't had some awful, embarrassing moment. No one was cruel. They just . . . lost interest.

Another time, during her third year at university, when she'd been at her absolute lowest and loneliest, something similar happened. Like a lightning strike, Vera had a group of friends overnight. She dated. She had fun. And like before, there was an abrupt and silent agreement that they would all move on without her. It didn't matter as much then because she found Vincent during that last spell. He didn't forget her.

And now he was gone, too.

It wasn't normal, but Vera didn't know anything different. To her, a life of insignificance was absolutely ordinary.

She brought fresh tea out for the late risers. They scrolled their phones or read the morning paper, except for one man who was markedly out of place in his sharp, grey tweed waistcoat over a crisply pressed shirt. A silver chain looped from his lapel to his breast pocket. He had no phone or reading material.

He looked wise, yet not old. And stately, though not stuffy. His attire matched his perfectly manicured beard, dark and strikingly speckled with silver, and long hair kept in a tight knot at the nape of his neck. People roamed Glastonbury in all manner of clothing. That wasn't why the hairs raised on Vera's arms every time she turned in his direction. It was . . . well, it was hard to say. He sat with his hands folded in front of him, only moving to pull out a pocket watch attached to the end of the silver chain. He inspected it, put it back in his pocket, and resumed doing nothing.

It hit Vera as she delivered his steaming tea kettle and milk: he'd been watching her. No one watched her.

"Thank you, Vera," he said.

She'd been turning back to the kitchen but froze mid-turn and looked back at him.

She faltered before finding her voice. "You're quite welcome. I'm—I'm surprised you remembered my name," she said, though she didn't recall introducing herself.

He had bright green eyes that met Vera's with a startling intensity. The man cocked his head to the side, and his eyebrows knitted together.

"Of course I remember you." He smiled, and something about him looked sad.

Neither spoke for an uncomfortable stretch as Vera hoped she'd recognize him. No memory came to her.

"Well," she said, breaking the leaden silence. "Let me know if you need anything."

He nodded, mouth quirked up quizzically at the corners as he turned his attention to his tea.

By the time Vera returned with his check, the man was gone. His payment left on the table was the only evidence that he'd been there at all.

Vera moved on to housekeeping duties, the interaction forgotten as a momentary oddity. The daily linens race, as Martin called it, was his favorite duty. Vera was only temporarily in charge of it until Martin was well enough for it again. But she'd inherited his love for the simplicity of a morning spent setting the rooms. She listened to her favorite music in her earbuds, and when the best bits of the song came up, she paused mid linen-tucking to dance with abandon. In such an old hotel, having music served another purpose, too.

The 500-year-old building stretched and groaned. Its porous wooden beams soaked in the memories of pilgrims past—and every so often, they leaked back out. Anybody who had ever worked at the George and Pilgrims and many guests would attest with their own experiences that the place was haunted, and thoroughly so. Being alone in the George amongst the ghosts and noises didn't feel so unnerving with music in her ears. But there was almost always something a touch abnormal.

Today, Vera was changing sheets in Room One, particularly known for being haunted, when the television turned on of its own accord. Then, the massive old wardrobe doors slammed open while Vera sanitized the washroom. Both things were easily explained away to aged wiring or wiggly latches on old furniture.

But she had seen her fair share of less explicable happenings, and once, she'd seen a ghost. It was another Tor sunrise nearly a year ago on the Winter Solstice. As she sat in her usual spot with a blanket wrapped around her shoulders to stave off the cold, movement drew her eyes away from the horizon to a spot not fifteen feet before her. A little cloud had been mysteriously left behind by the gathering mist in the field below, a puffy sheep of fog that wandered too far from the flock.

It took shape as Vera watched—a person. A man who paced half a dozen steps before turning and doing the same in the other direction.

"Holy shit," she had whispered.

He had stopped when she spoke, as if he heard her. And he turned and looked directly at Vera. He had facial features, but they were weathered like a garden statue left outside through years of wind and rain, worn down and indiscernible. She was transfixed on the spot as the sun broke the plane of the horizon. When that first beam rose, and its light hit the specter, he dissolved into mist, and the mist was gone in a whisper.

Compared to that, odd occurrences like the ones this morning were more than manageable. Vera finished the rooms without further incident and moved on to her midday lunch shift in the pub.

By the time she even had a moment to think, the last guests had gone and she'd cleared all the tables. It was four p.m. She weaved through the empty tables, working from the back toward the front window, pushing in chairs and wiping down tabletops. She noticed a few spots of heavy crumbs on the floor and turned to get the broom from behind the bar but was startled to realize she wasn't alone. Where moments before had sat an empty chair, now it was occupied by someone wearing a hooded robe, their back to her.

After the initial jolt, she continued toward the bar.

"So sorry," she said, "dinner service doesn't begin until five. Tea's available in about a three-minute walk in any direction if you—" She stopped as the man tilted his head up, revealing his face.

Though he was in a cloak and not smartly dressed anymore, it was unmistakably the man from this morning. The corner of her mouth tugged upward. She hadn't pegged him as the druid, new-age type. Vera was pleasantly surprised to have gotten him wrong.

"Oh. Hello again," she said.

He smiled, and it was just like that morning. He looked sad. "May I have a word, Vera?"

She stiffened. He'd called her by name this morning, too.

"Erm, all right," she said. "Is . . . is there something I can help you with?"

"A great many, many things, I should think." He gestured at the chair across from him. "Please, sit."

Very hesitantly, almost in slow motion, she sat across from him and positioned her chair farther from the table, creating extra space between them.

"Vera," he said, "you aren't who you think you are."

Her eyebrows shot up as the hairs on the back of her arms sounded the beginnings of an alarm.

"Sir," she said, forcing the politeness, "you've never met me. You don't know me. As I said, the pub's closed."

She stood quickly and was ready to tell him off further when he fixed her with a piercing gaze. It stopped her.

"I know a great deal more than you do," he said, his voice barely above a whisper.

Chills rose on both arms now. Vera had dealt with drunks and creeps of all ilk but never anyone whose focus centered on her. As every ounce of her gut screamed at her to leave, she stood rooted on the spot, trying to figure out what to say to someone who had so entirely disarmed her.

His eyes flashed away from Vera's toward the doorway behind her. She heard a clatter and the crash of porcelain before she turned to see. Allison was standing there with silverware and broken plates splayed about her feet. Vera's instinct was to rush to help her mother clean up the pieces, but she was transfixed by the horrified recognition on Allison's face.

"Good gracious. It . . ." Allison's voice wavered, thick with emotion. "Is it—it can't be time already?"

Vera's eyes ping-ponged back and forth between them. There was pity on the man's face. He nodded at Allison, a minute gesture.

Her mum looked as shattered as the dishes on the floor.

"What's wrong? What's happening?" Vera asked. She heard the panic rising in her voice, and she hated it. She dropped her hands on the table to steady herself.

Allison stood there, shaking her head in tiny, frantic movements. Something was deeply wrong. In all of Vera's life, she'd never seen her mum like this.

The man lay his hand on top of Vera's fingers. She wasn't sure why she didn't pull away.

"Why don't you sit back down?" he asked quietly, gently. "Allison, you should join us, too. And maybe a medicinal drink would be wise?"

Vera pulled her hand away from him as she sank back into the chair. Allison crossed the pub like a ghost. The joy that usually lit her face, crinkling around her eyes in deep lines from years of laughter, was gone. Allison grabbed three glasses and a bottle of whiskey from behind the bar and set them on the table.

She gave each of them a robust pour. Vera hadn't noticed how much grey streaked through her mother's hair before now.

Allison took a drink and stared at the man, so Vera turned to him too.

"There's no way to say this without sounding completely mad, so I'm going to say it bluntly," he said when Vera met his eyes.

"Vera, dear, I think you know that Allison and Martin are not your birth parents?"

Vera nodded. Her parents had been forthright that they'd adopted her in infancy.

"I'm not sure how much you've searched for your biological parents, but if you have, I'm sure you've come away empty-handed."

This was also true. The agency her parents used for her adoption had undergone some mysterious scandal and abruptly closed when she was young. At least, that was what her parents had told her. Did this man know something about her birth parents? Something that Martin and Allison had kept from her?

He went on. "Yes, well, there wouldn't be any records. I'm going to ask for your uninterrupted attention now. You'll want to shout down my madness, and you're welcome to do so. But first, I need you to listen. Is that fair?"

Vera scoffed. Fair didn't factor into this. She glared at her mother, the sense of imminent betrayal burning in her chest.

Allison was now rather tearful. "I'm so sorry, darling."

Vera's imagination ran wild with what this secret might be, a secret that was tearing her mother to shreds before her eyes. She fixed the man with a hard stare, resolving to stay calm through whatever was coming.

"All right," she said.

"All right." He nodded. "You can't find your birth parents because they don't exist anywhere you could search."

Vera steeled herself. This had to be something huge. Tragic death? Maybe they were murderers or some other kind of awful criminals.

The man's eyes drifted down to his hands. "You weren't born twenty-two years ago. You were born in the year 612."

With that pronouncement, every spinning thought in Vera's mind stopped. She'd agreed to hear him out not half a minute earlier, but this was almost certainly the last thing she'd have guessed the man would say, and it was nonsense.

Without lifting his gaze, he raised his hand as he correctly guessed that Vera was within a breath of interrupting him. His eyes flicked back to her face.

"When you were twenty years old, you were injured far beyond anyone's capacity to heal. For any of this to make a lick of sense, there is one major point you need to know, which will also sound ridiculous to you. Magic is real in our time—in your original time. It's not something everyone has, nor that those who have can equally access. I have magic and, forsaking humility for the benefit of your understanding, I have considerable access to its gifts." He shook his head as if the thought vexed him.

"But I couldn't save you. I could, however, save your essence and revert you back to a very early life stage. It's the same you, but it was like pressing a reset button. You were made an infant again."

He must have noticed Vera taking a sharp breath and clenching her jaw. "I promise," he said, "I will answer your questions to the extent I can but let me say this: you are irreplaceable to the future of England at the exact time when you first existed. Even with all the magic out there, you can't rush a human's generation. There was no way to make you who you were before without waiting, allowing you to grow to the right age again. By then, it would have been far too late.

"So, I found an unusual pathway . . . a workaround, if you will. I could bring you to this time, allow you to grow here, and then, once you were the correct age, I would have a small window during which I could bring you back and reinsert you after your initial accident. It requires precise spell work, but if executed perfectly, no one around would be any the wiser that you'd been away more than a year—and we'd be able to repair all that had gone awry. We are in that window today and today only."

He folded his hands on the table and watched her expectantly. Vera didn't break eye contact as she grabbed her whiskey and took a deep slug that stung her throat. The tangibility of its burn was a relief that grounded her in reality.

"So," she said, "is this the part when I get to say you're out of your fucking mind?"

"I believe that would be appropriate, yes," he said reasonably, the faintest hint of amusement playing at his mouth.

"Right. Okay," she said, any of hundreds of retorts swirling in her mind. But Vera's mother's hand was holding hers, and it was quivering. And Allison had silent tears slipping down her cheeks, which kept Vera's tongue at bay. She wished Martin were home.

"Okay." This time, she said it with finality. "You said the future of England depends on me? Which, like, let's not even get into that we are already in the future of your England right now . . . but . . . pretending any of this is possible, what's so important—"

"About you?" the man finished for her.

Vera nodded. Of the man's absurd tale, that was the part she found least believable.

"Well, for starters, you're married to the king."

She laughed, but Allison's palm sweated and shook as she squeezed Vera's hand.

When Vera met her eyes, she found her mother again, not the shocked ghost moving in slow motion. Her face was tear-streaked, but some of her spark had returned. Allison looked intently at her daughter.

"Vera was the nickname we gave you, my love," she said. "Your name is Guinevere."

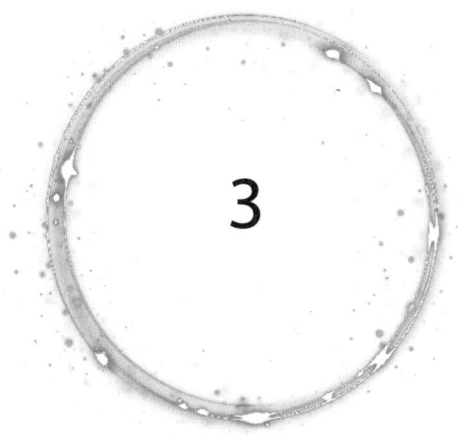

3

Vera snatched her hand from Allison's like the touch burned her. She looked desperately at her mother, the person she trusted most in this world.

"Mum, it's impossible! This doesn't make sense. You've got to know this doesn't make sense."

Allison nodded, her eyes wide. "It doesn't. It really doesn't. At first, I didn't believe it either. Merlin had to show us—"

"Merlin?" Vera croaked.

This seemed as good a time as any to throw back the rest of her whiskey. She choked on it and hastily wiped the escaped dribble from the corner of her mouth.

"Ah, yes." The man cocked his head to one side and raised a finger. "That would be me."

Vera leaned back as she took him in. "You don't look like Merlin."

"Oh?" he said with a raised eyebrow. "It's my hair, isn't it?"

"A bit," Vera said as she breathed a laugh. She'd have pictured a long silver beard and not his dark, manicured facial hair with only glimmers of grey through it. Vera thought better of saying that she'd have expected someone claiming to be Merlin to be far older, too.

"I try not to dabble too deeply in knowledge of your time, but I'm well enough acquainted to know that my name is rather familiar in your legends. They have gotten little else about me correct." He offered both hands, palms up in front of him. "I'm sorry for not introducing myself sooner, but I thought it would only hinder our conversation."

Vera shook her head. This was madness.

"It was only after Merlin showed us that we believed any of it," Allison said. "Your father and I thought he'd kidnapped you at first. I was ready to ring the police when—"

"He showed you . . . magic, or showed you time travel?" Vera asked.

"Magic." It was Merlin who answered. "Proving to someone you're from the past is considerably harder than you might imagine. I can tell you many things about our time that your history books have gotten wrong, but my word proves nothing."

Vera eyed him skeptically but spoke to her mother. "What did he show you?"

"He," Allison shrugged sheepishly and turned her glass in her fingers, "he turned water into wine."

"You're kidding," Vera said. "Like Jesus?"

Allison let out a short laugh and nodded.

"And what will you show me, Merlin?" Vera said, a sharp emphasis on his name.

Merlin cast his eyes down, grinning at his hands. She thought she heard a snort of laughter. But he sobered and grew focused. Without moving or answering, the lights went out in the entire room. Though the sun hovered in the sky, its light didn't fully penetrate the front window. The pub took on a heavy darkness. Merlin held his hand out, palm up, and a glowing orb formed millimeters above his fingers. At first, Vera thought it was white, then she saw the edges were black, and in some moments blue. But at the center, she saw a vision.

She couldn't place if the orb projected an image in her mind or if it played like a film inside the ball of swirling light. Vera saw herself clearly there. It was her face and body, but she wore a medieval gown, deep green with gold trim. Her eyes were dark even as she smiled. It was a grim expression Vera recognized, one she herself had worn on trying days. The ball faded from Merlin's hand, and the lights flickered back to normal around them.

Vera blinked and shivered. "Fuck." She exhaled the word more than saying it. There wasn't any way around it. That was magic. And, though she had no memory of being in that place, that had been her in the orb. No, not her. It couldn't be her. But . . . it was certainly someone exactly like her, down to the expression.

"Am I her clone?" Vera asked, grasping to make sense of it.

"No. That was you. You are her. That," Merlin looked pointedly at his now empty hand where the ball had been, "is your body—everything about you before I reverted you to an earlier life stage."

"But why?" Vera asked in exasperation. She'd never even liked Arthurian legends—though she'd attributed her annoyance with them to her father's obsession with consuming every film, book, and show on the matter, an obsession which now made more sense. She knew that the legend was about Arthur and his knights, not Guinevere. Why would the king's wife have any vital role—

Vera's lips parted with dawning dread. "Was she supposed to have his child?" The notion was a vise grip on her throat. She wouldn't do it. She'd sooner fight the wizard and die than be some time-traveling broodmare.

"It's nothing like that," Merlin said emphatically. "That's not the way succession works for us. Magic chooses the king, not blood. Whether or not you decide to have any children will be your choice."

"What is it, then?" Vera asked. "What is she supposed to do that's so important?"

"It's not she. It's you. You bore witness to an act that is draining magic from the kingdom. You were the sole witness. It is not a matter of if it will destroy our world; it is when. And your memories are our only chance of fixing it."

"You need me to remember what she saw?"

Merlin stared at her, considering it. He seemed like he was choosing his words carefully. "You need to remember everything."

Vera had never had any notion of a life other than the one that she'd lived. No visions of battles or castles. "I don't remember anything."

"You used to dream about it." Allison had been quiet so long that Vera jolted at the sound of her voice—and more so at the content of what she said. "You must have been three or four years old, and you never remembered in the morning, but you'd wake up in the middle of the night talking about him."

"About who?" Vera hadn't meant to whisper.

"The king. Once, you said you went on a walk with him and that everyone knew him and wanted to talk to him." Allison laughed a little. "You thought he must be tired after carrying on as if he liked them all."

Vera never had more than a passing hello with strangers on the street. She agreed with her toddler self's assessment. Still, that was a child's dream. Glastonbury was reputed to be the ancient Isle of Avalon, and the thirteenth-century monks at the abbey had claimed they unearthed Arthur and Guinevere's tombs. Even with her aversion to Arthurian legends, she could hardly go about town without hearing some reference to it. She was an imaginative child. She could have come up with some King Arthur story. That proved nothing.

"You talked about Merlin, too," Allison said.

Merlin straightened in his seat, and Vera thought he gripped his whiskey glass more tightly. But when he spoke, he merely sounded interested. "Really?"

"Yes," Allison said. She shook her head and offered a half grin. "She said you made . . . water balloon animals to cheer her up. It sounded like nonsense. Does that ring any bells?"

"It does," Merlin said.

"Do you remember what her favorite was?" Allison asked as she leaned toward the wizard. It seemed an odd question to Vera.

Merlin considered a moment before he flicked his wrist at his whiskey glass. The liquid soared out of it, and, at the twist of his fingers, it gathered into the unmistakable shape of a monkey, bulbous and fluid though not sweating a single drop.

"Oh," Allison cooed at the whiskey sculpture. Vera felt the unbidden smile on her lips. It did resemble a balloon animal, and it was indeed made of liquid.

Merlin turned his fingers downward, and the drink flowed like a wave back into the glass as Allison relaxed into her chair. Vera realized with a jolt that her mother had been testing him.

She turned back to Vera. "And there was a woman called Matilda. You woke up crying once and asked me to braid your hair . . . that Matilda lived in the castle and plaited your hair when you were sad."

"She's your chambermaid," Merlin said. "You see? The memories have always been within you. It might take some time, but when you're back home, we'll be able to begin unlocking them."

It was jarring to hear somewhere else, sometime else, referred to as home. This was home. Vera was not a queen. She wasn't—she couldn't be—Guinevere. But she couldn't deny that they were made from the same (what was the word Merlin used?) essence, nor could she deny her own childhood memories. Perhaps she was some sort of . . . container for Guinevere's story.

Accepting that brought the possibility of actually leaving into sharp relief. It frightened her. "If I go back with you, will I be stuck there forever?"

Merlin frowned, and there was pity in it. "If you can remember and get the course of history back on track by late spring, we will have another chance for you to return. If returning to this time is what you want."

"But I can come back?" Vera asked, with a glance at her mother. Allison seemed to be working to keep her face impassive. "It wouldn't rip the fabric of time or whatever?"

Merlin took a careful sip of his whiskey. "After you've helped us set things right, I can bring you back—if that's what you want."

Vera clenched her teeth together to keep from grimacing. He kept saying that: "If you want." Of course she would want to. But as much as the timing was important for Merlin and Arthur, it was for Vera, too.

"Will that bring me back to right now, or will six months have passed here, too?" Vera asked.

Allison gave a sad hum as she reached over and squeezed Vera's shoulder. "My love, you cannot map your life around his treatment."

Vera yanked away from her. "Can you guarantee he will survive six months?"

"The treatments are going well—"

"We won't even know if they've worked for another month." She glared at her mother to stifle her rising tears.

"Ah . . ." Merlin said quietly. "I gather Martin is ill?"

Vera rubbed at the side of her glass. She'd rather chuck it at the wall. "Yes. Fucking cancer."

As soon as she said it out loud, she froze. What was she thinking? This man had saved Guinevere from death. "Could you heal him?" Vera asked. "Show me that magic, and I'll do whatever the hell you want."

He smiled sadly, and her hope turned to ash. "Cancer differs from mortal flesh wounds. I'm sorry."

It was back to the essential question, then. "How long would I be gone?"

"You cannot touch any time that you've already lived, so I couldn't bring you into your past here, but I can deliver you back to Glastonbury after the moment we depart this evening," Merlin said. "I do not wish to mislead you; there is risk. I can't bring you back unless you've—until you've helped us fix what's broken. That is imperative. Whether or not you decide to come with me is your choice."

"And if I choose not to come, what happens?" Vera asked.

He heaved a sigh and stared down at the table before he met her gaze. "Time is," he clicked his tongue as he searched for the words, "immeasurably complicated. But the present as you know it is contingent upon you, upon your life and your actions . . . upon your returning to where you came from. If you stay here, the kingdom will fall. And I can't say how soon or the way it will happen, but this time, this life as you know it will eventually cease to be."

"You call that a choice?" Vera gaped at him. "Fuck. I have a life here. I'm—" She gestured around at the pub. What was she going to say? Cleaning toilets and changing bedsheets? "I'm happy."

"I'm sorry," Merlin said. "If it weren't for this, death was the alternative. You would have died the day you were injured and lived none of this life. This was the best I could give you."

Allison had managed to stave off a steady stream of tears, but her eyes were rimmed in red from the fight. "I have to go, don't I?" Vera said. Part of her hoped Allison would so staunchly object that the choice would be made for her.

"You do, my love," she said as she took Vera's hand in both of hers.

"I love you to the end of the world." Allison tried to continue, but her voice faltered. She cleared her throat and tried again. "Listen to me. You are not happy. And this is not a life. I want better for you."

It stung, but it was true enough. She hadn't been happy since Vincent died. She hadn't quite been able to slip back into herself, and Martin and Allison had seen that. In that way, Merlin's timing was a gift. Vera couldn't escape her memories of Vincent anywhere here, though she'd tried. She'd fled from Bristol, where they'd met, where they'd fallen in love, where they'd lived together, and where he died . . . back to Glastonbury.

She fled up the Tor nearly every morning. She fled into the regularity of cleaning rooms and serving breakfasts. No matter the distance or distraction, pain caught up and claimed her. She was typically good at tucking away hard things, shoving them beneath the place her conscious thought and feeling would reach, but this . . . this wouldn't go away.

It all only compounded with Martin's diagnosis just months ago. Vera had taken on the weight of his treatment schedule in a way she knew wasn't healthy. But she couldn't stop herself from thinking of his healing as her responsibility.

And she knew why. When it came to Vincent, she couldn't escape the truth of her culpability. When his car skidded off the road and careened into a tree as he came home from the pub quiz, she had been asleep on the sofa. He'd bled in a ditch for nearly two hours before someone found him. It was too late by then. Vera usually went to the weekly pub quiz with him but had stayed home that night because she was tired. If she'd been there, she could have gotten help. Even if she hadn't dozed off on the damn couch, she'd have realized he never got home. She'd have phoned the police. He wouldn't have died.

Vera got to the hospital before they lost him. It haunted her that she hadn't forced her way through the emergency department to get to him. She let him die surrounded by strangers.

And now, she was helpless as her father wasted away, day by day, with nothing she could do but watch.

Fourteen hundred years was a long way to run from her guilt. But they needed Guinevere's memories, and evidently, Vera had them. Maybe . . . maybe if she could fulfill this purpose, maybe if she could be the vessel that they needed, maybe—what? It wouldn't bring Vincent back.

But maybe you could forgive yourself.

How many lives would Guinevere's locked-up knowledge save? Surely, surely that deed could absolve her, and she could go back to her unnoticeable life. Her father's treatments would work (they had to work), and loss like Vincent's wouldn't be at stake. She could climb the Tor or read a book or stare at the stars and feel cheerful without being shredded by pain.

Vera laughed a little madly. She never dreamed she'd yearn to clean sheets for the rest of her life, but there was a simple joy to be found there. And if she had to travel fourteen hundred years and unearth some lost important woman's memories to reclaim it—so be it.

"I'll do it," she said.

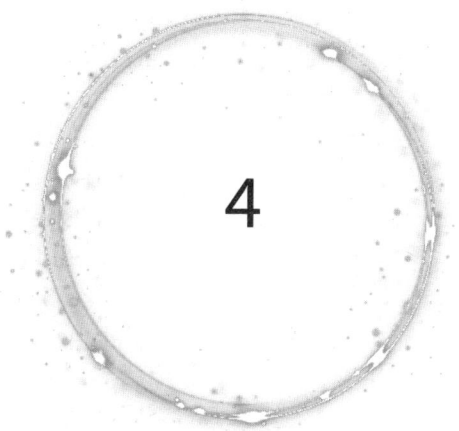

4

Allison shifted in her seat and spoke up sheepishly. "I hate to think of this, but what should we do when people notice she's gone?"

"They won't notice. It's been part of the spell—part of what made it possible for Vera to be here for so long," Merlin said. "Have you ever noticed the way people interact with her?"

Allison caught Vera's eye as she nodded. They'd only had conversations about it when she was little—and never since. She had cried about not having friends and her mum soothed her, stroking her hair, telling her it was normal to feel uncertain and insecure.

"I tried to pretend it wasn't happening," Allison murmured. "After a while, though, it became rather undeniable."

She couldn't decide if it was better or worse that her mother had noticed all along, but the admission stung as a betrayal that Vera swallowed. She didn't want to leave angry with her mother.

"They forget you here," Merlin said to Vera. "But no one has forgotten Guinevere in our time. You won't be ignored or dismissed there. It's where you belong." He tugged the chain of his pocket watch, lifting it from his pocket to peek at its face. "The voyage is possible until sundown. We have an hour and thirty-four minutes." He picked up a satchel from the floor next to his seat and passed it to Vera. "You'll want to change into this before we go."

She opened it and peered inside. All she could see was green fabric. A dress, she presumed.

An hour and a half wasn't nearly enough time to prepare, let alone say goodbye to her parents.

Shit.

Vera craned her neck to get a glimpse of the door as if looking would make her father materialize. Martin was in hospital in London for two more days. She'd been planning to leave first thing in the morning to sit with him during his treatment.

It was a three-hour drive.

"Fuck." Vera dropped her head into her hands. Tears blurred her eyes.

"I'll try to ring your father so you can at least . . ." Allison trailed off.

Vera nodded. "You could have given me more than an hour's warning, you know," she said, reserving some fury for both Merlin and her mother. "And just to be totally clear, this . . . king who she's—who I'm married to, it's . . . ?"

"King Arthur. Yes."

"Right." Vera scooted her chair out and held the bag up in place of a wave. "I guess I'm going to go change."

She threw the shoulder strap across her body. The well-worn, soft leather bag bounced on her leg as she climbed the stairs to her apartment. How was this real?

She upended the bag over her bed and shook it until a rolled-up dress dropped out with a pair of leather slippers flopping down on top of it. It was a mercifully simple garment. She didn't realize until after pulling the dress over her head that she'd kept her underwear and bra on.

"Fuck it." Her first act of rebellion would be transporting elastic contraband into the Middle Ages.

The irony of Vera's distaste for Arthurian lore made her feel sick as she glanced at her bookshelf, already knowing she didn't own a single iteration of the story. She mentally flipped through what little she knew about the legend: Arthur was the king's illegitimate son, identified by Excalibur to take the throne. There were the knights of the round table, including Lancelot, who had an affair with Guinevere in almost every account she could recall. That part unnerved her. A quest for the Holy Grail—or had that only been in Monty Python? She did like that version . . . And a strange name jumped to the front of her thoughts: Mordred. He was the villain, the one who killed Arthur.

Vera sighed, remembering Merlin's off-hand comment about how much history had gotten wrong. She focused instead on the gown, shifting it to sit correctly on her body. It was pretty, stretching down to the tops of her feet and a deep, forest-green color, with golden trim and embellishments along her waist that came to a triangular point below her navel. Vera smoothed the torso down and noticed a small tear on the hem of her sleeve. This gown wasn't new. Someone had worn it, though it fit perfectly along the curves of her body and was precisely the right length. She realized with a start that the person who'd worn it before was, in fact, her.

This was the very same dress from the vision in Merlin's hand. It wasn't entirely uncomfortable, either; no corset or boning, but there was some lacing in the back. Vera awkwardly stretched to reach around with one arm and managed to secure it enough. She turned and stared at herself in the mirror.

It was a funny thing, dressing in some ancient gown. She willed herself to laugh but stared at an expression uncannily similar to the version of herself in Merlin's vision.

Vera grabbed her phone and earbuds from the trousers she'd changed out of. It crossed her mind to bring them with her. It wouldn't work for contact, but she'd miss the comfort of music in her ears. She tapped the screen to see her battery was at 16 percent. Typical for the end of the day, but not worth trying to sneak the electronics past Merlin when she'd have no way of charging them. She sighed and set them and her keys on her desk next to her laptop before taking a pen and sticky note and writing down all the relevant passwords she could remember.

Vera wanted to bring something of her life with her, though. She scanned the room, and her eyes landed on a framed picture of her and her parents. Martin had put it on her shelves the day he'd assembled them for her. She popped the back off the frame, took the photograph, and tucked it into the leather bag. It was the only printed picture in the room. She'd gotten rid of her photos of Vincent on a day when she'd felt the pain of seeing them might kill her. Now, she was furious with herself for it. The anger sent roots of rebellion rushing through her as she eyed the otherwise empty satchel and made a beeline for the top drawer of her dresser. She grabbed underwear, two sports bras, and a few pairs of socks, confident the Dark Age counterparts would be woefully insufficient.

That was it. She straightened the throw pillow on her bed, replaced a book on her shelf, and put away the coffee cup from her dish drying rack. There was a hamper half-filled with dirty laundry, but that would have to be left to Allison. Vera grabbed her trainers from by the door and went to put them in the closet but stopped halfway there. Surely Merlin wouldn't allow it, but . . . these were fairly new shoes.

She shoved the trainers in the bag, too.

Vera switched off the light and closed the door without bothering to lock it.

She could hear the din of patrons beginning to gather in the pub before she reached the bottom of the stairs. Allison and Merlin were no longer at the table. They'd moved to the hallway right near the entrance, but Vera took a last look at the bar where she'd grown up anyway. It was jarring to watch people ordering a steak pie or having a pint when her whole existence had just been upended.

"Vera!"

She nearly jumped at Allison's voice. Vera hoisted the bag on her shoulder and went back to the hall. Allison had her phone pressed to her face. She held it away from her lips to say, "I've got your father!" and resumed her focus on the phone. "There's no time for that. They are walking out the door, Martin."

Vera could imagine her father on the other end, arguing against her departure. She took the phone and turned away for some semblance of privacy. "Dad?"

"Hey, love." Martin's voice, which used to be so quick to a joke and among the loudest in a room, was soft and somber. Vera didn't want to guess whether that was sadness or sickness. Both options wrenched her heart. "I'm so sorry I'm not there with you. You've—"

He stopped speaking. She knew he was crying. She couldn't stop the lump rising in her throat either.

"It's all right, Dad. I'm—"

"Vera, love, you're going to be okay. Just . . . be who you are. You're exactly who they need you to be."

They needed Guinevere. And that wasn't her, but the notion that fulfilling Guinevere's purpose might free Vera had already taken root. She didn't know how to explain that to Martin, who'd been even more alarmed than Allison by her recent shift in demeanor.

"If I can help them," she said, hoping against hope that he'd understand, "I can come home and help you finish your treatments. I'll be better. I'll have really done something that matters."

"You matter," Martin said emphatically. "Do you hear me?"

Vera didn't answer. He was a good dad. Of course he'd say that. She hastily wiped the tears from her cheeks, sniffing as she tried to keep her breaths from devolving into sobs. This was too much. "Okay," she said after a second. "I need to go, Dad."

"I know, sweetie." His voice was muffled.

Vera could imagine him in his hospital room, half seated in the reclined bed. She knew that his face was in his hand, that he was barely keeping it together. And the truth was, she probably could have taken a few more minutes to talk, but no number of stolen goodbyes would be enough. She couldn't take any more of it without collapsing in on herself.

"I love you so much," he said.

Vera's legs wobbled beneath her.

"I love you, too," she said, feeling foolish because there was no way to adequately say it. She leaned back against the wall and slid to the floor. "Thank you for being a ridiculous and weird and wonderful dad." She heard his chuckle, which was mingled with a sob. "I'll—you'll hardly know I was gone. I'll be back and—"

"It's okay. We'll talk soon, all right?"

"Yeah." She crushed her eyes closed. "Bye, Dad."

And Vera ended the call without waiting for him to answer. She could not stand. Every part of her trembled. She took one deep, shaking breath, focusing on facts: reality had changed. She had to go.

She took a second breath, and it was steadier than the first. Vera let Martin and Allison slip to the back of her mind. She focused on the next thing. She needed to walk out of this building. Her final deep breath filled her lungs without a hitch, and she exhaled a sigh before she stood up.

"I'm fine," she told herself out loud. Her body seemed to believe her and carried her back to Merlin and Allison. She gave Allison the phone. "Mine's upstairs. And I left my passwords and keys there for you."

Tears streamed down Allison's cheeks as she grabbed Merlin by both elbows and stared him squarely in the face. "You keep her safe."

He nodded, patting her arm. "I will. I promise."

Allison released him to pull Vera into a tight hug. "I love you," she said into Vera's hair.

"I love you, too. So much. So, so much," Vera said. She disentangled herself from Allison's arms. There was no room for a breakdown. She had to be okay right now. "Goodbye, Mum."

Allison bravely tried to stifle the sob that escaped from her throat.

Merlin held the door open for Vera. She took one final look at her mum, who reached out like she was about to grab her and pull her back. There would be no storybook ending to this moment.

Vera turned on her heel, walked out the door, and did not stop.

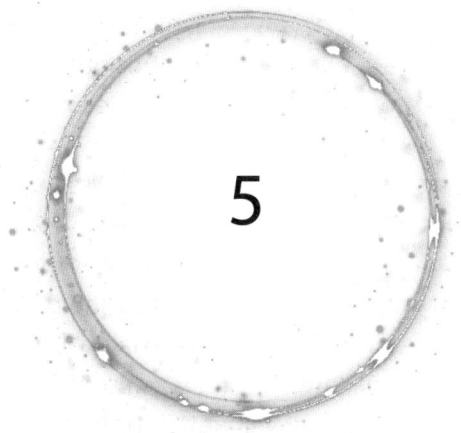

5

Don't look back. Don't look back, Vera silently instructed herself. She did not stop until she reached a bench in front of the old church a few buildings down. She didn't dare turn around to ensure Merlin was behind her in case Allison had stepped outside, too. He drew even with her and didn't stop walking but merely nudged his head, inviting Vera to join him.

She didn't know anything about him. Nothing about where they were going. She hadn't thought to ask what the accident was that brought Guinevere to the brink of death.

It was too much. There were too many pieces. Don't fall apart, she coached herself. Stay in it.

"Have you visited the White Spring Temple?" Merlin asked, not unlike how a visitor at the George might ask about the town. Vera softened toward him in the kindness of casual conversation. Perhaps he knew how delicate an edge her sanity balanced on as the distance between Vera and her home grew.

She nodded.

"That's where we're headed. It's . . . well, I suppose you could say there's a portal there, but calling it a magically stabilized wormhole might be more scientifically accurate," he said as if he were talking about what he'd had for breakfast.

Vera nearly snorted with mad laughter. On second thought, perhaps he'd overestimated her mental capacity. Nevertheless, if there were to be a portal (or wormhole or . . . whatever) in Glastonbury, White Spring was one of a handful of places that fit the bill.

The temple was in an old, unassuming well house at the Tor's base, built atop the spring to serve as a reservoir. They'd not updated the 200-year-old building with electricity, instead opting to light it with candles and tenacious bits of sunlight that could find an entrance in cracks and pinholes in the stone walls. It set the mystical mood along with the ever-present sound of trickling water and steady echoing drips from unseen sources. In every corner, shrines honoring the Lady of Avalon were erected that suited all manner of religious pilgrims. Some would call her Goddess, others the Virgin Mother, and still the rest Mother Earth.

The water that flowed from the spring had never dried up in recorded history. It provided for Glastonbury through famine and disease, and visitors devoutly attested to its healing properties, though when they'd tried to pipe it through the city in the late nineteenth century, it had blocked up the pipes. Scientifically, it was clear that the spring's high calcite content had caused irreparable damage to the metal. Others had their own answer: modern plumbing wasn't built for magic. Still, even if it didn't flow from their taps, anyone could visit the spring. Visitors were advised on a sign at the entrance to step into the shallow waters or fully submerge themselves in the deeper pools.

Oddly enough, White Spring was within a few hundred meters of yet another (and more well-known) ancient spring, Chalice Well. This one flowed red, reasonably explained by a high iron content to a rational mind but seldom seen that way by spiritual seekers. Christian lore purported that the spring and its healing powers were directly related to the Holy Grail. Legend held that the Grail was brought to England by Joseph of Arimathea and, at one point, buried in a cavern beneath the spring. They'd contend that the red waters signified the blood of Christ, once caught beneath the cross in that same chalice. The pagans believed it to be the earth's womb waters.

"I'm surprised it's not Chalice Well," Vera said, feeling compelled to say something. She took a right onto Chilkwell Street without even thinking about it. She'd walked this route so often that, were it not for the period clothing, she could almost convince herself this was an ordinary journey. They passed folks along the street heading in the opposite direction, but in an eccentric town like Glastonbury, where fancy dress was nothing exceptional, no one paid them any mind.

"Interesting you should say that," Merlin said. "The waters of White Spring come directly from the Tor. And that's where this particular kind of magic comes from. Vera." He stopped abruptly. "I noticed you still have that bag I gave you. You're wearing all the contents I provided, but it's not empty. What did you bring in the bag?"

Vera pursed her lips and only half turned toward him. "A picture of my parents, some socks and underwear, and . . ." Should she bother lying to him?

"Yes?" he prompted.

"My running shoes." She pulled her shoulders back and stood up straighter, daring him to argue with her about it.

He sighed heavily. "Nothing else? No electronics of any kind?"

"No."

Merlin chuckled and shook his head as he resumed walking. "Very well. But you must promise me you'll be careful to keep them concealed from anyone but those of us who know your situation."

This time, it was Vera who stopped in her tracks. "Other people know? Who all knows?" It hadn't occurred to her that others might be in on the scheme.

"Oh, Guinevere. I'm so sorry." Merlin's brow furrowed. "I should have said before. Arthur is aware, as is—"

"He knows?" She'd assumed she'd carry this secret alone, especially to be kept from Arthur.

"Of course. He also," Merlin heaved a sigh as he rolled his eyes, "against my better judgment, I might add, told his closest confidant."

"Who is that? Would I recognize the name?"

Merlin started walking again without a response. Vera ran the few paces to catch up with him. Now, she was intrigued. It was the first hint of frustration that she'd seen from the patient wizard.

"It's not, like, Lancelot or something?" she said facetiously, but Merlin's lips pressed together so tightly that they became a thin line.

Vera's jaw dropped. "Shut up. It is Lancelot!" Maybe it was because Merlin had turned her whole world sideways and backward in the space of an hour, but she delighted in his annoyance with the famous knight. She laughed. "And you don't like him!"

"I neither—" Merlin shook his head. "He is the king's oldest and dearest friend. And I've never known him to be anything but fiercely loyal, and for that, I'm grateful. But Lancelot is . . . loud and foolish." He opened his mouth as if about to add more but seemed to decide against it and clamped his lips shut.

It all felt distant enough to not entirely be Vera's story. But her mind flashed to that Arthurian storyline. Guinevere had an affair with Lancelot. Did Merlin know that part?

"I know you said you don't get too involved in our version of the legend, but there's a pretty consistent thread about Lancelot and Guinevere that might—"

"Yes, I'm aware." He waved her off. "Guinevere, you'll be shocked to learn how wrong this time has gotten things."

It took Vera a moment to realize that when Merlin said Guinevere, he was addressing her.

"About King Arthur?" she asked.

"About everything. Magic is commonplace in our time. It fuels our culture, our society—little will be as you expect. Magic leaves no archaeological trace, which is largely why you've grown up learning about this time as the Dark Ages." He gave her a sidelong glance, and the smile that rose to his lips was one of pride. "My dear, you will find it is nothing of the sort."

Merlin had stopped and looked across the street over Vera's shoulder. She'd been too caught up in trying to imagine a history that the books had gotten so woefully wrong that she'd not noticed where they were standing. They'd arrived at the well house.

The Victorian stone building was nestled against the wooded forest at the Tor's base. Foliage overtook it from above, giving the illusion that the building's roof was made of lush, green vines. An ever-flowing fountain trickled out of a stone pillar near the front corner. Even when the temple was closed, any passerby had access to the sacred waters. A squat stone wall lined a courtyard on the front end, with an opening meant to serve as a pathway from the road to the building's door—which wasn't solid, but a delicately designed wrought-iron gate of swirls and three vertical almond shapes up the center.

The temple only opened for a few hours each day. It was closed by this time in the evening, and the gate was locked. "Do we—"

Vera didn't have time to finish her question. Merlin fished a key from the pocket of his robe and moved past her to unlock the gate. He opened it enough for someone to slip through and politely gestured for her to go first. She started when she heard the key in the lock again and turned to see Merlin locking the gate behind them. Her throat tightened, and she tensed. She was trapped in here with a magical stranger. Vera clenched and unclenched her fist as she examined her situation.

What were the options? Decide everything to this point had been bullshit and that this was an elaborate scheme to murder her? Panic and demand he unlock the door so she could run home?

No. She'd decided to trust Merlin the moment she'd accepted the bag that now hung from her shoulder. That's why she was wearing this dress. She was in it, and there wasn't any turning back. Vera was either trusting a madman at her peril, or her life was about to become something she could have never even dreamed up. There was no in-between.

She squinted into the shadows, hoping her eyes would begin to adjust. The massive room was very dark, with the fading evening sun providing the only light through the doorway gate. Merlin waved his arm, and candles that had previously only been dark lumps to unadjusted eyes sprang to life all across the room: in dozens of candelabras, pillars on small shelves, candle arrangements surrounding shrines, and tea lights on any ledge wide enough to hold them. The room danced with a flickering glow set to the music of water over rocks.

Stone pillars rose from floor to ceiling, holding the building together while creating mystery, too. The room had nooks and crannies at every turn, each with more candles, pictures, statues of saints or deities, and glowing shrines that poked through the darkness. The floor was wet throughout, but stone basins caught the flowing spring.

Right in the center was a round pool where the water collected deep enough for someone to wade in up to the knee. At the back left corner was a three-tiered stone basin, the topmost of which was the size of a resort hot tub. It was here that visitors could fully bathe in the spring's waters.

"What now?" Vera asked, and her voice echoed through the chamber, feeling far too loud though she'd whispered.

By way of answer, Merlin carefully picked his way to the back corner to the three-tiered basin. "We'll need to climb into the submerging pool—"

"Why did I bother changing first?" Vera asked.

"It won't be an issue," Merlin answered as he gingerly stepped onto the first tier at the height of his knees. He climbed with the agility of a much younger man to the top of the basin.

Vera sighed, remembering she'd decided she was too far in to turn back, and followed him. It wasn't terribly high, not two meters to the top. She clambered awkwardly to sit atop the wall, her dress catching under her. She grunted with the effort as she spun her feet toward the waters. Clutching the bag still slung over her shoulder, Vera remembered the photograph tucked away.

"Merlin?" she said tentatively. She didn't see him at first. It was darker this far back in the room, and there was only one small candelabra lit up at the far end of this pool. After a moment, though, she saw that he had gracefully paddled to the center. "I'm not sure what to do with my bag. There's . . . there's the picture of my parents in there."

She couldn't see his face but could tell he'd turned back toward her. "It's all right. Your belongings will be fine."

She hesitated only another moment and then, clutching the bag to her body, lowered herself in. Half gasp and half yell escaped her when the cold water rushed over her skin. She'd never dipped in the spring herself but knew the waters were famously frigid year-round. Vera stumbled toward Merlin at the center of the pool, her soaked gown growing heavier with each step and catching around her ankles.

The Once and Future Queen

It was deepest in the middle. When she drew even with Merlin, their heads were the only parts of their bodies not submerged. Even as a disembodied head in freezing waters, he looked composed and stately. Vera, on the other hand, shivered violently and had to grasp Merlin's arm as she stumbled on her hem. He helped hold her to her feet and kept his hand on Vera's elbow to steady her.

"In a moment, I'll ask you to go completely underwater. And then I'll begin the spell." Merlin spoke deliberately and didn't break eye contact with Vera. "Once the spell begins, it's imperative that you do not come back to the surface. Do you understand?"

She nodded and tried to keep her teeth from chattering. "Stay underwater. Got it."

"We've only got one shot at this," he said. "Are you ready?"

"I guess so." She took a ragged breath. "Are you?"

"I am."

His ease soothed Vera some, and she found herself grateful for his steadying hand.

"Want a count of three or better to press on?" Merlin asked.

"Just go," she said.

"All right. And . . . go."

Vera took one deep breath and dunked her head beneath the surface. He hadn't specified how deep she needed to go, so she simply stopped fighting the drag of her dress. It pulled her down until her knees reached the bottom. She kept her eyes shut, and even had she not, it would have been too dark to see if Merlin was submerged, too. She felt his hand drift to her shoulder, pressing down firmly—not a shove, but a steadying tether to hold her in place.

It didn't feel extraordinary. It felt . . . like being underwater. Vera hadn't asked when to come back up or how long she'd need to hold her breath. The seconds stretched on, and nothing happened. She stayed perfectly still. After twenty seconds, the tickle of a burn bloomed in her chest. By thirty, Vera was beginning to panic. She couldn't hold her breath much longer in water this cold. What would happen if she tried to come up too early? Not consciously bidden, a survival instinct drove her feet beneath her, and the urge to stand became irresistible. As she pushed upward, the steadying hand on her shoulder shoved down with surprising strength.

Oh shit.

Her eyes shot open, and she looked into the dark water above her, searching for answers she would never see. Even in the dark, she could tell her vision was threatening to collapse on the edges. She was on the brink of losing consciousness when the water around her changed.

It was no longer liquid. Instead, it became a thick gel. Her frantic movements ceased; she froze. Everything was motionless, and then it was like a vacuum opened beneath her. Vera felt a great lurch and screamed into the gelatinous water as her body was violently sucked down, but she never hit the bottom. One second, her mind was vividly present in terror that she was certain would never stop.

From everywhere and nowhere, a voice she'd never heard before filled her.

"Ishau mar domibaru."

Then there was nothing at all.

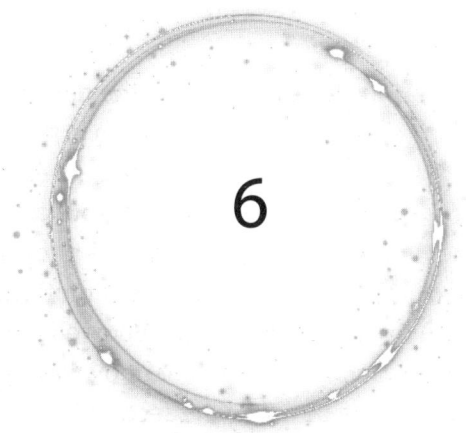

6

Vera's haze cleared as she stared at the sky, eyes already open, watching wispy clouds float above. There was one sound at her lips: ish. The sound of a summer breeze whispering through flowered fields. There'd been more words; she was sure of it. She chased it through her mind and tried to grab hold of it, but it vaporized into nothing as soon as conscious thought touched it. She sat up.

"Did you say something?" a man asked. She turned. Merlin sat on the ground behind her, looking as disheveled as Vera felt.

"I don't know," she murmured. Water. She remembered it changing and the sense of being sucked down, and then—what? Vera blinked. How had she gotten out of the water? Or the temple?

She sat on green grass in an open field. Vera heard flowing water before she noticed the stream to her side. Her left hand rested in its shallowest part, on smooth rounded stones that barely an inch of water trickled over. But her hand was the only part of her body that was wet. The dress and bag and shoes—everything that had been fully submerged was dry. Vera reached up and touched her head. Her hair wasn't even damp.

The stream meandered down the hillside before disappearing into trees and lush foliage below. Vera traced the waters back up the hill to where they came from, a gap in the rock not twenty feet above her. "Where are we?"

"Can't you tell?" Merlin asked.

She turned to find him on his feet, brushing dirt from his robe and adjusting his pockets. Vera began shaking her head, but the movement helped assemble the puzzle pieces.

The mouth of the stream on a lush hillside. She fumbled to her feet, and her eyes shot past Merlin to a forest grove behind him. There was no well house, and the trees obscured the view, but she was almost sure that, had there been a clear shot, she'd be looking right at the Tor.

"Oh!" Vera spun in place, trying to take in every detail. "Oh!" she repeated as she began to recognize the landscape.

Down the hill further on, the grass was well-trodden and formed a trail along what she guessed she used to know as the road. It passed in front of Vera and Merlin and curved around the trees where she assumed it wove to the top of the Tor. And in the other direction, Vera supposed it created the footprint for what would someday be the road leading into town.

"Shall we?" Merlin gestured to the path before them.

"Erm, I guess." Vera shifted the bag on her shoulder. "So that's it? We're here? It's the year like six hundred something?"

Merlin chuckled and patted Vera on the shoulder. "Precisely the year six hundred something. Now we walk down to Glastonbury, get our horses, and finish the journey to the castle."

Vera had assumed the time travel would also take them to their destination, wherever that was. She hadn't realized she'd get to see Glastonbury in its ancient form. Surely there'd also be people there, residents living their medieval lives. What did they do to fill their days? What did they talk about?

A prickle of worry pierced Vera's thoughts. "English is different now, isn't it?" she asked. "How will I be able to understand and communicate?"

"You needn't worry—oh, watch your step there." Merlin guided her around fresh horse manure in the path. "You'll understand everyone perfectly fine. And they'll understand you. It's—"

"Part of the magic?" Vera finished for him.

"You're a quick study," he said with fondness. "Any colloquialisms you use will be understood in the common tongue. No adjustments are necessary. Though," he added, scrunching his face as if he almost didn't want to say it, "you may want to say 'fuck' a bit less. It translates well but is decidedly less appropriate for a lady of your status."

"I'll do my best," Vera said as she cast a sidelong look at the mage.

He chuckled, seeming far more amused than annoyed by her antics. She was in awe of Merlin's ease in the face of everything that had to go right to get Vera here. All that remained on the daunting list was for her to regain Guinevere's memories. The travel itself hadn't jostled any to the surface. She was working out a way to bring it up when the gurgling stream nearby, the breeze through the trees, and the evening birdsong began to mingle with other sounds.

They'd emerged from the wooded area, and the bustle came from further down the lane. It was a din of voices—a lot of voices. And there was music: strings, flutes, and singing carried on the wind. There was a cottage to the left, and the two windows flanking its door had their wooden shutters open. A child of seven or eight ran with screaming laughter from behind the home and bodily dove through the open window, her pigtail braids flopping over her head. Right as she disappeared, what must have been her younger brother rounded the corner with a five-year-old's delighted roar. He had to work much harder to clamber through the window behind the girl.

It was comforting to see children behaving the same as they would in her time. A gust of wind carried the smell of food cooking over a fire. It was late evening by now, and Vera's stomach groaned in response. She smoothed her windswept hair back and realized her ponytail had come loose in clumps. Vera stopped walking to remove her hair elastic and fix it.

"That reminds me," Merlin said, fishing through yet another robe pocket and procuring a delicate circlet crown. It was made of thin metal woven together in a rounded pattern and finely shaped down to a point where there was a single oval-shaped moonstone. "You'll want to wear this."

Vera braided her hair and laid it over her shoulder. She wasn't sure how seventh-century hair would be styled, but a simple plait felt right enough. Merlin helped her position the circlet so the moonstone sat at the center of her forehead. She marveled at how it perfectly contoured to her head. Probably, she realized, because she had worn it before.

Merlin eyed her and shook his head. "Perfect. You look . . . like you."

The longer they walked, the more cottages were on either side of the ever-widening lane. Foot traffic steadily increased, too. Nearly every person who passed greeted them with reverent bows or curtsies, murmuring, "Ma'am" or "Your Majesty" as they did so. They whispered behind their hands and pointed from across the street. Vera's palms were clammy despite the evening chill. There'd not been a single time in her life when so many people paid attention to her.

She fidgeted with her skirt, making sure it lay correctly on her legs. "Is this sort of attention normal?"

"It's normal for you, dear," he answered kindly, taking her hand and looping it around his elbow. "They know you. I'd even say they adore you. Arthur is a well-loved king. You've been to Glastonbury many times. It makes quite an impression on people."

"Do I need to be responding in a particular way?" she asked, trying to move her lips as little as possible.

"You're doing well." He patted her hand. "Smile, say 'good evening' if you like. That's all you need do."

This must have been the heaviest residential section. Houses butted right up against one another with occupants scurrying in and out, cook-fires blazing, and groups sitting together at outdoor tables for their evening meal. Vera heard more laughter than she'd expected. The lane ended and she vaguely recognized that this was where the High Street would have been. They rounded the corner, and she was not disappointed.

Her feet stuttered to a stop. Disbelief stunned Vera into stillness. The lane was lined with buildings, all stone or timber, and quite a bit smaller than the structures of Vera's time. But it wasn't the structures that took her breath away. Glowing lanterns the size of footballs were strung merrily, crisscrossing above the dirt road and bathing the lane below in a soft warmth. There were carts and stalls every few feet. Vera smelled the spices before she saw them. Vendors were everywhere selling their goods: food, jewelry, clothing, and fine fabrics. And then, there were artists with paintings, sketch work, and embroidery. As the music started again, Vera searched for its source and found the troupe of performers past the spice stall, playing a lively song that quickly revealed itself to be about a mischievous fairy who snuck into homes and blessed children with magic.

And, indeed, there was magic.

On closer inspection, the lanterns that hung across the street were not suspended by string but bobbed in place of their own accord. And they didn't glow with fire, but some source unidentifiable to Vera. Across the lane, a young boy manned a cart. A woman behind him roasted sweet-smelling nuts on a blue fire. Vera noticed another woman further down, taking payment and levitating the customer a foot or so off the ground.

Everywhere she turned, there was something amazing. Merlin guided Vera through the throngs of people who all peered at her with as much interest as she did at them. She dragged her feet past two singers, a man and a woman, who mystically built a harmony of four parts between them. The Glastonbury she'd loved her whole life would forever be a special place. But this Glastonbury's evening market was the whimsical street fair of fairytales.

"We must keep going, Guinevere," Merlin said. The name was going to take some getting used to.

She let him lead her on without tearing her eyes from the happy spectacle around her. Too soon, they'd reached the end of the magical lane where the lanterns stopped, and the crowd grew thin.

"Arthur will meet us over there." He pointed to the end of the High Street, into the quiet darkness where Vera could make out a barn.

Her stomach flipped over on itself. Merlin must have seen her expression change.

"There's no need to be nervous. Reconnecting with him will help to loosen your memories. I expect you'll remember him before you remember the rest. This will be good," he told her.

His reassurance only carried Vera so far. She took a steadying breath and nodded. As they drew nearer to the stable, Vera saw that someone was seated on the ground outside it, his back against the wall. It was dark enough that she couldn't make out his features, but he must have also seen Merlin and Vera, for he stood up. It hit her in the gut.

It was him.

"Why don't you go ahead?" Merlin said. "I'll give you two a moment."

That really wasn't what she wanted. She didn't know how to make her feet work. How was she supposed to meet one of the most famous men in history as her husband? Jesus. Husband. She'd have laughed at the absurdity of it if it wasn't also so terrifying. Vera didn't have words or a voice to protest. She stood rooted on the spot. Merlin nudged her forward. She took a shaking step, then another.

Her heart thudded against her chest, and blood pumped so rapidly through her body that she'd swear she could feel it pulsing in her fingertips. She was sure the man could see how much she was shaking. Before she knew it, her feet were carrying her to him. He was handsome and tall, and his frame was neither broad nor narrow but lean, muscular, and fit. He wore a short beard cropped close to his chin, and his honey-brown hair was just long enough for a loose piece to swoop across his forehead. What she noticed more than all the rest was the kindness of his eyes.

As soon as their eyes met, a deep affection rose from her belly.

"Hello," Vera said hesitantly.

She didn't realize how rigid his mouth had been drawn until he relaxed at her greeting. The concern fixed into the lines of his face ebbed into relief, and his eyes glinted. He rushed to Vera and swept her into a hug. She tentatively let herself melt into it, experimenting with how it felt to lean her head into his shoulder and return the embrace, touching his back with one hand. He released his hands to her shoulders, bending his knees to drop to eye level with her. His brow furrowed as he carefully examined her.

"Are you all right?" he asked.

"I think so," she said with a nervous half-laugh. Though she had no memory of him, Vera instantly felt like she knew him. This might work.

"Goddammit!"

Vera jumped at Merlin's voice, cursing close behind her. "Where the hell is Arthur?" His glare burned into the man.

Vera tensed and turned back to the man holding her shoulders. This was not Arthur?

The stranger saw the shock on her face. He dropped his hands from her arms and stepped toward Merlin. "May I have a word?"

Merlin's steady demeanor, which Vera had witnessed only minutes ago, swung to palpable anger. She supposed, considering the gravity of the situation, it was understandable. The unknown man, on the other hand, genially guided Merlin away, an arm slung around his shoulders like an old friend. Vera couldn't hear their conversation but could see from his gestures and posture that the man was working to diffuse Merlin's ire. She watched them without any attempt to hide her interest. If there was some reason Arthur couldn't show up for a horse ride after she'd left her entire life behind, Vera felt entitled to know it. She'd assumed she would be the only obstacle to this plan's success, not anybody else. It hadn't occurred to her to wonder how Arthur felt about it, nor had she considered until this exact moment that Guinevere and Arthur's relationship might have been an unhappy one.

When Merlin turned back to Vera, the other man tailing a step behind him, it seemed his efforts had not been in vain. Merlin still seethed, but the aura of fury had dissipated.

"It appears I am urgently needed. I'll be riding ahead. Sir Lancelot will escort you to the castle. You'll be safe with him."

He wheeled about and hurried into the stable without another word, leaving Vera alone with Lancelot.

"Shit," she said under her breath. She was as clueless as she'd ever been about herself and this world, a maddening combination of concerned and offended by Arthur's absence, and wildly embarrassed by her interaction with the man she now knew to be Lancelot. He rocked from his heels to his toes, expression light and unfazed.

"Is something the matter with Arthur?" she asked.

"Oh, he's fine," he said with a dismissive wave of his hand. "Are you hungry? We've got a decent ride ahead of us. Maybe three hours."

Vera sighed, questioning if Merlin had intentionally couched the difficulty of this whole journey. To add to it, she actually was famished. After only toast and tea post-run and frantic bites of stew between serving tables at lunch, followed by having her existence called into question, Vera was wholly depleted.

"I really am," she said.

"Good, because I'm starving." He offered his arm to her, which she accepted before they walked back toward the evening market. "There's a stall with good hand pies up here. Ale or wine?"

"Oh, erm, ale," Vera answered. Water might have been a better option, but she wasn't sure if it was even readily available, and the shame of naivety kept her from asking.

Lancelot guided her through the growing crowd beneath the magical lanterns. He made a beeline for a particular food stall. While he spoke with the old man preparing the food, Vera slipped away from him and back into the street, careful to keep Lancelot in eyeshot. This version of Glastonbury was scrambled up, brightly lit, and magically buzzing. It was clearly the town she knew so well, but now she saw it as if reflected in a jeweled looking glass. The instinct to grab her phone and take a picture was so deeply ingrained that Vera even reached for where her trouser pocket should have been before she remembered it wasn't there. That was going to be stranger to get used to than the new name.

Vera felt Lancelot's presence at her elbow. He had a tankard in each hand with a steaming hand pie balanced on top and watched her with shrewd interest. She hurried to relieve one of his hands, taking a pie and a tankard, and followed when he maneuvered toward one of many long, shared tables with benches on either side.

Vera had only just sat down before she took as large of a bite as could be deemed polite and shook her head as she chewed. The insides were so scorching hot that Vera had to indelicately hold it in her mouth and suck air in through her teeth.

"What were you looking at back there?" Lancelot asked.

She could barely taste the pie filling beneath the blazing heat but would swear for the rest of her life that it was delicious. Once she managed to swallow, she answered. "It's so different from how it all ends up in my time. You only find magic in stories, and—I mean, this is our history. I learned about this time period in school, and we got it so wrong. What the bloody hell happened between now and then?"

"Nobody knows," Lancelot said, suppressing a grin with a sip of his ale. Vera only vaguely registered that it was likely in response to her colorful language. She was more focused on what he'd said. She hadn't expected him to have an answer. "Merlin can't access the time between now and nineteen hundred."

"How do you know that?" Vera asked.

"I'm very smart, and I know a lot of things," said Lancelot after swallowing a sizable mouthful. "The magic is limited."

"Really?"

"Yes, so many things." He leaned forward, eyeing Vera with a mock intensity. "Ask me anything."

She laughed, which drew a pleased smile from her companion. "No, I meant—"

"I understood what you meant. There's a full block on the next thirteen hundred years that magic can't penetrate. There's no knowledge beyond that," he said as if that was the end of it.

"Oh." Vera fell silent as she finished her pie and sipped her ale, trying to organize what she'd learned and what she still needed to ask. It was no small feat. It felt the more she was told, the less she knew. She was holding onto her tankard tightly, her body tense with the effort to stave off panic. Deep breath. Set it all aside. You're fine.

She didn't have to work at it long as her eyes snagged on one man, markedly out of place in the midst of celebration as he scrambled through the crowd, his brow slick with sweat and his sights set squarely on Lancelot. Vera's fear deflated with the distraction as she listed her head to the side. Lancelot followed her gaze as the man reached them, dropping both hands onto the table to steady himself.

"Sir Lancelot!" he said between heaving breaths. "I heard you were here. Bloody fine timing, too." He hastily shifted his focus to Vera, and she reeled with the unfamiliar sensation of being noticeable. "I'm so glad you're well and returned, Your Majesty. And please, pardon my intrusion. The matter is most pressing."

"Is it the thieves?" Lancelot asked. The atmosphere around him shifted before Vera's eyes. His features somehow sharpened and the twinkle of his friendliness hardened in an instant. The Lancelot across from Vera now was rather fearsome.

"They've been spotted approaching from the eastern road. I'll call for soldiers, shall I?" The man straightened, evidently eager to take action. "High time these boys were tossed in the stocks."

Lancelot sighed, seeming oddly reluctant, but he gave a nod, and the man turned to go. Then Lancelot's eyes lit, and he caught the retreating man by his arm. "Wait. Have they harmed anyone?"

"The thieves? No," the man answered quickly. "Nothing more than scrapes and bruises, thankfully."

"Hm." Lancelot drummed his fingers on the table. His eyes flicked briefly to Vera. "Garth, could you give the queen and me a moment?"

Garth, tense with his urgency, huffed a breath and pursed his lips.

"I know. Time is of the essence." Lancelot held up a single finger. "One moment."

He leaned toward Vera across the table as Garth took a few reluctant steps away.

"These thieves . . . they're boys. Barely more than children," he said quickly. "Little shits, no doubt about it. They've been ambushing travelers on the King's Road for three weeks—and successfully evading the local soldiers, which says something about the boys' cleverness."

"Or about the soldiers' competence," Vera quipped.

Lancelot grinned down at his hands. "Fair point. In any case, we didn't unite the whole damn nation and fight off invaders for ten years for those boys to make the King's Road unsafe. Word is that they don't have homes. They've clearly fallen through the cracks, but we can't allow their actions to continue. One of two things will happen; they choose to rob the wrong person and get themselves killed or . . . little shits grow up to become big shits. And big shits make for a mess that can't be cleaned up, if you'll pardon my language."

"No pardon needed," Vera said. "It's quite illustrative."

Garth cleared his throat and shifted his weight from foot to foot.

"I think I can scare the piss out of them and set them straight on our way out of town. If you're all right with it, that is," Lancelot said. "And if all goes to plan, they'll have a better life tomorrow than they had today. You won't have to do anything, and we'll keep you out of view. You won't be directly in harm's way."

Vera feigned disbelief as she raised an eyebrow, but a startling thrum of excitement quivered through her stomach. "Not directly?"

Lancelot's half-smirk nearly undid her façade. Shit. He was adorable—and too damn likeable. But it was the next that had her reeling. The smile dropped and he looked at her with ardent sincerity. "I will keep you safe, Your Majesty." He sounded far more somber than he ought to.

And she believed him.

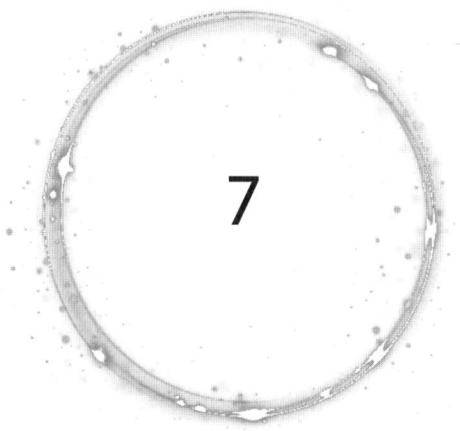

7

After Lancelot peppered Garth with a rapid-fire onslaught of questions, Lancelot picked up his pace to lead Vera to the stables. He kept casting sidelong glances at her as he tempered his strides to her far shorter legs.

"We could run," she offered before she had time to second guess herself.

His eyes went wide. "Really?"

Rather than answering, Vera started jogging. She heard his laugh before he joined in and drew even with her. Now it was Vera casting glances in his direction, satisfied that he looked delightedly dumbstruck when they got to the horses.

"Guinevere, this is Calimorfis," he said, brushing the neck of a sweet-natured brown-and-grey spotted mare. "Calimorfis, I'm sure you remember Guinevere." For the briefest of moments, Vera wasn't sure if Lancelot was being playful or if the horse might answer back. Talking animals didn't seem outside the realm of possibility here. But Calimorfis responded with only conventional horse noises, and Vera found that she liked Lancelot a little bit more.

He moved with impressive efficiency: digging through his saddle bag, procuring a traveling cloak for Vera to pull over her dress, helping her onto her horse, and gracefully climbing onto his saddle, all within about a minute.

As they rode away from town, Lancelot explained the plan. The boys' tactics had been the same each time they attacked. They waited outside town, and when their target approached, one pretended to be alone and injured. As the traveler helped the young boy, the other two came from behind and stole all they could. By the time the target realized what was happening, the thieving boys had made a run for it, and the one feigning injury would scurry off, too.

Lancelot's plan was a hearty dose of their own medicine. He would pretend to be in distress on the road, where he hoped they'd take the bait of an unexpected easy job. He'd catch them in the act of their thievery and, as Lancelot said, "scare the piss out of them."

Vera was to remain hidden with her hood up the whole time. He strapped his sword to her horse, committing fully to the bit of appearing unarmed and vulnerable. It was a decision that seemed risky to her as it, in fact, didn't merely create an appearance of vulnerability but a reality of it.

When Vera questioned him, he held his sword balanced on his palm, considering her query, and then assuredly holstered it behind her saddle.

"I think I'll manage," he said.

Merlin's description of Lancelot echoed in her mind, and it now rang as a warning: loud and foolish. But then there was her instant fondness for him that led to something Vera knew was more dangerous: she already trusted him.

The road from Glastonbury was a downhill stretch until it flattened out in all directions before them. Ahead, the only solid ground was a strip of road that cut through the countryside. Sparse groves of trees hugged close at the road's edges. But the surrounding terrain wasn't green. Beyond the hard-packed dirt road, stretching as far as she could see, the last light of day shimmered across the earth like a mirage in the desert, an illusion of water. In truth, it was no mirage at all. They were surrounded by marshland, the shallow water creating an expansive lake. She knew Glastonbury had long ago been an island and found herself staring at that reality.

"That looks good." Lancelot nodded toward an especially thick clump of trees and brush growth down the road. Vera guided her horse into the grove. She had only ridden a horse twice at summer camp but could tell this was an exceptionally well-trained animal. What Vera lacked in skill, the horse made up for in intuition. She seemed to know exactly where Vera wanted her to go, and once they'd gotten positioned behind the heaviest growth, Lancelot confirmed they were well enough hidden.

And then, they waited.

Vera leaned to her side to watch Lancelot through a gap in the branches. She wasn't supposed to be seen, but that didn't mean she wanted to miss the action. He dismounted his horse on the road and stood face-to-face with it, stroking affectionately between its eyes while crooning words she couldn't hear. There was a faint sound of raucous laughter on the wind. Lancelot stopped, looking over his shoulder. Then, he unceremoniously flung his sizable, graceful body down into the dirt. Vera had to cover her mouth with her hand to keep from laughing out loud. He turned his head in her direction with his own silent laugh.

"Keep it together," he said, just loud enough for her to hear. "Stay in it, Guinevere."

It was jarring to hear him say it. She'd admonished herself with that exact phrase earlier in the evening. Vera craned her neck to see the road as indistinct shapes grew nearer and took the form of three boys.

One was rather enormous. He lumbered along, moving more like a toddler than a man, with hands and feet bigger than his body knew what to do with. He was twice as wide as the littlest. They were a comical match-up, the one hovering around six feet tall, the other a full foot and a half shorter. The littlest one had mousey features and hair the color and texture of dirty straw. The third bore an angry expression on his acne-covered face, but he had the same nose as the mousey boy, and Vera suspected they were brothers. All were filthy and wearing clothes that desperately needed washing or even to be thrown away. Their shirts and trousers were more patch than garments. None wore shoes. Vera felt a pang of sadness.

They were so thoroughly engulfed in their boisterous bantering that they were nearly even with Vera's grove of trees when the tiny one cried out.

"Look!" His whisper was far too loud to keep any secret. They stopped, and their faces grew hungry.

"He looks hurt," the enormous boy's deep voice said, eyebrows knitted together.

"He looks rich." The smallest one plucked a dagger from his belt and spun it skillfully between his fingers. "And that horse could be sold for a fortune."

They stood in the road and debated about what to do. The boy with acne and his little brother wanted to check the injured man for money and take the horse. The big one argued they were being greedy and should take the horse and not chance anything else. They hadn't reached a conclusion when the mousey boy turned without warning and started toward Lancelot.

"Dunstan!" his brother hissed, his voice cracking. "Stop!"

But Dunstan did not stop. He marched forward, dagger poised to strike in front of him as the other boys stayed rooted on the spot. He kicked Lancelot hard in the side, and any sympathy Vera felt drained away in an instant. Lancelot didn't so much as flinch. She couldn't imagine how. Her heart hammered furiously.

Lancelot had two pouches at his waist and, satisfied that his prey wasn't conscious, the boy started fussing with the closure on one. When Lancelot's hand snapped up to grab his wrist, Vera jumped nearly as much as the boy did.

In one fluid motion, Lancelot was sitting up and eye-to-eye with the shocked child. Dunstan clumsily swung his dagger in retaliation. In the blink of an eye, the dagger was in Lancelot's hand, and their positions were swapped; Dunstan was now on the ground with Lancelot kneeling over him. His movements were so precise that figuring out how

Lancelot managed it was as fruitless as trying to describe a hummingbird's wings mid-flight. Vera's question of whether he should face the situation unarmed now seemed asinine.

To their credit, the other boys hadn't turned tail and run yet. In fact, Dunstan's brother was charging forward, drawing his own dagger. Lancelot didn't even turn around entirely as he thrust his hand out and caught the boy about the wrist. He stood to his full height, twisting the elder brother's arm until his dagger dropped to the ground.

"Oh shit," Dunstan's brother moaned, a flash of recognition lighting his pimply face.

Lancelot cocked his head and smiled ruefully. "Well said." He looked over his shoulder at the largest of the three. "If you want to have any chance of keeping your hands, get over here now." His voice was so commanding Vera almost wanted to hop off her horse and obey, too.

The large boy reluctantly trudged forward. Lancelot stowed the brothers' daggers in his belt. They'd all shifted enough that Vera couldn't see, so she edged her horse closer to the road. She wasn't as hidden but had a much better view. It was nearly dark, and the boys were facing away from her now anyway. As Lancelot turned back to Dunstan, the largest boy stopped halfway between Vera and Lancelot. He bounced on his toes, hanging in the balance of forward and backward movement. Lancelot's eyes shot up, sensing that something had gone amiss. The boy was about to do something stupid.

He turned and took off at a lumbering sprint down the road toward Vera. She didn't pause to consider the potential consequences. Vera kicked her horse into a run, urging her out into the road, where she drew up the reins and stopped so hard that her hood fell back. She unsheathed Lancelot's sword with both hands, wheeled it in a high arc over her head, and brought it down in front of the boy, halting his path forward. He skidded to a stop and fell back on his bottom, staring up at her in unbridled shock.

"I would reconsider," she said.

The boy mouthed wordlessly, scrambling backward like a scuttling crab.

"Is that the queen?" the boy with acne asked in horrified awe.

Lancelot gazed at Vera with one corner of his lips quirked up. "Yes, it is."

Vera thought she heard astonishment in his voice but decided she might have been mistaken as Lancelot shifted to glare at the largest boy. He lumbered back and joined the others.

"Sit." Lancelot spat the word.

Unsurprisingly, they all did so. None of them dared move. They likely hadn't even dared blink.

"I don't know what your lives are like," Lancelot began after an uncomfortably long stretch of glaring at them in silence, "but the mess you have created on this road has not gone unnoticed by your king. It will not continue." He paced in front of them, pointedly meeting each of their eyes. "You have a choice. Show up tomorrow at the armory, swear your allegiance to your king, and join his forces. You will have a place to live and food to eat, and you will learn to become good men rather than thieving boys. Or, if you don't show up, you will be found by the king's guard itself, and you will not be treated with the leniency I offer today. Do I make myself clear?"

They all nodded vigorously, like anxious chickens pecking for worms.

"Good," Lancelot said. "Now go—before I change my mind."

The boys scrambled to their feet and took off back toward Glastonbury at a run. They gaped at Vera slack-jawed as they passed her, except for the large boy, who stared at the dirt. Soon, they were formless lumps fading in the distance.

Vera turned back to Lancelot. His stern expression remained, but it fell away when he met Vera's eyes.

"Yes!" he shouted, thrusting both fists in the air. "You," he said, pointing at her, "you were fucking brilliant."

She was so caught off guard that she laughed. "It was a stupid thing to do," Vera said, "and this sword is insanely heavy. I about dislocated my shoulder." She held the sword out to him, both arms straining with the effort.

He accepted it, and where she'd had trouble wielding it with two hands, he easily sheathed it with one and mounted his horse as smoothly as if he were putting on a jacket.

"You were brilliant," Lancelot repeated. He clicked his tongue, and their horses obediently began to plod along. "I shouldn't be surprised. You always had a good tactical mind."

"Tactical mind?" Vera stared at him.

He nodded. "You and Arthur were married mere months before the final invasion. You came up with a crucial part of our battle strategy."

"I—I did that? You're certain?"

He laughed though he eyed her appraisingly. "Very certain. You wouldn't call yourself strategic now?"

"Hell no." That was the last way she would describe herself.

Half a grin took Lancelot's face, and he eyed Vera appraisingly for a moment. "You're different than—" He shook his head and clicked his tongue. "You're different."

She squirmed in her saddle. "In a good way or a bad way?"

"Just . . . different," he said, though he looked hopeful. "S'pose that's only fair, though. What's been a year for us has been a whole bloody life for you. What's it like? In your other time, I mean."

She wasn't sure how to answer that. How could she explain the phone she'd forgotten not to reach for about twenty times in the last hour? Where could she even start in describing the future? "I help my parents run an inn," she said.

Lancelot had loads of questions about how Vera occupied her time. She fumbled through a laundry list of interests, but when she mentioned running, he sat up straighter in his saddle.

"You run?" he said.

"Yes." Vera bit her lip. Was that an extraordinarily odd thing to say?

He fixed her with a delighted smile. "I shouldn't be surprised after that bit back near the stables. You looked comfortable running."

She hadn't thought about it, but Lancelot had seemed at ease, too. His stride and posture . . . Vera gaped at him. "Do you run? I didn't think people ran in this time."

"Soldiers do," he explained. "We were at war for the better part of a decade and ran every day to stay battle ready. Most soldiers have scattered to their corners of the country and lead much slower lives—and well deserved, I might add. I train the local forces and the king's guard, and I still run to keep fit. And I like it." He shrugged. "It calms my mind."

"Yes!" Vera nearly shouted it. "That's exactly it. Actually . . ." She remembered her trainers stowed in the saddle bag behind her and made a quick decision to show him. He positively gushed, twirling the teal laces between his fingers, and his eyes widened as he felt the cushion on the inner sole.

"Guinevere," his voice was hushed and reverent, "this has got to be the greatest invention of all time."

She laughed. "It's pretty high on the list."

There was hardly a breath's space of silence after that. Dark had fallen in earnest, and the velvety black night was bespattered with stars before it dawned on Vera that this was the easiest it had ever been to talk to someone other than her parents. This budding friendship was a pleasant surprise, but the more Vera warmed to Lancelot, the more her stomach churned. He watched her with a knowing look, his eyes kind.

"You thought I was Arthur when we first met, didn't you?"

She hoped the darkness could cover the heat that rose in her cheeks. "Yes," she said. "Why didn't he come?"

Lancelot searched Vera's face. "I'm sorry. This must be impossibly difficult for you."

Vera refused to fill the silence. He hadn't answered her question.

"I don't want to mislead you. We didn't know today was going to be the day that Merlin brought you back. He only sent word by messenger this afternoon, and Arthur had reservations about Merlin trying to . . ." Lancelot paused, his mouth in a tight line. "Well, about Merlin taking such extreme measures to bring you back."

He seemed to choose his words so deliberately. Vera might as well come right out and ask the direct question. "Does Arthur hate Guinevere?"

"No." This Lancelot said with certainty. "It's been . . . a difficult time." He shot Vera a heavy glance. "It's nothing to what you've been through, though."

She tensed, and the memory of Vincent bloody and dying flashed in her mind. How could he know that?

But he saw her reaction and clarified, his tone gentler. "You left your whole life."

"Oh." Of course. Funny she hadn't considered that, but it was true. And her ability to go home, to get her life back, to get herself back was contingent upon a task far more complicated than Vera had naively imagined. "What if I can't do what Merlin needs?"

Lancelot eyed her for a moment. "Merlin is single-minded in his commitment to the kingdom—to a fault, frankly. I'm not sure his expectations for you are reasonable."

Vera scoffed. "And I'm not sure he'd trust your assessment of the situation."

"Ah." Lancelot flashed a crooked smile, reigniting his spark of levity. "You've already noticed that I'm not exactly Merlin's favorite."

"You're about the only thing that broke his—" Vera searched for the right words to describe Merlin's powerful calm.

"Stick-up-the-ass demeanor?" Lancelot offered. Vera laughed. "Go on, then. What did he say about me?"

"He said that you were Arthur's dearest friend. And that you're very loyal," Vera said.

"Oh, that's quite nice. And?"

"And . . . that you're loud and foolish."

"That's—hmm." At first, she thought Lancelot was indignant, but he was grinning. "He's really coming around to me. Loud and foolish. That's probably the nicest way he's ever described me. Granted, he might have been edging it a bit trying to, you know, convince you to leave everything behind . . . but I'm calling this progress in the Merlin-Lancelot relationship."

They'd been riding for nearly two hours before an amicable silence fell, with Vera's eyelids close behind. They may as well have weighed a hundred pounds for the difficulty of keeping them open.

She woke with a start to a firm grip on her arm, holding her upright.

"About tumbled off there," Lancelot said quietly. "You've had a thousand-year day. Go on and lie forward on your horse's neck."

Vera's eyes were barely open. She nodded mutely and lay forward while Lancelot kept a steadying hand on her back.

She thought she heard him say "I've got you," but it may have been a dream, for she was already asleep.

"Ishau mar domibaru."

For a second time, unknown words reverberated through Vera's body, words that she would have no memory of when she woke.

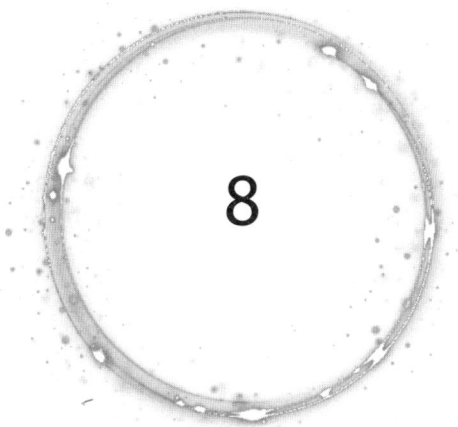

8

A soft glow brought Vera back to wakefulness, but it wasn't the moon. The side of her face lay on the horse's neck, and the light came from Lancelot's direction, not the sky.

Vera blinked, trying to make sense of what she was seeing. There was a lantern, a ball of light not unlike the ones she'd seen in Glastonbury, this one the size of a grapefruit and bobbing along between the two horses of its own accord. It didn't create any harsh shadows nor hurt to look at directly, but lit the space around them in all directions, like a traveling bubble. She sat up and rubbed her face.

"Good morning, there," Lancelot said. "Did you have a nice nap?"

She didn't know how long she'd been sleeping. Long enough for her neck and back to be stiff from the awkward position and for the moonstone on her forehead to have indented her skin where it pressed against her. Her ears perked at the distinct clip-clop sound of hoof on stone. They'd left the marshland and arrived on a cobbled street. They passed a farmhouse with a thatched roof, and she saw a concentrated cluster of light not far ahead atop a great hill, guessing that it marked their destination. "Is that where we're going?"

"Yes. Once we pass through the village gates, it's only a few minutes to the castle."

A few minutes to the castle. Vera's stomach gave a jump. This was really happening.

They switch-backed along the path up the hill to a towering stone wall extending in either direction. If the wall stopped or curved, it was far enough away that Vera couldn't see. She understood straight away why this spot might be chosen for a castle—the high ground for miles, defensible and fortifiable. The gates to town were shut and guarded, with men posted at alternating pillars atop the stone wall, only their dark silhouettes visible from the ground. The road was blocked by a massive wooden gate in the shape of an arch, split into two doors. With both swung open, it would be wide enough for most modern vehicles. Two soldiers were posted at each side of the gate. Lancelot called out to them, and they immediately recognized him.

The guard atop the wall shouted out, "Two on foot!"

The left side swung outward with an angry moan. The cobbled road snaked through the town. Homes were frequent in patches interspersed with shops and market stalls; a blacksmith here, maybe a pub there. The smell of smoky peatmoss fires rose from rudimentary chimneys, and the glow from hearths peered through cracks in window shutters where households stirred. Some lights through the town emanated a familiar sunset color, unmistakably the type of magic light that Lancelot carried.

They rounded the corner, and she saw it. She couldn't imagine how she hadn't noticed it sooner—perhaps clever placement of the structures on the hill. Even in the dark, though, the castle was unmistakable. It was not the cold medieval fort structure Vera expected. It was taller, the stone a light pearl color with an opalescent sheen in the moon's glow. The same wall surrounding the town carved another path in front of the castle for an added layer of protection, each section divided by a turreted watch tower. Four much taller towers rose behind it, marking the castle's corners. Three reached an equal and impressive height, topped by a round stone silo with a pointed cone roof. The fourth tower, farthest from Vera and Lancelot, was even taller and capped with a solid, flat-topped cylinder. Peaked roofs poked up from behind and between the wall and towers. There weren't spires reaching twelve stories high, nor was there a moat with a draw bridge or cascading fountains, but it was beautiful in its simple and shining form.

"Camelot," Lancelot said as Vera gaped in awe.

She raised her eyebrows. The stories had gotten the name right.

Lancelot led her through yet another gate into an expansive courtyard. There were stables to the left, and Vera smelled the horses before she heard them or turned to see their heads and hooves poking out above and below stall doors. One other structure in the vast field was jutting out on her right. It was the same pearl stone with a high peaked roof, but with one primary difference from any other structure. The door was flanked by a stained-glass window on either side and a triplet set of windows above.

Differently shaped glass panels in sea greens, evening blues, grey-tinged white, and a sharp, stark red were chunked out by thick ribbons of some sort of dark clay between them. It didn't form a picture, but the effect was a pleasant mosaic of colorful, shining pebbles. A squat stone cross was at the topmost point where one side of the roof met the other.

Beyond the chapel opposite Vera and Lancelot was the castle proper's main entry. Lancelot dismounted his horse, and Vera followed suit. She hadn't noticed the sleepy stable boy behind them until he handed her the satchel from the back of her saddle and led both horses toward the stable.

"It's nearly midnight." Merlin's voice cut through the silent courtyard, sounding cross. He stood expectantly in the doorway to the castle. "What took you so long? You're two hours later than I expected."

"Pardon my chivalry," chided Lancelot, hands at his hips. "You brought a woman through a thousand years and didn't bother to ask if she was hungry." He conveniently avoided any mention of their run-in with the thieving boys on the road, and Vera didn't chime in either. She couldn't tell for sure from where she stood beside Lancelot, but she thought he might have given her the tiniest hint of a wink. He palmed his light ball, which faded to darkness before shrinking to the size of a plum. Lancelot pocketed it as naturally as one might tuck away a five-pound note.

Merlin sighed. "I'm sorry, Guinevere. It's been quite a day."

She followed the two men into an entry chamber with high vaulted ceilings that made the echo of their footsteps louder than the steps themselves. There was a door on each side—one to the left, one to the right, and a grander door straight ahead on the opposite wall. With a flick of Merlin's wrist, the fixtures along the walls filled with light.

"Is he . . . ?" Lancelot asked.

"He's coming," Merlin said quickly, but uncertainty colored his voice. "Wait right here." He hurried off toward the grand door opposite them.

A flutter rose in the lowest part of Vera's belly. She was suddenly very conscious that she'd been on a horse for hours and had her face pressed against it. She straightened her circlet, making sure the moonstone rested in the center of her forehead, and she tried to flatten her dress around her legs.

"Do I look all right?" she asked without thinking, then felt immediately stupid and wished she could take it back.

Lancelot, however, answered without hesitation. "You look beautiful."

A flame of affection warmed her chest again. His Adam's apple bulged with a heavy swallow. He was anxious, too.

Through the open door where Merlin had disappeared, a faint sound from the hall beyond grew louder and more distinct. It was the sound of footsteps. Vera stiffened. She wished she could hold Lancelot's hand for support. She glanced down. His hand nearest her was poised on the pommel of his sword, a stance he seemed to take out of habit rather than a defensive posture. He, too, watched the doorway but took a small step toward Vera so that his bent elbow grazed her arm.

Merlin rounded the corner first with another man on his heels. He had to be Arthur. His eyes were trained on the floor in front of his feet. He didn't wear a crown or any finery and was dressed simply in an off-white shirt and dark trousers. And he wasn't a small man. He towered over Merlin. Everything about Arthur was more intense than Lancelot; his shoulders were broader, and his hair much darker. It looked like it came to his chin but was pushed to the back of his neck, and it had the slightest curl, making it hard to tell its exact length. The wave at its ends may have made him seem boyish if not for the severe line of his mouth. He stalked across the room behind Merlin and stopped three steps away from Vera and Lancelot before looking up.

Vera hadn't expected a tearful, joyous reunion, but she was still shocked. She took a reflexive half-step back before stopping herself. Arthur's face was a cold slate, humming with anger, though he held his features in a way that felt determinedly expressionless. He might have been handsome, but Vera couldn't see past his barely contained rage.

His eyes were a hazy grey when the light hit them right. They shone, a little watery, but not as if he were teary, more like . . . more like he'd been drinking. Fear prickled at the back of Vera's neck as Arthur stared at her. She knew she must look exhausted, and she wondered if she looked afraid, too.

Merlin also watched her, expectant. Hopeful.

She shifted her gaze back to Arthur and tried, really tried. But there wasn't a single thing that was familiar about the man before her.

No one asked Vera for confirmation. Her silence spoke volumes.

Merlin sighed. "It's not unreasonable that remembering His Majesty will take time."

Then Arthur looked away from her and spoke for the first time, his voice deep and with a low growl that made him sound frightening.

"That's not her," he said to Merlin.

Without a word or even a gesture to Vera, he turned and left through the same door he'd entered.

Lancelot had been as still as a statue the whole time, but now he moved quickly. He shifted his hand to Vera's elbow. "I need to—" he said, his jaw clenched as he took a step toward the door. "But do you want me to stay here?"

Vera did, but she shook her head. "Go."

"I'll find you tomorrow!" he called as he hurried after Arthur.

The heart-thumping nervous energy that had pulsed through her all congealed and lodged as a lump in her gut.

"What now?" she asked Merlin.

His eyes were closed, and he took a breath before opening them. "This isn't going how I hoped."

"No shit," Vera mused, letting out a bitter chuckle.

He smiled and cocked his head to the side like Vera was a painting (or an oddity) he was seeing for the first time. "I think many of us would be served well by a second chance at childhood with parents like Allison and Martin. It has clearly done your spirit good."

Vera couldn't help but feel gratified by his praise. And she'd only thought of Vincent once in the hours since she arrived, which was a far cry better than any other day since his death. Even as she congratulated herself, she pushed his memory away, afraid that she'd catch the virus of pain in this time, too, if she let his name linger in her thoughts.

"I thought Arthur would have responded more stoically." Merlin patted her arm. "I'll show you to your room. Your chambermaid will be there to help you. She's helped run castle matters while you were away."

"Does she know about me?" Vera asked.

"No," Merlin said sternly. "Matilda, like all others, believed you to be away at a monastery the past year recovering from an accident. In any case, she will help with your duties as you get readjusted." They wove through a maze of corridors with wall sconces that lit as they passed and dimmed in their wake until they reached an open doorway leading to a spiral staircase up one of the stone towers Vera had seen from outside.

The tower was so large that the stairs wound their own hallway up through it. Every story they ascended had a landing with a corridor cutting across the width of the tower. They stopped at the top, the fourth landing, where a lovely woman stood waiting.

Her wildly curly hair was a shade of red that reminded Vera of maple leaves in autumn. It was mostly tamed in a low twist at the back of her head save a few coiled strands that escaped and framed her forehead. Her simple, indigo-blue apron dress over an ankle-length white tunic complemented everything from her skin to her hair to her eyes. Vera guessed this was Matilda, though she didn't recognize her. She must have been in her early forties, and she was also one of the most effortlessly beautiful women Vera had ever seen.

Matilda's brow drew together with concern, and her disbelieving eyes were trained on Vera. "Your Majesty, I can't believe you're . . ." She trailed off. Her arms flinched upward as if to hug Vera. Instead, she stiffly clasped her hands together in front of her. "Well, I'm so happy that you're home."

"Thank you," Vera said, unable to stifle a dull pang at the word home.

"I trust you have things well in hand from here?" Merlin asked.

Matilda nodded, and the mage bid them goodnight before he disappeared down the stairs. Silence fell. Matilda's eyes searched Vera for a moment before she led her down the corridor to a door on the left. She unlocked it with a key that she fished from her smock's pocket.

Vera stepped into the room behind her. It was clean and well-lit by a chandelier hanging from the ceiling, speckled with tiny, glowing orbs. Centered against the wall on Vera's left was a large four-post bed with thick, navy-blue curtains hung from each post. On the wall to her right, next to another door, was a dark wooden desk.

The sound of a slam, wood against stone, pulled Vera's attention to the wall opposite, the curved wall of the tower's exterior. She saw the sound's source almost instantly: a window, taller than her, carved up into the wall. Three stone stairs led up to it, where there was a blue cushion on a bench in what she thought would be a quaint reading nook. The window had no glass pane. Instead, wooden dowels crisscrossed one another to make a trellis of diamonds, each the size of Vera's face. A gust of wind whistled through them, and again, the window's unsecured wooden shutter crashed against the wall.

Vera started toward the window, but Matilda cut in front of her. She hurried up the steps to snap the shutter closed and secured it with a metal pin at the top. Matilda's anxious eyes flashed to Vera as she descended the stone stairs. "I'm sorry, Your Majesty. That should have been closed. Would you like a fire to take the chill from the air?"

There was a great hearth next to the window. Vera was as enamored by the inviting fireplace as she was by the window seat. Poofy cushions surrounded a short wooden table in the middle of a lush fur rug.

"No, thank you," Vera said when she realized that she'd been gaping with wonder at a space that Guinevere would have known well.

When Matilda offered to help her change into the nightgown that sat folded on the bed, Vera frantically said no, remembering her out-of-place undergarments. Matilda was rightfully confused when Vera backtracked and asked her to loosen her gown's laces. Matilda stared at her with a keen eye before unconvincingly brushing it off as traveling weariness.

"I've laid some things out if you'd like to clean up after your journey," she said, fingers working swiftly at the woven cords of Vera's gown. She gestured to the corner nearest the door where they'd entered. There was a square wooden pedestal that looked bewilderingly like a tap.

"Are you certain I can't help with anything else?" Matilda asked more slowly.

Vera shook her head, and Matilda did nothing to hide her disapproval.

"All right," she relented with a sigh, hands on her hips. "My quarters have been moved up here until you feel more settled. I'll be right across the hall."

"Thank you," said Vera.

Matilda stood in front of her for a few seconds longer, waiting—for what, Vera couldn't say. Then she shook her head and left.

Vera waited, holding her breath, until she felt confident Matilda wouldn't return. She first dropped her bag on the bed and changed into the bedclothes laid out. She was accustomed to a T-shirt and leggings, but the white tunic, not so different from what Matilda wore under her blue apron dress, came down to her shins. It was soft and thick enough to keep her warm.

Then she began exploring the room in earnest. She opened the wardrobe next to the bed to find gowns in gorgeous jewel tones with elaborate embroidery. Vera traced the intricate threadwork on the sleeve of one, took the fabric between her fingers, and held it to her face, breathing in the scent, searching for any hint of familiarity, and finding nothing.

This seemed as good a place as any to tuck away her discarded sports bra and the bag she'd commandeered from Merlin containing her other contraband. She shoved them behind the gowns, hoping no one would care to dig back there. Not sure what else to do with it, she hung the circlet crown unceremoniously from the knob on the wardrobe's door.

Next, Vera investigated the pedestal. Sure enough, what she'd thought was a tap was indeed so, albeit a rudimentary one. The handle reminded her of a pump at an outdoor campground spigot. When Vera tentatively lifted it, a steady stream of cool water flowed from its mouth and into the smooth basin, where it swirled down through a drain at the bottom. Her mouth went dry as she let the water stream through her fingers. She was desperately thirsty. She grabbed the cup conveniently sitting next to the tap and filled it up but hesitated before she brought it to her lips. Was it even safe to drink?

Thirst nearly won out over caution, but Vera sighed and set the cup down. She distracted herself from her thirst by wandering over to the desk.

Wedged between a round rock on one end and a brass candlestick on the other was a neat row of leather-covered tomes lining the back of the desk. Books. She tried to remember when writing made the leap from papyrus and scrolls to books before it occurred to her that any information she could recall from what she'd been taught in history class was likely wrong anyway. After all, she was almost positive a sink and tap with plumbing didn't belong in the seventh century. Yet the clothing had no elastic, and the window didn't have clear glass. In fact, the only glass she'd seen was the stained window in the chapel. She couldn't pin down when things were as they should be and when they diverted riotously.

Vera pulled a book from the middle, one with a mossy green cover. She flipped it open and choked on her breath as she took in two significant things. First, the words on the title page were typed, and second, the font at the center read The Hobbit. As if she needed more confirmation of the impossible before her, she read the following line in a smaller type: Or There and Back Again by J.R.R. Tolkien.

She laughed in disbelief as she snapped it closed and examined it again. The leather book cover felt right in this time period, but The Hobbit was over a thousand years out of place, much like herself. Vera pulled another book from the dozen or so and opened it. Hamlet by William Shakespeare.

She opened each one in turn. The Iliad and The Odyssey, All Quiet on the Western Front, Kindred, Death of a Salesman, Pride and Prejudice, Beloved, The Stranger, Frankenstein ... Vera had read all of them in secondary school or university.

She knew The Hobbit best, so she flipped through the pages of it as she sat down on the bed, scanning for her favorite passages. Everything seemed in place. It was the familiar story she loved, and that she, Martin, and Allison made a tradition of reading aloud together every Christmas season.

Vera shut the memory out as she closed the book and instead paid attention to where she sat. The bed was inviting to her weary body, with space to sprawl out and plenty of pillows—

Her eyes flashed to the wardrobe filled with her clothes, and she scanned the room. There it was.

Another wardrobe. And there were stacks of parchments on the desk, too. A quill lay unceremoniously next to one. Of course. This wasn't just her room, and it wasn't just her bed. After Merlin reassured Vera that she was not brought here to bear a child, she'd put it out of her mind. But how had she not recognized before now that she wouldn't be sleeping alone?

It was like her thoughts acted as an invitation. The door opened. Arthur came in, locked it behind him, and took two steps into the room before he noticed her there. She stood, feeling it somehow imperative that she not be on the bed at this moment. He looked nearly as surprised to see her as she did him, which made Vera feel slightly better on the whole.

His eyes were still glassy, and after the initial rush of shock, his face was once again a sheet of ice. She opened her mouth only to close it.

Arthur didn't speak either. He collected himself and began walking toward her. Vera instinctively backed away from him, and Arthur stopped mid-step.

"I'm not going to hurt you," he said. His voice came out in a low rumble even when he spoke quietly. He started walking again, giving her a wider berth as he went to the second wardrobe. He took out a few garments and draped them over his arm as he crossed to the desk and filed through the books. His finger ran down their spines twice before he selected one. Finally, Arthur turned to face Vera. His eyes flicked to The Hobbit, hanging from her hand. Vera held it out to him, suddenly feeling like she'd violated his privacy.

Arthur shook his head. "They're yours. Merlin brought them for you from your time. He thought they might comfort you." He looked at Vera's shoulder rather than her face. "Leave the door to the hall locked through the night unless you need something. Go to Matilda if you need help." The unspoken was also clear: don't come to me.

Arthur turned to the door beside the desk, his fingers on the handle.

But she did need help, and she couldn't ask Matilda. She didn't know what to say to get his attention. Should she call him "Your Majesty" or "my lord"? Owing to necessity and rising panic that her only source of informed help was leaving, Vera found her voice.

"Arthur," she said.

When he looked at her, his face was a stone mask of displeasure.

"I—can I drink this water safely?" She hated that her voice shook as she spoke to him. "And I don't know how to turn off or, um, put out the light. I couldn't ask Matilda because I should already know . . ." Her words petered to silence.

Arthur's expression slipped for a fraction of a second. Vera was nearly certain that something other than blank anger, something softer, rippled through the muscles of his face. He nodded curtly.

"The water is safe. And the light . . ." He crossed by her to the side of the bed with Vera's wardrobe and gestured to a marble-like tile on the wall beside the bed. "Hold your hand here until it's as dark as you like."

He kept his cold eyes on her only long enough for Vera to mutter, "Thank you."

Arthur gave another swift nod and stared at the floor as he strode back to the door by the desk, and without another word, he left. She heard the scrape of metal on wood as he locked it behind him.

Vera was certain by Arthur's response to her and by Lancelot's carefully couched words that there was far more to Guinevere's story than Merlin had let on. The looming task of unearthing her memories seemed an impossibility. She'd been naïve to think she was up to the task. An acrid taste rose in Vera's mouth. She was afraid and felt utterly alone.

Vera downed the cup of water, refilled it, and brought it to the bedside table. She pressed her hand to the marble tile and watched the light fade to black and back up to daylight bright, settling on a dim glow as the darkness of having it completely off unsettled her. She crawled under the heavy covers, lay on her side with her knees curled up by her chest, and, not knowing what else to do, began reading The Hobbit. Vera didn't notice that, as she read the dialogue, she imagined the voices her father used to perform for all the characters during their Christmas readings. His voices had always delighted her.

And so it was that on Vera's loneliest night she slipped off to sleep, her hand limp on the open book, with the voice of someone who loved her drifting through her mind.

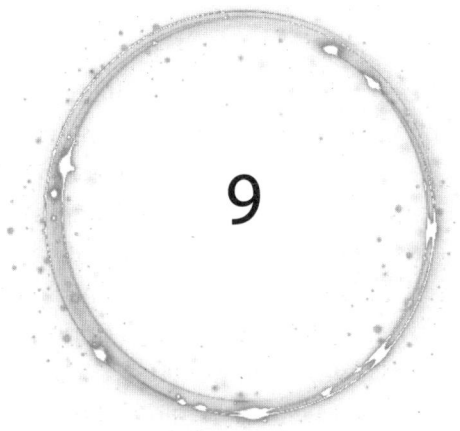

9

It was still night when Vera first woke. She only partly noticed that The Hobbit was now on the bedside table and the light overhead extinguished, but she didn't think to wonder how they got that way before she rolled over and was asleep again within seconds. The next time she woke, it was to Matilda's hand shaking her shoulder, and it was nearly midday.

There was no jolt, no momentary confusion about why she hadn't woken up in her bed at the George and Pilgrims. She knew where she was. More importantly, she knew when she was. Her eyes flicked to the door next to the desk, now slightly ajar. Curiosity about what lay beyond purred within her.

"Merlin wishes to speak with you," Matilda said, "and he insisted it can't wait."

If Vera had expected Matilda to do anything other than wait attentively, expectantly, she was sorely mistaken.

"You'll want to help me get ready, won't you?" Vera said, and Matilda nodded. "I don't mind doing it myself, I—"

"Your presence is urgently requested, and this will take much longer without my help," Matilda said. "Your Majesty, I'm not certain what it is you're afraid I'll see that's any different than it was before. It doesn't matter to me if you have scars or deformities or . . . multicolored spots on your skin. If I promise not to say a word or ask a question, will you allow me to help you?"

Vera sighed. "Oh, all right."

True to her word, Matilda didn't betray any expression of surprise or confusion at Vera's knickers as she helped her into a burgundy gown with sleeves that opened dramatically at the wrists, making Vera feel like she had delicate wings when she held her arms out. Matilda combed the tangles from her hair and arranged the circlet crown on her head over a tidy plait. She was ready in all of five minutes.

Under the guise of a detour to put The Hobbit back in its place on the desk, Vera pulled the side chamber door open a few inches more and peeked inside. There was no one there, and the room was all but empty save for a neatly made bed with the book Arthur had taken atop the blankets.

Matilda led Vera downstairs and into another courtyard, this one flanked by the tower with Vera's room and the one with the rounded roof that didn't match all the rest. Pipes she hadn't been able to see in the dark came from the top, tracing their way down the sides and running along the castle walls. She followed Matilda through an arched doorway in the tower's side. The inside couldn't be more different from the tower with Vera's quarters. No stairs climbed up, though there was a much narrower stone staircase descending into darkness. On the wall opposite was a ladder from the floor to the high ceiling, clearly visible because this tower was hollow.

Right in the middle of the dirt floor was a brick-walled well with a bucket pulley system. Wooden buckets rose from the well on one side, filled with water that sloshed as they rocked and clanked upward before the ascent stabilized and the buckets steadied. The filled buckets disappeared into one of two holes in the ceiling and reemerged from the other, upended and empty as they lowered down to continue the cycle. Vera gawped at the medieval brilliance before her. This was a water tower.

Merlin's study was down the staircase at the end of a narrow hallway. Matilda left Vera to enter on her own, and it was something like entering a pristinely ordered kaleidoscope. She wanted to look everywhere at once. One side housed a chemist's kitchen, with a large sink basin next to a chunky wooden worktable—and within arm's reach, a cauldron near the fireplace. Lining the back wall were shelves and shelves of glass vials and jars, filled with a rainbow of contents: a cerulean paste, red pellets, flaky green herbs, inky black goo, and hundreds of containers.

She heard water trickling over rocks. The chamber was so expansive that Vera strained to see where the sound came from in the farthest corner. Water flowed from the sculpted mouth of a stone boar's mouth into a bathing pool below it. In between where she stood and the pool was a veritable excess of treasures. There were baskets of rolled-up scrolls, wooden gears, metal globes, and delicate instruments ordered in cabinets from floor to ceiling, crystals in every color and size imaginable, and at the room's center, seated behind one of two desks pushed together, Merlin was bent over a book so enormous it nearly covered the entire desktop. He stood as Vera entered.

"You look well-rested," he said, a twinkle in his eye.

"I am. Thank you," she said.

He gestured at the seat next to his desk and she obligingly sat down, eyes still combing over the treasures of his study. "You inevitably have questions, and I owe you answers."

That pulled her attention back. "Yes, only about a hundred." She hoped she was smiling in a way that didn't betray her fear.

"Go on, then," he said encouragingly.

Vera went straight to the one that had bothered her most. "Why didn't you come to tell me who I was sooner? You can travel through time. That's the one thing we should have plenty of!"

Merlin chuckled. "The irony of it all is not lost on me. But the magic of time travel is not so simple, and it is limited. There are only certain times when the wormhole is accessible, and even then, the magic stabilizing it is different from the gifts most are born with. It was developed by mage study, and it is finite. Once it's spent, it is gone, and travel will become impossible."

If something happened, and she couldn't get back to her parents—to her father. Vera looked at her hands in her lap and squeezed her fingers into her thighs as a physical shiver of fear seared through her. What if she was stuck here?

"Which is why I didn't use it more than was necessary," Merlin added more quietly, his eyes tender with understanding. "I promised I'd give you the option to leave after your work here is done, and I'll do everything in my power to keep that promise. Now," he said more brightly, "what else would you like to know?"

Vera groaned. "I don't know where to begin. I don't know anything about magic or this kingdom . . ."

"All right. Basics," Merlin said. "When the Romans departed after a long occupation, it left what you know as England as thousands of scattered tribes, vulnerable and enticing to conquerors. That much is likely in your history books. After years of relative chaos, magic intervened and chose Arthur, and he brought the kingdom together."

"Was it Excalibur?" Vera asked, unable to stop herself from interrupting. "Did he pull a sword from a stone or a lake or . . . whatever?"

Merlin smiled like he was speaking to a child. "It wasn't so dramatic as any of that. A mage met him and was able to see him—to really see him and sense that he was chosen.

"Miraculously, all the other mages in the land who met Arthur confirmed it, too. That was a compelling testimony, as it didn't benefit any of them. But that's just it. It was undeniable. Anybody with even a less powerful gift could sense it when they met him, and that's no meager part of the population—nearly one in four. It gave him a firm foundation for ruling."

"Sorry." Vera stopped him. "A quarter of people here have magic? Is everyone with magic—or the gift—is that what you call it? Is everyone with magic a mage?"

"No. In fact, nearly all with the gift are born with one ability, and that's that. Mages are far rarer. We have multiple gifts, and we acquire more throughout our lives. Most towns in the kingdom have a mage who provides powers for their citizens. The greater the castle and surrounding town, the greater the mage. Our largest cities often have two." He waited, looking at Vera expectantly.

The implication dawned on her. "Are there two here?" she asked.

"There used to be. We shared this study." He gestured to the other desk. "She betrayed the kingdom by trying to kill the queen and nearly succeeding." Merlin folded his hands in front of him as Vera realized that, by the queen, he meant her.

"You said what happened was an accident," she said.

He nodded gravely. "The official story from the throne is that you were in an accident and that Viviane, our second mage, happened to be on a mission in Saxon lands when she was killed by captors. Only Arthur, Lancelot, and now you know the truth; Viviane attacked you, and she died for her crime. But we have kept it from our people."

That raised hairs on Vera's arms. "Why?"

"Peace, and even Britain itself, is young. The wars ended three years ago, and here we had an unprecedented force of unity, a land and a people rich with magic, and more mages with greater power than any nation has ever seen. The people are building infrastructure, knowing they're a part of something different, something bigger than themselves. This time is golden. Have you noticed how few guards there are roaming the castle grounds? That you only have the one chambermaid? That Arthur isn't constantly accompanied by a king's guard?"

She had noticed, but she'd thought it merely a coincidence that there'd been no guards in the corridors last night.

"We're not yet so established as to be confined by the structures and formality demanded by an older and larger country. It's a special time of growth and prosperity that few nations enjoy, and we only have it this once. Can you imagine how that would have shattered when the king's own mage, the most trusted and powerful position at court aside from the king himself, betrayed him? We couldn't sacrifice what we'd built, so we made the difficult decision to keep it all a secret."

"But you can't keep it a secret for long, can you?" Vera leaned back in her seat as if this would help her absorb the blow of this information. "You said yesterday that magic was draining from the kingdom. Won't they begin to notice?"

"Yes, and noticing will be the least of our problems, I'm afraid," Merlin said, and his face drew taut. "When I said that the magic rate was one in four, it was a misrepresentation of our current situation. It is the number most know and will say offhandedly, and it was true . . . before. Viviane cursed us. The magical birthrate is closer to one in ten now. This nation was founded on magic, and we will not survive without it. I can only imagine the designs she must have had for the kingdom to lay such a curse."

Merlin tilted his head to the side. "But you knew. You found her out, and you alone know what she did. She locked up your memories because they are our key to undoing her wrongs. It is a miracle we didn't lose you in her attack." He closed the massive book before him and opened his hands palms up toward her. "You're a one-of-a-kind anomaly, my dear. The type of magic I used to save your life has never been used before."

"Then how do you know it will work?" she asked, and with a swallow, mustered the nerve to voice her fear. "Merlin, I'm not her. I don't know how I could possibly have her memories."

"They're your memories," he corrected. "And I know because you've already begun to remember."

"No, I haven't," she said adamantly.

"You have." There was that measured patience in Merlin's smile. "I saw it."

Vera stared at him. There wasn't a single point in the last twenty-four hours when she had been anything but dumbfounded. The closest she had come to a memory was her unnerving affection for Lancelot, something she hoped Merlin hadn't noticed.

His eyes glinted. "How much horse riding do you recall doing during your life in Glastonbury?"

"Horse riding?" She blinked. "Hardly any."

"Any formal training?"

She shook her head.

"Guinevere, there's a particular way a lady wearing a gown is trained to dismount her horse. I watched you do it last night precisely as you were trained as a young lady in our time. You did it as if it was second nature to you because it is."

As soon as Merlin said it, she realized it was true. At the time, Vera had been consumed with what would come next. She hadn't noticed getting off the horse at all, and if someone had asked her to recount step-by-step how to do it, she wasn't sure she could. But Vera felt an easy conviction that she could do it again. "That's enough for you to feel certain the rest of it's in there?"

"It is enough, and I am certain," he said.

"Is there some magical way to make me remember?" Vera heard desperation creeping into her shaking voice. "Can't you pull it out of my head or something?"

Merlin steepled his fingers in front of his lips. She thought he wanted to say yes, but he sighed and clicked his tongue. "Ultimately, we'll need to use a magical procedure to penetrate the final barrier—to get to the heart of what Viviane didn't want you to remember. But . . ." He took a slow breath before he nodded, resolved. "The more you can wear away at what she's done to block you, the better magical intervention will ultimately work."

"How am I supposed to do that?"

"Familiarity is fundamental to unlocking both your conscious and unconscious memories. Immerse yourself into what was your ordinary life as thoroughly as possible. As queen, you're responsible for all matters in the castle, so you'll be well-equipped to perform those duties. I didn't plan it this way, but it works out rather well that you helped run the hotel with Martin and Allison. But the most important thing you can do is reconnect with Arthur—in every way you can."

She inhaled sharply. Her eyes flashed to Merlin. Did he—was he implying something . . . physical? She was probably blushing.

Vera cleared her throat. "Why would that help me remember?"

"There was no one you were closer to than the king. That's why this is so difficult for him." Merlin smiled sadly. "He scarcely dares to hope he might have you back. His love for you is the core of breaking through to your memories."

Vera had a hard time believing that the man she met last night, so cold and intimidating, would ever want to have anything to do with her, much less reconnecting. Still, she resolved to try.

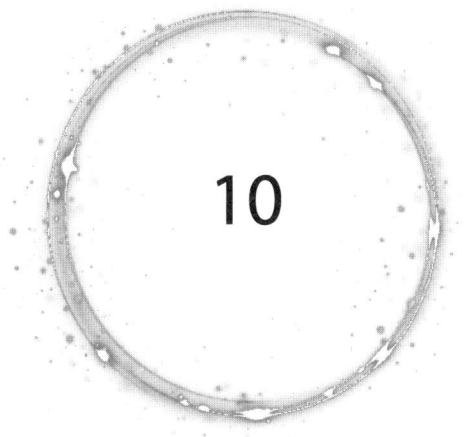

10

At the very least, Vera could throw herself into Guinevere's life.

Matilda took her to nearly every corner and crevice of the castle grounds throughout the afternoon. They started in the kitchen and caused a stir as Vera pretended to know the cook and the half-dozen kitchen staff members who flooded her with their welcomes. They visited the gardens, went to the stables, and met with the castle staff.

Matilda turned to Vera before each stop. "Would you prefer to lead the conversation, Your Majesty?" she'd ask. Or, "Please chime in as you like."

Vera smiled politely but observed in silence, knowing she'd betray her ignorance if she opened her mouth to say more than greetings. And each time, Matilda's offer became more of a formality.

When it was time for dinner, Vera let out a long sigh, assuming that Arthur would be there and that this would be her opportunity to finally speak with him. Her relief was short-lived. The great hall was the largest room in the castle, with two tables that ran the length of it on either side. They were already more than halfway filled with people.

A much shorter table was perpendicular to the rest at the front atop three short steps. There were only six seats at this table, and the two center chairs were more ornate than the rest, throne-like. They were all empty—save for the one next to the smaller throne. Lancelot occupied it. When he saw Vera, his eyes lit up. She nearly stopped in her tracks.

He remembered her. He wasn't the only one. All the gathered diners' eyes shifted to Vera as she took her place on the throne next to him.

But they remembered Guinevere. Lancelot remembered her.

"Good evening," he said with a cordial bow of his head as he passed her a goblet of wine. "Arthur sends his apologies. He will not be here this evening." Vera thought she heard frustration, even accusation, beneath his words.

So there it was. Arthur was continuing to avoid Vera, and evidently, Lancelot didn't approve. Her affection for him bubbled. She scanned the room as she took a sip, and her eyes found Merlin, his mouth fixed in a frown as his gaze darted from Vera and Lancelot to the door.

"How was your first day back?" Lancelot asked, pulling her attention to him.

"It was fine," Vera said, more a habitual response than an answer. He turned his whole body and squared up with her, his eyebrow raised.

"A bit overwhelming," she said.

Lancelot propped his chin on his hand. "How so?"

"Do you really want to know?"

"I do, if you're inclined to share." He seemed to mean it, too.

"All right," Vera said. Maybe it was loneliness that drove her, or maybe the warm tug of kinship with him. Either way, honesty came forth in a hurried whisper. Lancelot leaned closer. "I don't think I have Guinevere's memories and all of magic and the kingdom as you know it and likely even the future that I grew up in is going to be doomed. And I spent the afternoon behaving like a daft fool who doesn't know anything because, as it turns out, I don't know anything."

"I see," he said, matching her volume. "Why are we whispering?"

"I—" She hadn't done it on purpose. Vera looked out across the hall, finding far too many pairs of eyes staring back at her. She swallowed and told him about how it had been before, how no one could remember her. "I'm not used to being known or even noticed by anyone. And who even are all these people?"

Lancelot let out a long exhale. "Overwhelming is an understatement," he said gravely before he turned to the room, and his severity dropped away. "And these are all the noble folk in town. Most helped to fund our war efforts, some are successful merchants. And that man who just sat down over there . . ." He inclined his head toward the recently occupied seats on the other side of Arthur's empty chair. "Don't look," he added a half second after Vera had turned.

"Sorry," she said, whipping back to face him.

"It's all right." He grinned. "My fault. That man," he went on more quietly, "has brought his daughter in an effort to tempt me to marriage."

"You aren't married?" Vera had assumed that people from the Middle Ages married young. She couldn't exactly place Lancelot's age, but she was sure he was at least a few years older than her.

"No. I was eighteen when the invasions started, and life became war for the better part of a decade. Ordinary things like getting married were postponed. You and Arthur only got married three years ago," he added in a way that felt practiced, as if he'd mounted this defense before. "I haven't gotten around to it. Most of the knights haven't, for that matter."

Much more nonchalantly this time, Vera adjusted in her seat as if she were merely repositioning herself while the food was being served instead of what she was actually doing: getting a glimpse of the hopeful lord and his dejected young daughter.

"There are three more planning to come this week," Lancelot said through gritted teeth that he was somehow able to keep in the shape of a smile. "I am not being modest when I say that I am really not a catch."

Vera battled the sudden urge to argue that point as she noticed the muscles in his neck tense and his teeth lock together. He hated this.

She leaned toward him seriously. "If one of the others this week catches your fancy, shall I sing the praises of Lancelot the loud and foolish?"

His eyes flashed to her, a surprised smile playing at one side of his lips.

"Or, perhaps," Vera continued innocently, "I should tell them that, if the lady is lucky, he might bring her along to scare the piss out of some little shits at sword point?"

Lancelot laughed in earnest. "You may have noticed I left that bit out when we met Merlin last night." He stared down at his cup, turning it in his fingers.

"I did," Vera said, and before she had time to overthink it, she kept going. "And what about Arthur? Did you tell him?"

Lancelot grimaced. "I, er, hadn't gotten around to that."

This time, it was Vera who laughed. "A convenient theme for you, it would seem."

Eating dinner on what amounted to a stage in front of a hall of courtly attendants, craning their necks for a view of the long-awaited queen, was a much more pleasant affair with Lancelot at her side, distracting her with courtly gossip. Vera didn't even notice that the hall had begun to empty and even the seats on the other side of Arthur's empty chair had been vacated by the lord and his daughter by the time Matilda was standing next to her.

"Matilda," Lancelot said with a twinkle in his eye. "Will you please marry me and save me from the parade of lords desperate to be rid of their daughters?"

She pursed her lips, feigning annoyance, though a sly grin seeped through. "As tempting and romantic an offer as that is—no."

Lancelot shrugged as he pushed out his chair. "Worth a shot. Good evening, lady Matilda." He bowed to each in turn and winked at Vera. "G'night, Guinna."

She pressed her lips together to stifle her smile as he departed. Maybe he'd always called Guinevere Guinna, but the endearment was brand new to Vera.

Matilda watched with her head cocked to the side and her expression unreadable. "Let's retire, Your Majesty," she said.

After Vera's mission of connecting with Arthur had been so thoroughly thwarted, she held out hope of even a short interaction in their chamber like they'd had the previous evening. This time, she was prepared. She'd decided that when she saw him, she'd be blunt as a mallet and tell him that she didn't believe she was actually Guinevere either. They weren't—they couldn't be—the same person. If Arthur knew she had no designs to try to replace the woman he'd lost and that all she wanted was to unearth those memories for the kingdom, for him, surely he would help her.

But when she returned to their chambers, the door to the side room was already locked. The next morning, Arthur was gone before she woke.

Matilda knew everything that happened in the castle, so Vera was positive that she'd noticed the strange situation between what should have been two reunited lovers, but she didn't let on. She dutifully accompanied Vera in the tasks of running castle life and murmured kind corrections in her ear when she got details wrong, which she frequently did. That too must have sounded some alarm bells that Matilda ignored, save a raised eyebrow here and there.

By far, the highlight of Vera's first week came on her third morning when she was woken before dawn to a knock at her chamber door. She sat up in bed, thinking she'd imagined the sound in the silence that followed when it happened again. Three sharp knocks. Vera crept from her bed, her bare feet hissing along the cold stone floor, eyeing the locked door to Arthur's chamber as she considered whether she should call for help.

"Who's there?" she asked in an awkward half-whisper.

"It's Lancelot!"

She opened the door right away, worried something was wrong, but there he stood with a broad smile. "Fancy going for a run?" he asked.

"Yes!" Vera said. She left him in the hallway while she dressed.

A quick rummage through the wardrobe produced a tunic shirt, heavier and more blousy than the one Lancelot wore, and a pair of thick brown trousers. Neither was ideal, but Vera was so desperate for the release of a run that she'd have gone in her nightgown if it was all she had.

They left through a back gate in the castle wall, an ordinary and underwhelming wooden door (that didn't at all match up with the rest of the main gate's defensive measures), and set out.

The sun had not yet risen, and the trail they ran on was dark, but Lancelot's orb bobbed along between them. Their pace was easy and left air in their lungs for conversation, which came rather effortlessly.

Vera nearly ran Lancelot off the trail in panic when a squirrel burst out of the bushes near them, prompting him to yell out an overly loud warning for any animal he saw after that. "Bird!" he'd shout and point, even if it was high in the sky. But his dedication to the joke served him poorly when he was mid-point and stumbled on a root that stuck up in the path, only barely avoiding a face-first wipeout.

Vera grinned to herself in the darkness, patiently waiting for her moment as they ran on. Then she saw it lying in the path ahead.

"Stick!" she shouted when they came upon it, a puny thing no bigger than her arm. Lancelot jumped at her voice and then had to full-on stop to recover from his laughter.

She'd started hundreds of mornings running. This was like every one of those runs, except this time, she wasn't alone. Vera was so grateful she didn't even think to complain about how heavy her clothes were and how quickly she was drenched from head to foot in sweat.

After about an hour, Lancelot guided them to the back gate where they'd started as the sun was beginning to peek over the horizon. He flopped down on the grass outside the wall and held out his hand as his orb zoomed back to him and shrunk in his palm.

"Is that your magic?" Vera asked, nodding toward his light as she sat down next to him.

"What? Oh, this?" He spun it in his fingers before pocketing it. "No. No, I don't have a scrap of magic. Merlin provides all the lights . . . well, most magic for Camelot, truth be told."

"And what about Arthur? Does he have magic?" Vera asked, making a great effort to sound casual.

"That," Lancelot said emphatically, "is a much more interesting question altogether. Not explicitly. But when the invasions began, and Arthur started uniting the people . . . I wouldn't have believed it if I hadn't been there. So many things had to come together just right for us to stand a fighting chance. And we'd have been thoroughly fucked without the mages, but," his eyes clouded with admiration, "I don't say this because he's like my brother, but this country and this peace—none of it would exist without Arthur."

"He sounds remarkable," Vera said, feeling like something leaden had dropped into her stomach.

Lancelot smiled sympathetically at her. She could read in his face that he knew far more than he was willing to share.

"What's wrong with him?" she asked, more bluntly than she meant to.

"Ah," Lancelot leaned toward Vera so that his shoulder pressed lightly against hers. "It's . . . not my story to tell."

Fiercely loyal. Vera heard Merlin's words in her mind as Lancelot shook his head and picked at the grass near his feet. "You should talk to him, though," he told her.

She scoffed. "He'd have to be willing to be in the same room with me first for that to happen."

He set his jaw and an unspoken exchange passed between them as their eyes met. He wouldn't say it out loud, but Vera felt like, at least in this matter, he was on her side. He reached up to pat her back but quickly pulled his hand away. "Gross. Gods, you are dripping in sweat, aren't you?"

Vera laughed as the wave of tension broke between them. "This shirt is so damn heavy."

He raised his eyebrows. "Then let's get you better clothes."

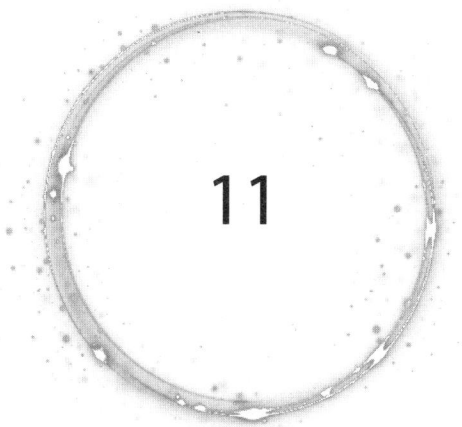

11

It was only two mornings later that Lancelot led her through the cobbled streets of Camelot straight to the armory. Vera had expected some royal seamstress or a clothing shop. Instead, they were greeted with a sharp glare by the scruffy middle-aged man (who Vera felt unreasonably sure would ride a motorbike if he were born thirteen hundred years later) deftly weaving tiny metal circles into chain mail. He set his work down in front of him and scratched his mostly grey beard with thick fingers as his eyes searched Vera. She felt he could read every lie she was living as if it were written plainly on her face.

"Your Majesty. Lancelot," he said, more grunt than words. He rose and picked up a neatly folded pile of garments and pressed them into Vera's hands. Right to the point. She could appreciate that. "Change over there." He pointed to a makeshift changing curtain in the corner.

After struggling to untie the strings of her dress, Vera pulled on the startlingly comfortable garments. The trousers were rust-brown with loose-fitting legs and buttons just below her knees to keep them from flapping about while she ran. The long-sleeved shirt was more fitted than the tunics she had seen but made of the same soft fabric as the trousers.

"How does it feel?" Vera started at Lancelot's voice as her fingers fumbled with her new trousers' buttons.

She stepped out from behind the curtain. "They're perfect."

It was no surprise. Lancelot had filled her in on their walk over.

"He made garments for me? In all of two days?" Vera had asked incredulously. "How did he know my measurements?"

"That's Randall's gift," Lancelot had said. "It's a sensory power. He's never needed to take your measurements. He saw you at dinner the first night and instantly knew them. He can hear better, see better, smell from farther, and he's got this thing with his hands, too. He has these massive sausages of fingers, but he weaves the finest, most intricate armor. Quickly, too. It was all dead useful in battle, even the smell part. He's a bit rough about the edges, but don't let him fool you. Randall's one of Arthur's most trusted knights, and he might be the sweetest man to walk this planet."

Vera couldn't speak to the armor nor to Randall's sweetness, but Lancelot's assessment of her new running kit was certainly true. Randall made a circle about Vera, eyeing her as he rubbed at his beard. "The shirt's based on what our soldiers wear underneath their chainmail. The whole set's a wool and silk blend. It should handle moisture well."

"That's good," Lancelot said, "because she sweats loads. Buckets, really."

"It was a heavy shirt!" Vera protested, glaring at him. He was seated at a workbench, bent over Randall's chainmail with metal tools in hand, grinning in satisfaction as he worked. "I sweat a normal amount," she added to Randall.

He continued his inspection, checking the seams of Vera's sleeves. "You're very bad at that," he growled, and Vera only realized he wasn't speaking to her when he glanced over his shoulder at Lancelot. "Yes, you," he added when Lancelot looked thoroughly scandalized. "Going to have to redo all of your work. And you're slow, too."

Randall lifted his gaze to Vera's face for the first time, and his left eyelid flinched just enough for her to realize he was winking at her as he joined the banter on her behalf.

She smiled. "I can't believe you made these so quickly. Thank you."

She touched his arm, and Randall awkwardly ducked his head in a bow, color rising above the whiskers on his cheeks. Perhaps Lancelot had been right about Randall's gentle spirit, too.

Lancelot guided Vera via a different route back to the castle: a winding footpath through a section of town where the structures thinned out and gave way to a lush green field speckled with purple heather and with benches along the side. Between the benches were practice swords, spears, and shields hung on wooden racks.

"This is our training arena," Lancelot told her. "We run drills with the castle soldiers every day."

An enclosure caught Vera's eye on the farthest end of the field. It reminded her of a petting zoo pen she'd once visited on a day trip during school, made of picket boards and the height of her hips.

There were no goats bleating their demand for children to feed them, but the pen wasn't empty. There must have been a dozen people corralled in it: boys barely old enough to have scruff on their chin, men who could have easily been their fathers, and two teenage girls—all running, laughing, and shouting. Onlookers crowded the picket board wall, cheering them on.

Vera heard a loud THUNK, and soon she could see a roughly sewn-together football. They were playing some sort of keep-away game. Players could kick the ball or smack it with their fists, but when it bounced off the wooden pickets and whacked someone in the leg, or when a player took a directly kicked ball to the bottom, they'd hop the wall, and the game continued with those who were left. It ended when one person remained, who was clapped on the back in congratulations of their victory before anyone wanting to join the next game clambered into the pen.

"That's the pit. The game is rather a favorite in town." Lancelot eyed her. "Do you want to play?"

"What? Me?" Vera looked around her as if expecting there to be someone else that he was asking. "Is that even allowed?" There were plenty of women joining in the game.

"Sure," he said. "Granted, I'm probably not the best judge of propriety, but . . . I don't see why not."

Lancelot didn't wait for an answer. He took Vera's hand and escorted her to the pit, where they both joined the gathered players. Nobody spoke directly to her, but a general hum of excitement rippled through the crowd as they took notice of Vera and Lancelot's presence in the game. The winner of the previous match had the honor of kicking the ball first, and then they were off.

And it was riotous fun. Lancelot jumped high to dodge a particularly well-aimed zip of the ball, and Vera held up a ready hand to congratulate him.

He looked at her fingers and back to her face. "What's that? What are you doing?"

"A high five," she explained, tickled that, to the best of her knowledge, she was performing the first ever high five with the legendary Sir Lancelot. "You slap my hand with yours." She mimed it for him, clapping her raised hands together. "It's like a 'Well done!' sort of congratulations thing."

"Oh," he said as he gamely slapped his palm to hers. He grinned. "I like that."

Play carried on around them, and Vera was caught with a ball to the shoulder while still laughing about rewriting the high five's history. The players grew rather quiet in the seconds following until she threw her head back in playful frustration and climbed over the wall. That was permission enough for the fun to resume. She mercilessly rooted against Lancelot, and when he was pegged by a poor bounce off the wall, she roared with glee, and he rolled his eyes in the first sign of annoyance she'd yet seen from him. This delighted Vera even more. Her new friend evidently liked to win. But he wasn't a poor sport and was soon cheering on the remaining players.

During the next game, with luck and a hefty amount of hiding behind larger competitors, Vera found herself one of four remaining. She vaguely noticed that the crowd grew quiet but was too focused to try to figure out why. The ball was in her area, and she kicked it as hard as she could. She'd been aiming it at one of her opponents, missed, hit the wall, and it ended up ricocheting conveniently off two remaining players, leaving only Vera and a sturdy man across the pit vying for victory.

The ball stopped near her opponent, meaning he would start the volley. His eyes darted from the ball to Vera and back to the ball before he lobbed the most pathetic kick at her. She pursed her lips as if that could contain the indignation coursing through her. Vera marched forward, picked up the ball that had stopped rolling not halfway across the pen, and went over to the man.

Murmurs rippled through the surrounding crowd, but one voice carried to Vera's ears above the rest.

"What's she doing?" It was familiar, and she would have turned to look, but Vera had recognized her opponent. In fact, he wasn't a man at all . . . just a boy in a man's body.

"It's you!" she said. It was the boy she'd stopped at sword point on the road—only he'd clearly had a bath and haircut and was no longer dressed in rags. One feature from before remained: the fear on his face. If it was possible, he was more petrified now than he had been during their first encounter.

"You're the queen! I can't play against you, Your Majesty." He said it so softly that Vera had to lean in close to hear him. And his eyes darted up every few seconds.

"Of course you can," she said. If only he knew how very insignificant she was.

"Not in front of Sir Lancelot . . . and definitely not in front of the king."

Vera's neck would hurt later from how quickly she whipped around. Next to Lancelot, who leaned casually against the wall, stood Arthur. Her stomach dropped. She hadn't caught more than a passing glimpse of him since her first night. He wasn't dressed formally, but his hair was pulled back at his neck, and he wore a gold crown. His hand rested on the pommel of his sword as he watched. At least he was in the same vicinity as her, and Vera noticed he wasn't scowling. She turned back to the boy, very much needing not to think about Arthur's presence.

"He'll kill me," the boy went on. "Especially after what happened—after what I did," he corrected himself, his words dripping in shame.

His eyes were pained, tortured even. She smiled sadly at him, wondering exactly how young he was. "What's your name?"

"Walter," he said, staring at Arthur.

Vera lowered her voice and moved closer to him. "Look at me, Walter." She waited for him to tear his eyes from the king. "He doesn't know about that. But if you let me win this game in the name of some misplaced chivalry, I will march right over there and rat you out." She said all this with grave severity, but she ended it with a goading grin. "Come on, now. Show me what you've got."

She pushed the ball into his hands. Vera wished she could convey to Walter that she was as nervous as him. Arthur stood precisely at the spot on the wall opposite Walter, which, of course, was the place it made most sense for Vera to stand in front of. She could feel his eyes on her back as Lancelot's voice joined with the crowd's cheers. "Stay in it, Guinevere!"

When Walter smacked the ball into play, Vera jumped out of the way and heard a resounding thud behind her as the ball slammed into the wall. He wasn't holding back this time. Good. She gave a good show of it, successfully dodging a handful of strikes and even getting in a few solid whacks at the ball, but she wasn't much of a match for Walter. Vera was off balance and distracted after catching a glimpse of Lancelot and Arthur, their heads inclined toward one another. Lancelot was talking quickly and gesturing at her as Arthur's lips pressed flat together into an unreadable line.

Walter swiped at the ball, and amid her preoccupation with Arthur, it bounced off the wall behind Vera and nailed her forcefully, dead on in the middle of her back. She fell gracelessly forward onto hands and knees in the dirt and heard a collective gasp from the crowd as Walter launched into a stream of horrified apologies.

"I'm sorry, I'm sorry, I'm so, so sorry!" He rushed to her side and reached out toward Vera's shoulders, then pulled back, then reached out, apparently unsure whether he should touch her. Vera grabbed Walter's hand to settle the matter, and he pulled her to her feet.

Her dress must have been filthy, and strands of her hair had escaped her braid's valiant attempt to restrain them. Vera also felt the heat in her cheeks. There was no scenario in which falling in the dirt in front of strangers, let alone a real-life mythically famed king, was not humiliating. She'd forgotten they'd all keep looking at her once the game was over.

Nevertheless, Vera could sense that this moment was precarious for Walter. She beamed at him and raised his hand to signify victory. The tension in the crowd broke as the onlookers cheered and clapped with more enthusiasm than before.

"Thank you," Vera said to Walter. "That was great fun."

The soft-spoken boy in a man's body blushed scarlet and bowed to Vera while backing away.

As many from the crowd clambered over the walls to join in for the next round, Vera made her retreat. The crowd had grown, no doubt, due to Vera and Arthur's unexpected presence. Having spent her whole life being markedly, even unnaturally forgettable, the attention heaped upon Vera made regret swirl within her at having played in the first place, especially after insisting on a competitive end to it. She'd no sooner swung her feet to the other side of the wall than, everywhere she turned, she found someone vying for her attention.

"Welcome home, Your Majesty!"

"Quite a fall. Are you all right?"

"Fine game, Ma'am. Well played!"

She smiled sheepishly at the well-wishes, but there were whispers from some, too. She distinctly heard "inappropriate" and "shameful" as she made her way through the crowd. Vera felt a hand on her elbow and turned to find Lancelot with Arthur a half step behind him.

Lancelot bestowed Vera a slack-jawed chuckle. "I was not expecting that," he said.

She chanced a glance at Arthur and was relieved that he didn't look angry. He wasn't smiling, though.

"Are you injured?" he asked in his stony way. It was the first time he'd spoken to her since the night she arrived. A tight flutter shot through Vera's chest.

"Only my pride," she said, managing a smile.

She thought Arthur's mouth twitched at the corner but surely must have been mistaken, for his face remained cold.

"I didn't know you were here," she said.

He tilted his head in a gesture toward the training field. "I'm training with the soldiers today." Arthur looked Vera up and down and opened his mouth as if to say something, but a bent old man with a cane beat him to the punch.

"Your Majesty," the little man said in a squeaky voice, bowing low.

Arthur instinctively reached out to support the man at his elbow and smiled kindly at him. It was jolting to watch Arthur's expression soften so dramatically. She'd only seen his face set and cold, controlled as a granite statue.

"I had no idea the queen was such a fierce competitor!" The little man said with no small measure of pride.

"Indeed," Arthur agreed, turning his warmth toward Vera but only looking as high as her shoulder. Still, it nearly toppled her. "She was quite impressive."

The old man waggled his cane at Vera. "I'd hope for nothing less from you, Your Majesty. And we are all glad you have returned to us." He patted her arm and hobbled off with impressive agility. Watching him was a good cover for figuring out what she should say next to Arthur. This was her opportunity; he was right here and warmer than he'd yet been.

But when she turned to Arthur, it was to see his back as he strode away toward the training field.

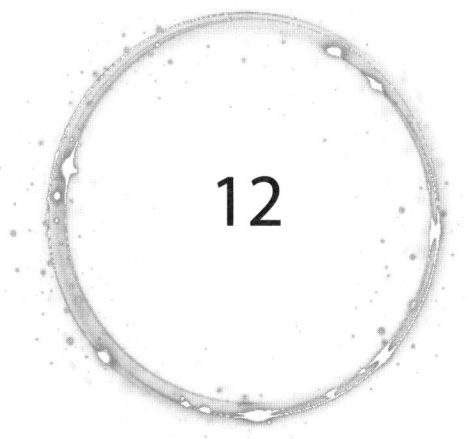

12

Perhaps the one had nothing to do with the other, but it had been their friendliest interaction yet, and that night, Vera stopped mid-stride on her walk through the great hall when she saw Arthur's seat occupied. There he sat, dressed far less formally than Vera expected. Nonetheless, his presence noticeably changed the room. There was an electricity in the energy of everyone present. And it was louder. The prior evenings when Arthur was absent, she'd been uncomfortable speaking much above a whisper. Tonight, a pleasant hum of conversation and bawdy laughter surrounded her.

Vera's eyes flicked to Merlin, wondering if he'd had any hand in this. He smiled encouragingly.

From how Arthur was seated, angled toward Lancelot, who sat in the chair on his left, Vera's approach around the table had her facing him. He kept his eyes on Lancelot, who was talking animatedly.

"And it wasn't the only way we might have—" Lancelot stopped mid-sentence, diverting his attention to Vera as she stepped into his view. "Good evening, Your Majesty," he said, and it forced Arthur to acknowledge her presence, too. He turned in his seat and inclined his head in a bow of greeting, stiff and formal.

As soon as she sat down, though, he bodily turned to Lancelot, his back an impassable wall that shut her out, leaving Vera to soak in her frustration—but not for long. As the meal was being served, a trumpet blared, and a melodic voice took command of the room.

"Our king welcomes this evening, for our courtly entertainment, the North Wind Players, performing The Most Tragic Tale of Dorchester." The castle's herald stood at the back of the hall and took a great step aside as he opened the door with a flourish, and an acting troupe entered to polite applause.

The room went silent as the actors took their places in the open space between the two tables. They held their poses for nearly too long, and precisely when the first antsy audience member shifted in his seat, they all began moving. The two on their knees in front pattered the floor with their fists. An enchanting woman in all grey with streams of fabric tailing behind her swirled through the room, and as she passed, a true sound of wind, the kind that meant rain was coming, followed in her wake. One actor jumped atop a table, holding a glowing yellow orb high above his head before he heaved it down at the floor. It shattered not into shards but with a final bright flash and a puff of vapor. The accompanying sound was the real rumbling crash of thunder. The vapor swelled and rose, darkening and expanding until the great hall's ceiling was covered with a blanket of storm clouds.

The clouds continued to rumble above their heads as a scrawny girl emerged from the chaos and began to spin the tale. She was the lone survivor in a village massacred by a young mage gone mad.

As she told the story, the actors performed around her, bringing the sad tale to life with striking beauty. The entire audience was captivated, more than one with tears on their cheeks as the young girl was hidden by her brothers in their animal feed trough before watching them be slain by the mage through cracks in the boards. It was a fairytale trope, one with a moral lesson pasted on at the end, lauding how Arthur's rule brought unity and an end to violence against the people. They held their final poses in perfect stillness. The clouds above sank toward the audience's heads.

Since they were seated higher than everyone else, the blanket of clouds first reached the royal table. Vera glanced at Arthur, who was grinning as he reached up and touched them with his fingers. Like he'd sensed her gaze, he turned to her. His eyes didn't have time to darken, and Vera knew her expression mirrored his amazement. Her skin prickled. It was almost intimate—and gone in a flash as the descending clouds reached their foreheads and obscured Vera's vision entirely.

A murmur rose around the hall with surprised oohs and ohs, and a scant few who sounded genuinely frightened. After the clouds reached the floor and faded, leaving only the faint smell of rain, Vera noticed that the acting troupe had risen and arranged themselves together under the cover of the descending storm clouds. They bowed, and the court followed Arthur in his enthusiastic applause.

"That was most impressive," Arthur said when the applause dwindled. "I'm honored by your telling of my part in this. Forgive me for my memory, but the massacre of Dorchester was twenty years ago, was it not?"

The ensemble looked at one another and nodded.

"I was a boy of ten and, humbling though it is to admit, probably convincing my father I was more likely to create havoc than ever unite any kingdom," said Arthur modestly.

The actors' eyes flitted back and forth among one another until the troupe's leader, the woman in grey who could make the sound of wind with her body, stepped forward with a flourish and bow. "My liege, we believe the spirit of the crown moved among us before it found you. But it was you all along."

The gathered court applauded once more.

"That's lovely," Lancelot said graciously to the performers. Then, leaning forward so Vera and Arthur could see him, he spoke much more quietly. "What the bloody hell does that mean?"

Arthur was more equipped to absorb his friend's humor. His lips merely curled up further on one side, and he inclined his head in a bow to the departing performers. Vera, on the other hand, snorted with laughter. The nobleman to her right glared at her. She quickly turned away from him to find Arthur watching this exchange, the glint of a laugh in his eye. No sooner had Vera caught his gaze than his eyes flitted downward, and he was rising from his seat.

"Pardon me," he said. Without a nod or bow or another word, he abruptly walked away. She was left staring at Lancelot, his eyes wide and the corners of his mouth dipped into a frown.

"I take it that's not normal," Vera said.

"Er." His eyes followed Arthur as he exited the hall. "No," he said.

Vera let out a single, ridiculing laugh.

After a long moment, during which Lancelot twiddled his fingers and scrunched one eye shut with his mouth in a nearly comical grimace, he looked up at her brightly. "So," he said, "Do you want to run tomorrow?"

Now fully outfitted, rising before the sun to run was the one constant between Vera's life before and her life as Guinevere now. This time, though, she had company. Like tonight, Lancelot would confirm at dinner whether they'd run the following morning, and most days they did. They met at Vera's door, ran for the better part of an hour, flopped onto the grassy hillside by the castle's back wall, and talked until the sun rose.

Routine took its course in many aspects of Vera's life in the early days of her new normal. Run with Lancelot. Household duties with Matilda. Dinner. It was the ample amount of idle time in between that prodded Vera's anxiety awake. Merlin was scarcely around the castle. He was almost constantly in a neighboring village, fixing their magical problems. Vera was eager to begin the work of recovering Guinevere's memories. She couldn't possibly pull off this ruse for long—a nobody draped in the body of a queen. But when Merlin summoned her to his study after nearly two weeks, her relief was short-lived.

"What are you—?" Vera started, but it was obvious. Merlin already wore his traveling cloak as he carefully tucked potions into his saddle bag. "Why are you packing?"

He sighed as he glanced up at her. "There is trouble in Exeter." At Vera's blank stare, he explained further. "It's a two-day ride from here. Larger towns have mages. In places like Exeter, however, they rely on the gifts of the many, pooling the collective resources of all born with a gift in that area. Exeter supplies grain to Camelot and the next four towns. But the reason they could claim that role was down to the gift of a woman who crafted a rather ingenious irrigation system.

"The complex turbine system that rerouted the water came from her magic. She died shortly after its construction, and, for the most part, the town's folk have been able to maintain it and repair it when it broke. But now the whole system has stopped. There's no water flowing, no one with a suitable gift nearby that can fix it, and the late harvest is in imminent peril without intervention. So . . ." He shook his head as he continued shoving tomes and bottles into his bag.

Crestfallen, Vera dropped into the same chair she'd sat in during their first conversation. "Why did it stop working?"

"When a person has made something with their gift, they obviously can't sustain it once they're gone."

"The magic dies with them?"

Merlin rushed to the baskets of scrolls and began rifling through them. "Not exactly," he said as he plucked two rolls of parchment from the bundles. "The work of the magic will fade from what they touched without that individual's force sustaining it, but the gift itself returns to circulation. In theory, babies are born all over the world with gifts every day. It should stand to reason that somewhere, a child was born with her gift the day she died. As long as we've studied it, magic functioned like air, a resource we use that recycles itself."

She nodded. "But not since Viviane?"

Merlin stopped packing and looked at Vera in earnest. He seemed older than she remembered. "Not since Viviane," he confirmed. "I've spoken with Arthur, but . . ." He shook his head. "I'm sorry that this is on your shoulders, but he needs to hear it from you. If you tell him you need him, I don't believe he will refuse you."

"I hardly see him. I don't know how to even get a word in—"

Merlin dropped to his knee in front of Vera, his eyes rent with desperation. "Please," he said. "Please try. The situation is being gravely underestimated."

Vera swallowed, alarmed that the plea was as evident in his face as it was in his words. "I will. But what if he says no?"

Merlin sighed as he rose and resumed gathering his things. "We'll consider magical intervention when I return."

Under different circumstances, the lengths to which Arthur went to avoid speaking with Vera might have been amusing. She'd thought dinners might be her best option to corner him now that he attended them. After all, they were in the same room and right next to each other for at least the length of a meal. But the performance from the acting troupe hadn't been a one-time visit. Every subsequent evening brought yet another performance, which would have been infuriating if each wasn't as wonderful as the last, some with magical elements and some without.

A minstrel who sang the kingdom's legends. A band of musicians who ended up playing far beyond the dinner hour. More acting troupes. Dancers. The night Merlin left for Exeter, there was a storyteller who painted while he regaled them with legends. Vera felt this had to have some kind of magic to it, though she couldn't pinpoint the mystical quality. There was a lull when the storyteller grew quiet to make adjustments to his painting, and Vera made a snap decision that this was her chance.

"I have to unlock those memories." She said it quickly, leaning closer to Arthur. She didn't wait for him to acknowledge her; she knew he could hear. "Merlin thinks that connecting with you is the best way to start remembering." She hesitated, embarrassed to say the next part. But she thought of Merlin's plea, and the words tumbled out. "I need you."

Arthur flinched. He hadn't turned toward her as much as he'd angled his head in Vera's direction. He opened his mouth to interject, but Vera put a hand on his arm and plowed on even as she felt his muscles stiffen under her fingers.

"Just listen, please. I won't try to replace her—"

She stopped—because he looked at her. But it wasn't with interest or even politeness. He was furious.

"Guinevere." He snarled the name. "I can't." His voice was strained and low, and behind the rage in his face, Vera saw it in his eyes and a tremble through his rigid form: a flash of fear. The performance wasn't finished, but Arthur stood and left the hall, an action which didn't go unnoticed through the room.

She tried to keep her face composed as if this was ordinary. Heads turned toward Arthur until he disappeared through the side door, and then they turned to her. Even the artist faltered and paused, looking at Vera as he stuttered to a stop. The room was uncomfortably quiet. Her palms went slick, and nausea swept over her. Did they expect her to speak? She wasn't—she couldn't pretend to be their queen. She was a broken projector of a memory. That was all. She stared down at her hands.

Lancelot leaned toward her. "Guinna . . . ?"

"Help me," she whispered, hating how pathetic she sounded.

Lancelot's brow furrowed. He turned to face the waiting watchers, plastering on a dazzling smile. "The king offers his apologies. He has been called away and requests that we all enjoy the remainder of this superb performance on his behalf. Carry on, good sir."

Vera didn't remember another second of the performance. As soon as the applause began, Matilda ushered her from the room, and Vera followed to her quarters in a fog. There had to be a reason for Arthur's behavior.

As Matilda unlaced the back of her gown, Vera glanced at the closed door to his chamber. She knew he didn't believe she was Guinevere; neither of them did. But was that enough for him to respond to her like this? There had to be more to it.

She was changed into her nightgown, and Matilda was two steps from leaving the room when Vera made a decision.

"Matilda?" she said, and Matilda turned toward her in surprise. "Would you like to have a drink and . . . talk?"

She stared at Vera for a long while, her eyes soft. "I would be honored."

Vera gestured to the seating area by the fire, where Matilda sank into one of the comfy poufs. Vera fetched two glasses and the pitcher from the desk, which was always filled with fresh wine (presumably by Matilda herself). She poured Matilda's and then filled her own cup. Matilda shook her head as she took her first sip.

Vera wasn't sure where to begin. She had a plan for this conversation, but it felt unnatural to jump right to it. Her eyes landed on the vase of flowers on the low table. They were replaced with new ones at least once a week. When Vera left this morning, they'd been blooms of yellows and golds, and during the day, those had been swapped for large burnt orange blossoms mixed in with smaller white and cream flowers so lovely and perfect that Vera wouldn't have been surprised if they'd been made of silk. She fingered a petal in an unnecessary confirmation that they were real.

"Thank you for these. They're lovely," Vera said. "I always enjoy seeing the week's bouquet."

"I—" Matilda became keenly interested in her glass of wine. She stared down into it, swirling her goblet as she answered. "You are very welcome, Your Majesty. But you should know—"

"I was hoping you might call me Guinevere instead of Your Majesty," Vera said.

Matilda pursed her lips. "It would be improper for me to address you so informally."

"What if you just called me Guinevere in private?"

Matilda sighed a slow, deliberate breath. "I'll try, Your Majesty, but it's a rather big adjustment." Vera smiled at the first lapse. "Your—Guinevere," she said it stiffly, "your sense of propriety has been . . . relaxed since your return. And," she shook her head as Vera refilled both cups, "you should not be serving me."

"I'm sure you've noticed many things that are different," Vera said. She'd been thinking about this since her first night when she couldn't ask Matilda her most pressing questions, certainly during all their work together around the castle. After tonight, it was unavoidable. Vera needed more help. More importantly, though, she needed to be less alone. Maybe there was a good reason Matilda had been left in the dark about all that happened to Guinevere, but they clearly trusted her to care for Vera and to be around her so much. She must have noticed the books while tidying up, not to mention Vera's undergarments.

"Matilda, I need to tell you something."

Matilda set her cup down and leaned forward. "I think I may already know."

Vera blinked. "You do?"

"You have memory loss, don't you? From the accident?"

"I—" Why hadn't she thought of that? Come to it, why hadn't Merlin or Arthur thought to feed Matilda that story? "Yes. That's it. I do."

"I'm not sure why anyone thought that needed to be a secret from me." Matilda smoothed her skirt, somehow conveying her irritation with the gesture. "Arthur knows, of course?"

"Yes," Vera said, noticing how easily Matilda called Arthur by his name.

"He hasn't been the same since it happened."

"Did I do something before the accident?" Vera asked. "To make him so angry with me?"

Matilda frowned as she lay a comforting hand on Vera's arm. "No," she said. "I was with you nearly always, and in the times when I wasn't . . ." She shook her head. "I can't imagine what you could have done."

"Then why does he hate me?"

"He—" Matilda went silent, and Vera thought she might not answer at all. She leaned forward to straighten the flowers. "I don't get these, you know."

Vera laughed in stunned discomfort. She wasn't sure what that had to do with anything. "Who else comes in here?" Her eyes shot to the wardrobe where her bag of anachronisms was now carelessly tossed. Her photograph with her parents was on the bedside table, tucked into The Hobbit as a bookmark.

Matilda looked at Vera pointedly. Why wasn't she answering? If there was someone other than Matilda and Arthur coming in the—oh.

They were the only ones who ever came into the room.

Matilda nodded as Vera's eyes landed on her.

"Is that . . . has he . . ." She thought back on her chamber, on how everything had remained the same except the flowers, the only physical evidence in the room that time had passed these first few weeks.

"Every time?" Vera asked, her voice breathy.

"Every time." Matilda finished straightening the flowers with a frown. "I don't understand his behavior since you returned, but he has never, not once, hated you."

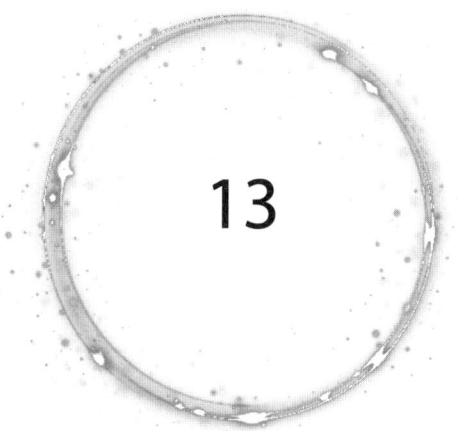

13

Vera felt an irrational certainty that, the strange kindness of bouquets aside, something had happened to make Arthur treat her so poorly. And she knew who she really needed to ask. Based wholly on her experience so far, if there was something Guinevere had done, Lancelot would know—because it would have happened with him.

It was unseasonably warm when they set out in the early morning darkness. Lancelot didn't mention Arthur's behavior the previous evening, but he did watch Vera more closely. Like she was a tea kettle on the edge of boiling, one that would scream out any moment. She was used to their route now, but he turned right instead of left at the fork in the road, and Vera followed without question. It would be nice to have a diversion from the conversation she knew needed to come at the end of their run.

She enjoyed the new trail and could understand why he'd held off on it until he knew she was capable. While the other wove between and around hills, keeping the loop submissively flat, this trail was narrower and took them into the woods, where it climbed and fell frequently. But it was lovelier, even in the dark. The trees they ran through were rich with their autumn leaves, and Vera could hear flowing water nearby.

Twenty minutes in, Lancelot stopped. He'd not done that during their runs before.

"What's wrong?" Vera asked.

He turned off the trail and held aside a bendy branch, beckoning Vera to follow. "Nothing," he said. "Wanted to show you something."

She followed him down a well-trodden game trail, the sound of rushing water growing in her ears until the branches thinned and gave way to a grove straight out of a fairytale. A pond lay before her with water so clear that she wasn't sure where it began until a frog jumped in, and the widening ripples traced the outline of the shore. On the opposite side was a tree so vast and ancient that the trunk was the size of a small cottage. She turned to match the sound to a stream gurgling down the rocky hillside and falling into the pond from ten feet above, a narrow curtain of a waterfall.

Vera turned back to Lancelot, her joy at this place on her lips, just in time to see him taking off his shirt.

"What are you doing?" she asked, aghast but laughing.

"Going swimming," he said, as if it were the most obvious answer to the silliest of questions. "Can't imagine we'll get a day warmer than this before spring. And I have a rule that I follow fastidiously: when you come upon a beautiful body of water, always go swimming. Always."

He took off his shoes and dropped them in a pile with his shirt, leaving him only in his trousers. He tossed the orb light underhanded in a high arc over the pond, but rather than falling after reaching its highest point, it stopped and hung there, a miniature moon that only answered to the tide of the sacred grove.

Lancelot scrambled up the rock next to him and unwrapped a rope from the tree branch above. He held tight just above a hefty knot at the end, swung from the side, and dropped, his body in a tight cannonball, right into the middle of the pond. An impressive splash exploded in all directions around him.

He resurfaced moments later, positively howling and gasping the specific sound humans make when shocked by cold water.

"Catch the rope, Guinna!" he called between gasps.

Vera, obligingly, did as it swung back toward the shore. Lancelot laughed loudly into the night, especially when he saw her disbelief.

"It is rather cold, Your Majesty," he said. "Not suited for a lady's disposition." He ducked his head underwater and swam away without giving her time to retort.

"Dammit," Vera muttered. He had her number. There was no way she was staying on dry land now. She climbed up on the rock and secured the rope before taking off her trainers and socks. She hesitated with her hands over the buttons of her trousers. She could stay fully clothed but then would have to finish the run dripping wet. Or she could undress as fast as possible and get in before Lancelot caught a glimpse of her mostly naked body.

He was still underwater. She heard the splash of his kicks as he swam away from her and saw the ripples extending in his wake. Vera sighed. She fumbled with the buttons at her waist and wiggled her trousers off. She flung her shirt over her head and tossed her garments into a pile, save for her sports bra and underwear, before grabbing the rope. Vera held tight with both hands and swung. Her drop into the water was less coordinated cannonball and more indelicate flailing.

She hit the surface with a slap and a splash, and the cold surged over her, waking up every inch of her body. Vera came back up, gasping and shouting gibberish as Lancelot flung both fists into the air.

"Yes!" he shouted, bobbing up and down as his legs treaded water beneath the surface. He left one open hand raised and stared at Vera expectantly. She shrugged while doing a breaststroke in place to keep afloat.

"I know I'm new to this, but I'd say that's a high five–worthy action," Lancelot said.

"Oh!" Vera laughed. She swam over to him and clapped her hand to his. She deliberately kept her eyes above his chin, away from his bare chest. A week ago, she wouldn't have had a second thought about seeing a man shirtless, but context was everything. Vera was surprised by many aspects of seventh-century life, yet she felt confident that this was dangerous territory.

Lancelot swam toward the waterfall, and despite her misgivings, Vera followed. With each stroke, the water became more bearable. By the time they reached the far side, she was almost of the mind that it was pleasant. He waited for her outside the curtain of water until she drew even with him.

"Can I show you something on the other side?" he asked her.

Vera nodded.

"It's a bit dodgy here. Stick with me," he said. Beneath the water's surface, Vera felt him take her hand. They took a deep breath together and plunged under. She immediately knew what he meant. Beneath the waterfall, the water churned in a way that could have easily disoriented Vera and tossed her upside down without the tether of Lancelot pulling her forward. It didn't require swimming far to pass beyond into the calm shallows. She found the rocky ground beneath her feet and stood up, her neck and shoulders breaking the surface as Lancelot dropped her hand.

It was very dark. The light that he'd suspended over the pond didn't reach back here. Vera could barely make out his form, scurrying ahead of her.

"Just a moment," he called.

Vera blinked as a new orb glowed to life. It took her a second to make sense of what she was seeing. First, it was merely the orb. Then, she realized that Lancelot was holding it and smiling—and he was standing on the dry rock ahead of her, but they weren't outdoors. They were in a cavern with smooth rock walls. The only discernable opening was the way they'd come in, under the waterfall. Vera half walked, half swam, and clambered onto the shore. Lancelot was already rummaging in a box at the base of the wall.

"Here." He held a blanket out behind him without turning to face her. He kept his eyes on the wall until Vera had it wrapped around her, holding it closed beneath her chin. He procured a second blanket and did the same for himself, both of them like children playing dress up in makeshift capes. Lancelot sat on the ground, using one corner of his blanket to dry his hair. Vera sat next to him and raised her eyebrows, bemused. She was not the first person he'd brought here.

If he noticed her reaction, he ignored it. He beamed at her. "What do you think?"

"This is . . . amazing. How did you find it?"

"A mixture of good luck and mischief, I suppose." Lancelot absently ran his hand over the smooth pebbles at his feet, picked one up, and began tracing his thumb over it. "Come to think of it, that's how I've found damn near every good thing."

Vera fished through the pebbles, too, until her fingers found a small, flat rock. She picked it up and skipped it across the water. It zipped along the surface until the pebble took its final skip and disappeared into the waterfall. He gave an appreciative hum and nudged his shoulder against hers. That was it. She couldn't put it off any longer.

"There's something important I need to ask you about," Vera said, nerves adding a quiver to her voice.

Lancelot sat up straighter. "Are you all right?"

"I'm fine." She took a deep breath and felt her heart begin to quicken. "Before the accident, did we . . . do something? You're the one person who has felt familiar since I got here. And I really like you."

"I really like you, too," he said quietly.

It urged Vera on. "Well, I wondered if that meant . . . did something inappropriate happen between us?"

Lancelot blinked, stunned as he took her meaning. "You think we had an affair."

"I—well, I don't know." Shame rolled through Vera before she made up her mind and said firmly, "Yes, actually, I do. In the legends about you lot from my time, Guinevere and Lancelot had an affair . . . one that rather wrecked the kingdom, I think. And this feels so strong. Based on what we're doing right now . . . Lancelot, we're sitting together with barely any clothing on in a cavern where you have obviously brought women before—and don't try to deny it. You have an entire box of blankets, a light at the ready, and I wouldn't be surprised if you have some wine tucked away somewhere, too."

He'd opened his mouth to argue but closed it as he chuckled and stared down at the rock that he turned in his fingers.

"I can't help but wonder if you've brought me here before. And it also might explain why Arthur can't stand to look at me, much less speak to me." Now, her voice was barely more than a whisper.

"You haven't been here before, and we did not have an affair of any kind," he said. He was silent for a moment before he fully turned, repositioning his body to face Vera. She turned, too. They each sat cross-legged, knee-to-knee. "Guinna, this does feel strong now. You're right. And this is going to sound mad, but I hardly knew you before. Of course, I knew you. But you and I never had more than a five-minute conversation between the two of us."

"We didn't?" Vera asked, utterly flabbergasted. "But this is so easy. I don't think I've ever felt this comfortable with anyone. And if we didn't even talk before, why were you waiting for me in Glastonbury when I came back?"

"I didn't want you to be alone." His jaw stiffened, and he stared down at his feet.

She could feel it; he was holding back. "What do you know that you aren't telling me? Please," she urged at his silence. "How am I supposed to do this if I don't know anything?"

Vera groaned when he didn't answer.

Lancelot shook his head. "Guinevere was—you were sad before the attack. And I knew Arthur was struggling after, and Merlin is . . . Merlin," he said offhandedly with a half-smile. Then, he grew serious. "I didn't want you to be alone without anyone who knew what happened. Without anyone who could be your friend. I'd have never guessed it would be like this, though. This is different."

His face shone with unbridled adoration. She understood what he meant. Vera would have called this sort of friendship magic before she even knew magic existed. But the way he'd corrected himself when he referred to Guinevere as another person needled at her mind.

"I think I'm only a container for her memories," Vera said. "I'm not really her."

He cocked his head and met her eyes, searching her. "Maybe not. The way you move and talk, even your expressions are the same. But Guinevere often seemed like she was walking through a dream, and you're . . ." He exhaled a laugh before he finished, "Not that. I can't imagine her stripping down to her undergarments and swinging into a pond, but there were glimpses. Like when she came up with the battle strategy. She was rather fearless. That part feels like you."

Vera laughed. He wasn't seeing her clearly. Perhaps it felt harsh to him to face the truth: the only part of her that was important was

Guinevere's memory. "That's kind," she said, "but I'm far from fearless, and I certainly shouldn't be anywhere near commanding anyone. I still have Matilda address the kitchen staff for me."

"I'd follow you into battle," he said. "And I mean that."

"Thank you," Vera said, blushing under his gaze and the compliment. "What do you have there?" She reached out to steady his busy fingers on the stone.

He grinned as he handed it to her, aware that she was asking solely to change the subject. "It's a nice shape, isn't it?"

Vera turned the stone in her hands and smiled. "It's a heart."

And so it was, a smooth black river stone in the shape of a heart that fit comfortably in her palm.

"A heart?" He leaned closer for a better look. "I've seen a heart. That is not what it looks like."

Vera laughed. "Well, in my time, this is the shape that's used to represent a heart or love. People draw them, make jewelry with them . . . My mum actually finds heart-shaped rocks everywhere she goes. She has a whole vase full at home." As Allison's face came to mind, the sting of it was instant. Vera held the stone back out to Lancelot.

"You should keep it. To remind you of her," he said.

"I don't want to be reminded of her," Vera said, sharper than she meant to. If she thought of her parents, if she thought of her own life at all, she'd think of Vincent. So much for being fearless. All Vera could do to make the painful things bearable was hide from them.

"All right. I'll keep it." With one hand, Lancelot took the rock and put it in his pocket. With the other, he took Vera's hand and gently squeezed it.

His gaze drifted from their entwined fingers up Vera's blanket-wrapped body to her face, and it was as if their proximity occurred to him for the first time. He pulled his hand back.

"You know I didn't bring you here to seduce you, right? I don't have any interest in . . . I have no physical desire for you," he said. Then, hastily, as if that might have offended her, "You're a beautiful woman, but it's not like that."

"I know." And as Vera said it out loud, the knot in her stomach undid itself because she knew it was irrevocably true. "Do you worry, though, that our friendship is suspicious to others? I mean, I questioned if we'd been together."

He considered it only briefly. "I don't know how it was in your time, but it's rather scandalous for a woman to be alone with a man who's not her husband or father. But you and I have some fortunate latitude. I've been named your escort. I'm trusted with you because of my station in the kingdom and my friendship with Arthur. Granted," he surveyed the cave and the nest of blankets surrounding them and squinted guiltily, "this might be pushing the boundary."

"Pushing the boundary or absolutely trampling it?"

"It could be worse," Lancelot said, his lips turning up at the corners. "I usually swim naked."

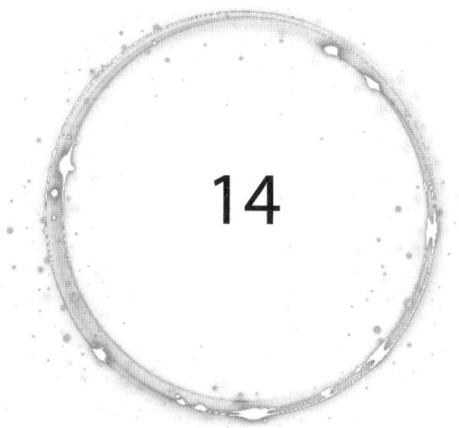

14

Vera made a choice. Since her efforts to get closer to Arthur had only ever backfired, she decided to stop trying, and the freedom that followed was a marked relief.

She reassured herself with Merlin's promise that they'd begin magical intervention when he got back. And he had encouraged Vera to reacclimate. Since Arthur removed himself as a point of connection, she took that as the go-ahead to spend her idle time precisely as she pleased. She had no delusions that she could be more than the conduit for lost memories—but she could at least try to enjoy herself along the way.

Over the next two weeks, she started seeking out nooks of delight. The first was the chapel Vera had noticed in the courtyard on her first night here. The inside was beautiful. Light shone through the stained glass in corridors of color, especially lovely when it bathed the many statues in its beams.

The sculptures with their draped clothing carved onto precisely chiseled musculature reminded Vera of the Roman statues she'd seen on display in the British Museum. But one statue, the one closest to the front on the left side, was a very pregnant woman whom Vera associated with Glastonbury's imagery for Gaia, Mother Earth. It was something about how she stood, one foot slightly in front of the other as if walking. Her shoulders were back and chest up with her stare trained straight ahead, an expression of strength and wisdom forever fixed on her face. She had one hand below and one above the globe of her pregnant belly, pointedly framing it.

Vera had never seen the mother of Jesus sculpted with this aura of power before, but she was positive that the woman frozen in marble was intended to be Mary. She loved the chapel the second she saw it, and she had plenty of time to admire it when she'd attended Sunday services with a stalwart and silent Arthur at her side.

She'd been failing to resist the urge to look back at the chapel door every time it opened.

"He isn't coming," Arthur's low voice had rumbled near her ear. He faced forward, his face impassive, but he'd inclined his head ever so slightly toward Vera.

"Who isn't?" she'd replied instinctively.

"Lancelot," he said, correctly guessing who she was expecting. "He follows the old faith."

"Oh." No one seemed to mind that the kingdom's general followed the "old faith" as Arthur had called it. In fact, Vera learned that Camelot's population was nearly an even split between Christians and pagans—and, evidently, they weren't yet at a point in history when that had become contentious. Vera wasn't sure whether this peaceful, seventh-century cohabitation was recorded in the schoolbooks collecting dust on her shelf back in Glastonbury.

Matilda was perhaps the most delightful surprise. Initially, her sense of propriety had her holding Vera at arm's length, stiffly guarded in her presence. Vera tried including her in after-dinner banter with Lancelot, but she merely gave them the smile of a mother patiently indulging her children's uninteresting stories.

She cracked the code of Matilda quite by accident the next week, as the young stable hand she'd met her first night (who she learned was called Grady) gave his weekly update. Grady's father, the stable master, left him in charge while he was out training their newest horses. The boy was all of fourteen and took his role very seriously. He wore his father's too-large boots and had slathered some sort of oil through his unruly dark curls that only partially smoothed them. Grady must have been told how sweet his dimply smile was all his life, for he hardly showed it during Vera and Matilda's visit. Like all young boys, he wanted to be seen and treated as a man. Yet he was the least intimidating of all the castle staff, so Matilda encouraged Vera to resume her duties here first.

"Our feed schedule is right on target." Grady pitched his voice lower than was natural as he led them through the stables. "And father tells me the new lot are training up exceptionally well. There is one small matter." He paused, looking at Vera with concern. "With Calimorfis."

It took Vera a beat longer than it should have to remember that was her horse's name, as she'd not ridden since the night of her arrival. "What's wrong with her?"

"Nothing is wrong," he said as he led them both into Calimorfis's stall. She was pristinely groomed, and she whinnied, tilting her silky neck toward Grady. He forgot not to smile as he stroked her head. "Since your return, she hasn't been ridden much, and she's getting antsy."

"Oh." Vera was ashamed she hadn't thought a thing about that. "Who rode her while I was away?"

"Mostly the king, Your Majesty. Occasionally, he'd ask me to. She's an incredible horse. It was my honor." Grady chuckled as the horse leaned her head into his shoulder. He nuzzled her back. "Any time you wish to ride, I will gladly ready her; just say the word. I can do it in minutes," he said with pride. "And in between, if you'd like, I can ask one of the knights to ride her." He sounded mournful at the idea of it.

"Would you mind riding her for me?" Vera asked.

His eyes lit up. "Me?" His low-pitched voice had vanished and was replaced with squeaky excitement.

"Certainly. But only if it isn't an imposition—"

"Your Majesty, I'd be honored!" In his glee, he hadn't even realized that he'd interrupted her.

"Thank you, Grady," she said, grinning broadly as Calimorfis continued to lean into him. "She clearly adores you. I think I've lost her favor."

"She's easily won with only a bit of love. The king showed me,"

Grady said. "Give her one good brushing, and you'll be back in her graces. I could get a brush and show you?" He was so hopeful that Vera found herself nodding enthusiastically.

Grady tore out of the stall and ran down the stable row.

"He's always fancied you," Matilda said. "And now he'll love you forever."

Vera blushed and buried her face in her hands. They were both laughing, so they didn't hear the ruckus immediately.

Grady must have been returning with the brush, but the moment's peace was upended by angry shouting and the slam of a fist against wood.

"What the fuck is wrong with you, boy?"

Vera didn't recognize the voice. Whoever it was shouted so loudly that she was sure it could be heard all the way to the entrance hall.

"My horse! My horse should have been ready an hour before my departure. You stupid fuck, what are you staring at?"

"I—my lord, I—" Grady stammered. "I was not informed of your departure."

Vera helplessly looked to Matilda. She wanted to intervene in defense of Grady but was worried she might humiliate him by preemptively coming to his rescue in a situation he could handle on his own.

"Oh, like bloody hell you weren't. Do it now, boy. Now!" The man sounded more furious by the second.

Grady, admirably, maintained his composure. "My lord, I will be there in a moment. I'm with the—"

Heavy footfalls stomped closer to the stall. Closer to Grady. "I don't care, you insolent shit!" There was the distinct sound of a fist on flesh, the whimper and grunt of a boy, and Vera was in motion in half a heartbeat. She rounded the door. Grady was on the floor, his arms up defensively above his head, a pitchfork in one hand and a brush in the other.

An impeccably dressed nobleman who was short but more than twice the size of Grady owing to height and girth stood above him, poised to take a kick at the boy's face.

"Stop!" she shouted. Vera could feel the blood surging through her,

her face blazing hot with rage. She didn't remember how she closed the distance between where she'd been and where she now stood, close enough to grab the wrist of the man in front of her.

He had a puffy face that looked extremely ugly with a scowl fixed upon it and a smear of something stinking and brown across the bottom half of his left cheek. It must have flung off the pitchfork as Grady was thrown to the floor. The nobleman's hair was inky black, and he wore the sort of long velvet tunic and tights that Vera had imagined Arthur and Lancelot would wear before she met them. He paused and tore his glare from Grady, his lips curled with cruelty, ready to aim his vitriol at Vera until he saw her clearly, and recognition softened his features.

"Your Majesty." He stumbled backward a step. "I did not realize you were—"

"How dare you disrespect a member of this castle?" Vera snarled.

"Disrespect?" the man blustered. "I have been disrespected. I have a four-hour ride ahead of me, and this stupid—"

"Don't." Vera's voice was pure ice. "Not another word."

He stared angrily at her but remained silent.

"Grady," she said, continuing to glare at the man, "please ready his horse. It is best if he leaves sooner than later."

"Yes, Your Majesty." Grady's voice was quiet behind her.

"Sir, you will wait there." She pointed to a bench halfway down the stable. "And you will not speak to this young man again except to apologize."

Vera suspected he'd rather slap her than listen. "Do you know who I am?" the man said in a dangerous whisper.

"No," said Vera, and she turned her back on him.

Grady's face was covered in dirt with streaks cut through it by his silent tears. He scrambled to his feet, pitchfork and brush still in hand. Vera wished there was something that she could say to him, anything that would make him feel less small at this moment. When she heard the man grumble away to the seat where Vera had relegated him, she reached out to take the brush from Grady's hand. "I'll be with Calimorfis."

He fixed his tearful gaze on the floor.

"Grady." Vera put her hand on his shoulder and waited until he reluctantly met her eyes. "He is thrice your age and not half the man you are now."

He was on the brink of tears, his chin quivering mightily.

"Fuck him," Vera added.

Grady let out a bark of a surprised laugh. He nodded and set his chin before he set off to work.

"Well said, Guinevere," Matilda said. She stood in the stall door, keeping her eyes fixed on the nobleman as Vera began brushing Calimorfis. Tears burned at her eyes as if they'd passed from Grady to her like a potent virus.

"I don't care if I have to brush this horse twelve times. We aren't leaving this stable until that man is gone," Vera said.

"I quite agree."

Thankfully, Grady's work was quick. When Vera heard the man stirring outside the stall, she feigned taking the brush back to the tool shelf to hover near him. Grady walked the man's horse out, his face set as he passed the reins to him.

"I'm sorry, boy," the man growled, not at all sounding as if he meant it. Grady bowed his head respectfully before hurrying to busy himself with ropes and tack at the farthest end of the stable.

Vera crossed her arms on her chest, watching the man mount his horse.

"I'd consider finding a new stable boy," he said as he tugged his riding gloves on, unable to resist vying for the final word. "This stable smells far worse than any I've ever visited. It needs a good cleaning. It's shameful that this is our king's stable."

Vera wordlessly crossed to the stack of cleaning cloths, snatched one, and marched back to the man. She held it out to him as his eyes darted from Vera to the cloth and back in bewilderment.

"You have horse shit on your face."

She was satisfied that the man looked rather like his head might explode.

"When I return," he said, face crimson with fury, "I will take this up with the king."

"Oh, please do," Vera said, and the man road away in a huff.

Matilda had put forth quite the effort to keep the corners of her mouth from turning upward, and from that day on, her guard dropped. Her laugh came readily, and even the time spent helping Vera dress became more punctuated with conversation. In short, the two became friends. She barely protested when Vera insisted on serving her during their evening visits.

"Do I have more blankets?" Vera asked her one chilly evening. Matilda had just gotten a fire roaring in the hearth and settled back into her cozy pouf.

"Yes, in that chest." She gestured to a trunk behind Vera and started to get up, but Vera waved her off.

"I'll get them," she said. Matilda merely smiled and shook her head.

The trunk was filled with heavy blankets, neatly folded. Vera took two in her arms and noticed a corner of thinner fabric sticking out from beneath the blanket pile. She gave it an experimental tug, and something attached to the material scraped against the side of the chest. With a steady pull, out came more fabric attached to a wooden embroidery hoop. The project was barely started: a simple cloth napkin. All that was completed was a thin line of green vines and four flower petals sewn with tidy blue stitches.

Vera added it to her armload of blankets. She dropped one on Matilda and pulled the other over herself as she ran her thumb over the bumps of Guinevere's stitches, feeling like she held a ghost in her fingers.

"Do you remember how to do embroidery?" Matilda's voice pierced the trance of this thread between Vera and Guinevere.

"Actually, yes." It was true, but it wasn't a recovered memory. Embroidery had had a moment in Glastonbury a few years back. Vera and Allison attended a kitschy sip-and-sew workshop where they'd giggled and shared pinot noir while a grandmotherly woman instructed them on various stitches. Vera had enjoyed it and taken it up as a hobby over the following months until she lost interest. Forgotten embroidery was something that she and Guinevere had in common, for Vera knew she had a partially completed project tucked in a drawer somewhere, too.

"I'd guess you had plenty of time for that sort of activity at the monastery," Matilda said. Vera stared vacantly at her. "While you were recovering at the monastery," she clarified.

"Oh! Yes. Right. Erm, a bit." That's what everyone had been told; that Guinevere spent the year recovering at a monastery in the farthest southwestern corner of the land, an order devoted to healing.

"What was it like there?" Matilda asked. "I've heard the monks like to play games to fill their idle hours. Is it true?"

Vera remained so thoroughly delighted by this newfound friendship that she heard herself reply, "Yes," even though she knew nothing about the monks who were supposed to have cared for her.

"Will you teach me one?"

"Erm . . ." Of course, she had no idea what games the monks played (if they played them at all). So, Vera taught Matilda the only one that came to mind. "It's called rock, paper, scissors."

After sharing a pitcher of wine in the warmth of a fire with a friend who kept forgetting which beat what at rock, paper, scissors, and falsely proclaiming victory time after time, it turned out the game was rather funny.

"All right, all right. I've got it. This time, I've got it," Matilda said confidently.

"Fifth time's the charm." Vera laughed. "I believe in you."

Three slaps of fist to hand followed by the reveal. Matilda balled her hand as rock, and Vera laid hers out flat as paper. Matilda squealed in delight before Vera had a chance to say anything.

"I won, didn't I?" Matilda all but shouted. Vera couldn't speak. She shook her head, tears rolling down her cheeks as she devolved into the sort of laughter that produced no sound at all.

"I didn't win?" Matilda cried. "That doesn't make any sense! Those monks are fools." This only sent Vera further into her hysterical collapse. And then Matilda was laughing, too.

For the moment, the embroidery hoop had fallen aside from Vera's lap, forgotten, but it had sprouted an idea.

Dinner the following evening proceeded as was now usual. They ate, the performers performed, then Arthur made an excuse to leave. They arrived at his exit like clockwork.

He nodded to Lancelot and then to Vera as he muttered, "Good evening."

That was one of a few positive shifts. Since the night when he'd been so harsh, he'd at least acknowledged Vera before he departed each evening. She wasn't sure if this was owed to her new "could not give a shit" attitude, if Lancelot had said something to him, or if he just felt guilty. Once she had stopped seeking Arthur, however, he seemed to relax. He even laughed at Lancelot's jokes in her presence or forgot to harden his gaze when he accidentally met Vera's eye, but only ever for a moment.

Though his gaze had drawn goosebumps on more than one occasion, Vera made a point to give it little of her attention. She'd find the memories without him and never have to go any deeper to figure out what his problem was. After all, she had her newest plan to tend to. She scanned the hall until she found Matilda in the back corner. Matilda smiled knowingly as she wove her way to Vera, an unassuming bag hanging from her shoulder.

By all appearances, she was escorting Vera to her chambers. In truth, they crossed the grounds in long strides, raindrops beginning to splash off the tops of their heads and bursting in tiny explosions on the stone path around them. From the castle's entry chamber, Matilda passed Vera the bag as she continued alone to the chapel. With a quick wave of confirmation from Vera when she got there safely, only Matilda retired.

She'd initially been hesitant when Vera pitched the idea, thinking it was unwise to send Vera off alone. But by late afternoon, Matilda had an abrupt change of heart. Vera was so pleased that she didn't bother asking why.

After the first chapel service, the priest encouraged her to come to pray any time, that the chapel would be empty and unlocked in the evenings should she wish to use it, and indeed she did. Vera wasn't sure if she would call it praying, exactly. But as soon as the idea took her, she knew she wanted to sit alone in that chapel and bathe in the jewel-colored sunset beams streaming through the stained glass, embroidering in the shadow of the exquisite Mary statue. It was all as lovely as she'd imagined.

After that, any evening not spent with Matilda, Vera rushed to the chapel where she embraced the benefits of solitude, of not having to worry about who was watching or listening. While she stitched, she sang whatever she wanted. Vera didn't have a voice that would make anyone hold their ears, nor would it bring an inspired tear to anyone's eye, but she liked music and didn't want to forget the songs from her life before. She sang through the ones she'd loved with a broad catalog of whatever suited her in the moment: The Beatles, Adele, the Mamas & the Papas, Ed Sheeran, Whitney Houston—even the Spice Girls.

This night, Vera's fifth of such a routine, a soft rain tapped a percussion on the high roof above her. She was so deep in song that her fingers fumbled, and she pressed the needle through the fabric with too much oomph, driving it deep into her thumb. Vera loudly yelped and hissed "Fuck," as she wrenched the needle free.

And then she heard a noise from the front of the chapel. She sat stock still as fear pulsed in her gut. Maybe she wasn't alone after all.

Vera realized now that she'd never walked to the very front. There might have been an alcove off to the left. She hadn't thought to check.

She stood and took a few wary steps forward. "Hello?" she called.

Silence, heavy and ringing, answered.

The sun had set by now. Vera bit her lip, remembering the marble tile controlling the lights on the opposite end of the room. She wished she'd set them brighter. Out of habit, she nearly reached for her phone (that wasn't there) to use as a torch.

"Is someone there?" Vera called more forcefully.

"Good evening." The man's voice came from behind her. She jumped and spun so quickly to face him that she nearly fell over.

"Sorry, Your Majesty. I didn't mean to startle you," he said. He stood just inside the door and was around Vera's father's age with mostly grey hair save for darker spots clinging to their youthful nut brown. "I saw the light and thought Father John might be here. My name is Thomas. I was appointed deputy treasurer during your time away." She was relieved he'd introduced himself and that this wasn't one more person she had to pretend to remember. "I'm sorry to intrude. I was hoping Father John might scribe a letter for me, but it appears you're alone here?"

"Yes," Vera said. "Sorry."

Thomas twisted his hands together, seeming torn between further entering the chapel or leaving. He bobbed for a moment and, with a deep breath, decided on the former.

"Would you pardon a moment of boldness?" Thomas asked.

Her curiosity stirred. "Gladly."

He came toward her and happened to stop in a chink of blue light reflected from the stained glass. He did not notice that his face was awash in blue, and Vera did well not to chuckle at the sight. "It's awfully heartening to see a lady spending her idle time in prayer," Thomas said.

He meant it as a compliment. Vera murmured her thanks, curious what he would have said if he'd heard her cursing after stabbing her thumb.

"I know we choose with the grace of Christ to be tolerant of all," he said hastily with a dismissive wave. "But with so many who follow the old pagan ways, I, for one, am grateful our king and queen follow the Christian path. You are the queen our people need."

Vera had to consciously coach herself not to bristle at Thomas's comments. Nearly everything about this time had been more free-thinking than she could have dreamed. And she was moved by his earnest conviction and generous compliments, even if she felt it was misplaced by being directed at her.

"You're too kind," she told him honestly as she searched for the right words to say. "I'm . . . not sure my prayers would satisfy the Lord."

He beamed. In her attempt to be subtly truthful, Vera had unintentionally fit further into Thomas's demure caricature of her. "You're a sweet girl. It's an honor to meet you, my queen."

As she watched him leave, Vera remembered what Lancelot had said about her being alone with a man and wondered if the protocol breach registered with Thomas.

She never thought again about exploring the alcove at the front of the chapel, and she forgot to wonder: if not Thomas, what, indeed, had made the noise she heard on that rainy night?

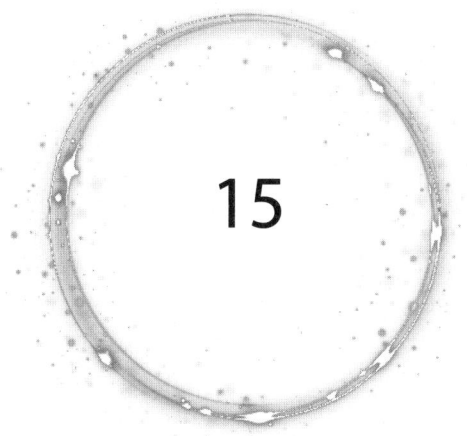

15

In the three weeks since Vera's first night in the chapel, she estimated that she and Lancelot had run more than one hundred and fifty kilometers over six different routes. They were both surprised when Randall was waiting for them on the outskirts of town as they returned to the castle one morning. Completely unprompted, he'd made Vera two more sets of running clothes, including one thicker shirt, which was much needed as the perfectly crisp mornings of fall had shifted to the biting chill of winter.

"I see you running nearly every damn day," Randall said, pushing the bundle of clothes into her arms. "Having some extras might be helpful, and Matilda won't need to collect the laundry as often."

Vera thanked him profusely, which he waved off as he hurriedly made an excuse to leave.

"I like those shoes, Your Majesty," he called over his shoulder. Vera and Lancelot stared at one another, wide-eyed.

The two had also gone back to play the keep-away game a handful of times, but they had not returned to the sacred grove. With December winds whipping up and rain pattering their heads more frequently, they moved their end-of-run chats from the hill to a well-shielded patch of wood near the castle wall with a perfect clearing for comfortable lounging.

Seated in the chapel, Vera completed three embroidery projects. Thomas stopped by at least once a week, always with polite conversation. He brought her a flower on two occasions, which she tucked into the bouquet in her room even when it did not match. He'd often wax on about her piety or purity, but he was kind to her, albeit slightly scathing about any other members of her sex. She cringed inwardly and reminded herself, magic or not, it was the Middle Ages, and politely tolerating him until he left was likely the least confrontational outcome.

Thomas was there the night she finished her third embroidery piece. It had been nice to have someone to celebrate with. She'd proudly passed him the hoop, and he'd fussed over it.

He traced his thumb across her tidy stitches. "If you give this sort of attention to your sewing, I can only imagine what you pour into your husband. Our king is blessed to have your devotion."

Her smile had faltered. She doubted Arthur would share his admiration.

Beyond a muttered "Good evening" at dinner, Arthur had entirely avoided speaking to Vera. So when he sat down for the evening meal and straight away turned to her, Vera knew something was coming. Her cup had been raised nearly to her lips. She set it down without even taking a drink and arranged her hands folded in front of her on the table. In a blink-and-she'd-have-missed-it moment, she was positive she caught Arthur's lips ticking up at the corners before he had time to cover it.

"Did Merlin tell you about court?" he asked her so seriously that Vera was convinced she'd imagined his flash of lightness.

She looked around the room. This was the court, wasn't it?

"It's not all this." Arthur waved his hand toward the dinner gathering. "We've been on a pause since your arrival, but each week we usually hold court. Anyone in the kingdom can come to address us—address me. Merlin had planned for you to attend like Guin—" He clenched his jaw. "Like you used to before."

Every time he stopped speaking, he clenched his teeth together and then relaxed them—a pattern performed on repeat. Vera wouldn't have noticed if she hadn't been so near to him and hadn't been studying his face with the fervor of a field botanist, waiting for any change in the foliage with patient diligence. The muscle in front of his ear lobes bulged and contracted with the rhythm of the clench-release cycle.

When he stayed silent, Vera noticed he was watching her closely, too. Their eyes met, and, for once, Arthur did not look away. Her stomach fluttered under the intensity of his gaze. Dammit. After weeks of his appalling rudeness, why did she care if he looked at her? Certainly, he was remembering Guinevere from before. Maybe her time here was making Vera seem more like her.

"I don't mind coming," she said quickly, anything to break the hold of this moment. "When is it?"

"Tomorrow." She heard Lancelot's voice before he leaned forward so she could see him on Arthur's other side. "Tuesday. Every bloody Tuesday. Most kingdoms hold court once a month, but not this one. A solid six hours of complaints and queries and asinine requests every week," he said brightly. He clinked his cup against Arthur's before draining its contents and heartily slamming it on the table with a performative eyeroll. "It's so fortunate for you to get that experience back."

Vera peppered Lancelot with a steady stream of questions about court during their run the next morning. "It is valuable and incredible for the kingdom's morale," he relented breathlessly as they crested a steep hill in the woods. "But of course, everyone thinks what they have to say is the most important thing in the universe. They all want to feel understood by their king, and I'll be damned if Arthur doesn't deliver. It just takes so long, Guinna, and it's usually mind-numbingly boring."

She'd instinctively been connecting what was to come with the judicial system. "But isn't that where you'd address crime or violence?"

Their eyes were trained on the ground in front of them while they ran, ever ready for rocks and roots, but Vera could feel Lancelot looking at her out of the corner of his eyes. "Well, yes, but things have been remarkably good since the wars ended. It's been a bit like living in a bubble . . . there's been little crime."

"And . . . ?" Vera prompted, sensing there was more.

"And it's a carefully cultivated culture. There's no way it will last. We're going to outgrow the idealism of it. But if you tell Arthur I said that, I will deny it to my grave. We keep as many sentencings out of court as possible. When crime does happen, it's a battle with Arthur to punish offenders appropriately."

"Is he harsh?" asked Vera, remembering Arthur's sharp glare and glassy eyes from the first time she'd seen him. And it didn't take an historian to know the Middle Ages were a cruel time, chopping off hands for theft and heads on a whim. She'd been scared to even ask. Scared to find out how Arthur wielded his godlike power to keep the land in such a utopian peace.

But Lancelot laughed so loudly that Vera stumbled. She huffed and ran on in silence.

"I forgot that you don't really know him anymore," he said more gently. "He isn't harsh. That's the problem. We spent so many years on the battlefield. Justice in war was unforgiving and brutal. Arthur had a different vision. When justice needed to be dealt, it could be done with mercy. He always wants to find a way to choose mercy."

"And you don't want him to?"

"He can't, Guinna. You can't rule and have everyone go home happy. When a criminal complaint arises at court, Percival—you'll meet him later today. He's the youngest knight and easy to pick out as he has a scar across his whole face. Anyway, Percival and I work to convince Arthur when it comes time for sentencing. Arthur's no fool. He knows what needs to be done, but hearing it affirmed by the ones you trust most . . . well, in the end, he's laid the groundwork for the country he hopes for. More often than not, if he extends a fair justice, he can trust that his people will come through with mercy.

"But it's rarely ever anything interesting. We get a lot of announcements of marriage, farming issues, magic gone sideways, someone quarreling with their aunt's brother's cousin over land . . . It will be more interesting when you begin retaking queries," he added the last with a baiting tone that Vera knew without looking was accompanied by a sly grin.

"You're joking," she said, endeavoring to keep her voice flat and not give him the satisfaction of rising to his taunt. She hadn't considered that she might be expected to participate in the proceedings.

"Yes, but not entirely," he said. "Once you're feeling more yourself, Merlin thinks you should. But that seems like it might be a while, doesn't it?"

Vera couldn't even imagine it.

Court was in a chamber she had never been in before. She sat on the throne next to Arthur's atop a dais at the front of the room. Several other chairs were behind them, one occupied by Matilda, the rest by advisers and attendants: the crown's treasurer, two citizen representatives (who Lancelot told her changed each week), Lancelot, and Percival. She recognized the latter by the prominent scar beginning under his eye and tracing across the bottom right half of his young face before it disappeared beneath his tunic. Merlin was the last to come in. He'd only gotten back the day prior. There were dark circles beneath his eyes, and he moved more slowly than usual.

Vera had stumbled upon him in the courtyard on the way back from her run. She'd been worried he would want to exchange pleasantries and belabor the conversation, but Merlin was nearly as eager to broach the heart of it as her.

"Has Arthur—" He stopped. Vera was already shaking her head.

"I did try," she said at his look of disappointment. To her surprise, she found she actually cared that he knew that. "Can we try magic?"

Merlin pinched the bridge of his nose as he sighed. "I don't think we have another option."

She'd been ready to follow him to his study right then and there.

"After court," he'd said wearily. "I need to consider how we do this. I'll have more time soon." It was cryptic, but his meaning became clear as soon as court began.

Merlin's was the day's first audience. He and Arthur announced they'd sent for a second mage to fill Viviane's position. "He is the youngest among the council of mages. He is very smart, though a bit odd." Merlin smiled fondly before he carried on. "The demand of maintaining the current magical structures of Camelot has kept me from attending to the kingdom's long-term needs. This will help." At that, his tired eyes flashed to Vera, and she averted hers, feeling senselessly guilty. Arthur was the one who should be ashamed.

The pettiest part of Vera relished that she might get to see him under pressure today. There could be a complaint about him that he'd have to answer, that he couldn't turn away from with an icy glare.

But it was nothing like that. He was nothing like that.

She'd seen so little of him beyond a cold expression, and he'd said even less. Here, he was an entirely different person than the man who slept in the room adjacent to hers. This man listened to his citizens with interest and respect. It had no bearing if they were dressed in finery or rags, whether they approached Arthur with dire concerns about their farm's survival, a dispute when the equivalent of pennies was owed, or even a baby's birth announcement. Arthur asked thoughtful questions and engaged each in conversation. His voice, which Vera had thus far heard in only a few sentences at a time, was now the anchoring sound. She was startled when she realized that the sound of his voice, commanding, steady, and deep, soothed her.

Depending on the subject, Arthur consulted with each member of his gathered council. Lancelot and Percival provided advice about military matters, and the two citizens served as a catch-all for interpersonal and daily life issues. All were regularly included in the process except for Vera, who watched silently from Arthur's side.

He never grew weary as the hours crawled on and person after person filed into the throne room. Vera's mind would occasionally drift, and her eyes glazed over, but the low tenor of Arthur's voice drew her back. The image that Merlin and Lancelot painted of him came into focus. Perhaps this was the magic they had described. Even Vera could feel it: Arthur was made for this. Made to build and rule and love his country. It was extraordinary to witness; here was a man who measured up to his legend.

The sting of it was immediate. Vera had done so well at burying fear and loss and any manner of unpleasant things. Even Vincent. Tucking his memory in an unreachable place was easier here, so far from the world where she'd known him. Vera had decided to detach from Arthur's cold distance, and that should have settled it. Usually, she could master such a task, but this gnawed at her. Why didn't he feel compelled to help her, or know her, or even show her basic kindness?

But now Vera had seen him. She'd seen him among friends, seen him interacting with his people: witnessed his softness, his easy smile, his warm face. He chuckled at a joke Vera didn't hear and quipped a jovial response that brought a scattered chorus of laughter from everyone else in the throne room. This was the real Arthur—and he gave it to everyone but her. That was the piercing blow. It lodged in Vera like a forgotten axe wedged into a stump and left there to rust.

But court wasn't simply Arthur getting to be a doting ruler. Issues with magic were prevalent. Mourners announced that a brilliant performer who'd had a gift of perfect vocal mimicry for any voice he'd ever heard had died after a lengthy illness. A sweet old man asked for assistance rebuilding the enchanted goat fence that his late wife constructed. Then, a bee farmer, afraid his hives might have contracted a disease. He hoped for a potion or spell to save his bees and their honey. The most alarming came next. Rumors of mage violence in France, which they called the Frankish Kingdoms.

Vera's eyes shot to Arthur. The abruptness of her movement drew his attention—or perhaps the nature of the topic. He looked at Vera from the corner of his eyes before he addressed the man standing before them. "How did you hear this?"

The man swallowed as he fished in his pocket and procured a folded piece of paper. "My sister lives in Normandy. She sent word of the whispers in her letter. I wanted to tell Your Majesty straight away."

The sister was most helpful. She'd heard various versions of attacks along the southern coast, each one slightly different from the last. All employed brutal usage of magic. All were devasting. But it was also all conjecture, and there was nothing to be done about it save for sending a scout to investigate and for the lot of them to feel uneasy in the meantime.

The next woman came forward so quietly that it took them all a moment to notice her as their minds drifted to imagined battlefields on foreign shores. She wore a black dress and veil to match, and it struck

Vera with a jolt that her round face and kind eyes reminded her of Allison's.

She took a shaking breath. "My son has died," she said, and that was as far as she made it. She sank to her knees with a wail as if the weight of loss collapsed atop her.

Lancelot and Percival looked at one another, stunned. The two townsfolk whispered behind their hands. The treasurer stared all about the room, anywhere but at the woman. Vera turned helplessly from the observers to Matilda, whose expression mirrored Vera's sadness for the woman, and then to Arthur.

His eyes set on the woman who sobbed alone on the cold, stone floor. He stood and went down the steps, knelt beside her, and tentatively wrapped his arm around her. When the woman leaned into Arthur and cried into his neck, he embraced her with both arms.

"I'm sorry. I'm so sorry." He spoke barely above a whisper. Arthur stayed on the floor with her, only ending the embrace when she initiated it.

"I know there's nothing I can do to ease your pain," he said. "Could we ease your burden? Are there things you need help with that your son used to do?"

The devastated woman nodded, and with tears streaming down her face, she told Arthur. "My husband has been gone for some time. My son tended our animals, and he harvested the grain. We have a crop that's ready in the field, and I—I don't know—"

"It's all right," he soothed her. "We can help you." He looked to Lancelot, who nodded.

"It's done. We'll send men today."

The woman choked back a sob as she accepted Arthur's outstretched hands to help her stand up. He hugged her and spoke so quietly that Vera could only hear the low timbre of his voice, a hum with no words. Whatever he said, the woman smiled a little and patted his shoulder. And then, Vera saw the most remarkable thing.

Arthur cared for this mother with a tenderness as if he were her own child. It was like it all slowed so Vera could see it clearly. In this exact instant, she felt she was seeing Arthur for the first time. He was beautiful.

She hurriedly averted her eyes when he turned to come back to his seat and instead watched the grieving mother leave while another man was escorted forward. There was something familiar about his waddling frame, dressed in finery and with three attendants who trailed behind. Someone coughed from the seat just behind her. After a few moments, she heard it again and turned. Matilda glanced meaningfully from the man to Vera.

Vera whipped around to face forward.

"Shit." She whispered it slow and drawn out, a sharp emphasis on the T.

Arthur's head tilted in Vera's direction, but she kept her eyes on the man. He wore a crooked, one-sided smirk that didn't reach his eyes and read of smug satisfaction. He was only slightly less unattractive without the smear of manure across his face, because his cruelty was a permanent feature.

It was the man from the stable, and, as promised, it appeared he was ready to bring his grievance before the king.

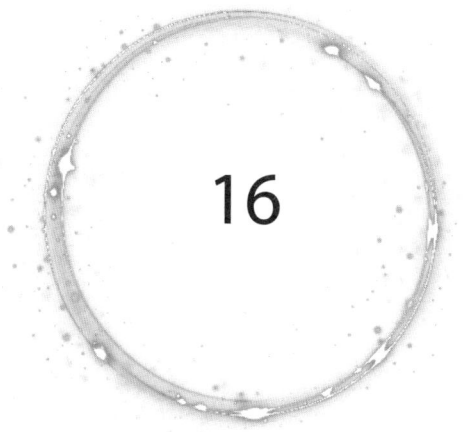

16

Vera leaned toward Arthur. He mirrored the gesture, inclining in her direction on the arm of his chair.

"This is probably about me," she murmured, moving her mouth as little as possible.

"Are you sure?" Arthur asked.

"Erm . . . yes."

The nobleman found his place and stood there expectantly.

"Welcome, Lord Wulfstan." Arthur greeted him cordially, divulging nothing of Vera's whispers. "This is a surprise. You've never attended court while in Camelot for trade before."

"I've never had cause before now, Your Majesty," Lord Wulfstan said. Now that he addressed the king, a show of reverence replaced his smirk, all pious concern with his conceit well-concealed.

Shit. A nobleman in the business of trade and barter would know how to manipulate a situation well. Vera should have told Arthur what happened before (as if she'd had a chance). She'd been foolish to believe her actions would stand on their merit and her word alone.

"Tell me what troubles you," Arthur said.

Lord Wulfstan licked his lips, and vengeful glee flashed through his expression as he shot a glare at Vera. "I regret to inform Your Majesty that, on my departure from the royal stables concluding my last visit, I was treated with disrespect and disregard by your stable boy."

His audacity had Vera gripping the arms of her chair so tightly that her knuckles were white, and the edges of the wood dug into her palms. She knew the fury would be written on her face. Vera clenched her teeth to keep from outright snarling as she listened.

"And most appalling of all," the brazen, awful man continued, "was my encounter with Her Majesty the queen, and the vulgar language she used. It pains me to say it, having traded with her father in the Northland for many years. He would be appalled."

Vera momentarily forgot her anger. For the years she'd spent searching for her birth parents in vain, it hadn't occurred to her that she might be able to know them here. She'd have to come back to this because Lord Wulfstan charged onward.

"Her Majesty told me, and forgive my language as I quote her directly, that I had," he paused dramatically, "horse shit on my face."

The room and all in it were more still, and the silence deeper than any other time at court. Vera imagined she could feel Merlin's eyes on her back.

Arthur looked at her without speaking. When Vera met his gaze, his eyebrow quirked upward. She gave the tiniest indication of a nod in confirmation.

A single laugh burst from behind her, convincingly covered with a cough. Had it not been Lancelot, whose laugh she knew so well, Vera would have been fooled.

Arthur's face revealed nothing at all. The control he exhibited was masterful as he turned his attention back to Lord Wulfstan.

"And did you have horse shit on your face?" he asked evenly.

It was the last thing Vera had expected Arthur to say. She barely managed to contain her reaction to just her wide eyes. Lord Wulfstan, on the other hand, had gone from composed to having cheeks the color of a ripe tomato. He huffed loud breaths through his nose.

Finally, he replied with a curt "Yes," hissed through his teeth.

Arthur turned to Vera. "What exactly happened?"

If she didn't tell it all and tell it right now, there likely wouldn't be another chance. Her chest tightened, but she forced herself to find her voice. She told him all that she could remember. The foul insults Wulfstan hurled, the way he'd not listened when Grady tried to explain that he was with the queen, and how hard he'd struck the boy. She would not be intimidated by the man before her.

"I demanded his apology to the young man," Vera said. "And . . . I have no qualms about how Lord Wulfstan told my part in the rest of the story. His portrayal of my language is accurate."

The silence that followed was thick as Arthur studied Wulfstan. Someone shifted in a seat behind Vera, and Merlin's voice chimed in. "I might offer, sir, that the queen has been recovering from—"

Arthur held up a hand to stop him, his unreadable stare focused on Wulfstan. Vera's heart slammed against the inside of her chest. She didn't know what to expect or even what outcome to hope for. Arthur let the hush linger for longer than was comfortable before lowering his hand.

"While I cannot say if I would have addressed the manner in the same language as Lady Guinevere, I share the queen's sentiment."

Vera sat up straighter, her eyes shooting to Arthur. Fuck yeah.

"No one," Arthur paused for a breath, "is to lay a hand on a member of this castle's staff nor to raise their tongue in undue cruelty. To do so against a stable boy is to do so against me."

Lord Wulfstan tilted his chin down, appropriately cowed.

Arthur turned to Vera after another stretch of quiet. "Would you like to say anything else on the matter?"

She wasn't sure if he was asking her to apologize. Vera searched for any ripple in the still waters of his face and found no hint of what he expected from her.

"Yes," she said.

Wulfstan's smirk curled back into place. He certainly thought an apology was coming, which was a shame as Vera had genuinely been considering it until she caught sight of his smug face. Rage boiled anew within her.

"My lord," she started, impressed with herself at how calm she sounded, "I should never have used such unladylike language, especially not in the presence of a gentleman." She meant Grady but resisted the temptation to clarify that. "I am heartily sorry. It was not my place. I should never have informed you that you had manure on your face." It took everything in her not to add, I should have let you leave it there and smell it the whole ride home, but Vera allowed the statement to hang in the air and speak for itself. She didn't dare tear her focus from Wulfstan, keen to see if he was mollified or if he caught the thinly veiled insult.

Arthur stared quickly at the floor between his feet. Was that a smile he hid? He'd caught Vera's meaning and started speaking before the nobleman could catch up. "There we have it. You have apologized to our stable boy, and your queen has offered her apologies."

Wulfstan bowed his head. "I suppose that settles the matter for me," he said, somewhat begrudgingly. He made to leave, flicking his wrist to signal his attending servants, but all motion stopped when Arthur spoke.

"Not for me, I'm afraid." Goose flesh rose on Vera's arms. Arthur sounded perfectly blasé, dangerously so. "Sir, have you yet apologized to your queen?"

Vera sat so still that she even held her breath. Did Arthur really say that? Lord Wulfstan spluttered meaninglessly, the color rising again to his cheeks. "I—pardon me?"

"To your queen," Arthur repeated slowly. "The language you used in her presence was untoward at best. By your standard, you owe an apology. Surely you wouldn't hold yourself to a lesser expectation of conduct than the lady. Did you apologize?"

"I did, sire," he said hastily. "As soon as I realized she was present."

Arthur looked to Vera for confirmation. She stared blankly back. She didn't remember what he'd said in those seconds right after he struck Grady. She'd been too angry.

"He did not, Your Majesty," Matilda cut in. "Pardon me, but he did not." She then spoke directly to Lord Wulfstan. "My lord, you said you did not realize the queen was there. You did not apologize."

Arthur turned back to Wulfstan. "Additionally," he said, "you came to the seat of this throne with full knowledge of the expectations of how you are to treat our staff and, believing you were alone with our youngest member, knowingly defied those rules. When called out by your queen, you deigned to argue with her. The queen's authority is equal to my own." The venom was potent in Arthur's every word.

"I—I am sorry, Your Majesty—" Arthur's cold glare stopped Wulfstan mid-sentence.

"Do not apologize to me. Apologize to Guinevere." His tone remained even, but his voice was noticeably more of a growl, and there could be no doubt that Arthur was livid.

Wulfstan physically stepped back and clamped his mouth shut as he swallowed heavily. "I beg your forgiveness, Your Majesty. I was wrong to disrespect you. I—I am sorry."

"I accept your apology," Vera said.

Arthur gave a curt nod. "Very well. Let us be done with it and move forward."

Wulfstan's eyes cast toward the floor. He bowed stiffly, turned on his heel, and stalked out of the chamber, his servants fumbling and hurrying to follow his less-than-ceremonious departure.

Vera didn't give herself time to think about it before she reached out to gingerly touch Arthur's arm—only long enough to draw his attention. Still, he flinched and stared down at her fingers.

"I'm sorry," she whispered. "I should have controlled my temper, I—"

"I'm not angry," Arthur said tersely before he looked away.

Then what the hell is wrong with you? She almost asked it out loud. Say it, she told herself. Go on. But the words never came. How could he defend her and go right back to this?

"This is horse shit," she muttered under her breath. The only reason Vera could see in it was that Arthur defended the throne and its authority, the kingdom's delicate balance, and not her. She crossed her arms and leaned back in her seat, feeling rather like a petulant nuisance and wondering for perhaps the hundredth time why her presence in this world even mattered.

But court wasn't over yet. There was already another person entering the throne room, and it took Vera a moment in the wake of Wulfstan's departure to realize that something was amiss. A uniformed soldier bearing the king's coat of arms emblazoned in red upon his chest ran the room's length. Lancelot and Percival stood, their hands instinctively moving to their swords.

"Your Majesty," the soldier said. He did not wait to finish bowing before he continued. "There's flooding. Word has spread quickly. We need aid."

"Where?" Arthur said.

"Exeter."

Now it was Merlin who stood and moved next to Arthur. Doubt wrinkled the mage's brow. He'd just been in Exeter, hadn't he?

"What's happened?" he said.

"I—I'm not sure what's gone wrong, but—"

"The magic?" Merlin asked sharply.

"Yes. The water continues to flow, but now it's flooding, and we've no way to stop it."

"I put barriers in place," Merlin said to Arthur. "They must not have held."

"And word is out?" Arthur asked the soldier.

He swallowed heavily. "It is. Even here in town, everyone's saying that the harvest can't be saved."

"Is that true?" Arthur said.

The soldier hesitated.

"What's your name, soldier?"

"Marcus."

"Marcus, your job is not to deliver good news to me," Arthur said. "I need the truth, and I need it immediately."

"Yes, sire," Marcus said with more confidence. "It's not all lost, but we must act now. We need men to salvage what's left, and we need magic to fix the problem. We need it fast—as soon as possible."

"Understood," Arthur said.

"Your Majesty, I can leave immediately and take a unit of men with me," Lancelot offered.

"No," Arthur said. "I want you and Percival to remain in Camelot. Percival, find Sir Bors. Tell him to gather his unit and make to leave. Marcus will bring their orders to the armory. Come directly back here. We have more to discuss."

"Yes, sire," Percival jumped into action, dashing from the room without delay. Arthur looked to Merlin without a word. He nodded gravely.

"I'll leave straight away." Merlin glanced at Vera as he spoke. The light of hope dimmed in his eyes, a candle flickering in the wind seconds before its suffocated.

Arthur next addressed the two stunned citizen representatives, a man around Vera's age and an older woman with her silver hair wrapped in a bun and perched atop her head like a bird's nest. "Thank you for your service today. You've been privy to especially delicate information. I trust your discretion as you return to your homes."

"I'd say the chances of discretion are slim," Lancelot said as soon as the door closed behind the two townsfolk. He picked up his chair in one hand and gestured to Matilda's. "May I?"

She stood, and he moved both into a semi-circle next to Vera and Arthur's seats. She was surprised when Lancelot took the chair next to hers, leaving Matilda the one by Arthur rather than the other way around. They could all see one another now.

"We're waiting for Percival?" Lancelot asked Arthur. He nodded distractedly and rubbed at his chin.

Lancelot was deep in thought, too. He leaned back in his chair, staring at the ceiling. "What was it you said?" he asked abruptly. His eyes were twinkling as he set them on Vera. "Horse shit on your face . . ." he said, relishing the shape of the words. "You truly said that to Wulfstan?"

Vera glanced around at each of them. "Yes."

Lancelot grinned. He held his hand up expectantly for a high five. Matilda and Arthur watched in bewilderment as they slapped palms, Lancelot enthusiastically and Vera reluctantly.

"But I didn't know who he was," she said.

"Well, I'll tell you. He is a self-important prat and a colossal ass with too much money and far too much economic influence. So, there is actually no one in this realm who could get away with what you did except for you—and maybe Arthur, but he'd never," he added dismissively. "I didn't think I could love you more, but here we are." He rocked back in his seat as if he had not just told Vera that he loved her and done so in front of her husband and chambermaid. Arthur had heard all this, but he remained focused on the closed door on the other end of the hall.

"Matilda," Lancelot continued, "I'll be jealous for the rest of my days that you got to hear that happen in person."

Matilda suppressed a grin and pushed a curl back from her forehead. "I don't personally know the man, but it was not unsatisfying."

The door to the room swung open, and Percival hurried in. Lancelot fetched a chair for him, and he dropped into it, barely winded though he must have run the whole way to the armory and back.

"The troops are making ready," he said. "They'll depart this afternoon."

"Good." Arthur looked at all of them in turn. "We need to do what we can here. This is our first crisis since my rule began. Fear is potent, and panic spreads like a plague. Everyone in our realm remembers how it felt to go hungry during the wars. They must feel certain their children will not starve over the winter. Matilda, can we tap into our food stores to bridge the gap? A show of abundance between now and the harvest's arrival could help ease fears."

Matilda cast a furtive glance at Vera. The question should have been asked of her, but she wouldn't have known how to answer anyway. "Yes, Your Majesty. The queen can make that order today."

"Good. We need our soldiers on board, and we need ambassadors to make trips to the other towns impacted as we send supplies. The damage will be worst here, though. Our town's troops need to know what to say. And the two of you," he said to Lancelot and Percival, "should stay visible to reassure our people. I'll do the same."

"What about a public address?" Percival asked.

"I think that would be wise. And the queen—" Lancelot began, but he stopped short as Arthur glowered at him. God, how he must hate her. "We need her, Arthur. If you want a show of solidarity to boost morale, she can't be absent when the whole city knows she's here."

"What do you think?" Arthur asked Matilda. She glanced at Vera, her lips set in a thin line before answering.

"I'm fairly certain you know what I think, Your Majesty. It would be beneficial for the queen and me to be present at supply pick-ups, as it has been for her to resume her duties and be at meetings with castle staff. Lancelot is right. It's good for morale. I would guess it's done damage that we weren't doing it sooner."

"What do you think?" Percival asked Vera.

She didn't know much about Percival, but with his earnest eyes set on her, awaiting her answer while the others had talked around her, Vera liked him already. She noticed just how young he was simply by the contrast of sitting next to Lancelot. It was clear that Percival was strong, but he had more the body of a teenager than that of a man. His shoulders were narrower than Lancelot's and his facial features softer, not as sharp as either Lancelot's or Arthur's. He couldn't have been any older than her, and if he'd fought in the wars as Vera suspected from the scar across his face, that meant he'd been at battle in his teenage years.

"I'll do whatever you need," Vera said.

Arthur sighed. He likely had the same hesitation that Vera did; the concrete knowledge that it was a farce, and that she couldn't possibly fill the queen's shoes.

17

Taking swift action had been wise. The atmosphere of Camelot changed overnight, with panic threatening to boil over at any given moment. Arthur's public address went well, and the soldiers did their part with impressive dedication. Lancelot and Matilda had been right about their instinct that Vera should also be involved in the campaign. The three were greeted like heroes by most as they had the pleasant task of accompanying the food relief deliveries into town. Matilda and Lancelot smiled, passed out supplies, offered reassurances, and played games with children. Having decided she'd already caused far too much trouble with Lord Wulfstan, Vera did her best to be visible while engaging as little as possible.

Hopeful gratitude marked the first few days. But it did not last.

Despite Arthur's reassurance, coupled with his and Vera's constant presence throughout the city, there were struggles at every turn. Ruthless merchants thought to profit off insecurity and gouged their prices. They had to be tracked down by the troops and set right. Some with the resources to do so stockpiled more food than they needed for fear that there soon wouldn't be enough, which temporarily created a legitimate shortage and left the poorest in the city without a way to buy food. Arthur put ration limits on how much each household could buy. While it ensured no one went hungry, it did nothing to improve the people's spirits.

A cold front slinked into town in the early morning on the sixth day. And with frost lingering on the tips of every tree came a chilling amongst the people, too. Vera didn't expect anyone to continue throwing parades of gratitude as their anxieties ballooned. The frequency of tense encounters with citizens felt reasonable, but she kept catching Matilda and Lancelot sharing worried glances when they thought she wasn't paying attention.

They'd been at their morale-boosting work for nearly two weeks when what Merlin was able to save of the harvest began to arrive. Prices started righting themselves, and while it wasn't the economy of abundance the kingdom had grown accustomed to, fears of shortage abated. But like the colder weather, which seemed to have gotten comfortable and planned to stay awhile, the chill remained in the people, too.

Lancelot had adopted a casual way of keeping his hand on the pommel of his sword at all times. He accompanied Vera and Matilda on every excursion into town now, and though he'd join in on their conversation, his eyes continually scanned their surroundings.

They were picking up firewood for the week when Lancelot distractedly grabbed at empty air before finding Vera's hand to help her down from the seat of the horse-drawn cart. They'd stopped at the end of a long line, the equivalent of half a block from the woodcutter. No sooner had Matilda clambered down from her seat than four more groups tucked into line behind them.

Lancelot glanced at the newcomers, his lips pressed hard together. It was no bigger a crowd than the one at the pit on Vera's first day, but size wasn't the problem. The happy sounds of laughter and excited shouts to friends across the square had been frequent before. They'd have felt foreign and inappropriate now. People stood together in clumps, talking in low voices and casting uneasy glances at anyone outside their groups. It was alarmingly different. Lancelot was like a dog with his ears pinned back—and clearly displeased that he couldn't watch everywhere at once.

Voices raised from near the front of the line, accompanied by a rippling murmur of discomfort.

"We need guards posted here." Lancelot looked around in exasperation as if one might appear. They'd never needed to have soldiers posted through town before. This was all fresh territory. More voices joined in what had boiled over into an argument near the front.

"Go help," Vera said. "Babysitting me is certainly the lesser of your duties. That's actually your job."

He sighed, but he didn't argue. "I'll be right back." He and Matilda shared that worried look over Vera's head before he disappeared into the crowd.

"What?" Vera snapped. "Why do you keep doing that?"

"Do you honestly not know?" Matilda asked.

"I know everyone's a bit on edge, but—" She stopped at Matilda's look of pity. "What?"

"Lancelot and I started noticing it about a week into all this. People aren't just on edge, they're treating you poorly."

"That's not true. They're—" But she stopped. This morning in the market, a woman's laugh had stopped abruptly when her eyes fell on Vera. Her face had hardened as she hastily grabbed her husband by the arm and left in a huff. Vera had been deliberately ignoring it, but all the glares these past weeks had been directed at her. "But . . . why?" she asked.

"I don't know," Matilda said, but she must have noticed how Vera tensed. She laid a hand on her arm. "We've told Arthur, and he's asked Percival to put his ear to the ground. We'll get it all sorted out. People behave strangely under stress."

"Don't make me talk to them." Vera tucked in against the cart, yearning for the invisibility that once felt like a curse.

Almost simultaneously, the atmosphere shifted. It didn't take but a few moments for grumbles to morph into electric murmurs and for all eyes to point in the same direction. Vera knew what she'd find before she turned to see.

Arthur was there. He alone had that impact on a crowd. He and Vera had never gone on these endeavors together, though he'd been out amongst the people constantly. Their eyes caught for a second. He gave a stiff nod to Vera, and she returned a fleeting smile, her heart stuttering.

She pressed into her nook behind the seat, her back lodged against the cart, avoiding eye contact with anyone. But she was constantly aware of Arthur. The other times she'd seen him in town, he stayed on the opposite side of the square from her. This time, he weaved in. Closer and closer until Vera could take a few steps, reach to her right, and touch him.

She could hear him even through the crowd's noise, sometimes only the tone of his voice, not quite loud enough to form words. As his volume raised in laughter or to call to someone farther off, she'd make out a few words. She was entranced in listening, soothed by his presence—and unnerved that he had that impact on her.

He shifted as Lancelot called out to him, pulling him out of Vera's view. She peeled herself from her hiding place and moved forward as if her adjustment were to tend the horse.

Arthur's eyes found her immediately, as if he'd known her every move as she'd tracked his. This time, his brow was furrowed as his attention was drawn back to whatever Lancelot was saying.

Then Lancelot pointed at Vera, and the couple they'd been speaking with turned around with bright faces—and it wasn't just a couple. There was a cherub-faced toddler with mussed curls like he'd been freshly woken from a nap as he nuzzled into his father's trousers, and the mother cradled a bundle of white cloths in her arms, which proved itself to be a baby as it thrust a tiny fist into the air.

They were coming toward her now. Shit. There'd be no avoiding this. The man, who must have been the one to bestow his son with curls (though his were not so unruly), closed the distance with a few strides and bowed. "Your Majesty, my name is Roger, and this is my wife, Helene."

Helene ducked her head and drew her dress out with one hand in as best a curtsy as she could manage with the baby in her arms. Lancelot smiled with a glint in his eye from behind Helene while Arthur stood tense at his side.

What the hell was this about?

"It's . . . it's a pleasure to meet you." Vera didn't know if she should ask the couple a question, but Roger solved that for her.

"We know you aren't taking queries, but... we hoped you would bless our new daughter," Roger said.

"Oh." If this had been one of Guinevere's duties before, it could be added to the countless other things Vera didn't know about.

Arthur cast Lancelot an uncharacteristically unguarded glare before he sighed and stepped close to Vera, between her and all the others. He leaned next to her ear and spoke quietly, raising goosebumps on her neck. "This is quite customary, and you're fully capable if you'd like to say yes," he said. "But I can do it if you'd rather."

Vera hadn't ever been this close to him and had his eyes locked on hers for this long. There was no cold mask in place. This was a matter of ruling well, and no loathing or bitterness could stand in Arthur's way of loving his people. She wanted to show him that she could do something that might be helpful.

"I can try," she said. Arthur nodded as he stepped away, and Vera turned back to the couple. "Just, erm, a standard sort of blessing, then? For a, er, healthy life and the like?"

Roger smiled. Helene nodded.

Did Guinevere have religious training that she didn't know about? Helene wore a veil. Was that a religious choice? Vera licked her parched lips. "Shall I use Christian or pagan prayers?" She didn't know many of either.

"It doesn't matter to us," Helene answered. "We'll be honored by whatever blessings you offer."

Vera swallowed. "May I?" she said, with a gesture toward the little bundle.

Helene's rosy cheeks dimpled with her smile as she passed the bundle to Vera. The baby, barely older than a newborn, wore a white christening gown. The tiny perfect fingers of one hand waved through the air occasionally, and the other fist balled up under her button of a chin. Her face, with its delicate nose, lips, and closed eyes, was relaxed as she slept.

As if she'd sensed the transfer into a stranger's arms, the baby started fussing, fitful cries piercing the newfound quiet of the square. Vera bobbed her in rhythm with a soothing "shh-shh-shh" until she calmed back into her deeper sleep.

"What's her name?" Vera asked quietly.

"Guinevere," Roger said. "We've named her after you."

Vera's breath caught. "Thank you," she mumbled, surprised to be fighting back emotion. After all, the baby was named for the real Guinevere. Not Vera.

"Our town was nearest the final battle. We love our king," Roger said with a glance at Arthur, "and we have not forgotten it was our queen who saved us."

Imposter. Liar. Vera couldn't stop berating herself. But the baby was beautiful and the family sweet—and people were watching.

"God of all," Vera began with her eyes on the baby, unsure how loudly she should speak. "We ask your blessing on this wondrous child. May she live a long life of health, safety, prosperity—and love and joy all her days."

The parents thanked Vera, but her attention shifted to the little boy. He'd been hiding behind his mother's skirt but had inched much closer to Vera, standing on tiptoes to try to get a peek at his sister.

Vera crouched down so he could see. "What do you think about your new sister?"

The boy pouted, his eyes threatening to flood with tears.

"He is frustrated that he can't pronounce her name," Helene explained.

An idea tumbled into the front of her thoughts. Helene had turned back to her husband and Lancelot. Arthur was with them, too, his attention focused on whatever it was they were saying. Nobody was paying attention to Vera. Good.

"Can you say 'Vera?'" she whispered to the child.

"Ve-ra," he said, breaking it apart into two words.

She nodded encouragingly. "That's what my parents used to call me. Do you think you'd like that to be your special name for your sister?"

His eyes lit up. "Yes!" he said. "Vera." He murmured it three times and clumsily kissed his sister's head, stumbling over a stick he'd wedged into the pocket of his trousers.

"What's that you have there?" Vera asked.

He pulled it free and brandished it, all shyness forgotten. "My sword!" he proclaimed. "Watch!" His chubby arm waved the stick about. Lancelot caught sight and jumped in to play with the boy. Vera laughed as she stood to pull the baby free from the game's danger zone, just as she was knocked in the back of her shoulder and stumbled forward.

It was a man who'd bumped her. He carried on with an askance glance back at Vera.

"Pardon me," she said instinctively, though she'd not done anything wrong.

The man stopped in his tracks and turned back with a taut and nearly purpling, incensed face. Vera recoiled a step as he lurched toward her and hissed, "I won't pardon a bastard babe."

He started to stalk away as Vera's mind slowly made sense of his words. Maybe he knew these sweet young parents, and they hadn't been married in a way he approved of. Whatever the case, Vera's cheeks went hot as a quick anger erupted from her. She could have let it go, could have let the man leave with his petulant judgment in tow, but he kicked dirt at the little boy as he passed.

"What's that supposed to mean?" Vera snapped.

He stopped and wheeled about to face her. She thought the way his eyes narrowed was a hesitation. People around had started noticing the scuffle, stopping what they were doing and watching. The man's hand lingered in his pocket as he stared at the ground. If it was guilt and embarrassment, then good. He deserved it for insulting Helene and Roger. It emboldened Vera.

"Not words you care to stand behind?" she quipped.

"It's a child of a whore," the man said, and Vera's jaw fell. But he didn't sound as certain or convicted with the attention on him.

Vera's blood boiled. How dare he? She'd tear into him for coming after Helene, but he kept going.

"You haven't fooled anyone." The way his loathing stare seared into Vera frightened her. "Convenient you were gone a whole year. Time enough to grow and bear your shameful bastard. You're no queen. You'll bring our ruin!"

Wait.

What?

There wasn't any extra time to process the madness as the man pulled his hand from his pocket, reeled his arm back, and hurled what looked like an egg at Vera. She clutched the baby to her chest, trying to shield her from the blow.

But the impact never came. One moment, Arthur had been fully engaged with the couple, his back turned. And the next, he'd lunged in and caught the egg, which shattered into his hand.

"No!" The man who threw it dropped to his knees and screamed out in terror, the remnants of his anger melting into a pitiful cry. "It was for her," he wailed.

Vera did her best to ignore him, made easier by the overwhelming and putrid smell that erupted the instant the egg broke. It must have been rotten, but then—it was a puff of greenish smoke that emanated from it and none of the expected oozing mess. Other than the smoke, the egg was empty. But Arthur's skin started to blister and bulge, rolling like the surface of boiling water.

Vera stared at it, but Arthur was focused on her. With his uninjured hand, he took her shoulder, eyes searching her and the baby in her arms—blissfully unaware and still sleeping.

"She's fine," Vera said.

"She's a witch!" The man screamed out through his tears as Lancelot tackled him to the ground. The man's face contorted with his wild rage. "She's brought a curse upon us! Burn her."

He wrenched his arm from Lancelot's grasp only long enough to point at Vera. And the faces of the listening crowd weren't what they should have been on hearing the ravings of a mad man.

They were afraid—but they were looking at Vera.

They were afraid of her.

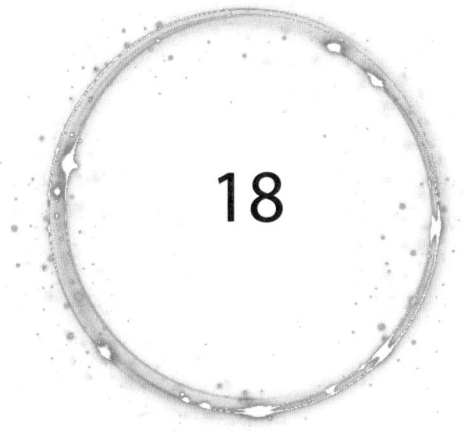

18

It was eerily quiet. They sat in the throne room, Matilda close at Vera's side. Lancelot, on her other side, was uncharacteristically somber. He'd taken the man to the dungeon before joining them in the throne room and made a beeline for Vera when he arrived.

"You're unharmed? Truly?" he'd said, his brow furrowed as he took her hands and studied her face.

"I'm fine." She felt sick, and her skin prickled and burned in the wake of the shock, but she wasn't hurt. Lancelot's breath shook as he exhaled. He kissed each of her hands. Vera glanced across their circle at Arthur. He paid Lancelot's brazen affection no mind.

It was only the four of them, with one empty seat left for Percival. Percival, who had all the information. Percival, who'd been sent to question the mad man. It would have been Arthur, but his boiling hand kept him from it. Camelot's physician had insisted on treating it immediately as the rolling blisters inched up his wrist and threatened to overtake his forearm.

His hand and wrist were bandaged now, though the angry red blisters continued to spread. A new one was rising above the dressing. He had to be in agony, though his mastery over his expression nearly concealed it, except that his jaw had been clenched since he arrived.

There were guards outside the throne room. There never had

been before. They flung the doors open for Percival when he arrived. He dropped into the one remaining seat and heaved a deep breath as Arthur inclined his head at the youngest knight in a clear invitation for him to begin.

"There's some good news," Percival said, though his face was grim. "Let's start there. The work in Exeter is done. Our troops have already begun returning and should all be back by morning. Merlin will be with them. The harvest would have been exceptional. We're lucky for it. They were able to salvage a decent amount. We'll almost completely deplete our reserves when it's all said and done. It's a gamble that next season's harvest will be good . . . but no one will go hungry over this winter. For now, that's cause for celebration."

Vera heard the nerves in Percival's voice. Something had changed in him. And in Lancelot—a hardness that betrayed their fear. Arthur kept his face carefully blank.

"The attacker?" he prompted in a soft voice.

"He's out of his mind," Lancelot mumbled.

"He is," Percival said. "But that doesn't change the accusations that he levied. Dangerous accusations. And I'm sorry to say it, but they're shared by others."

A deep line formed between Arthur's eyebrows as they drew together. "That doesn't make sense."

But Vera innately understood. She'd been thinking about it all morning. "The trouble started after I came back," she said.

Percival nodded. "You're different than you were before—though who could expect otherwise? None of our soldiers, present company included, were the same after the wars. Why should you be after you nearly died?"

"Of course she's changed," Matilda put in with a note of defensive pride. "And she's the better for it. We're all the better for it."

"Agreed." Lancelot's eyes flashed to Arthur before they settled on Vera with his familiar warmth.

Heat rose to her cheeks, and she stared at her toes. She felt less flattered and more like she'd successfully run a con on them. She wasn't brave enough to see how Arthur reacted.

"I feel I know more of you now after mere minutes of conversation than I ever did in the years of being in your presence before, Your Majesty," Percival said. "You seem stronger."

Arthur shifted in his seat, and Vera thought she saw a flash of anger blaze through him. Percival ignored it. "That's one of the issues, though. They take offense that the lady is outspoken."

Fuck. She'd not once taken this seriously enough. Vera had behaved like Camelot was a playground . . . all the moments she'd laughed inappropriately at dinner with Lancelot, that day when she'd made a scene playing at the pit. And then her sharp tongue, both with Lord Wulfstan and now with the man locked in the dungeon.

"By contrast," Percival went on, "there have been the last few weeks when the chief complaint was that the lady doesn't interact with the people. They perceive her as—" he paused with an askance glance at Vera.

Oh god. What else? "Say it plainly," she said, her stomach churning.

"Standoffish," he said. "That you feel your northern upbringing makes you better than them." Percival gave a grim smile. The corner of his lips that were crossed by his scar didn't lift with the rest. "It's an unfair expectation, leaving you with a narrow corridor of acceptable behavior."

"What about the infidelity?" Matilda's voice was quiet and apologetic. "Do others think that, too?"

Percival dropped his elbows to his knees and clasped his hands between them. He looked like he was fighting to get the words to come out or like he was trying to keep from throwing up. "There are some rumors that the queen is spending her nights with other men. I've been unable to find the origin."

Vera and Lancelot caught one another's eyes. Their early mornings together. It had to be. It was exactly what she'd known to dread all along.

She was alarmed to notice that Percival had shifted his focus to Lancelot, too.

Lancelot actually laughed. "Oh, come on. She is allowed to have friends." He knew better than anyone in this room that their particular friendship, though it wasn't romantic, wouldn't be seen as innocent by any suspicious party.

"She is always with you," Percival said, his voice carefully even. Vera slumped in her seat.

"She's also always with Matilda," Lancelot shot back. "I don't see—"

"That's different."

"Of course," he drawled sarcastically, "because two women have never taken up—"

"Stop it," Matilda said sharply. "Right or wrong, it's different. And you're behaving like a child to act like it's not."

Percival's face reddened as Lancelot, not ready to give in, rolled his eyes and went on. "She's with Arthur plenty, too. Every court. All the meals. For the Gods' sakes, they go to the same chamber every night."

"But she's happy when she's with you!" Percival barked back, his volume mounting with his frustration. "That's what's really at the heart of this. The queen—" He seemed to remember himself. Percival looked at her, then at Arthur, who'd listened in cold silence.

"Go on, Percival," Arthur said with infuriating calm. "Tell me."

Percival inhaled to begin but stopped himself.

"I mean it," Arthur said. "Give me the truth. All of it."

"She—" Percival paused and instead addressed Vera directly. "You look terrified at the king's side. And Your Majesty," he shifted to face Arthur, "you look like you're being tortured. The people watch carefully. They watch everything you do carefully. And they have taken notice of your apparent displeasure with the queen. The people love you, and they will follow your lead when it comes to her." He swallowed hard. "They have followed your lead."

Arthur's face changed for a shade of a second. From sitting by him, listening to him, diligently observing him all these weeks, Vera realized that she'd begun to be able to read the minuscule breaks in his carefully crafted exterior. She recognized the expression that rippled across his features. It was the same one she had seen her first night when she asked him if the water was safe to drink.

Arthur was ashamed.

Good, Vera thought with a savagery that only reached as deep as her hurt and perhaps was merely a placeholder for it.

"And there's the accusation that she's a witch," Percival added.

Vera scoffed and surveyed all their faces. None of them took it lightly.

"But . . . aren't there witches everywhere?" She'd assumed, apparently incorrectly, that any woman with a gift would be considered a witch. It was probably something she should have known. Percival's raised eyebrow was confirmation enough.

Arthur covered it. "You use a different term in the north. In the south, a 'witch' is a woman who uses dark magic. Unsanctioned magic."

Percival nodded. "The coincidence that the harvest's wreckage came on the heels of the queen's return . . ."

"Shit." The light of Lancelot's laugh and indignation was gone from his eyes as they fell on Percival. "There's no way around this, is there?"

Percival shook his head.

"Arthur," Lancelot said quietly, "ten years ago, maybe even five, that would have been enough evidence. She would have already been burned for it." He looked to Percival, and Vera realized that they'd begun talking to Arthur in tandem. They were working to persuade him about something but what? To burn her? The thought had barely crossed Vera's mind before she tossed it aside. It may have been naivete, but she trusted Matilda and Lancelot completely and was surprised to realize that she trusted Arthur not to harm her, either.

"I wish I could say this wasn't an issue, Your Majesty," Percival said, taking the thread of conversation he'd been passed, "but this belief goes deep. For some, it started while the queen was gone and festered there. Few gave it merit. But it planted a seed, and our current reality gave it roots. The people who believe this aren't small in number anymore. And that man attacked her today. He meant to disfigure her." Percival gestured to Arthur's injured hand. "He told me a witch should be as ugly as the harm she's inflicted."

She didn't need to know that. Vera's head swirled. She'd begun to reckon with the hardship she'd brought on the kingdom, but she hadn't understood before now that her life might actually be in danger, too.

"I have to do it," Arthur finally said.

Lancelot let out a sigh. He and Percival had succeeded, though neither were pleased. "You do."

"It should be done today," Arthur said. He'd never looked like he carried a heavier burden than right now. "Belaboring it will only draw more of a crowd. I want to send a clear message without stirring up undue fear."

"What are you—" Vera's words came out so quietly that no one heard her.

"It'll be the first in your reign, won't it?" Lancelot asked with a frightening gentleness.

Arthur nodded.

"The first what?" Vera asked. Trepidation had driven breath behind her voice, making her question sound like a demand.

At last, Arthur met her gaze. He held it steadily. "Execution."

She couldn't make sense of the word at first. On her arrival to this time, she'd assumed a brutal society, a reality rife with cruel punishments. It was a notion she'd quickly been dispelled of. They'd built a different world. Arthur dreamed of a new sort of nation, and he'd made it and—

He was going to execute the man who attacked her.

It was all shattering, everything they'd fought for. Everything she was supposed to help them save. And it was Vera's fault. That man was going to die because she hadn't held her tongue. It was her fault.

A pained sound escaped Vera before she found any words. "No. No, you can't." Camelot was different. This England, it was better. It had been better . . . until she arrived. She would fix it. She would beg. She would plead. "I never meant for any of this to happen. I'm sorry. I should have stayed silent. I shouldn't have pretended to be her—"

"You haven't done anything wrong." Lancelot spoke over her, trying to cover her slip before Percival or Matilda heard it.

"There must be another punishment. He—" her eyes shot to Arthur's wrapped hand, "he didn't mean to hurt you. It wouldn't have killed me—"

The Once and Future Queen

"You were holding the child, Guinevere," Matilda said this, and gently. "If he had hit you, it certainly would have killed the baby."

Conscious thought was gone from Vera's mind, replaced by rapid bursts that didn't quite connect with one another. She crammed her eyes closed, trying to shut it all out, but all she could imagine behind her eyelids was death. A dead child in her arms. The man. Vincent.

Her fault.

Arthur could fix this. He loved his people. "I'm sorry. I'm sorry. Please. Please don't—"

"It's not your fault." Vera thought Arthur said it. It may have simply been what she wanted to hear. Her vision went blurry. She couldn't see him clearly.

"I don't want this." Her voice was rising, heedless of what she was saying. "I'll leave. I'll go back to Glastonbury—I should have never come here. I can't be her—"

"It's not about you!" She heard that. Arthur yelled it so forcefully, so furiously, how could she not? Vera sucked a deep breath in, and her vision cleared enough to find revulsion etched in the lines of his face. "It is my decision. That man committed treason. His actions are a threat to my rule and the kingdom we have built. He dies. You have no say in this."

It wasn't about her. It never had been. It was about his rule. Of course. That shouldn't have made her angry. Vera knew she was nothing more than a placeholder for Guinevere.

She gritted her teeth and glared back. Anything softer than anger would have left her sobbing.

When Arthur spoke, his voice was quiet though startlingly stern. "It has nothing to do with you. Do you understand?"

She'd break. She'd cry if she spoke.

"She does—" Lancelot began, but Arthur stopped him with a glare before turning it back on Vera.

"Do you?"

It was a lie. It had everything to do with her, and Vera despised herself for it. But in that moment, she hated him, too, and that made it easier.

"Yes, sire." She threw the word like a dagger.

"Who performs the execution in the absence of a mage?" Percival broke the overlong quiet that followed. "Merlin won't be back until tomorrow."

"I'll do it." The response came from the door, startling them all. Lancelot and Percival rose automatically and assumed defensive postures, unmatched by the man who stood by the closed door with his hands clasped in front of his dingy brown robe. His eyes were deep-set in his skull. It might have been this that emphasized the perturbed scowl carved into his features. His inky dark hair wasn't long or short. It lazed about down to the middle of his ears, the distinct appearance of someone who meant to have short hair but couldn't be bothered to maintain it. Coupled with the scowl, the eyes, and a sharp nose, Vera found him rather alarming.

Percival's open-mouthed shock made Lancelot crack a half smile, though his sword was also half unsheathed. "Who the bloody fuck are you?" Percival barked. "How did you get in here?"

The man didn't answer. Instead, he said flatly, "I'll perform the execution."

Percival's lips moved in exasperation, though no sound came out.

"That's a generous offer from an unidentified stranger," Lancelot said with a quirked eyebrow, "but all executions must be performed by a mage."

"I'm aware," the sullen man answered, followed by more thick silence.

A hum of recognition came from Arthur's direction. "You're Mage Gawain."

Vera jolted. That was a name from Arthurian legend. A knight, one of Arthur's knights. She was sure of it. For the hundredth time since her arrival, she loathed herself for never taking enough interest in the legend to have read a single damn book about it. But this man wasn't a knight.

Gawain stared at Arthur's injured hand as he gave one curt nod, his hair curtaining his eyes with the motion. "I've only just arrived."

"I thank you." Arthur inclined his head. "And I'm sorry this will be your welcome."

"Treason is the highest crime against you." Gawain's dark eyes scanned them and pointedly lingered on Vera. "It's my duty in Merlin's absence, but I must insist on seeing to your wound first."

"It's already been tended by the physician."

Gawain shrugged. "If you're content with being permanently maimed." He offered no further explanation.

"Are you being deliberately obtuse?" Percival stared at Gawain, aghast. "Please elaborate on what you mean."

Gawain's sunken eyes stayed on Percival for a long moment. "The wound was caused by magic. It must be healed as such."

"You have a healing gift?" Lancelot asked with his head cocked to the side.

Gawain nodded. "They are rare. I am fortunate."

They must have been extremely rare, for even Percival was cowed enough by the revelation to go slack-jawed with awe. It brought Vera's dread back, though. The hands that would heal would soon perform the execution. She wanted time to slow down. She wanted his work on Arthur to take hours ... something that would save them from what was to come. There had to be a way out of this.

But it all moved in a flurry. No one had to tell Vera that she needed to attend the execution, that Guinevere needed to stand by Arthur in the wake of Percival's revelations. It was a foregone conclusion, though she couldn't remember how she got to the town square. They didn't have a designated site for executions, but the square was chosen for its logistics; a place for Arthur to oversee the act with Vera at his side (a raised box that had ironically been built for observing Camelot's many celebrations) and ample surrounding space for ... spectators. The square was nearly full, speckled with dejected and frightened faces who'd grown comfortable in a time of exuberant peace. At the very center was the man with his hands bound, knelt on a makeshift wooden platform.

She couldn't see the tears from where she stood, but Vera heard his weeping. He was flanked by Lancelot in full formal regalia and sharply contrasted by Gawain on the other side in his dingy, brown robe. Vera also recognized Father John, the castle's priest, who stood over the man, offering last rites before he backed away and disappeared into the crowd.

Soldiers were situated in a wide ring to make a bubble of space between the spectators and the main event. Percival and Randall bookended a cluster of soldiers guarding her and Arthur, their backs to them.

And then it was time. Vera's legs shook so violently that it was a wonder she could stand. She clenched her teeth shut to keep them from chattering.

Arthur stepped forward to make the pronouncement. "Joseph, son of Cuthbert the carpenter," he said, and Vera's breath hitched. She hadn't thought to ask his name before now. "You are unquestionably guilty of treason for attacking your king and queen, endangering not only their lives but those of countless witnesses present. You are hereby sentenced to death." There was no direct mention of his verbal assault, but it was the reason that he would not be offered last words.

Lancelot's face was taut and his expression hard as he stepped behind the man—Joseph—and held him by the shoulders. He nodded to Gawain.

It was going to happen. She caught Arthur's movement in her periphery and felt the weight of his stare on her. She couldn't bear the thought of seeing his hatred.

She told herself it was curiosity, but the truth was that loneliness had her turning to him. In his eyes, she found fear and was overcome with the unnerving sense that he needed her. No, not her—Guinevere.

But she reached for him on instinct and would have stopped herself short if he had not moved toward her at precisely the same moment. The fingers of his bandaged hand met her untarnished one and closed around it, holding tightly.

Joseph's crying rose and shifted to shouts, and the tender moment was gone like mist on the wind.

Gawain looped his left arm around Joseph's head, bracing his neck firmly in place beneath the chin. In his other hand, he held a thin-bladed silver dagger.

Vera gasped. When there'd been no guillotine, no rope, no massive sword, she'd assumed the mechanism for the deed would be magic. Never a dagger. Sweat beaded on the back of her neck, though the day was cool.

"Close your eyes," Arthur murmured, his lips hardly moving. "Please don't watch."

Her shock at his gentle plea nearly stole her breath, but Vera had to watch. She couldn't look away when that man's blood was on her hands.

Gawain struck swiftly, piercing Joseph's chest in the center, all the way to the blade's hilt. Joseph screamed, and it was the sound of an animal caught and made prey. He gasped and squirmed beneath the mage's grasp. With every pull and cry, blood spurted from the wound, but Gawain remained motionless for one long inhale and exhale before he jerked his own head to the side.

It was as if the motion pulled the thread of life cleanly from Joseph's body. The tension collapsed from his muscles, and he crumpled from man to corpse in a single blink.

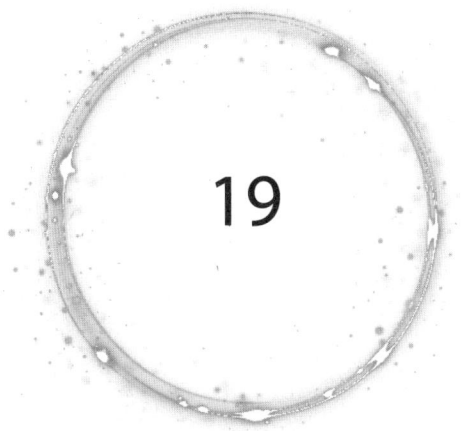

19

Vera hardly slept that night. Waves of anxiety pushed through her, followed by a sense of dread so overwhelming that she felt it in her pounding heart and pulsing through her skin. When even her blankets grew damp with sweat, she kicked them off.

The day had been awful, so nightmarish to even elicit pity from Arthur. Her mind flashed to his hand holding hers far too many times, but it was one of two things from the day that didn't leave her staring at the ceiling in abject horror.

The other was the note on her bedside table. Matilda had crept through Vera's door to deliver it just before midnight, needlessly worrying about waking her. It was from Merlin. He was back. Vera was to report to his study in the morning. Finally.

She'd been intent on waiting up for Arthur, somehow knowing that, after yesterday, he'd listen to her. She'd ached to apologize and, more than that, have one real conversation with him. But he never came back. Even when morning broke at last, and Matilda came to help Vera dress, the door to his sleeping chamber was a few inches ajar in the exact position as it had been last night.

It might all be done after today anyway. Vera hadn't questioned whether she could survive here until spring when time travel would be possible again. Insulated by castle walls and the likes of Merlin and Lancelot and even Arthur, with her nighttime reading lit by literal magic and her dinners colored with spectacles of storytelling, she'd treated this more like being in a storybook than a real place on the brink of disaster—where her life was in real danger.

But of course, it was. Guinevere met her end here.

So today, she'd magically retrieve the memories and then . . . what? Actually go into hiding at some monastery in the countryside and wait out the winter? They could pretend she'd died. That would go over well. She shoved away the pang of sadness at the thought of leaving Lancelot and Matilda. Their lives would be better, and they'd forget her soon enough. And she would go home.

Home. Seeing her parents was too good to even think of. But picturing herself back in Glastonbury as she knew it . . . back at the George, running alone every morning, back to her forgettable life. It was what she wanted, so why was it so hard to imagine? Vera didn't belong anywhere.

It wasn't a long walk to Merlin's study, down the steps of her tower, past the guards that now flanked most corridors, and across the back courtyard, but she and Matilda stopped short at the bottom of the stairs. Because the quiet morning air was shredded by the sound of screaming. A pit dropped in Vera's stomach. Oh God. What now?

There were many voices, the loudest one a woman's, wailing with primal terror. Before Vera knew her feet were moving, she started running toward it.

"Guinevere, wait!" Matilda called from behind her, but she followed, too, all the way to the throne room. There were four guards in the thick of things with Arthur and Lancelot, and the woman screaming . . . Vera recognized her. Though her face was a twisted-up mask of itself, she held the bundle of her baby tightly to her chest. Helene, the mother from yesterday.

Roger was there, too, facing away from Vera. He held the cherub-faced toddler. The boy looked frightened and had a perfect tear clinging to his cheek, but his eyes brightened when he saw Vera over his father's shoulder. He waved a chubby fist at her.

Arthur and Lancelot were huddled tight with the parents, both working to calm Helene, when Arthur saw Vera. His face darkened, and he grabbed Lancelot's arm and pushed him in her direction.

Lancelot only seemed confused by the gesture until he turned and saw Vera and Matilda. He hurried over to them. "The baby is sick."

"What do you mean? Where's the physician?" As Vera asked it, Percival ran into the courtyard with Gawain rushing behind him.

"The baby is very sick," Lancelot said. "Come on." He was trying to hurry her away with a hand on her elbow. Vera shrugged him off.

Gawain made a beeline for Helene and took the child from her. The bundle hardly moved, nary a wiggle as one tiny hand slipped limply from it. Vera's knees buckled, and Lancelot caught her beneath the arms to steady her. "Is she dead?"

But then the little fingers curled into a fist.

Her hands now empty, Helene spun about, and her wild eyes fell on Vera. They transformed, clouding with rage. "What did you do to her?" she screamed.

"Helene, please," Roger said through his own tears. Arthur tried to restrain the woman, but she had the force of a mother's aching fury behind her and moved straight through him. Lancelot lunged out to stop her with one haggard glance over his shoulder at Vera and Matilda. He was so worn down. He and Vera had such fun together during their runs. They laughed. He understood her. But they never went deep. They never talked about any of their difficult realities, and now it was all they were left with. She expected it wouldn't be long before he got sick of her, a petty thought next to a mother actively losing her child.

Matilda tugged at Vera's arm. "We need to go."

This time, she didn't fight leaving. She followed Matilda in the opposite direction, Helene screaming behind her. Vera tried not to hear the words, but they echoed her own thoughts. She was selfish. She was ruin. She was a curse.

She shook with nausea and only kept moving, eyes trained on the ground in front of her, because she'd collapse if she stopped. How had she ever been so deluded to think she could do this?

She didn't even know where Matilda was leading her. They'd made it to the entry hall. Vera heard the chatter of whoever was there but paid it no mind until Matilda abruptly stopped. "No," she said in a horrified whisper.

"What's wrong?" Vera asked.

"It's your father."

Vera followed Matilda's gaze to the finely appointed man approaching them with sure strides, leaving a cluster of servants in his wake. She did not recognize him, yet fear filled her, and she had to fight the urge to cower. His eyes were set on Vera without even a flash in Matilda's direction.

It was her first glimpse of her biological father.

He was younger than she'd imagined, with hardly any grey streaking his hair and merely touches of it in his neatly trimmed beard. She'd dreamed of knowing him and now wished she could be anywhere but in his cold sights. Wished he weren't so tall and imposing a figure. Wished she didn't instantly and nonsensically crave his approval.

"My lord," Matilda said, "the queen has—"

The thin line of his lips tipped downward at the corners, not a frown but a scowl set on Vera. "I require a private word."

He grabbed Vera's upper arm, his fingers digging in painfully. She cast a helpless glance over her shoulder at Matilda as the man—her father—dragged her into the side corridor, out of any bystanders' eyeshot.

"You have shamed the north," he spat as he yanked Vera's arm to pull her around to face him. "You have shamed me."

She had imagined she'd feel something if she met her father. She never expected him to be frightening. His face was inches from hers, and she couldn't help but fruitlessly search for something recognizable in his features.

"Wulfstan would have been bad enough. And now I hear you've been playing the whore," he said through gritted teeth as he bore down upon her. Vera stumbled backward against the corridor wall. "I swear to you, child, if you have defiled yourself, I will make sure you wish you'd died in that accident."

Vera stared back, speechless, bracing herself against the stones behind her.

It wasn't the right response. Her father reeled back and surveyed her from toes to head, disgusted. "You stupid cunt, did you open your legs?"

She should have categorically denied it. Of course. But she sputtered meaninglessly and, unable to bear his judgment, tore her eyes from him.

He grabbed her by the chin and forcibly turned her face toward his.

A deeper, more primal instinct than her need to pacify him rocketed through her. She yanked away to stare at the floor. She knew it was a mistake only a heartbeat before the back of his hand ripped across her face. Vera cried out when the ring he wore bit into the corner of her lip and stung even once it was gone.

His slap had pulled her face back in his direction. "I raised you for this. You must be perfect." He grabbed Vera's shoulders and gave her a violent shake. "You—"

"Lord Aballach!" Arthur's voice came from the end of the corridor, and while it wasn't a command, it sounded like one. Vera's father obeyed by falling silent and dropping his hands to his sides. By the time he and Vera looked at him, Arthur had already closed the distance between them, but he drew up uncomfortably close to her father, his chest nearly touching Aballach's shoulder as he exhaled a forceful breath.

"Do not," he said with a growling fury that left Vera stunned, "touch my wife again."

Aballach took a reflexive step back. "She is my daughter and—"

"And now she is your queen." Arthur's face quivered in his barely restrained ire. He shifted to stand in front of Vera, turning to face her and entirely blocking her view of her father. His eyes didn't reach hers; they stopped at her lips and darkened. Vera touched the spot where the ring had struck and drew her fingers away. Blood. She felt a flash of pity for Guinevere—the real Guinevere—who'd grown up with this man.

"Go," Arthur said, as quiet as a breath, before wheeling back around on Lord Aballach.

Vera had no delusions about the purpose of his intervention. He had to protect his rule. Still, she was grateful. Giving her an escape was the kindest thing he could do for her. She didn't know what would have happened without his intervention.

If there hadn't been guards at the gate to stop her, she'd have wandered out of the castle and kept going. Disappearing would be the best she could do for all their sake. But her feet took her to the chapel free of her mind's guidance. Out of habit, she supposed, she wandered next to the statue of Mary and sank to the ground. She drew her knees in close, wrapped her arms around her legs, and lay her head atop them. It was as small as she could be.

Vera didn't cry. She stared vacantly at the floor. She'd spent a lifetime learning how to steer her mind away from sadness, but now there was nothing else. So she stared at nothing as the weight of her transgressions pressed down on her. This was worse than being worthless.

When the door opened and the sound of footsteps followed, she tucked her head to her chest and closed her eyes. That would likely be Thomas. She wasn't sure she could manage a conversation with him just now.

But it wasn't him.

"Do you want me to get Lancelot?" Arthur's voice, gentle and soft. He must have seen her come in this direction.

Vera's eyes snapped open. She expected to find him angry or pitying her. But the stony mask was solidly in place. Anger sparked and pulled her from her stupor.

"No," she said, "I need you"—she felt unbearable shame at the admission and hastily added—"to be able to be in the same room as me. Running to Lancelot is exactly how I've wrecked this so terribly." Vera dropped her forehead into her arms. "I know you hate me—and at this point, you have every reason to. I am worse than an imposter. I have smeared Guinevere's name and her memory. I've broken everything you made. I—I'm so sorry. I can't do this. I can't fix this."

She waited for his voice to fill the silence long enough that she started to think she'd imagined him ever being there. She looked at him, utterly still except for his shoulders raising and lowering with his breath. His jaw shifted to the side, and he seemed to decide something.

"You're right," Arthur said, and dread flooded her, but he came over and sat on the floor next to Vera. "You cannot fix this. And you did not break it. There are some things that you need to understand. What you've heard—that Guinevere saved us in the final battle—is true. But a lot of people died because of it. It worked because it was so deadly, and no matter what I said, she bore the weight of it.

"I was meant to care for her. To protect her. I failed her so many times." He swallowed and turned his head against the stone wall to look at Vera, and there was nothing cold or calculated there. Only anguish. "I thought if I stayed away from you that it would . . ." Arthur shook his head. "That it would be better for you, but I failed you, too. I need you to hear me. None of this is your fault. I have done everything wrong. All that's happened these last few days, it's because of my behavior. These are my failings."

"But that baby," Vera said, her throat instantly tight. "I held her, and now she's dying. Maybe there is a curse—"

"That wasn't you."

"It was, though—"

"No," he said firmly. "It was the fumes from the Venovum. The cursed object that man threw at you. That's what made the baby sick. Gawain already had the potion ready from treating my hand. She's going to be fine."

"She is?" Her voice quivered. "You're sure?"

"Look." Arthur held his left hand up so Vera could examine it. The bandages were gone. It was only faintly pink in a few spots. "Gawain is good at what he does. The baby started improving immediately."

"Oh. That's good. That's—" Her breath came in a lurch. Push it away. She tensed her muscles. Don't think of it. Vera took three deliberate breaths and swallowed heavily.

She was about to say, "I'm fine," when Arthur slid his left arm around the back of her shoulders and wrapped the right around the front of her shins, encircling her balled-up form in his arms. Perhaps it was the mere shock of encountering such tenderness from him, or perhaps the rickety barrier Vera had constructed to hold the horror at bay within her simply snapped, but a gasping sob ripped through her. She didn't know where relief stopped, and fear and sadness began. They might have all been the same, and they crested out in her tears. She dropped her forehead onto his shoulder, heedless in that moment of what his care meant or why he'd given it, only knowing that it felt safe, and she wept. She wept every tear that she'd been swallowing since the day she left home—and some from before then, too.

There'd been no place for them. Vera had floated like the misty specter from the Tor, and Arthur's arms had somehow caught her and given her a shape, a container she could collapse into. He didn't utter a single word. It was only when her tears slowed that she began to question it. It was too intimate, especially with him. Vera sat up, and Arthur pulled his hands back to his lap.

"You don't have to do this." She swiped her fingers beneath her eyes, a fruitless effort to erase the evidence of her tears. "I'm grateful you're talking to me, but I don't want you to pretend to like me."

"I'm not pretending. I'm—I'm quite fond of you."

"No you aren't," Vera protested, though she wanted to believe him. "Maybe you were fond of her, but I'm not her."

"You don't need to be her. Be you."

Vera glowered at him, which, for some reason, drew a fleeting half smile from Arthur. "I sort of tried that. It didn't go well before."

He nodded. "I was a colossal prat before."

Vera nearly laughed at that. She hadn't yet been able to hold his eyes like this nor see him so unguarded. "I don't know how to do this," she said.

"I don't either." His hand flinched, and she'd thought he might have been about to reach for her, but now he seemed hesitant to touch her. His face went rigid, and he dropped his eyes to her chin. "I'm sorry. I owe you many apologies. I don't deserve your forgiveness, but I have to fix this. I don't see any other way than, at least publicly, I'll ask you to endure my affections . . . to spare you from poor treatment and for the good of the kingdom. And—" She was relieved when he met her eyes again, even though sadness marred his face. At least it was real. "And privately, I would offer you friendship if you're willing to entertain it. I wouldn't blame you if you're not."

"That's all I've wanted from you. This whole time, that's all I've wanted."

"I'm sorry," he said.

He rubbed his right hand where his knuckles were swollen and awfully red. Vera hadn't realized the boils left such swelling. But it was his left hand that he'd caught the egg with. It bore only light pink spots where there'd once been blisters.

"What happened to your hand?"

"Oh. Erm . . ." He tried to hide it at his side, but Vera gingerly grabbed it.

His knuckles were so terribly swollen, especially by his index finger, that Vera could feel the bulge of it at a cursory touch. "What happened?" she asked again.

He pursed his lips. "Well. I, er, lost my temper. With your father."

"How would that—" Oh. Her lips formed the word, though she didn't say it. "You punched him?"

He slid his hand free and tucked it back by his side. "Er. Yes."

"Hm." She tried to suppress a grin, the same tingling sense that she'd felt at his protective affection with Wulfstan blooming in her chest before she remembered that it was about his rule. Not about caring for her.

He must have noticed the way her expression changed. "Does that upset you?"

She didn't know how to answer. "That was the first time I ever met my biological father." She wasn't sure why she was telling him that, except it felt important that someone knew. "Is he always like that?"

"I'm afraid so. He's . . ." Arthur shook his head. "He's an ass. Guinevere told me that her childhood was not a happy one."

"What did he say?" Vera asked.

"Hmm?"

"What did he say to make you take a swing at him?" She forced her voice to be light, but she craved to know.

"Oh." Arthur's eyes drifted up to the ceiling. "It was nothing."

Vera scoffed. "Don't spare my feelings. Tell me."

Arthur sighed, and his cheeks went pink. "He said I should get you pregnant to tame you."

The tingle flared in her chest. "That made you punch him?"

"Right in the mouth," Arthur said. He looked at her lips, and Vera reflexively reached up to touch the cut that still stung. "It only seemed fair."

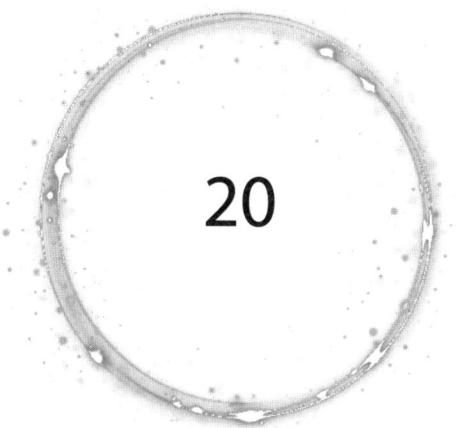

20

Lancelot had found them in the chapel with a summons for Arthur from Vera's father and the local lords. Arthur offered to send Percival instead, but Vera had insisted she was fine. They all knew Arthur was the one who was needed. She planned to head to Merlin's study alone after that, determined not to delay their session, but Lancelot fell in step with her rather than following Arthur.

"You aren't needed for whatever diplomacy is about to happen?" Vera asked.

"Oh no," he said. "Arthur's far better suited for it. It doesn't take being pushed beyond the brink of offense and exhaustion for me to start taking swings."

She thought he'd bid her farewell at the door to Merlin's tower, but he was right on her heels and looked at her expectantly when she stopped at the threshold.

"You've seen me safely here," she said. "You don't have to walk me all the way down."

"Oh, I'm not just walking you. I'm staying."

She'd been so certain that all the trouble she'd caused would have him running to get away from her. "I'm sure you'd rather be with the soldiers at training or—"

"Guinna," he said sternly. "I want to be here."

"Only if you're sure . . ."

"I am. I insist." His intensity fell away as an ornery grin stole over his face. "In case someone needs to take a swing at Merlin."

At first glance, Merlin's study remained the same: oddities dangling beneath hooks, piled on shelves, stuffed in baskets. It was a pleasant sort of mess that was actually tidy, with only the appearance of whimsical disorder—except for one island of pure chaos exploding from the epicenter of what was once Viviane's empty desk. Bits of rumpled parchment and discarded piles of rubbish littered the floor around it. The desk was transformed into a makeshift stronghold, fortified by stacks of hefty tomes lining the edges of it on three sides and partway on a fourth, leaving a gap in the middle where Gawain now worked. Well, presumably, it was Gawain. All that was visible beyond the gap in the book walls was the seated lower half of a robed man.

Vera imagined completing the desk fort with a handwritten Keep Out! sign and smiled—until she caught Merlin's eye over in the kitchen area. She'd imagined countless versions of what he might say to her, of how he might be angry. Disappointed in her. She'd wondered if there'd be pity.

But he simply looked a little bit frightened, which might have been worse than the alternatives. He busied himself, carefully combining ingredients on the counter. Lancelot plopped down in Merlin's chair, going so far as to open the giant tome on his desk and flip through the pages.

"What are you doing?" Merlin snapped once he noticed.

"Reading," Lancelot said innocently. "Merlin, what's—" he bent his head low over the book, "the defensible transference postulation?"

The top of a head and two eyes barely crested the fort walls as Gawain sat up and blinked at Lancelot, his interest apparently roused.

"Hullo there," Lancelot said to him. "Wasn't sure that was you in there."

"I'm leaving," Gawain said. "I've been instructed that this is a private matter."

Lancelot smiled pleasantly as he folded his hands on the desk.

"Yet you are staying," Gawain added with no small amount of disapproval.

Lancelot's grin widened.

Merlin crossed the room and slammed the book shut. Lancelot barely pulled back in time to spare his nose from being clobbered by it.

"The king has ordered it, Gawain," Merlin said.

"There you have it." Lancelot threw his hands in the air in mock annoyance. "I'm here on orders. Nothing I can do about it."

Gawain tipped his head forward and glowered up at Lancelot through his eyebrows. "I do not find you amusing."

This only further delighted Lancelot. "That is a shame."

"We should be finished by supper," Merlin said, putting an end to the conversation.

Gawain stared, fixated on Merlin's hand—but no . . . Vera could see he held a glass vial. He adjusted so that his fingers covered it, drawing Gawain's attention up as the elder mage delicately tilted his head toward the door.

"Of course," Gawain said quickly, his chair's feet raking across the floor as he scuttled from his seat, a rectangular plank of wood clutched in one hand. Vera had only noticed it because she'd thought it was a cellphone at first glance. It was exactly the right size. But he tucked whatever it was into his robe's pocket and strode out the door without so much as a greeting nor a goodbye to Vera. She wasn't sure he'd noticed she was there at all.

"He's a good lad," Merlin said. Then he sighed and shook his head. "I'll have to think of what to tell him about you soon. He's uncannily perceptive."

"Oh yes," Lancelot piped in, comfortably twiddling his thumbs in Merlin's seat. "Really has a knack for nuance, that one."

Merlin wasn't any more pleased about Lancelot's presence than Gawain had been. Their dynamic was that of a toddler who could smell the annoyance of his caretaker and who would now prey upon that weakness mercilessly.

He chuckled when Merlin snatched the closed book and turned away.

Stop! Vera mouthed in exasperation, though she smiled, too. She was nervous. His mischief was a welcome distraction.

Merlin led them over to the bathing pool in the darkest corner of his study. It was larger than it appeared from a distance and eerily the shape of a coffin. "We'll be trying an enhanced form of sensory deprivation," Merlin said.

"To, like, put me in a trance?" Vera asked.

"It serves that function and then some. With the aid of magic through a potion, your regular brain function will be nearly stilled. It lets the unconscious part of your mind take control."

"How does she come out of it?" Lancelot asked as he inspected the tub and ran his fingers across the water's surface. It was a good question. Being stuck in her unconscious mind would be its own form of hell.

"Mostly, it will take its course," Merlin said, "but we can also set a limit, and I can pull her back if we go over."

"And this will definitely work?" Vera asked.

Merlin quested his head back and forth. "It is the less invasive option. I don't believe the block on your mind has been adequately loosened. This should help. I can't say for certain that it will reveal a memory from your life before, but it will reveal something of your unconscious mind. At the very least, it will be a step in the right direction."

Fear rippled through Vera. There were many things tucked away that she'd rather not touch, but her drive to recover Guinevere's memories was stronger. She stole a glance at Lancelot. He'd stopped cracking jokes and stared at her with a tight smile and a furrowed brow. If he was here, she'd be fine.

"All right," she said.

Merlin procured a heavy white gown that reminded Vera of a choir robe. She didn't hesitate when she asked Lancelot to loosen the cords of her dress (though Merlin pursed his lips and minutely shook his head) before stepping around a privacy barrier to change. When she returned, Merlin passed her the small bottle and a thick, black loop of fabric.

"When you're ready to get in, drink all of this. You'll have about fifteen seconds before conscious thought fades. It should be enough time to safely get in the water, lie back, and put your eye mask on. Once you've drunk the potion, neither of us can touch you or the effects will be negated. I am ready when you are."

Lancelot gave her shoulder a squeeze. "Bottoms up, love," he said as he knelt down next to the basin.

Vera stared at the palm-sized vial of clear liquid in her hand. It was less than a shot of liquor, so she took a deep breath and threw it back as if it were vodka. There was no smell—no flavor, though her throat went numb as the liquid slid down it.

She climbed into the comfortably warm waters and pulled the blindfold over her eyes as she lay back. The water held her weightless, with her feet hovering above the tub's bottom and only her face above the surface.

"The salt and potion I've added to the water might feel strange," Merlin said. The sensation that rose over Vera's skin prickled pleasantly. She heard the mage's words as if from a long way off, and as she drifted further away, a last conscious thought occurred to her. She heard words, the same words, every time she fell asleep. It had started with her journey back to this time and happened daily, but she could never remember them even a moment later . . . like a rubber eraser scrubbed them away as soon as she heard them, leaving only a smudge of dust, the sole hint that they'd been said at all. And there they were.

"Ishau mar domibaru."

Vera's thoughts grew hazy, sense and fantasy bleeding into one. And the words were gone. And all the world was darkness.

Until it wasn't.

Vera was barefoot in a field. She felt the prick of pebbles and the scratch of dry grass beneath her toes. There were low mountains in the distance, and between her and the mountains, a river's tributary, and closer, a field rich with spindly yellow flowers as tall as her knees. Hundreds of them. They waved at her as they swayed back and forth. She heard the babbling river and felt the breeze kissing her cheek. The sweet smell of life springing from the dirt was vivid, but there was a second note of rancid rot.

And the sound changed.

It started softer than the water's friendly ruckus but stood out because the two noises were at odds. It grew louder and louder until Vera could hardly hear the river anymore.

Screaming. Petrified screaming that didn't need words to be a cry for help. Vera whirled around, and all breath left her body, for there was her mother. Allison knelt in the field, clutching her stomach below her naval, and as she wailed, blood gushed between her fingers.

Vera tore over to her mother. Allison's face flitted through a range of emotions from the fear she must have felt to being appalled that Vera was here and then to a stalwart reassurance that only a mother could manage, and then—her face shimmered like it was under water. It wasn't Allison anymore. For a moment, Vera stared into the mirror image of herself. Another shimmer.

The new woman was a stranger, though her expression hadn't changed across the three iterations. But she was just as real. Vera's sobs joined hers, her heart just as wrecked as when it had been Allison. There was so much blood pumping from the gaping wound. She hadn't known that freely flowing blood was so thick and, as it congealed, it was nearly purple.

Vera pressed her hands to the wound, but they were too small, or the wound was too big. Her fingers slid through the slick mess of blood. Her hands were covered in it after seconds, and the sharp smell of rust overwhelmed her. All she could see and smell and feel was blood, and the only sound was screaming, though now it was her own, for the woman was silent.

Vera's eyes shot open, and she rose from the tub with a gasp. There was a hand clutching her wrist and another on her shoulder.

"You can't touch her!" Merlin scolded.

She ripped the blindfold free. The hands on her were Lancelot's. His breath came in heaves. "You were screaming," he said.

She couldn't spare a moment to reassure him. Vera grabbed Merlin by the wrist. "It's my mum—I saw her dying. I have to go back. I have to—"

Merlin cupped her face in his hand. "Guinevere," he said sternly but not unkindly. "Allison is fine. Nothing has happened to her. You were dreaming. It is not uncommon to fall asleep during this process."

She was shaking her head to protest even as she remembered the way Allison's face had morphed. It had all been real except for that.

"Her face turned into mine, too. Do you think . . . was I remembering Guinevere's death—Viviane's attack from before?" Vera asked.

Lancelot's hand tightened on her shoulder as Merlin cocked his head thoughtfully to the side. "Where was the wound?"

Vera pointed to the spot on her stomach.

Merlin shook his head. "No. No, that's not it." His eyes glazed like he saw nothing in front of him. He was quiet so long that Vera was surprised when he spoke. "Your previous injury was to the heart. You were dreaming. That was a nightmare."

It had felt like more than that. Vera dropped her forehead onto the tub's edge, and Lancelot rubbed the back of her neck. She took a slow and rattling breath. Put it away, she instructed herself. Another deep breath, this one steadier as the memory of what she saw receded. One more breath, smooth and deep. She lifted her head to meet Lancelot's wary gaze.

"I'm okay," she said.

"Shall we try again?" Merlin asked.

Vera said "Yes," as Lancelot barked a hard "No."

"This feels dangerous. I do not like it," he said through gritted teeth.

"I was asleep," she insisted. "I'm fine."

He pressed his lips together and shook his head.

"I have to do this," she said. "After the last few days, you must understand that."

She thought he wanted to argue. If he did, he might convince her to change her mind. She didn't want to do it again, but she had to.

Vera grabbed both of his hands to peel them off of her and firmly placed them on the tub's wall. "I'll be fine."

"We'll have to do a bit more potion," Merlin said, "to get you back under."

Fear lurched in her stomach. "Can we try without it?"

Merlin pressed a second vial into her hand as he answered. "It won't work. You've been touched."

It was a pointed jab that landed how he'd meant. Lancelot cast his eyes down. She didn't want him to feel guilty.

"I don't mind." Vera drank the second vial's contents. This time, she didn't remember lying back and the blindfold was barely over her eyes before the words came. In the final seconds before her consciousness fully evaporated, she felt a swell of trepidation. This was wrong.

She was back in the field. The dying woman only bore the third face: the woman Vera recognized in one breath and felt certain was a stranger in the next. This time, she found herself squinting into the morning sun. Too bright. As she walked toward the woman like before, the grass beneath her feet that before only gently scratched her weathered soles felt sharp as shards of glass.

Come to that, everything was . . . more than it should have been; colors oversaturated, edges sharper, smells overwhelming.

It was all worse.

When the woman wailed, her screams pierced Vera's ears to the point that she thought if she reached up, she'd find blood trickling from them. The woman's fear of death that held her with a sure grip, the woman's attempts to be brave, her whimpers . . . it was so unendurable that Vera tried to help far more frantically than before. She tore her skirt to use as a compress, but there wasn't enough of it—it was only a light summer dress. She pressed it to the wound. The stench of blood was so strong that it covered Vera's tongue, and she began choking on it and sputtering.

Helpless and defeated, she lay on the ground next to the woman whose breathing crept to a stop until Vera gazed at the empty shell of a human. She closed her eyes. Something else would happen now. It had to. And if it didn't, Merlin could pull her out. When she opened her eyes, it would be gone.

Vera inhaled through her nose, relieved to smell only fresh air instead of the heavy odor of blood, and opened her eyes.

She was still in the field.

In the spot where she'd started both times before. She turned to look, and there it was.

The woman, her hands on her abdomen. Bleeding.

It was starting over.

There was nothing for Vera to do but live it again, in its new hyper vibrancy that made the scene, already so real, even more so. She was on her knees, clutching at her hair, unsure whether the screams in her ears were hers or those of the poor dying woman.

When the screaming stopped and the smell abated and only the sound of the breeze cut through the air, Vera dared to open her eyes.

Again. In the field. And two times more after that.

It was torture.

The next time, Vera didn't even stand. She curled into a tight ball on the ground and screamed into the nothingness, into the void of sinking despair that the potion had gone wrong, and she was doomed to relive these awful moments until she lost her mind and there was nothing left of her.

So it came as a shock to Vera when the cycle stopped with the smallest shift.

There was a hand in hers. Like a lost deep-sea diver finding their rope, it led her out of the ill-fated loop. The next moment, Vera was somewhere else.

The hand was still in hers as they walked beside a stream. She couldn't explain it, but it was like the feel of his hand had a smell, and she knew without having to look it was Arthur. She turned for confirmation and there he was, face taut with nerves as he stared out at the horizon. Vera knew, in a distant way, that they hadn't known one another long. A glance behind her gave more evidence: her father and Merlin trailed some ways behind them. Chaperones. Merlin's presence brought a rush of feelings—Guinevere's feelings. He was the only one she trusted. He was the one who cared for her the way her father never had.

A flash. The stream was gone. They were in the throne room for court. Guinevere had made a comment that Arthur found amusing. He squeezed her hand and gave a sly smile.

Then it was the great hall. Vera recognized the men of the king's guard gathered around a table in the middle—not the one on the dais, and no one was their usual self. Lancelot slumped in his chair, his head only kept from slamming onto the table by the way it was perched on his hand. His hair was unkempt, and his eyelids seemed to require a great effort to keep open. Vera felt pity, but this wasn't her memory—it was Guinevere's. And Guinevere felt the strangest guttural surge of disgust toward him.

Lancelot wasn't the only exhausted one in the room. Another older man with wavy silver hair, unkempt and hanging loose, dozed in his seat and snored softly there. The ones awake enough bore more severe expressions. Percival chewed at his thumbnail as he looked at a map unfurled before them, and the way his eyes darted to the more senior leaders in the room betrayed his fear. Randall had a ghostly expression of resignation from his spot in the corner. And there were other faces interspersed among the ones she knew so well. Two more men and women at their sides, focused and forlorn. Vera turned to Arthur. He studied the map, too, his face hard and determined. Under the table, though, he'd taken Guinevere's hand. She rubbed her thumb over the back of it, a gesture of comfort in this moment that tasted of hopelessness.

It was the end of the war—one way or the other, it would all be over soon. They'd withstood innumerable invasions and the largest was yet to come. The faces in this room were a microcosm of Arthur's forces. Even the best among them had little left to give.

The sense of knowing struck her like lightning. Guinevere knew what to do—Vera could access that in her mind but couldn't penetrate deeper . . . couldn't know the what of her thoughts.

"I have an idea," Guinevere said. Vera's voice said.

The room was gone. She lay in bed, and Vera had no context as to why, but she felt what Guinevere felt, and it frightened her. Even in her darkest moment, even the day of—of—ugh. What was his name? She'd loved him and he died. Vera was nauseous as the dualities of her life and Guinevere's competed within her.

Then the name came to her. Even on the day of Vincent's death, she had never felt this deep of despair. Arthur sat next to the bed, his hand over hers, eyes filled with regret and an odd glimmer of awe.

The edges dimmed like night was falling on the visions. Vera wondered if that meant the potion's effect had begun to lose its hold. Blackness closed in from all sides until her mind's eye was only a pinprick of light at the center—and then nothing. Sensation returned to her waking body.

    Vera came up with a spluttering gasp, the last vestiges of the vision gone except one piece which remained: her hand wasn't empty.

21

Vera ripped the blindfold off.

Arthur knelt next to the tub, holding her hand, his sleeve wet up to the elbow. Why hadn't he rolled his sleeve up? Vera's brain was foggy. Was she still dreaming—remembering—whatever it was?

Water dripped from her soaking hair in quiet splatters, and for a moment it was the only sound. Arthur and Vera stared at one another. She wanted to ask him what he was doing here but couldn't get the thought into words. Something in her wasn't working right.

"You are here?" she said with immense effort, surprised by the rasp of her own voice. "How?" Vera swallowed and cleared her throat, which she noticed was sore.

"I—felt like I should be," he said. His eyes searched her. She didn't understand why he looked so frightened.

But the other man did, too. Her friend. It was silly, really. Vera couldn't summon his name. She knew it . . . of course she knew it. "It was different the second time," he said. Lancelot. That was his name. "You screamed for half an hour straight."

Then she noticed Merlin, next to Arthur, nearer her head. A sheen of sweat coated his brow as one pearl broke free and tumbled down his face. She'd not yet seen the mage sweat.

"What happened?" Merlin asked. "Do you remember what was so awful?"

Vera wiped water from her face with her free hand. She did not let go of Arthur. "I—" She meant to tell them about the field and how it wouldn't stop, but it took so much effort to form words. Too much.

"I felt stuck" was all she could manage.

"You were stuck," Lancelot said, his eyes uncharacteristically wild and wide, shirt splotched with patches of wet. "We both started trying to pull you out—maybe ten minutes in. Positively shook you, to be honest. Merlin sort of zapped you with magic. You kept screaming. Nothing worked until . . ." He looked at Arthur.

"His Majesty showed up after we'd tried everything and tried it a second time," Merlin said. "When he took your hand, you stopped screaming, but you didn't come out as you should have." His weary face bore a glint of hope. "Did you remember anything?"

The fog of being in two minds at once was lifting, and for that, Vera's answer came quickly and assuredly. "Yes. I remembered."

Dried and dressed, she sat by Merlin's desk with the three men. Merlin had suggested they gather near the fire, but Vera nearly passed out from the mere idea of it. She sweated from the moment she left the water, and her skin burned fiercely. At least the mental fog had mostly dissipated. When she tried to speak, words came. So she told them what she'd seen.

"That was before the final battle," Arthur said when she got to the scene in the great hall.

Lancelot let out a breath. "Not our best day."

The memory of Guinevere's disdain for him came crashing back. "She didn't like you," Vera said.

"No," he said with a sad smile. "She did not."

"I thought you hardly knew each other," Vera said. "Why wouldn't she like you?"

He shrugged, and his eyes glimmered as they flashed to Merlin. "Probably something about being loud and foolish." Merlin sighed and Lancelot chuckled, but Vera did not entirely buy his unbothered response.

She hesitated before finishing with the memory in their chamber, when Guinevere was bedridden with despair.

"And that was after the battle," Arthur murmured. She wanted to tell him that she now knew with certainty, having borne witness in this strange way, that there was nothing Arthur could have said to alleviate Guinevere's pain. They hadn't felt like her own memories, more like eavesdropping in someone else's.

"It stopped there," Vera said.

"That couldn't have been more than a few weeks before the attack," Merlin said. "That was more fruitful than I expected. You're getting close."

His hunger for answers was plain in his eyes. It matched her own drive. "When can we try again?" she asked.

Lancelot made a strangled sort of noise, but Merlin smiled. "The magic takes a toll. Let your mind rest a few days."

Lancelot shifted in his seat, ready to argue, but Arthur beat him to it. "You're not doing that again."

"I am fine!" Vera protested, a blatant lie. She was sweating. Her voice was weak, especially as she got more worked up. And when she wasn't actively speaking, she fought to keep her eyes open. "It's working. We can actually fix this!"

"No," Arthur said. She wanted to kick him in the shin. It wasn't bravery to persist, it was necessity. This was her one purpose. This was the reason she existed. She could handle the pain. She had to.

"His Majesty is right," Merlin said. "Not today."

"Not bloody ever," Lancelot mumbled. Vera wanted to kick him, too. She scoffed, prepared to launch back in.

"I require a private word with Merlin," Arthur said.

"Now?" Lancelot raised an eyebrow.

"Right now," Arthur said as he stood, the motion deeming it final. And that was that.

They'd been so close to unearthing the truth. How could Arthur not share her urgency? An idea stole through her thoughts, fleeting but present, nevertheless. For the first time, Vera wondered whether he might not want her to remember. And a question came on the thought's heels: why?

Vera couldn't get her eyes to focus when she settled into her bed to read that night. She couldn't have even finished a page before she must have fallen asleep, but she jolted awake when Arthur came in. Before, he'd always gone right to the side room, occasionally with a detour to his desk to pick a new book. But the past two days (God, had it really only been two days?) might as well have been a decade for all that had changed.

When he saw that Vera was awake, he crossed to the bed and sat down on it next to her ankles.

She sat up straighter. This was very new. And . . . it made her heart flutter. Also new. She didn't like that. His care after such deliberate avoidance left her with a pathetic sense of longing to be close to him. She would fight it with her frustration.

"I would have been fine for one more go," Vera said.

"I have no doubt that you are capable of enduring, but that procedure should only be a last resort." Arthur had a far-off look, the shadow of earlier. For how the three of them had reacted, Vera's suffering in the tub must have been a jarring sight. "Merlin's dedication to the kingdom is commendable, but it has skewed his judgment. We must proceed more carefully. He's going to do more research on how to offset the toll the memory work took on you. We can try after Yule and Christmas."

"We can't wait that long!"

He fixed her with a sad, knowing smile. "It's only two weeks."

"I—" She was dumbfounded. Vera knew it was winter, obviously. But without checking a phone or computer every day, she hadn't realized the date.

Arthur parted his lips, inhaling as if to speak, and then shook his head. What was he not telling her?

He looked at the book in Vera's lap. "The Hobbit?" he asked, surprising her with the change of subject.

She nodded. Of course he recognized it. It was the only book from the desk with a mossy green cover.

"I read all the books Merlin brought for you. At first, to learn more about the world you came from. Selfishly, I just . . . enjoy them."

"It's one of my favorites," Vera said. "My parents and I used to read it aloud at Christmastime together."

"Would you like to—?" He gestured sheepishly with the tilt of his head toward her, then toward the book.

Warmth bloomed in her chest. "You want to read it together?"

"I'd like that," he said.

"All right."

Arthur started to shift his weight, but he paused. "Would you be comfortable if I sat close to you?"

Vera focused on keeping her expression even despite the way her pulse had jumped. She silently counted to three before she answered. "That's fine."

She scooted to the middle of the bed to make room for him to sit next to her. They were shoulder to shoulder, both sitting up and leaning against the headboard.

"We could start at the beginning," she offered. She'd been partway through.

"No, that's all right. Let's pick up where you left off."

Vera opened The Hobbit to the page she'd marked with the photograph of her and her parents. Arthur ran his thumb across the image.

"That's you there," he said. "What is this?"

"It's a photograph. It's like . . ." Vera thought about how to explain it. "It's like a painting, but it's made with light using a clever thing called a camera. Someone points it, you press a button, and it takes a picture."

"Are these your parents?"

"Yes." He kept staring at the photo, so she went on. "Mum's name is Allison. Dad is Martin." There was a pang in her gut at saying his name.

Arthur held it close to his face. "That's extraordinary," he said, and then his voice softened. "You look so happy."

She did. It had been taken after her university graduation some half a year earlier, a girl who would never imagine what was to come sandwiched between Allison and Martin, her arms slung around their necks. Allison gleefully held out Vera's diploma, and Martin wore her graduation cap lopsided on his head, the tassel dangling down in his face while Vera was caught mid-laugh. She wouldn't have laughed at all if she'd known about the cancer already growing inside her father on that very day.

"Who made the photo?" Arthur asked.

"Hmm?" Vera said absently.

"You said someone holds the camera and presses a button. Who had the camera?"

She understood why he might be curious. In the photo, Vera seemed like she was staring right through the picture, sharing a private joke with the viewer. Arthur correctly guessed that the moment had been shared between Vera and the photographer.

"I don't remember," she mumbled as sadness threatened to overtake her. She felt his eyes on her and deliberately didn't meet them.

"Shall I start?" she asked, overly brightly.

Vera held the book between them so he could see while she read aloud. Her voice came out more hesitant than it ever had when reading with her parents. But she soon slipped into the story, and out came her voices for each character. At her silliest dwarf voice, Vera felt the deep rumble of Arthur's laughter reverberating through his shoulder. When the chapter ended, she passed the book to him. He looked at her in confusion.

"It's your turn."

Arthur licked his lips and cleared his throat, flustered—but he started reading in his deep timbre. His happened to be the chapter when Gollum showed up. Vera's jaw fell open in delight as Arthur pitched his voice into a scratchy whisper for the creature.

"That is a splendid Gollum," she interrupted.

Arthur tucked his chin to his shoulder with a grin. "Aside from my tutor and my parents, I haven't actually read out loud to anybody."

"Well, you're very good at it."

"My father would be proud," he said. He found his place and resumed reading.

The Once and Future Queen

Arthur's voice was so soothing. She didn't remember choosing to close her eyes, nor how her head came to rest on his shoulder. In a half-awake moment of clarity, she realized that her cheek nuzzled into him, but with his steady voice rumbling through her and the heat of his broad shoulder beneath her skin, she couldn't bear to turn away from such contentment. It almost felt like being with Vincent. She could nearly pretend it. Perhaps he might be able to imagine her as Guinevere—the real Guinevere of his memory. Maybe this would be their way forward . . . a broken and imperfect way that Vera and Arthur might bring one another comfort.

Eventually, he must have stopped reading. She came around as he was easing her down onto her pillow, and then his weight was gone from the bed. She opened her eyes in time to see him slipping the photo back into the book and setting it on the table before he touched the slab to lower the lights. Vera let her eyes fall shut as she felt the blanket being gingerly laid over her shoulders.

She'd always thought, always assumed, that Matilda was the one who came to check on her during the night, lowering the lights and putting her book away. Now, she wasn't as sure.

22

That night marked the start of their careful friendship and an immediate shift in Vera's life in Camelot.

"It's probably best to display some affection," Arthur had said the next day as they headed into town. "May I hold your hand?"

Her heart nearly leapt out of her chest. "That would be fine," she said.

But by the week's end, he inclined his head toward her to share private jokes at dinner. She would lay a hand on his arm as she laughed. It was a convincing act partly because there was no pretense in it for Vera. She liked him. His nearness felt like breathing fresh air after being too long in a cellar. And the people of Camelot began to notice.

It wouldn't all be fixed in a snap, but the change had already begun to undulate out from them. Most of it was surprisingly due to Gawain, who Vera was convinced absolutely loathed her. Lancelot had insisted she was imagining it, but she would swear his scowl darkened with suspicion when he looked at her.

She didn't have much cause to encounter him, though. Gawain was regularly dispatched to repair magical deficits through Camelot and the neighboring towns. It was a charge he apparently performed well, for the magic complaints in court significantly dropped the next week.

On the loveliest winter morning, Vera and Arthur watched Lancelot and Percival playing a game at the pit as the castle's cooks prepared ingredients nearby. Yule was two days away with Christmas on its heels, and Vera and Arthur would travel with a small party (as she delightedly learned was customary) to Glastonbury for the Yule festivities the following morning. All seemed right in Camelot. The celebratory boar hunt was underway outside the town walls, and a great horn blasted in the distance, signaling that the party was closing in on the boar. The gates should soon be opened so they could parade the carcass back to the cook site.

Margaret, the head chef at the castle who was sweet and grandmotherly about all things except for the business of running the kitchen, paused her onion chopping at the sound.

"They'll be back with the beast soon," she said, gazing off in the general direction. "I thought we'd have a bit longer." She wiped her hands on her apron and left her chopping post, calling out as she went. "Oy! Call up the butcher's boy to magic up the meat. Let's get the fire stoked for the spit!" She gave one final shout over her shoulder, "And for the love of God, someone finish chopping that veg!"

Vera looked to her left and right. All the other castle staff were already occupied. She wasn't sure anyone else had heard Margaret's orders.

She left the wall of the pit without a word to Arthur, stepped up to the vacant spot at the table, and took up the knife. She'd not chopped even a turnip in months, but years of kitchen work at the George were not so easily forgotten.

"Should I be alarmed at your proficiency with a blade?"

She broke her focus only momentarily to find that Arthur had left his spectator spot and was watching her instead.

Vera laughed. "I was trained by the best."

He tilted his head and raised his eyebrow.

"My mum," she explained, surprising herself by sharing so readily. She'd mostly avoided any conversation about her parents and certainly hadn't willingly brought them up before now. "She had me chopping veg before it was wise to put a knife in my hands. I take it your mother didn't recruit you in the kitchen?"

The moment the question cleared her lips, she wanted to pull it back in. His smile hadn't fallen, nor his shoulders tensed, but there was something inscrutable that shifted in him and made Vera feel sure she'd touched a tender place.

"No," he said, and he dropped his gaze to the table as he rolled a bulbous white onion beneath his palm. Just like that, the shadow fell from his features. "Care to teach me?"

"Don't you want to watch the game?" She nodded at the pit, trying to give him a kind excuse to walk away. But he didn't budge.

"We can see from here." His eyes glimmered a little as his lips tipped to a smile. She found she couldn't look away from them. She was struck by the realization that Arthur knew very well what it was like to kiss her. He knew the taste of her lips when she had no idea the taste of his.

She shoved the thought away as she found an extra knife for him and began showing the proper chopping technique as Allison had once taught her. He wasn't accustomed to being so close to onion fumes and tears streamed down his cheeks in seconds, reducing them both to fits of laughter before Vera swapped his onion out for a cabbage.

People had begun watching them, pointing at the king and queen preparing vegetables for the town's dinner. Grady waved to her as he passed by with one of the newly broken horses. She smiled and inclined her head, grateful for the friendly face. Chopping veg for dinner wasn't exactly a proper royal activity, which nearly gave Vera pause, but Arthur was with her. Anyone watching saw that they were having fun, that he was being so warm—ah.

It hit her with a pang. The flirtation was an effective show.

It wouldn't have bothered her if she stupidly hadn't been swept up in it. He was far too charming.

When the sound of a horn cut through the air again, she was lucky her knife didn't slip. It sounded again, only this time, it stopped mid-blast.

What happened next all went very quickly. Vera wouldn't have seen anything amiss except that her eyes were already on Lancelot in the pit when his expression hardened. He stopped playing and, trancelike, climbed onto the pit's wall, holding a post as he balanced on the slim ledge. No one reacted much at first save for askance glances at him.

"Two blasts means the hunt's over," Arthur said, but he also stared up at Lancelot. "They'll open the gates over there." He gestured in the direction Lancelot was looking, where there was an expansive field between Camelot's wall and the forest. "So the party can parade into town with their prize."

But Lancelot was shaking his head. Arthur set his knife down and went to Lancelot's side. Vera followed.

"That blast didn't sound right," he murmured.

"What do you mean?" Arthur asked.

"I don't know . . . just . . . Arthur, I think you should have them close the gates."

Arthur didn't hesitate to ask questions. He flagged Percival down and sent him running for the town's wall. It wasn't far, only down the lane and around the corner.

But they were already too late.

"Shit!" Lancelot jumped down from the ledge as a cacophony of shouting rose from where Percival had disappeared. "The hunt's not over. The bloody boar's gotten loose. It's within the wall."

All at once, everything was in motion.

"Get inside!" Arthur bellowed.

He and Lancelot shouted repeated warnings as Arthur scooped up a fallen child and passed him to a frantic mother, and Lancelot sprinted to where they had left their swords, but they were out of time. He had barely lain a finger on the hilt of his weapon when the furious beast rounded the corner and pummeled through the square.

Vera gasped. She couldn't have guessed how fast and ferocious a boar would be. It was no pig. It was closer to the size of a bull, and its eyes were so wide in rage that they were more whites than pupils. It trampled past her, near enough that she could see that its black hair was coarse and oily, that it had worked up a lather around its mouth, and that its short tusks were wickedly sharp. Arthur jumped down next to her, able to do nothing more than take hold of her arm as the boar thundered by them. The panicked shouts mostly came from inside houses as, mercifully, most people in the square had gotten to safety.

Percival rounded the corner, sword drawn, shield ready. Lancelot was already sprinting toward the boar when it skidded to a halt. Even if he'd had a spear in hand, ready to throw, he was too far to get enough power to pierce its hide. And anyway, he didn't have one. None of the armed warriors running after the beast did.

Lancelot's gait stuttered to an unexpected stop. Vera heard the horse's whinny before she followed the boar's grunting stare to see it. Grady had one arm around the newly broken stallion's neck, the other clutching its lead with all his might, but the barely trained horse's terror was far more powerful than a fourteen-year-old boy's grip. The horse reared up on its hind legs, sending Grady tumbling backward onto his bottom with a grunt. Freed from his grasp, the horse galloped away at full speed, leaving Grady alone and dazed on the ground, stuck in a corner between two buildings on either side and a frothing monster in front of him.

"Grady!" Arthur shouted. The boy looked up at once, eyes searching for Arthur but first finding the boar and widening. Arthur, armed with absolutely nothing, tore toward him, but there was no way he would get to Grady in time. Lancelot was closest. He wouldn't get there either.

The boar snorted. And again. And again—in a quickening rhythm like a battle drum before it charged. Grady scrambled backward until he could scramble no further when his back hit the wall behind him. He raised his arms helplessly in front of his face.

Oh God. She couldn't watch, but she couldn't turn away. Vera dropped to her knees with a cry, not feeling the sting of rocks digging into them, only a rush of burning sensation over her skin that did not come from the winter air. Even if Grady didn't know she was there, even if it was horrendous, Vera would not look away. She would not abandon him to die without someone who cared for him at least bearing witness. A distant part of her noted what a dismal thought this was, but the heat raging through her scorched it to ash.

When the boar was about to slam into him, when Grady should have been taking his last breaths, there was something else. It started at Grady's chest and exploded out from there—a blue-white disk of light that burst from him with a colossal exhale of wind, so powerful that the boar was tossed in the air like a rag doll, thrown onto its back.

The explosion sent a shockwave like a string threaded through them all, stretched tight and thrummed. If the beast hadn't been stunned by the impossibility of what had happened, it still would have struggled to find Grady.

Every loose piece of wood, be it the handle of a tool, a spare board, or even a wagon for hay, zipped toward Grady and formed a wall in front of him. It gave Lancelot and Percival time to get to the dazed boar and swiftly end it.

Vera ran to catch up with Arthur. They were all left staring at an unharmed Grady behind his makeshift fortress. He stared at it in shock.

"Looks like somebody used their gift for you," Percival called over as he tied the dead hog's feet together. Vera caught Arthur's eyes and knew he'd seen it all, too.

"I—I did it," Grady said in awe. To confirm it, he swiped his hand, and all the gathered wall clumsily disassembled into a pile in the dirt. "I felt like something in my body exploded and then . . ." He shook his head, and his jaw hung slack. "I knew I could do it. I knew I could, and I knew how."

"That's not possible," Percival said. His eyes searched the gathered men for answers. "That—powers don't just show up. You have to be born with them."

No one present had ever seen someone exhibit a new gift after infancy, but there was no denying it. Impossible or not, Grady now had magic, a gift that had saved his life.

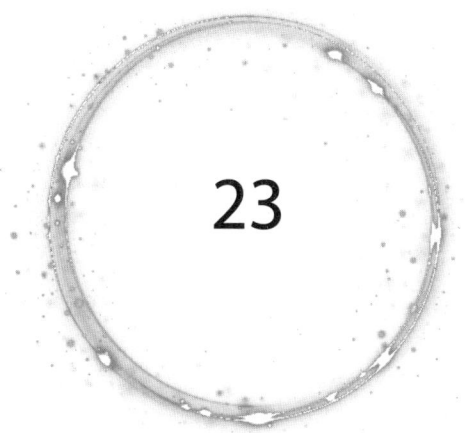

23

The story of the hunt gone wrong and its aftermath tore through town as quickly as the boar itself. The horn's call, mistaken for the end of the hunt, was meant to be a series of emergency blasts warning that the beast had broken loose, but it was cut short by sharp tusks to the crier's gut. Thanks to the quick work of Gawain, who had arrived barely in time to keep the man on this side of the brink of death, the crier would survive.

The next morning, before their departure to Glastonbury, Arthur sent Percival out to find the mage and bring him back so the king might thank him, but it wasn't so easy a task.

"Well, I found him after searching the whole bloody castle and half the village." Percival rolled his eyes. "And you aren't going to believe this, but he flat-out refused to come. Said he was too busy."

Annoyance flashed through Arthur's eyes, but Vera saw the way his lips tugged up at the corner.

They decided to go find Gawain themselves.

Percival led Arthur and Vera straight to the training field and past the keep-away pit. At first, Vera thought that Percival got it wrong. She didn't see anyone, save the townsfolk, who all cast disconcerted glances toward the spot where Grady had nearly been killed yesterday. Was it superstition that captivated their attention? Nothing was there —

Vera's thoughts screeched to a stop as she saw a man in a dingy brown robe crawling in the dirt. Gawain.

Percival cleared his throat. Gawain ignored him.

"Mage Gawain," Arthur called.

"Yes," he said, barely audible as he lowered the side of his face to examine the ground without so much as glancing at Arthur.

Percival stared at Gawain, aghast as his eyes narrowed. "Mage Gawain," he barked. "Your king addresses you. Another ruler would lock you in the stocks for far less than this display of disrespect."

He blinked as he sat up.

"I was supplicant on the ground, was I not?" he asked dryly, only addressing Percival.

"Yes," Percival said with exasperation as he gestured toward Arthur. "And yet you continue to ignore your king and queen."

Gawain's sunken eyes stayed on Percival for a long moment. Percival's face reddened. He might have even stopped breathing. Arthur looked on in bemused silence.

"You're right," Gawain muttered. He cleared his throat. "Your Majesty, I apologize." He sounded about as engaged as if he was reading the phone book. Vera wished Lancelot was there to witness it because she would swear that Gawain's scowl deepened as he addressed her. "And to you, my queen."

She dipped into a poor curtsy, expecting that to be the end of it. But he kept his shadowy eyes on her like he was making a silent accusation.

"Why didn't you come when summoned?" Arthur asked, his tone even as he cocked his head to the side.

"An unprecedented magical break happened right here yesterday." Gawain dropped his face back to the ground, resuming his study of the ordinary-looking dirt. "Magic leaves a trace, but it doesn't linger. I couldn't afford to delay."

Percival scoffed loudly.

"What are you hoping to find?" Arthur asked.

Gawain sighed and sat up, Arthur's attention evidently an annoyance to him. "This is my area of study."

"What? Dirt?" Percival shot back.

Gawain smiled, thick with condescension. "Patterns in what gifts show up and where. But most of all, how the magic break happens."

"What's a magic break?" Vera asked.

"The exact instant a person first exhibits their gift. I used to only study infants, but the war changed my mind."

"Why?" Arthur said.

"Something I saw once."

"What," Percival pressed emphatically, "did you see?"

"An execution on the battlefield. Not just one, of course. I saw many, like both of you, I'm sure. But as the sword fell on his neck this time, I saw him have a magical break."

The skin on the back of Vera's neck prickled. "Did it look like a light exploded out of him?"

Gawain nodded. "Out of his chest. Is that what happened to the boy yesterday?"

"Yes," she said. "I saw it. Arthur and I both saw it. Then Grady used it—his gift."

"What was the man's gift on the battlefield?" Percival's annoyance had given way to genuine interest.

"No idea," Gawain said. "He died."

They stared at the mage, though Percival voiced their shared sentiment. "Are you being deliberately obtuse?"

He carried on as if Percival hadn't said anything. "The soldier likely never even knew it happened. But the boy yesterday," Gawain said. "Could either of you see his eyes when it happened?"

"I could," Vera said.

"What did they look like?"

"Frightened." She shuddered as she remembered Grady's face, drawn with a horror that no fourteen-year-old should ever know.

"Panicked? Petrified? Desperate?" Gawain's voice rose in excitement with each suggestion.

"Yes, of course. All of those things. He thought he was about to die."

Gawain sat back on his heels as he sighed wistfully. "I wish I'd seen that."

Vera recoiled. "That was the worst moment of his life."

"Yes, but with all due respect, Your Majesty, he didn't die and now has a very useful gift." Gawain must have found what he was searching for on the ground as he procured a vial from the pocket of his robe and scooped it full of dirt before he turned his attention to Arthur. "And especially since I didn't witness the event, it is imperative that I study the trace of what was left behind. It could not wait."

"I understand," Arthur said. Vera shot him a glare that he either did not notice or didn't acknowledge. "But if you cannot meet a summons, I expect you to send word to explain your absence."

"At the absolute least," Percival added, though he clearly would have liked to say more.

"I am sorry, Your Majesty," Gawain said. "That was thoughtless on my part. It won't happen again."

"Good," Arthur said.

"You were here yesterday when the incident occurred," Gawain said. "Were you able to see the boy clearly?"

"Yes," said Arthur.

"Tell me, in as much detail as you can, about the terror on his face."

Vera decided she'd prefer not to know Gawain better, but as Arthur's traveling party gathered mere hours later at the castle stables, it became clear she'd have trouble avoiding him. Like a misshapen piece pressed into an already completed puzzle, there Gawain was, standing at the edge of the cluster that buzzed with excitement, a bulging travel pack at his feet and his face sullen.

As they readied their horses, Percival and Lancelot led the festivities with a bottle of some amber liquor passed around amongst them. Beyond Arthur, Lancelot, Percival, and Matilda, just four other soldiers would accompany them. And Gawain. The soldiers each wore some variation of a dazed expression, gleeful disbelief at being fortunate enough to travel with the king's party. Then, there were the few who came to see them off: Grady, his father, and Randall.

As Grady and his father ensured the horses and tack were suitable for the journey, Lancelot bawdily encouraged Grady to show off his newfound gift. He started by sheepishly restacking a few sticks of firewood. His initial reluctance melted under the soldiers' enthusiastic praise, and he was soon juggling the logs midair without physically touching a single one. Gawain inched closer, surely trying to sort out how to corner Grady and interrogate him on his recent trauma.

Randall, who reasserted that no, he was not attending the festival, hung close to Matilda. As she knocked back a hearty swig of the amber liquor and passed it along to him, his tension slackened, and he too grinned and took a drink.

Percival ambled toward Vera and Arthur, his eyes on Gawain. "Here, Your Majesty. This is the parcel from Merlin," he said, offering a bag with some heft to it. Arthur's eyes darkened on the package, but he accepted it and tucked it into his saddle bag.

"Why on earth does he think he should come?" Percival grumbled petulantly with a sharp nod toward Gawain, interrupting any notion Vera had to question the package from Merlin. Arthur glanced over at the mage before he tied his bag off and gracefully mounted his horse.

"Probably because I invited him," he said.

Percival's mouth fell open, but he caught himself and pursed his lips. He revered Arthur far too much to say anything aloud, though his face said plenty as he went back to his own horse. Vera rather shared his sentiment.

Arthur chuckled. "I invited Gawain to be polite," he said when Percival was far enough not to hear. "I didn't expect him to say yes."

"Pardon me. Your Majesty?" Randall's voice called out from behind her. Vera continued securing her bag on her horse. Randall cleared his throat. Apparently oblivious, Arthur was pulling on his riding gloves until he noticed Vera eyeing him.

"He means you," Arthur said with a one-sided grin.

"Me?"

The grin spread to both sides as he nodded.

"Your Majesty, may I have a moment?" Randall said, and Vera whipped around to face him this time.

"I'm so sorry. I thought you meant the king."

Randall didn't answer. He shifted the bulk of his weight from one foot to the other. "I gave Matilda something for you, in case you want it." Then, after another pause, he said, "Do you have a gown for tomorrow's celebration?"

"I brought one I like." It was the red one with the wide sleeves.

"It's a dress from before?" Randall asked. It took Vera a moment to realize what he meant; from before the accident. Before she'd been "away" for a year (and an entire existence).

"Yes," she said.

"You should have a garment other than your training gear that's been made for you, Your Majesty. I've made you a gown. You don't have to wear it," he added quickly. "But you should have the option."

"Of course I'll wear it," Vera said quietly.

Randall's blush crept above his whiskers. "Only if it suits you."

"Randall, you've been so kind to me. Thank you." Vera would have liked to hug him, but he didn't give her the chance.

He nodded to her and bowed to Arthur. "Safe travels, my liege. Happy Yule, happy Christmas, happy whatever the hell we're celebrating now. We'll make sure Camelot doesn't go to shit while you're away."

The celebrations continued once the party set off. It wasn't a quiet ride by any means. Chatter was abundant as they traveled in clumps, sharing their excitement by retelling stories from previous Yule festivals.

Vera stayed near Lancelot and the soldiers. Even as she laughed along with the others, she looked ahead at Arthur and Matilda, noticing the ease of their conversation. Noticed that Matilda gazed at him with such love. Why hadn't she seen it before? It had never occurred to her before this very moment that they might have found love together since Guinevere's death. She couldn't possibly fault them for it.

And still. It stung, a startling confirmation that she'd not only grown fond of Arthur. Vera had begun to long for him.

She cast about for something else to focus on and found Gawain riding farther back by himself, his head low and dark eyes staring vacantly, an especially sharp contrast with the enthusiasm in the rest of them. Vera was well acquainted with being the one left alone to witness the friendship of others.

She sighed and mumbled, "Dammit," as she steered her horse close to Lancelot and casually took the jug of mystery liquor. They'd passed it around all morning, so he merely spared her a smile as he handed it over, not missing a beat in his conversation with the soldiers.

Vera pulled up on the reins and hung back until Gawain drew even with her. He looked up in surprise, which suited his face more pleasantly than his standard scowl. She offered the jug to him.

"What is this?" he asked, peeking skeptically in the mouth of the jug.

Vera shrugged. "Alcohol. It doesn't taste half bad."

"You drank this without knowing what it is?"

"Yes." She laughed but prickled at the judgment in his tone. "Percival brought it. I trust him."

Gawain continued to study the bottle. A green-tinted light, just a faint aura of a glow, started at the base. It spread from beneath his fingers across the jug's surface. His eyes were closed in concentration, and his lips moved silently in the shapes of words that were nonsense to Vera. When the last wisp of green glow faded, Gawain opened his eyes.

"It's safe." He tipped the jug to his lips and took a deep slug. Then, abruptly, "I met your aunt, Cecily, on my way from the Magesary. She said your cousin's wedding will be this spring."

"Oh!" Vera said, playing along as had become her custom. "That's wonderful news." She mentally filed the new information about Guinevere's family.

Gawain stared at her.

"What?" she said.

"You don't have an aunt. At least, not to my knowledge. I made that up." Vera's chest tightened at the revelation and more at the way he looked at her. Like she was being measured and coming up short. "Merlin told me you had memory loss from the attack, but I thought you might be faking it."

Vera tensed. "Why would I lie about that?"

"To avoid responsibility for your actions," he said, as if it were obvious. "But you remember nothing."

"I remember how to mount a horse." A poor attempt at humor to skirt her discomfort, but Gawain cracked a condescending smile.

"That's not much. All the same, you don't have to pretend to remember in front of me. And if you have questions, I can be someone to answer them."

It might have been a generous offer had it not been accompanied by the affectation of a concrete brick. He was the last person Vera wanted to share anything with. Her guard had been up before. This conversation fortified it.

"I was under the impression you didn't like me much," Vera said.

"You were correct," he said bluntly. "But that was before I realized your mental deficiency." Vera barked a laugh. Gawain looked at her and blinked. "But not remembering . . . perhaps that's a gift. You get to start again."

"I have to remember." Merlin had told her the mages knew about Viviane's betrayal. Gawain should understand better than anyone. "You know that I have to remember."

He was silent for a stretch before he took another drink, wincing as he swallowed and passed the jug to Vera. "I'm not so sure. Magic's been behaving peculiarly for some time now . . . since well before Viviane's attack on you."

Her mouth took on a strange taste and her head swam. "How long?" she asked, forgetting not to give him the satisfaction of her interest.

"Since before the wars," he said. "I don't have evidence to prove it, but I'd conjecture at least since the Massacre of Dorchester."

Why did that sound familiar to Vera? And why did she see a descending mist in her mind's eye as she thought of it? Descending mist, thunder, and a dancer . . . Then it hit her. It was the story the performers shared on one of her first nights here.

"When the whole town was massacred by a mage gone mad?"

Gawain gave her a slow, sidelong look. "It wasn't the whole town. It was the efficient extermination of every non-magic person in Dorchester. A dark experiment on population. If people with the gift only bred with others who also had it, the hypothesis was that it would increase the number of magical births."

"And . . . did it?"

"No," Gawain said. "I doubt recovering your memories will make any difference." He forged onward as if he'd not savagely taken a mallet to Vera's one goal in her new existence. "By my census studies, the magical birth rate has been steadily dropping for nearly a decade. Its rate has simply increased enough recently that we've taken notice."

Vera sat stiffly in her saddle. She clenched her muscles to shield the way fear descended on her. Oddly enough, that tickled Gawain. His eyes even briefly lit as he chuckled. "You're wise to be mistrusting. You shouldn't trust anyone."

Vera was taken aback enough to find her voice. "What about the king? What about Merlin?"

Gawain merely shrugged. "Certainly not him." He pointed at Lancelot. "He reeks of lies."

Vera laughed. "I'll keep that in mind. Look, I really just wanted to apologize for being the reason you had to execute that man." She'd not known she was going to say it before the words tumbled out of her.

"It's my duty," Gawain said.

"Yes, well, it's not one you've ever had to officially perform, is it?"

He gave her another sidelong look. "Not officially. But it was not uncommon on the battlefield."

He'd been so skilled and precise. It stood to reason that he'd performed that task before.

"How do mages train for such things?" she asked.

"How?" Gawain chuckled. "You're asking the wrong questions, Your Majesty." A loud laugh erupted from Lancelot and Percival's clump of riders, and Vera glanced wistfully at them.

"You don't want to talk to me anymore, do you?" he asked.

She was so startled by his blunt (and correct) assessment that she wasn't sure how to respond.

"I'm done talking anyway," he said. "I'd heard you were strange, but I like you better than I thought I would."

And with that, Gawain pulled up on the reins of his horse to fall back and ride alone.

Still in shock, Vera caught up with Percival and Lancelot, now on their own, apart from the other soldiers.

"Been watching you back there. What was that about?" Percival asked.

"That guy's a fucking weirdo," Vera said.

This set Lancelot to howling, so she felt compelled to continue. "He said he was done talking to me and wanted to ride alone."

Percival muttered a few choice insults under his breath.

"Ooh, I've never seen anyone get under your skin like that," Lancelot said to him. "You like damn near everybody."

"I've never met anyone with such disrespect for Arthur. And now for the queen, too. He's an egregious, pompous—"

"All right, all right. Point taken," Lancelot said. "Don't you feel a tiny bit sorry for him? Off on his own in this rowdy crew?"

"No," Percival said.

"Also," Vera added, joining in Percival's annoyance that Lancelot clearly didn't get it. "He told me that you reek of lies and that I shouldn't trust you."

"Really?" Lancelot's eyes glimmered with delight. "That's fabulous. I'm going to go annoy the shit out of him. Cheers!" He made a soft clicking noise, and his horse was trotting off toward Gawain before either could attempt to stop him.

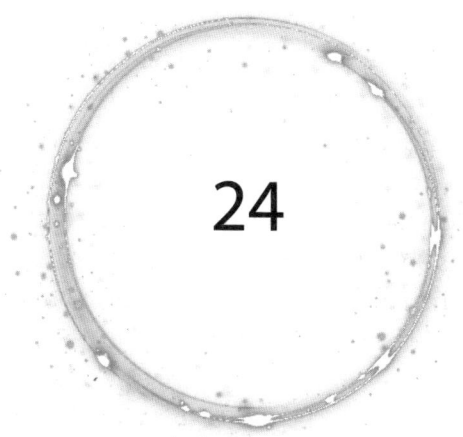

24

In opposition to Vera's abysmal familiarity with Arthurian legend (a rather hilarious joke of the universe), she was well acquainted with Glastonbury's history. Based on all accounts that she'd been taught in school and during class trips to the abbey, all the buildings and lodgings should have been made of wood, simple structures to keep less civilized ancient peoples out of the elements. As had become the custom of her new life, her knowledge was wrong.

The party arrived on the High Street of Glastonbury in the early afternoon, as a cold rain began to fall in a broken spit like the sky was talking excitedly and couldn't keep from at least a few drops flying free.

A merry woman met them at the edge of town with a dramatic "Good morning!" that rose and fell, sounding like an arch.

"That's Maria. She's the master of festival," Arthur murmured to Vera.

Maria was lovely, with a pile of golden curls arranged atop her head and a bright magenta gown that didn't feel like it belonged in the seventh century. She excitedly led them all to a stone building that was, as best as Vera could tell, about half a block from where the George and Pilgrims would stand in some 800 years.

"Leave your horses here with Harding; he'll see that they're cared for. Don't you dare touch those bags," she barked at Lancelot, who grinned and raised his hands from the bag on his horse. "Tawdry will bring them to your rooms. Your Majesty, may I steal you away for a titch? My queen, you can carry on to your quarters if you wish. I'm sure you need a rest after your journey."

These were the lodgings they'd used every year when in town for the festival. The king's party had the entire ground floor.

"This one's yours," Matilda said in Vera's ear, reaching past her to open the first door on the left. She peered into the quarters, her eyes first drawn to the blazing fire in a grand hearth on the wall opposite, with all the necessities for a bedroom between here and there.

"I'm the next one over. Lancelot is directly across the hall," Matilda said. "Shall I help you get settled in?"

Vera assured Matilda she was fine and sent her on her way. Strangely, she noted with her head cocked to the side, the room was entirely lit by fire—from the robust one in the fireplace to the flames of candles all along the walls. There was a chandelier of orbs hanging from the ceiling, completely dark, and the marble panel that would have been used to light it was in its customary place by the door, but it was covered with a cloth.

"We only use firelight for the solstice." She jumped at Arthur's voice behind her. "Sorry to startle you." He smiled. "No magic lighting for Yule. It's all of the earth to celebrate the light of the sun beginning to return." Concern crept into his features as his eyes swept the room. "Is this going to be all right?"

Vera glanced at all the furnishings. "It's beautiful."

But Arthur remained tense. "There's . . . just the one room for us."

Ah. She hadn't thought about it, hadn't worried about it. They'd not shared a bed before. "I don't have to—" Arthur started. "I can stay in Lancelot's room."

Vera laughed. "That would be horribly unfair to him." She imagined at least one of the girls he'd snuck away to his sacred grove might be in attendance. "It's all right," she said earnestly, hoping her reassurance might unfurrow his brow. "I trust you." And a knot in her unknitted, too, because she meant it.

The Yule's Eve celebration would be tonight, an evening of food, drink, and fine performers. When they walked under an enormous stone archway into the festival grounds, Vera's entire field of vision was taken by high-standing torches, their open flames casting a bouncing light in all directions. There were also candelabras throughout the courtyard, campfires with clusters of revelers gathered around them at the back of the space, and in the middle, near the front, a stage cleverly lit by shallow basins of flames. Tables and chairs skirted the courtyard's edges, and every corner had a makeshift bar serving wine and ale.

A prickle rose on Vera's arms, and it took her eyes adjusting to the surrounding light to see past the courtyard area. At first, she could only make out a looming structure. Something was familiar about where she stood. The prickle turned to goosebumps as Vera spun toward the High Street, orienting herself. She stood on the grounds of what would someday be the abbey. Now, in 633 CE, if there should have been a structure here, it would be a humble wooden church. But she walked toward it, squinting into the darkness.

Arthur followed her. "What are you looking at?"

"This . . . it's . . ." She was going to say "impossible" as she gaped at an ornate stone cathedral towering above. Two towers were facing Vera with the bulk of the building in between—not in the gothic style she recognized from the abbey's ruins of her other time, all spiking points and buttresses. It was rounder and gentler, more in the style of Camelot's castle, though certainly as grand as any more modern structure Vera had seen. And since there was no record of it, no archaeology to mark this reality that Vera could have walked forward and touched with her own fingers, she knew it must have been made with magic. The stone structure they did have archaeological evidence of would be built more than a hundred years from now. What could possibly happen between now and then that would erase the gargantuan beauty before her?

"There are only ruins here in my time," she said. "Impressive ruins, but not of this. This is . . . no one from my time has seen the likes of this."

Arthur tilted his head to the side. "Except for you."

"I suppose that's true."

Vera followed Arthur back to the festivities. They wove their way to a table near the front where Matilda, Percival, Gawain, and Lancelot were already seated, watching the performers who had begun their show. Vera sat next to Percival, who looked especially miserable, his elbow on the table and his cheek squashed against his hand to prop his head upright, making the scar across his face even more pronounced than usual. He glanced to the stage fleetingly and otherwise stared down at his drink.

"They're doing Percival's story," Lancelot whispered to Arthur and Vera.

"This one's excellent," Arthur said, his lips so near Vera's ear that the barely subsided goosebumps rose on her neck again. He took two goblets from a passing server and gave one to Vera as they sat.

Percival groaned, and Lancelot rolled his eyes. "Oh, you poor suffering warrior. It must be so hard to be admired and beloved because you were such a heroic boy," he said as he took a goblet. He noticed that Gawain was the only one remaining without a drink in hand, picked up another, and passed it to him.

Gawain looked nearly as unhappy as Percival, though she suspected that was simply the nature of his face. He glowered at the stage, mumbling, "Thank you," to Lancelot almost inaudibly.

Vera turned her attention to the stage. An orator narrated as actors gracefully interpreted the story in dance to the musicians' accompaniment.

"There wasn't any dancing at all," Percival grumbled. She grinned and otherwise ignored him, eager to hear his story. They set the scene: it was the war's most crucial battle.

"That's not even close to true," Percival said.

Percival was only fifteen years old.

"Actually, I was fifteen when I joined the forces. I was sixteen at this battle," he told Vera. Matilda hushed him, and he sighed but remained silent after that.

His bravery and loyalty landed him directly in the king's service. They'd lost the previous battle, and things were grim. Arthur was in the thick of the fighting, and Percival courageously brawled to get to him to provide aid. Each was locked in swordfight, fighting for their lives.

Vera looked at the three warriors at her table. Percival bit his lip as he reluctantly watched the performance. Arthur and Lancelot bore proud smiles. They weren't trying to antagonize him. They were celebrating him like a most beloved brother. Arthur surveyed the gathered crowd, checking to ensure people were paying attention.

The story's climax came with Arthur and Percival battling a short distance from one another. Arthur was occupied, and his arms got caught up. There was another aggressor, though, and his sword was about to swipe across Arthur's throat from the side. Percival was also under attack. He could have easily parried the blow coming down toward his own face. Instead, he thrust his sword out to stop Arthur's attacker and knowingly took the blow directly to his head by his assailant's broadsword.

It should have killed him, but it didn't. According to the storyteller, Percival's mighty and selfless spirit served as a shield sent from God that kept him alive. All of Arthur's forces, witnessing this miracle, found untapped strength, and the battle was shortly after won. Arthur knighted Percival right there on the battlefield; the youngest person to ever be knighted.

"But that's not what happened," Percival told Vera. "Magic stopped that sword from hitting me with its full force, or my whole head would have been chopped in half, face first, rather than leaving me with a measly scar." It was hardly a measly scar, running nearly the full length of his face. Percival unconsciously scratched at the part of it beneath his eye. "It was like," he shook his head in frustration and stared into space as he remembered, "an invisible arm or . . . or like a rope or something pulled back on the soldier's sword arm right when his blow would have fallen."

"Who did it?" Vera asked. "Who saved you?"

"No idea," Percival said. "But it wasn't some God-sent miracle. It was someone's magic who was on the field with us." He looked around like his savior might reveal themself.

"Yes, and Arthur didn't knight you right on the field. He let the bleeding stop first," Lancelot said. "But that doesn't make for a good story!"

Percival shook his head and drained his cup in one drink. Nobody mentioned it again for the rest of the evening, which was spent with laughter and countless goblets of drinks at their table. Festival attendees came by to welcome them and especially to greet Arthur and Vera.

Vera held somewhere in the realm of a dozen babies, had her hand kissed more times than she could count, and her cheeks hurt from all the smiling. It wasn't at all unpleasant, though she grew tired as the hours wore on and had already hatched a plan for what to do with her solstice morning in Glastonbury. She could not be this near the Tor without climbing it for the sunrise.

Matilda noticed her yawning from across the table. "Are you ready to turn in for the night?" she asked.

Vera smiled gratefully. "Yes, I think so."

Matilda stood to join her.

And so did Arthur.

"You can stay. I'll be fine." She touched his arm. It was a gesture that didn't raise anyone's attention, but Arthur stared down at Vera's fingers as butterflies erupted in her stomach. She'd touched him before. Why was this different? She blinked to shake herself from it.

"You're doing me a favor," Arthur said. "Otherwise, this lot will try to keep me out until dawn."

"S'true," Lancelot said loudly. He grinned up at them with glazed eyes. "There are only a couple days in the whole damn year I don't have duties and obligations and—" He waved his hand, searching for the word. "And such. I fully intend to make the most of it." His speech ran together enough to betray his inebriation, though he made a valiant effort to sound coherent.

"I'm guessing you don't want to run to the top of the Tor in the morning?" Vera asked with a laugh, hoping her disappointment didn't show.

"Absolutely not," Lancelot answered. "But I will for you, Guinna." He slammed his fist on the table and pointed at her seriously. "Only for you."

"Don't you dare," she said. As much as she'd love to share that with him, Vera would not steal his one morning of respite. And she certainly wouldn't guilt him into the torture of a hungover run up a wickedly steep hill.

"I haven't ever been to the top of Tor," Arthur said. "I'd like to come with you."

"Really?" Vera asked. "Are you sure?"

"Only if you don't mind me slowing you down. I'm not much of a runner like the two of you."

"I don't mind at all," she said. "Thank you."

Had this really been the same man who would only fix her with a cold stare for the better part of the past three months? Arthur's face was now so flooded with gentleness, his eyes alight with concern. He'd known just how much this meant to her.

25

Running the Tor was as familiar as drawing breath, but this morning's venture may as well have been her first time making the journey. In many ways, it was. Chronologically speaking (in a way that positively bent her brain sideways), this was Vera's first run on what would someday become her well-trodden path. Also her first while knowing the truth about her past (well, knowing more of the truth). Her first with Arthur.

The bed they'd shared was large enough that they didn't so much as brush fingertips through the night. She'd thought that knowing he was so close might keep her awake, but she fell asleep quickly and slept more soundly than she had in weeks.

That part may have had something to do with being in a place that felt like home. And resuming her favorite morning ritual. He was already up and dressed when Vera woke. Unsure of the condition of the path to the top, they left earlier than necessary and carved their way through the landscape. They jogged up the lane, past the stream of White Spring where Vera had first emerged into this time, and onward, up the long slope. The way was clear. Enough pilgrims had made the trek to leave a natural foot-worn trail through the otherwise grassy hillside. Still, it was tougher terrain to jog. They charged up a particularly steep section, Vera but a half step ahead of Arthur. When he stopped, she felt his absence and stopped, too.

"Shit," he groaned, looking at the climb ahead. His face shone with sweat, and his heavy breaths came out in cold vapor puffs.

Vera grinned. "Yeah, it's rough. Do you want to walk for a bit?"

He chuckled through a heaving breath and looked at her with admiration. "No," he said.

It was a lie, one she knew he valiantly offered only for her sake. She had gotten faster after so many mornings running with Lancelot, and, in her excitement to be back on this trail, she may have pushed her pace more than usual. Arthur gamely kept in step with her until the final stretch when her excitement spilled over. She sprinted ahead to the top. Her breath would have been taken clean from her body even if she hadn't been winded.

Chest heaving, she marveled at the sight with an open-mouthed smile. St Michael's Tower wouldn't be built for hundreds of years. Instead, a single stone totem stood in the center of what would someday be the tower's footprint. It was taller than both of them, though not gargantuan. Arthur could jump and touch the top, which was like the rounded end of a dull crayon. Squat grey stones surrounded it at equal intervals. These looked like benches. Vera counted twelve and wondered if it formed a sundial.

Then she noticed the base of the totem in the center. It was surrounded by a collection of offerings, a makeshift shrine on the ground. There were candles, palm-sized paintings weighted down with rocks, tied cords and ribbons, Celtic knots made of thin, bendy branches, and a smattering of handmade clay statuettes.

Arthur crested the top of the Tor and joined her in the circle. He'd never seen any of this, either. "Is this here in your time?" he asked.

She shook her head.

He knelt to upright a miniature statue that had fallen over before he began looking at the other paintings and notes. Vera turned in place. The Tor was empty of any other people, and there wasn't a single direction in which the view did not stun. And there was her spot; the place she'd liked to sit (or, she supposed, the place she would someday sit in the distant future). She removed her shoes, left Arthur in the circle, and let her bare feet draw her to that place of comfort.

The mists gathered around the Tor's base. That part had always made it look like an island. Now, there actually was water and marshland underneath the gathered fog. Isle of Avalon. The words came to Vera as Arthur sat down next to her.

His face was set on the surrounding terrain, too, with the look of someone who had stumbled onto a wonder of the world, drunk with the splendor of it. "You can see for miles from here," he said, facing Camelot. "I've traveled all over this kingdom. I've passed this hill dozens of times. But I've never actually seen it before."

His careful mask was gone in favor of abject reverence, his eyes roving the horizon left to right as if it were scripture to be read. But even in his reverie, he looked so tired. And not the kind from waking up early to run. There were bags under those awestruck eyes and an almost permanent furrow to his brow. He was weary and stretched. It was something he didn't let show often but that he always carried. There was a lot he didn't let show.

"How often did you run up here?" he asked.

"A few times a week, at least." Vera shrugged, a casual gesture that didn't match the memory's importance. "Nearly every day since I moved back home after—" Her voice hitched in her throat. "After—" She desperately wanted to tell him. She couldn't keep doing this half-truth, half-living existence, but she didn't know how to unwind it.

Arthur let the emptiness hang there between them. "What would it be like if you finished that sentence?"

His invitation shrunk the gap between what had been and what could be.

"I'd like to know what you didn't say," he said.

She wouldn't allow herself to overthink this. If she hesitated, she'd wheedle a way out of the refuge (and the terror) of telling the truth.

"After Vincent died," she said. It didn't explain anything to him. Still, he waited. "I loved him." She was shaking, but she didn't stop. "He was the one who took that photo of me and my parents. It was less than two weeks later when he died."

"What happened?"

"Car accident," Vera said, and realized that was nonsense to him. "Erm . . . I don't really know how to explain that. It's a carriage without any horses—"

"I know about automobiles," Arthur said. She turned to him in confusion, and he clarified. "From some of the books Merlin brought you."

She was curious about what that discovery had been like for him but set it aside for now. His knowledge simplified things for this story. She swallowed and continued. "I got word that he'd been in a car wreck and was rushed to hospital. I knew it was bad, but they didn't say how bad it was. I got there in time to see them taking him back for care. It was horrible. He was . . . mangled. I should have known he was dying, but I was naively hopeful. He died alone. Then his parents arrived, and I told them their son was dead. It was worse than a nightmare."

Her words were yeast to the memory as she retold the story. It all swelled to life again: the frantic sounds, the florescent light shining overhead, casting everything in its putrid aura, and Vincent's mother . . . how it took extra seconds for her to comprehend the words after she'd heard them, and the way horror physically rocketed through her.

"I've never told anyone about that night."

He took her hand. "I'm so sorry."

"It made it easier to come here," Vera said, "which also makes me feel rather terrible."

"What do you mean? That's perfectly understandable."

Was she really going to tell him all of it?

"My father—my real father, the one who raised me, is very sick. He's undergoing treatment and he could survive, but it's—" she stopped. She'd meant to say unlikely but couldn't. "It's not good," she said instead, still needing to grit her teeth and stare at the horizon before she trusted her voice. "If I can help you fix things here, I'll go back and be with him and my mum until he's . . . better." She finished with the awkward lie of a smile.

At this point, they all might have wished she'd stayed put in the first place. Vera gave a scornful laugh. "Though I'm a hell of a lot closer to bringing your kingdom to ruin than I am to helping. Maybe if I can stop losing my shit every time I . . ." Her thoughts stumbled over the memory of Joseph and the moment he became an empty body. "A man was killed because he hurled an insult at me, and I couldn't hold my tongue."

But Arthur's face shifted to something like disbelief as his gaze bore into Vera. "That's not what happened. I was two feet from you. And I spoke with all the witnesses from that day."

He had? And she'd known he was that close, but she didn't think he'd been listening.

"You thought he was insulting Helene." Arthur rubbed his thumb across the back of Vera's hand, and a rush fluttered through her stomach. "That's not what happened with Wulfstan either. That's never been what's happened."

"How would you know that?" It sounded more accusatory than she'd meant it to. Vera let go of Arthur's hand in the guise of repositioning herself, regretting that she had before the warmth of his fingers had faded from her skin.

"Because you don't do that on your own behalf," he said. "I've given you a hundred reasons to lay out your wrath on me, and you haven't."

She didn't have any answer to that, but a glow was blooming on the horizon.

"The sun's about to come up." Vera nodded toward it. "You don't want to miss this part."

It effectively pierced the bubble of tension as he averted his expectant gaze from her. When the first petal of sunlight appeared, Arthur gasped.

"I've never watched the sun rise before," he said. They sat in silence until the sun broke the horizon's plane entirely, a coin of gold hovering low in the sky, bathing the land in its glow.

"It wouldn't have been wrong if you had spoken up in your own defense," he said, his eyes on the horizon. "I wish you would."

"I'd just as soon you not give me any more reasons to." She'd meant it as a joke, but his response didn't match her smile. It was like a weight was dropped on top of him.

The weight of his loss, perhaps? She wasn't the only one

grieving. Vera wrapped her arms tightly around her knees. "Is that what Guinevere would have done? Shouted at you?"

His breath came out a hard laugh. "I'm not sure. There were certainly many things she needed to say that died with her." He clenched his jaw. The tension was gone before Vera had time to decide what it meant. "You're like her in many ways. I like those things about you," he added when she bristled. "And you're different in as many ways."

"Did you love her?" she asked it quickly.

His response was nearly a grimace. Guilt? She thought of Matilda. If Vera and Arthur were being honest, she may as well lay it out. "Are you in love with Matilda?"

His grimace fell. Arthur looked as though ice-cold water had been dumped over his head. He actually laughed. "Is that what you think?"

Vera shrugged sheepishly and nodded.

"I do love Matilda," he said carefully. "But it's never been romantic. She's family. Our mothers were sisters. Matilda is the closest to a sibling I've ever had, except maybe Lancelot."

Now it was Vera who laughed. "You could have mentioned that before."

"I didn't think to because—"

"Because I used to know." She finished the thought for him and then corrected herself. "Guinevere knew."

Arthur sighed. He stood and took a few steps forward. He shook his head and started pacing, deep in thought. "I hate that your life has been stolen from you. This is such a mess."

"It is. I love my home. My parents. It's a simple life, but it's good." She wasn't sure how to reckon with her feelings but tried anyway. "But there are parts of being here that are rather lovely. I've never really had friends before. And . . . being in Glastonbury for the Solstice, getting to see it in a way no one from my time could even dream of?" She looked around and was re-stunned by the sunrise and the circle atop the Tor. Then her eyes fell on Arthur. Being here with him was the part that made her heart stutter. "This is spectacular. I'll cherish this morning forever."

Arthur smiled, though some of the mask returned, covering a flash of shame. He strode a few paces, turned, and did the same in the opposite direction. If she let the silence hang long enough, she knew he'd find the words he was struggling to churn up. But when he turned to pace in the other direction again, Vera realized she'd seen this before.

She gasped, and Arthur looked up at her, completing the vision, matching it perfectly.

"It was you," she whispered.

"What?" Arthur was bewildered.

"Last Solstice, I was here. I was right here, sitting in this spot, and I thought I saw a ghost." She swallowed. Her hands shook. "It was this. I saw this exact moment. I saw you."

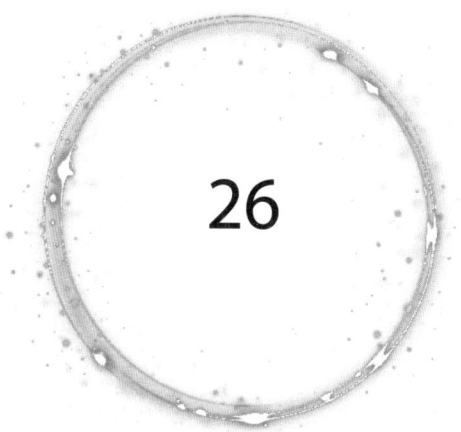

26

Vera regaled Arthur with the whole story on their way down the Tor—what she saw, how it matched up—all in great detail. "I know it was you," she said. "I'm sure of it. Is that completely mad?"

But he didn't think it was mad at all. Maybe the veil of magic and time was thin: same day, same place. Maybe it was luck. Either way, whatever it was felt like it meant something, that at least something that was happening was right with the universe.

They made a quick stop for Vera to change her shoes and throw on a dress before meandering on down the High Street. The street already bustled with the daytime revelers getting a jump on shopping the market's celebration wares. Arthur stopped at a food cart for sweet apple pastries, piping hot but so delicious that even when the steam singed Vera's tongue, she closed her eyes in bliss.

Wisdom would have been waiting to take another bite as the next one was more toward the middle and rich with even more gooey filling approximately the temperature of molten lava. The special drive of post-run hunger made a different decision. At that point, Vera had two choices, neither particularly graceful: let the bite fall from her mouth to the ground or do her best to suffer through it. Vera chose the latter and was inelegantly sucking fresh air into her scorched mouth to cool the traitorous apples as Maria approached. Arthur tore his concerned stare from Vera's antics (which, of course, she couldn't explain because she had a mouthful of food) to greet Maria.

For Vera's part, she did her best to smile without fully closing her mouth (the steam had to have somewhere to vent), nor appear she was in absurd, self-inflicted pain, which she obviously was.

Maria took no notice. "Good morning, Your Majesties!" she gushed, her voice arching melodically over the words. "Look at you two. To see you together again . . . and my goodness! Inseparable, it seems. Well, I suppose it only makes sense after being apart so long."

Vera squinted as she swallowed, another misstep as she now felt like her throat was hot enough to breathe fire. Maria, however, carried on. "We weren't going to ask because we know the queen has been recovering. But now that we've seen the two of you together—that's to say, we've seen how well the queen looks . . ." Maria beamed at her. Vera heard the hidden meaning. The rumors of trouble between her and Arthur had made it this far.

"Yes?" he prompted.

"Do you remember the year that the two of you opened the festivities? With the Yule Carola?" she asked.

"Yes," Arthur said, and Vera began nodding, too, trying to play along. He bit his lip to stifle his grin.

"It would be so wonderful if you would do that tonight. Would you? Would you please?" Maria's twinkling eyes settled on Vera.

"Certainly!" she said with a shrug, still in the tumult of her scorched mouth, but to the pleasure of an effusive Maria and to wide-eyed surprise from Arthur.

Maria practically squealed as she hurried off to let whoever know about whatever Vera had agreed to.

"What is that—the Yule Carola?" she asked Arthur. "Is it, like, a reading or procession or . . . recitation?"

"That—I cannot believe that just happened," Arthur said. "Erm, no. It's a dance."

"Oh," Vera said. "Shit."

The worry dropped from his face. He laughed. "That's all right. We have all day for you to learn it."

The Once and Future Queen

They didn't quite have all day. Maria made it clear that they intended to give Vera a more traditional royal treatment to prepare for the evening. But they had plenty of hours before that would begin, even after Arthur said he would need time to gather a few things. Vera and Matilda shopped the market for a while, where she found enough treasures to purchase that her full hands made the decision to return to her quarters easy. She hadn't been there long when Arthur returned with his hands full, too—carrying a lute.

Vera raised her eyebrows at him and sipped the drink she'd poured herself. "Are you musically inclined?"

But he didn't respond in kind. His eyes darkened and locked on her goblet. They shot to the corner where his saddle bags lay on the table.

"Where did you get that drink?" he asked with the edge of panic in his voice.

"I—bought some wine, apple wine, while I was out with Matilda this morning." Vera fumbled through her words. "Is that okay?"

The stiffness dropped from his posture. "Of course it's all right."

What the hell was that about? "Would you like some?" she asked. Apples were a Glastonbury specialty in Vera's time, too. The whole morning had felt like she was holding the end of a string in the seventh century with a kite on the other end in her time. Special. Mystical. She'd bought the wine intending to share it with Arthur.

"Er, yes," he said rather awkwardly. "Thank you."

He shifted the lute in his hands to accept the drink.

"So." Vera tapped the instrument with her index finger. "What's with the lute?"

"Ah," he said. "We couldn't exactly have a musician come and play the song for us while you learned." It was a good point. It would be strange that Arthur needed to teach her. "I asked Gawain if he could come up with a way for us to have music to practice in private for this evening." He held the lute up between them. "It's a brilliant enchantment."

Arthur laid the instrument on a chair and plucked a single string. The note rang through the room, and as it was about to fade to silence, the lute began to play itself, a short and happy melody that repeated twice.

"Is that the whole song we're to dance to?" Vera asked.

"That's it," he confirmed. "I'm not an especially gifted dancer, and even I think this one's easy."

Arthur undersold himself. He was a patient and pleasant teacher, calling out helpful reminders as they performed the movements. "Right hands together . . . Good. Switch to left, and—what was it you called this one? Fancy feet." He chuckled. Vera had taken to naming moves. Names that got suspiciously sillier as the bottle of apple wine diminished.

"Oh fuck!" Vera stomped after she got the same move wrong for the third time in a row.

Arthur lay his hand on the lute strings and stopped the music. "It's all right. Do you want to take a break?"

"Do we have most of it done?"

"We are so close," he said.

"All right." Vera nodded at the lute. "Let's try again."

But Arthur saw her smiling and paused. "What's funny?" he asked.

"Nothing. It's—nothing."

"Oh, come on."

"I've come up with some lyrics to the song," said Vera.

Arthur beamed at her as he plucked the lute string to start the music. "I hope you'll sing them."

They began the dance: a coming together, palms meeting, a step back. His hand across her waist and hers across his for a spin. Arthur watched her with mirthful expectation. It was Vera's turn to laugh. When the melody began its repeat, and they moved on to the next set of moves, she sang her words.

"Once upon a winter's night, the wild queen was all a fright.

She was not so fair and graceful; she agreed to lead a dance disgraceful."

Arthur laughed. "You aren't at all disgraceful. You're doing very well."

He taught her another step in the dance, and they started over with the new move tacked on. Vera thought nothing of it as the music came to a close with her hand in Arthur's. He held her fingers near his lips as she dipped into a curtsy.

He stared at her with the funniest expression.

"What?"

"That was the end of the dance. But I—didn't teach you that last bit yet."

He was right. He hadn't. And it wasn't just the curtsy. There had been two other parts before that, one when their right hands joined at chest height and left hands met overhead and another when Vera did a sort of promenade around Arthur. Neither were movements that might have happened by accident. She had remembered. Two signs of good in one day.

"Huh," Vera said as she sat down on the foot of the bed. She didn't consciously remember, but she knew the dance. She knew the steps. That much was certain. "I know I didn't learn that in my time. My dancing is nothing like that."

"What's your dancing like?" he asked.

"My dancing, in particular, might be better characterized as flailing." She said. "I . . . feel the music, you know?"

"No, I don't," Arthur said with a grin. "I think you need to show me."

"Seriously?"

He shrugged and gestured to the open space on the floor near him.

Vera shook her head and took a swallow from her goblet before she stood and moved where he'd beckoned. "It's sort of like—"

With the aid of being tipsy enough and with how much fun they'd already had together, Vera was surprised at the ease of her vulnerability as she broke out some of her silliest moves: hands above her head, a shoulder shimmy, jumping, and spinning. After a hopping spin, she found Arthur in mid-hearty laugh, a delightful and uninhibited sound. But it did not make Vera feel self-conscious or made fun of. His eyes were alight. For a breath, the flash of his face from the first night she had met him, expression hard and cold, jumped to her mind. She couldn't believe this was the same person. In truth, he wasn't. That man felt like a stranger, and Arthur felt . . . different.

"That's the first time I've heard you laugh like that," said Vera.

He smiled broadly. "I've seen a lot in the years since I met you, and that is certainly the first time I've ever seen you dance like that."

It was also the first time Arthur referred to Vera as if she and Guinevere from before were the same person. Her smile hitched, wondering if he would realize his slip. It was also in this instant that Vera understood she'd made a terrible assumption this morning when she hadn't given him time to answer about whether he'd loved Guinevere. If he had loved her, and now, he was gazing at a woman identical to her...

She couldn't think about that and, selfishly, was afraid the bubble of this sweet moment might be abruptly popped.

"How do normal people dance with each other in your time?" Arthur asked, feigning innocence.

"Rude!" Vera dropped her jaw theatrically, though she couldn't hold in a grin. "Well, it's not usually choreographed, and it's far simpler than what we're doing tonight. Just... swaying, really. There's not much to it."

Arthur peered down at his feet. When he looked back up, he was still smiling, but his eyes bore into Vera's. She wasn't quite used to that, him looking her right in the eye.

"Will you show me?" he asked.

Now she was nervous. "It—it's odd without music." Her voice was unwieldy in her throat. "The song on the lute wouldn't work. It's slower than that."

"What about the song with the bird in the Sycamore tree?" he asked.

Vera stared blankly at him. Then Arthur, the ancient king of Britain, began to hum the unmistakable tune of "Dream a Little Dream of Me." She couldn't believe it. Hearing his regal voice hum the song she'd grown up hearing performed by the Mamas and the Papas delighted her.

"You singing that song has to be the strangest thing in all of history," she said.

"Will that one work?"

Vera nodded and held out her hand to him. Her palms were clammy, and her heart was beating faster than it ought to. Arthur gazed down at her with a destabilizing intensity when his fingers touched hers.

"Here," she said, guiding his right hand to her waist. His fingers slid beyond to the small of her back, holding her closer than he needed to. She hadn't been expecting that, but it was also exactly what she wanted. Vera swallowed, self-conscious that he might feel her pulse quickening beneath his touch.

She began to softly sing the song, and they danced together. Vera couldn't fathom looking Arthur in the eyes when they stood this close to one another, so she lay the side of her head on his chest. Almost instantly, she doubted the decision. Was it too close to a full embrace? But then he responded in kind, resting his cheek on her head.

She couldn't say who backed away first—simply that the song ended, and they were not quite so close together anymore. He'd dropped his hand from her back and she from his shoulder, and though their other hands dropped too, Arthur delicately held her fingers in his at their sides.

"It's sort of like that." Vera could only manage a whisper as she tipped her head back to meet his gaze. "How did you know that song?"

"You used to sing it in the chapel," Arthur said. "I didn't . . . I wanted to be there for you without hurting you, and I didn't know how to . . ." His voice trailed off. "I went to the chapel after you and would sit in the alcove so you wouldn't be alone."

Words failed her. She stared at the floor, no notion of how to hold this care. Care that belonged to someone else, but she had fallen into its glow, nevertheless.

"I'm sorry," he said. "It was stupid and invasive—"

He stopped when Vera looked up at him. "It wasn't," she said.

He did not try to mask the pain in his expression. His lips parted, and he inhaled sharply. "I have to tell you something."

Vera was nearly certain she knew what it was.

She'd found it suspicious that Merlin agreed to let the memory work wait without anything in its place. And the way Arthur's behavior had changed toward her after that day in Merlin's study . . . Merlin had convinced him to try to connect with Vera. As he'd noticed her affection for him bloom, she guessed he was feeling guilty for not being forthright. That had to be it.

But he didn't get any further. A sharp rap sounded from the door just before it opened to reveal Maria, already dressed splendidly in a billowing cobalt gown and with sparkling teal and turquoise around her eyes. The top half of her face was painted like the feathers of a peacock.

"I hate to interrupt an intimate moment," Maria crooned as her eyes darted between Arthur and Vera, looking like she would have rather relished a more salacious interruption than this one. Vera disentangled her fingers from Arthur's, more like embarrassed schoolchildren than spouses. "But we must begin preparing for this evening if Her Majesty is to be ready on time."

"Can it wait a few minutes?" Arthur asked.

"No, Your Majesty! We are already behind schedule." For how scandalized Maria sounded, Arthur may as well have asked her to betray him and the country.

"It's all right," Vera said, leaning close to his ear. Her lips were millimeters from his skin. Goosebumps rose on his neck. "Tell me later?" Why spoil the moment?

He brushed a hand down her arm. "All right."

That was sufficient for Maria, who herded Vera out of the room with the tenacity of a border collie wrangling sheep. Vera risked a nip at her heels to turn for one last glimpse of Arthur, smiling as he watched her go.

27

Getting ready for the festival was not nearly as simple as getting ready for a day at the castle, the informality of which Maria bemoaned multiple times throughout the afternoon. To her credit, every complaint came with a suggested solution, usually including Maria's permanent presence in Camelot. Vera did her best to graciously dismiss the subject rather than shouting a panicked "No!" each time it came up.

For the festival, though, Maria planned the afternoon flawlessly, arranging for Vera to have her hair and makeup done in succession. She'd heard of lead being used in some ancient rouges and fresh animal fat in others, so she was both relieved and delighted that the cosmetics were mixed fresh before her eyes. The rail thin woman with sharp eyes and painted pink lips had carted in her two bags filled with supplies. She told Vera tales of her years on the spice trade route while she performed her alchemy using beets from Egypt as a base for rouge, berries Vera didn't even recognize for her lips, and dark dried leaves ground down to fine powder for her eyes.

Under Maria's sharp instructions, the attendants helped Vera into the gown Randall had made for her as they gushed over his craftsmanship.

Vera adored everything about the gown. It was a work of art, a masterpiece she was honored to wear. She would not have believed this gown was possible if she'd not known that Randall had literal magic in his fingertips. It was a creamy white, with swirling vines embroidered all down the fitted bodice. The threads were a gold that was somehow the color of light shimmering in a creek. The gown's neckline swooped deep, stopping below Vera's bust, but it came to a narrow point so it avoided being uncomfortably revealing. The back dipped low to her ribs, and the sleeves were fitted to her elbows where they split. The remaining length of the sleeve hung free, revealing a bolder golden embroidery on the fabric's reverse side.

They stood back to admire their work, looking satisfied, especially Maria. As Vera was wishing she had a mirror, Maria dramatically swept her arm across her body like an orchestra conductor. Instead of music swelling at her command, water from the trickling fountain followed her wave and formed into an upright column in front of Vera, creating a perfectly smooth reflection.

Vera hadn't seen her reflection since she'd left the George and Pilgrims, and she nearly didn't recognize herself. This was exactly how she hoped to look if she ever got married. Then she remembered that, indeed, she was living a life in which she already was married, so perhaps donning this lovely gown and dancing with a handsome king was enough.

Maria swept the water back to its place with a flick of her wrist.

"Is Arthur coming here?" Vera asked. Maria stared at her blankly. "To . . . escort me?" she added.

"Oh, goodness no," Maria said curtly. "His Majesty is fully occupied until after your arrival. Sir Lancelot shall—"

"No he's not," the makeup artist casually interjected as she packed her tools into a leather roll.

Maria blinked at her uncomprehendingly.

"The king," said the makeup artist. "He's outside the door . . . said he'd wait there . . . until we'd finished . . ." Her voice trailed off as Maria's expression transformed into one of horror.

"You left the king sitting in the hallway to wait?" Maria said, each syllable like a truncated slap. The makeup woman withered. They exchanged anxious glances, rooted to the spot before Vera rolled her eyes and marched to the door herself.

The Once and Future Queen

"Wait!" Maria called as Vera unceremoniously threw it open. Arthur leaned against the wall opposite. Maria groaned from behind her. "So much for a reveal," she said.

Vera grinned as his eyes met hers.

Arthur wore a much finer belted tunic than usual with threads and toggles that complimented Vera's gown. His dark hair was pulled into a knot at the top of his neck which, Vera decided in that exact second, was her favorite way he wore it. He stood up straight as he saw her, and with the pleasant, crooked smile he fixed upon Vera, something in his prematurely weathered face looked boyish.

"Hi," Vera said breathlessly. "You look very handsome."

Arthur blushed at the compliment, and Vera was thrilled by that. "Thank you," he said, his eyes roving over her. "You're stunning."

Maria had no choice but to send them off with minimal fanfare, mollified only by the assurance that they were planning to lead the opening dance. Arthur offered Vera his elbow, and they walked to the festival grounds arm-in-arm, where they found their friends seated at the same table as before.

Lancelot rushed over to them, clapping a hand on each of their shoulders. Then he turned his attention to Vera and kissed her cheek. "Guinna!" he said. "You look gorgeous. Is this the dress Randall made?"

"Yes. And thank you." She shoved her hands into the slits in the sides of her skirt, eager to show someone who would appreciate the best bit. "It has pockets!"

"Hell yeah," he said appreciatively.

She felt the heaviness of Gawain's stare before she saw him. Lancelot noticed and shrugged. "I think I've cracked him. He's actually pretty funny."

There wasn't time to argue Gawain's merits. Maria was already beckoning them to the front for the dance. It all happened very quickly. One moment, they were standing around a table with their friends, and the next, it seemed, they were out in the dancing area alone—with hundreds of Yule revelers' eyes on them. Vera's breath hitched.

"Are you nervous?" Arthur whispered.

"A bit," she said.

Arthur and Vera began the dance when the musicians beside the stage started playing. Her movements were stiff as she focused all her energy on not screwing up, but during the first part, where she and Arthur got closer, she heard his deep voice softly singing and looked at him, wide-eyed in her surprise.

"I made up lyrics, too," he said.

She shifted her focus to him, straining to hear the deep quiet of his voice following the melody.

"The king agreed to teach a dance, but His Majesty was full of shit,
And when the festival was ruined, Maria had a massive fit."

Vera threw her head back and laughed.

"Not exactly a masterpiece," Arthur said as he and Vera drew close to spin, but he smiled at having pleased her so thoroughly. The rest of the dance was looser and, unbelievably, even fun. The audience melted from Vera's periphery, and she saw only Arthur. Each time they came close enough to whisper, one or the other would mutter the made-up name for the next move. She was almost sad when the song ended.

Next came the presentation of the Yule crowns. It wasn't Maria who processed onto the field for this, but a band of four children. The two youngest were at the front, a girl and a boy, each carrying a crown on a pillow, reminiscent of ring bearers. They were at the end of their toddler years and had an older child attendant accompanying them to keep them on task when they wanted to wander or shy away from the surrounding crowd.

Vera squatted down to be at eye level, and Arthur followed suit. She smiled encouragingly, emboldening the little girl to close the gap.

"Happy Yule, my queen lady!" She held out the Yule crown to Vera. The beautiful and earthy things were made with quartz sticks and gold wrapping them together. The older attendants placed them on Vera's and Arthur's heads. His was simpler: woven wire with one dark, round crystal at the center. Vera's was a radiant eruption of crystals.

"Can we wear these every day?" she asked Arthur.

She was kidding, but Arthur said, "Yes," though his eyes more plainly said, whatever you want.

The feasting and dancing began in earnest after that. Arthur and

Vera retreated to their table to a bawdy welcome from their friends, who were clearly all feeling pretty good. Lancelot fussed and ensured she had food (because that was what he did, and she loved him for it), and Arthur got Vera a drink.

"I need to make a quick round to offer greetings, but you," he said, emphatically holding up a hand as she stood to join him, "should stay here and enjoy yourself. This isn't an official affair. No one would begrudge you that."

She had no desire to argue. This table of raucous laughter and no expectations for her to be anyone but herself was precisely where Vera wanted to be.

"Guinna," Lancelot said. "We're interrogating Gawain to get to know him better, and it's great fun."

Matilda leaned toward Vera to bring her up to speed. "So far, we've learned he's the youngest mage on the high council—"

"By twenty-two years," Lancelot cut in.

"Yes, I was getting to that," she said, batting at Lancelot with her napkin. "By twenty-two years, that his favorite gift he has is being able to do some healing work, and that he is well aware of how much his demeanor infuriates Percival."

"But only because Lancelot told him," Percival cut in with the exasperation he reserved especially for the mage. "Otherwise, he felt we were getting on fine."

Even Gawain cracked a reluctant smile, though he had a drink in front of him, too, and Vera thought it would be a fair guess that none of them were on their first round.

"I have a question." Percival eyed Gawain sharply. "You said you study who magic comes to and how the break happens and all that nonsense, right?"

Gawain didn't acknowledge the insult. He merely nodded.

"Isn't the magical birthrate one in every four people?" Percival asked.

Gawain listed his head from side to side. "It is lower than that now. Closer to one in ten, according to my research. But it would have been about one in four when you were born."

"Right." Percival rolled his eyes. "Here," he gestured around the table, "we've got four of us, and not one has a magical ability."

Gawain waited with a deadpan face. "Do you have a question?"

"Yes!" Percival's annoyance had them all stifling laughter. "My question is, what the hell? What gives? Shouldn't at least one of us have a power?"

"Statistics don't order themselves to our expectations." If Gawain intended to sound condescending, he succeeded. "It all comes down to the population dispersion, how people tend to group themselves, and what roles each party has to fill. I've found that the rates of magic in, say, leaders in armies tend to be far lower. Maybe they're threatened by their inability and prefer to keep those with magic in a more pigeon-holed role? Perhaps those who cannot do order others to do."

If Vera only had a blow dart and could have offered Gawain the mercy of tranquilizing him, she would have. Lancelot pressed his hand hard against his mouth, but she could see him laughing. Matilda patted Percival's arm, who looked like he'd enjoy nothing more than to punch Gawain. Thankfully, the table was between them.

Gawain forged on without any clue. "Whatever the actual cause, the truth remains that it's perfectly reasonable that none of you would have any powers."

"Let me get this straight." Percival leaned forward as far as he could toward Gawain, who finally took note of his precarious position and leaned away a bit. "You're saying that Lancelot and I are either talentless hacks who are afraid of magic or that we happen to have rotten luck and are statistical anomalies. Do I have that right?"

"Erm," Gawain said, his eyes darting between them. That was a yes. When Percival burst into laughter, they all followed suit.

"What about Guinna's knack for strategy?" Lancelot said. "That could be a gift . . . Though, if it is, it's a load more boring than being able to make fire or heal people or whatnot."

"No," Gawain said. "If Guinevere had a gift, she wouldn't have ended up queen."

"Why not?" Vera asked.

"You must have been too young to remember," he said quickly, his cover for Vera's ignorance so smooth even Lancelot didn't seem to notice it. "Right around the time you'd have been born, the Christian leaders near your familial home of the North Upton territories rounded up all children with the gift, no matter how powerful its manifestation, and sent them to vocational training to join the religious order. It was their attempt to respond to the foundation of the council of mages after the massacre of Dorchester. They wanted their own supreme board of power. And," he added gravely, "they wanted all trace of magic away from their populations. A knee-jerk to the horror inflicted by—"

"Oh! I've got it!" Percival pointed at nothing in particular. "Lancelot's like really lucky. Nobody ever died in battle when paired up with him. Come to think of it," he turned to Lancelot, "it's pretty damn brilliant to have you on the king's detail."

Lancelot snorted. "Thanks a lot, Perce. Let's conveniently forget that I trained since childhood and have dedicated my whole life to being a soldier. Can't be that I'm actually an excellent fighter. No, it's got to be magic."

Gawain eyed Lancelot appraisingly. "No one ever died when fighting at your side?"

He tipped his mug toward the mage. "Not once. Bit of a point of pride for me. But even in my big-headedness, I can acknowledge that much of that came down to luck."

"That could be a gift," Gawain said as he scratched thoughtfully at his chin. "Part of my theory about magic breaks that occur at an advanced age holds that even someone unaware of their dormant gift might exhibit latent magical traits. Like the specimen in Camelot—"

"His name is Grady," Vera said with a glare.

He halted and, after a pause, stiffly nodded. "Thank you. Like Grady, yes. His father told me that he'd always been naturally inclined to woodworking. Of course, it's not evidential proof, but the correlation between that and the manifestation of his power makes me wonder."

Lancelot nudged Gawain with an elbow and gave his most winning smile. "You think I've got some fantastic power lying in wait?"

Gawain cast his eyes upward as he considered it. "Mm. Magic is clever, and I believe it deliberately hides. If you did have a gift, we'd actually make it far less likely to appear by telling you about it. Later life magic most commonly breaks via the necessity of a disaster."

"There you have it," Lancelot said. "My life has been in dire peril somewhere in the realm of hundreds of times, so if my incredible secret gift didn't break during any of those instances, I'm fairly certain it doesn't exist."

"Seems about as likely as the original gifts' existence," Gawain admitted. "That's to say; highly unlikely."

"What are the original gifts?" Matilda asked. She leaned forward intently.

"Rumors, mostly. They're the powers that have been in myths and stories all across the world. One tells of the power to bring the dead back to life, another invincibility, and there are many different versions of the gift of immortality, the fountain of youth. In the Greek stories, it's ambrosia—"

Vera perked up as the threads connected. "The Holy Grail?"

Gawain turned to her, his sallow eyes suspicious. "How have you heard about that?"

Vera picked at the tabletop with her fingernail to stall for time. "They mentioned it at the monastery." Ah. Even with Gawain aware of her memory loss, she had to be careful not to betray the time travel bit. She wasn't sure how long her go-to excuse of "the monastery" would hold for all the things she shouldn't know.

Gawain held his stare on Vera.

"What's the Holy Grail?" Lancelot asked. Percival and Matilda were intrigued as well.

That answered one question. Arthur nor his knights had their sights on the grail. That part of the legend had to be false.

After a pause that felt longer to Vera than it was, Gawain answered. "It's rumored to be the cup Jesus of Nazareth used in his last meal and that caught his blood as he died on the cross. It's said to contain such gifts of immortality to those who drink from it, like all the other cultures' stories. Same ends—different magical mechanisms to achieve them."

"So, the item gives the power? You don't even have to have the gift to receive it?" Matilda asked.

"That's the myth," Gawain said. "But there's no logical truth behind it."

"How can you be sure?" Percival said. "If so many people all over the world have come up with the same thing, maybe there's something to it."

"What do all people who live have in common?" Gawain asked. He waited, like a teacher hoping his pupils would rise to the occasion. When they didn't, he forged on. "We're all afraid of dying. That's what frightened people do. They make up stories that make them feel better. In this case, humanity came up with a story of magic that can alleviate our biggest fear. It's an appealing prospect to believe in, especially when times grow dark.

"Even the council of mages has been caught up in that thinking. But unless we have actual, concrete answers, magic as we know it is doomed. I've not gained much popularity by saying it, but someone has to address the situation honestly. Magic's dying out. If it continues to dissipate at this rate, it will have completely disappeared from humanity within two generations. I'm not entirely certain the world can even survive without it."

Vera shifted in her seat, at a loss for how her life in the future made sense in all of this. Lancelot watched her keenly, chin propped up on his hand, and raised his eyebrows when she met his eye.

"There's a sect of mages who believe that the original gifts are our key to saving things." Despite the topic's gravity, Gawain's voice remained dry. "They're as deluded as whoever came up with the notion of original gifts in the first place. The notion that there's a power out there that we might find and use to fix things in a markedly bleak situation is soothing. It's also a farce."

"So . . . that's it?" Matilda asked. "We're doomed?"

They stared at him in the heavy silence that followed, only broken when Percival let out a low whistle. "Sheesh, Gawain," he said with a disbelieving laugh, "You're a real riot at a party, aren't you?"

"It might be hard to believe," Gawain murmured, "but I haven't been invited to many parties."

They weren't sure if he was joking until he looked up from his drink, and his sullen face bore a hesitant grin.

"A joke!" Lancelot yelled as he threw his hands in the air. They laughed and offered a toast to Gawain's efforts at party conversation, an unofficial welcome to his presence among them. Vera wasn't entirely sold on him after his theories rattled the purpose of her existence. But if Lancelot had made a friend of Gawain, that would be enough to call the man at least tolerable for the time being.

This last toast left many of their cups empty. Vera jumped up and began collecting their tankard handles between her fingers with the particular skill of a woman who'd waited tables since she was seventeen.

"Absolutely not!" Matilda reached to try to grab the cups, but Vera stubbornly pulled them away. "You are not going to serve us!"

"Rock, paper, scissors for it?" Vera asked.

Matilda rolled her eyes and begrudgingly agreed. As Vera sat the cups down and they began to play for best two out of three, Lancelot gaped at them open-mouthed.

"What the hell is this?" he asked. "Is this a game? Why don't I know this?"

Vera closed out the bout, covering Matilda's rock with her paper. She spared Lancelot a shrug. "Sorry! Matilda will teach you because she just lost, and I am off to get drinks!"

She'd forgotten that there would be no blending in. Not in this time, not on this night, and certainly not in her incredible gown with the shimmering crown on her brow, marking her as royalty. The barmaid seemed starstruck when Vera carefully set down their five mugs on the counter.

She looked about herself anxiously as she refilled them. "Please let me find someone to help you carry these. There are servers here . . . somewhere."

Vera tried to reassure her, but the mugs were rather heavy, and she hadn't thought through how she would manage it with all of them once filled. Thankfully for her (and further unnerving for the barmaid), Arthur stepped up to the bar beside her.

"I can help," he said. He procured his empty mug for a refill as well. "I've done my greeting duties satisfactorily enough. Think we can manage six of these between the two of us?"

"Easily."

When they returned to the table, Lancelot, Percival, and Matilda cheered Arthur's arrival.

"Perfect!" Lancelot said as Vera and Arthur took their seats. "Now we have an even number. Right: the game is rock, paper, scissors. Best two out of three wins. Loser drinks. Arthur, you'll catch on. Do this, this, or this," he mimed the three options, "on 'shoot.' It's all luck anyway."

Vera lost count of how many games she'd won or lost, but she was sure there'd never been a night in her life when she'd laughed more, never been a time when her name (well, sort of her name) had been called so often from someone—a friend—who wanted to talk to her.

She and Arthur had thrown rock simultaneously for the third time in a row when she laughed and leaned into his shoulder. He smiled as he gingerly touched her elbow, his fingers tracing around one of the embroidered swirls before he dropped his hand. Vera's heart sank as soon as he withdrew that gentle touch. She wanted to be close to him.

"Would you like to dance some more?" she asked, entirely on impulse.

He didn't remind her that she only knew the one dance. And she couldn't say how long they danced, only that Arthur called out the moves as he'd done that morning. No one seemed to care that their queen often made missteps or went the wrong direction—only that she often laughed with her head tossed back as their king, more jubilant than they'd ever seen him, didn't once tear his eyes away from her.

When the night grew old and the dancing music ended, the area was cleared to ready a bonfire for the dried trees of last year's Yule to be thrown on. The table of friends had dispersed through the party. Vera spotted Matilda and Percival over by the guards who'd traveled with them to Glastonbury. Lancelot proved harder to find. After a while scanning the crowd, Vera caught sight of Gawain as he skirted the edge of the lit festival area. She was nearly ready to give up her search for Lancelot when she noticed movement in the dark beyond Gawain.

He looked only a hazy specter until he broke the lantern's threshold and entered the light. Sure as day, it was Lancelot. She had seconds to wonder where he'd been when a pretty young woman, her locks of curling dark hair mussed about on one side, emerged from farther down in the dark, too. Now that Vera paid closer attention, Lancelot's tunic was also askew, and he hurriedly brushed the grass from his trousers.

It was a common theme. Others emerged into the light from various spots along the edges, giggling and breathless. Though they'd obviously been partnered up off in the darkness, many came back one at a time like Lancelot, making some effort at discretion.

Lancelot jolted when their eyes met, his expression tightening with panic.

She didn't want him to feel uncomfortable that she knew. Why should she care if he and this woman had enjoyed one another's affections? She raised an eyebrow, glanced at the dark-haired woman she suspected had been Lancelot's partner, and grinned knowingly back at him, hoping to assuage his concerns. His gaze ticked toward the lady, and now, caught red-handed, the fear dropped, replaced by a crooked smile and a roguish "What can you do?" shrug.

She didn't say a word when he joined them back at the table, and the others came along shortly, too—except Gawain, who aided in lifting the trees onto the fire with his magic. He held his hand in a fist in front of his face and worried his thumb back and forth between his fingers, his dark stare trained on the trees hovering above the bonfire. When Maria signaled him, he dropped his fist to his side, and the trees fell with it and slammed into the fire with a crackling thud. Flames leapt hungrily at the fresh kindling and swept it up into the fray in seconds, sending an upward explosion of fire high into the air. The crowd gasped, and clapped, and cheered as a rush of hot wind from the fire blew past them all.

The spectacular effect of it lit the festival as brightly as midday though it was much closer to midnight. Vera caught a clear glimpse of Arthur, his eyes glassy like she'd seen them only once before; the first night they'd met. Though that was the extent of the similarities. Tonight, she saw nothing but happiness in them.

"Your Majesty," she said coyly. "Are you inebriated?"

Arthur chuckled and raised his hand to show her the slightest sliver of air between his index finger and thumb. "Tiny bit," he said.

Vera laughed, leaning into him and dropping her head onto his shoulder, a casual gesture of affection. Her marked lack of inhibition reminded her that she wasn't entirely sober either. Arthur looped his arm around her waist as easily as if he did it all the time. She looked up from the safe crook of his arm and found Matilda watching them with a discerning glint in her eyes. Suddenly embarrassed, Vera sat up. Arthur pulled his arm away as casually as he'd placed it, mid-conversation with Percival on his other side. Still, he seemed aware of her every move.

His voice was at her ear when she could no longer stifle a yawn. "Guinevere," he said. She felt a pang at the name. She was used to it by now, but when he used it, guilt stirred. Once, it had been because it reminded Vera what an imposter she was, trying to fill his dead wife's place. Now, Vera ached for him to say her name. For him to want her, not Guinevere. "Are you ready to turn in for the night?"

"Only if you are," she said, though she was thoroughly exhausted. Arthur was already rising from his seat and offering her his hand. Like the night before, Matilda stood to accompany them to help Vera change for bed.

Vera stopped her. "I won't even rock, paper, scissors you for it. Stay here and have fun at the party. As your queen, I command it." She hadn't had the nerve to throw around her position's weight before and found she rather liked it.

Matilda laughed and shook her head. "Yes, your stubborn majesty. As you wish."

"Lancelot," Vera called, interrupting his animated conversation. "Running tomorrow?"

He mirrored her energy and raised his cup to her. "Not a chance in hell!"

Arthur grinned at the exchange, and as "goodnights" and "merry

Yules" were bid across the table to one another, he slid his arm around Vera's waist, and she did her best to pretend this was ordinary and that she wasn't thrilled by his touch.

It helped some that Arthur sang his made-up words to the song, Vera joining in and making them sillier. They wore the shadows of their laughter when they reached the room. Someone had come by and set a fire blazing in the hearth. The candles all along the wall were lit as well.

"That was so much fun!" Vera said. She took off her quartz crown and set it aside before she uselessly began trying to reach the ties on the back of her dress. It had her squirming and stumbling backward, which put Arthur in stitches so forceful he collapsed into the chair behind him.

"Be a gentleman then and help me," she chided.

"That's a first," he said with a smile. "A lady tells me to be a gentleman by demanding I help her undress."

She opened her mouth to protest, but Arthur held up a hand. "And I will gladly oblige."

They were both laughing as she turned away from him, and his fingers fumbled with untying and unfastening various parts on the back of her gown. "I might have been better off struggling through it myself," she teased.

He got it untied right after she said that. Vera felt the bodice loosen. It may have been her imagination, but she thought Arthur's fingers lingered on the bare skin at the small of her back for a second more than they needed to. She closed her eyes. A shiver rushed through her. She was glad he couldn't see her face.

She heard his footsteps retreating across the room and knew he'd politely turned away, giving her privacy as she changed into her nightgown.

When she turned to face him, it was to find him struggling mightily with the toggles beneath the neckline of his tunic. They made eye contact and burst into laughter.

"I suppose it's my turn to be a lady and help you undress," she said.

"I don't know," Arthur said as she closed the space between them. "Guffawing at my failure suited you nicely."

Vera grinned. She stood very near to him, but it felt different than when he was untying her gown. This had them face to face, an intimacy they couldn't escape, though she tried by slipping back into humor as she struggled with the toggles.

"Dear God, who are they trying to keep out? Someone should tell Randall about these fasteners. This might do better than traditional armor." She tugged so forcefully that Arthur nearly stumbled, laying a hand on her waist to steady himself.

He made a quiet chuckling noise, one Vera could feel through her fingers on his chest. She focused on his tunic until she made headway on the stuck toggle. She wasn't thinking about it as she continued to undo the others for him. When she reached the last one right at his sternum and was about to pull away, Arthur lay his hand over her fingers.

He wasn't laughing any longer. He'd closed his eyes as he held her hand. He drew it to his lips, softly kissed the tops of her fingers, and then froze, eyes shooting open as if awakening from a dream. She did not move a muscle as she held his gaze.

Then she felt it; his thumb moving up and down, a light caress on her torso. Her breath quivered. When Vera had dared to let herself feel anything relatively romantic since Vincent's death, it had been sorrow. So much sorrow and the weight of loss. But now, the pain was blanketed with longing, and longing felt good ... like being electrified awake.

Arthur looked down at the floor in a moment of hesitation. It was like he stood at the edge of a cliff, deciding whether or not to jump. The pause was agonizing, yet Vera wanted to hold it for an eternity, this time hanging in the balance when all things were possible, and there were no consequences to actions untaken. With her free hand, the one not encased in his, she reached up and traced from the side of Arthur's cheek down the curve of his jaw in a gentle stroke.

In one fluid motion, Arthur decided to leap. He slid his upper hand to the back of her neck, and his lips were on hers, kissing her with an insatiable hunger.

Vera hadn't realized she was on the cliff too, but she jumped with him. It was an explosion within her as she kissed him in return, her yearning quickly becoming a sense of need. Arthur pulled her closer, his fingertips weaving into the hair at the nape of her neck as they embraced. She wanted more.

She wanted everything.

"Tell me to stop," he whispered in a hurry.

But she would not. She could feel his lips curve into a smile under hers as she pulled his body toward her and pressed herself against him, the two opposing forces meeting.

An unwelcome part of Vera's mind interrupted the bliss: the memory of him not half an hour ago calling her Guinevere. He's seeing you as Guinevere. She could not bury the notion. As badly as Vera wanted this, wanted to be close to him, wanted to be with him . . . As much as she ached for him, she would never forgive herself if doing so was a manipulation of his love for the woman she couldn't be.

Her body must have betrayed the thought for an eyelash of a second, and Arthur noticed. He broke the bond between their lips but stayed close, his forehead resting against hers.

"Are you all right?" His voice was even deeper when he spoke so quietly, and Vera shivered at his chest rumbling against her.

"Arthur, I'm not her. I can't be her. I—" Vera fumbled. She knew she didn't have the right words, but she forged on anyway. "I would . . . If I could bring you comfort . . ." All wrong. She hated them as they came out of her mouth.

Arthur went rigid. He held her for a single deep breath.

"I'm sorry," he murmured, and he pulled away. Their bodies separating from one another was like being cleaved in two. He turned and took two quick steps away, then turned back, mouth open and eyes on the floor at her feet. He stood there as if about to speak but instead shook his head. His face darkened: all that was gentle moments before went rigid.

"No," he said through gritted teeth. Vera wasn't even sure he was talking to her. He turned on his heel and left the room.

"Shit," Vera said. She didn't go after him. She drank water. She paced the room. And she went to bed, knowing that he wouldn't be there in the morning, terrified she and Arthur had ruined every step forward they had taken with a few moments of tipsy impulsivity.

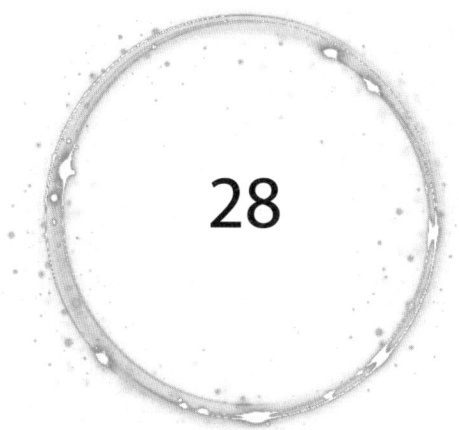

28

The unseasonable warmth of the last few days transformed under the influence of a north wind while Vera slept. She hadn't thought sleep would come at all. Not only was she in a strange place and alone, but the spot Arthur would have occupied was an unavoidable reminder of his absence, like the negative space in a painting. In one breath, she replayed the instant his lips found hers. In the next, her stomach fell with the memory of anger returning to his face before he left the room.

Vera didn't want to roll over when she woke to the soft light of morning, knowing his empty place would send her down the same path of cyclical delight and dread as she mentally replayed her every move from the day prior. She turned over, consoling herself that at least she might spread out or double up the covers to make her cocoon of blankets all the more insulating against the cold.

But the bed wasn't empty. Arthur was there, fast asleep, lying on his side facing Vera. His features were peaceful with the weight of consciousness lifted from him. She'd like to stroke his cheek with her finger as she'd done last night.

Instead, she got up, endeavoring to get ready quietly, but even dressing in her simplest traveling gown didn't lend itself to quiet. The skirt rustled no matter how deliberately she maneuvered it. When she finished, the unreachable ties at the back of Vera's gown hung loose, but it would be good enough until she found Matilda.

In her rustling around, she hadn't heard Arthur get up and cross to the fireplace. He knelt there, feeding logs onto the smoldering embers and stirring the flames back to life. She avoided looking in his direction, telling herself she wanted to give him privacy as he dressed for the day. Mostly, she was afraid that she'd find the shell of him from before if she saw him too closely. She knelt on the cold floor, folding her dress from last night and trying to fit it back in the bag without making a mess of things.

"Guinevere?" Arthur said from behind her. She jumped at his voice and played it off as she stood to face him. Anxiety flooded her: there was his masked stare. "I . . . had more to drink last night than was wise. I apologize." He didn't offer any more explanation, and a pit dropped in her stomach at his apology. They'd been so close to being something more than two people forced to share space—very nearly friends.

And now, she'd lost him.

"It's all right. We both did." Vera said.

He gestured to the laces hanging down on the back of her gown. "Would you like me to—?"

She didn't. It was too reminiscent of last night, of what they were now calling a regrettable mistake. But it would also be nice to be ready and not face Matilda or any uncomfortable conversation that might stem from their interaction.

Arthur was careful not to so much as graze her skin.

When they left their lodgings and stepped outside, the harsh wind stung Vera's face as she belatedly realized that she'd packed away her cloak. Arthur draped his over her shoulders. They didn't look at one another.

She'd let herself be foolishly swept up in her own fairytale, and now all that was left was a steady and subtle nausea churning in her stomach. He had deemed their embrace an act fueled by drunkenness and requiring an apology.

But there were bigger concerns. Truthfully, the prior night was a near-perfect model of what was happening in the kingdom; a sheen of happiness when all felt right for Yule—but it was a superficial layer atop a more sinister reality.

Their departure from Glastonbury was delayed as village leaders discreetly called on Gawain to repair a lengthy list of magical issues. And Vera overheard the report that Lancelot brought Arthur: another attack. This one was farther north along the French coast, much closer than the previous. Combined with the late night of celebration and the less hospitable weather, it made for a subdued journey to Camelot.

After Vera and Arthur's silent trek to their chamber, Vera was ready to crawl under the covers and sleep all day. She anticipated that Arthur would retreat to the side room, but he didn't. He unfastened his sword belt and hung it by the desk. Then, he just . . . stood there, staring at the floor and worrying at his chin with his thumb and forefinger.

"What are you doing?" she asked.

"I don't know how to tell you—"

There was a knock at the door.

Arthur let out a low exhale before he went to open it.

"May I have a word, Your Majesty?" Was that Gawain's voice? Vera leaned forward so she could see. Neither of the mages came into this tower. Yet there he was.

"Not now," Arthur said. "I will come to your study when—"

"No," Gawain said. "No. It must be here. Immediately. It's about the curse and the queen's memory loss. We cannot risk being overheard."

Gawain turned sideways and scooted past Arthur into the room without invitation.

Vera and Arthur shared a glance. She nearly cracked a smile before she remembered that he wasn't the one she could share that with anymore. Her face fell, and she swallowed.

The three of them sat near the fireplace, Vera leaving plenty of space between her and Arthur, and the young mage leveled his blank stare at them.

"I have my doubts about the nature of magic's demise, and I wonder if pursuing the queen's memories is the wisest course. I'm not sure if the queen told you about our conversation—"

"She did." There was a note of defensiveness in Arthur's voice that bewildered Vera. "She told me right away." It was true. She had told Arthur all about her interaction with Gawain. But that had been before last night.

Gawain barely nodded before he launched right in. "I'm guessing there's more to your memory loss than I know . . . more than Merlin is willing to tell me, I'm sure. From my observation, it seemed the potion had fostered some of the hoped-for attraction between the two of you but without any results on your memory. Am I correct?" he asked Vera.

Arthur had moved, his hand half raised as if to stop Gawain. But the words had already been spoken. Words that Vera didn't quite comprehend, but a singe rose over the surface of her skin—like she'd touched a scorching oven burner, but her mind hadn't yet recognized the damage.

A potion. For attraction.

Gawain had to be mistaken.

There hadn't been any potion. Well, except for the one for the memory procedure and that was only for the procedure, wasn't it?

But . . .

She'd never asked Merlin what was in it. And her attraction, that . . . desire, that need for Arthur was new.

Fuck. Her head swam. Her feelings for him had come from the potion. Did Arthur know? Did he know that Merlin had drugged her into desiring him? Her cheeks flamed with the shame of it as she tried to think through how pathetic and desperate she'd behaved with him. He'd certainly reciprocated, though. And it wasn't as if he'd had a potion.

Wait.

There'd been the package from Merlin. The one Arthur had grimaced at. The one his eyes shot to in their room when Vera had been drinking the apple wine.

No. No, no, no. He wouldn't lie to her about that. Gawain was mistaken. Or . . . Arthur didn't know. He couldn't.

She expected his denial or outrage, but he stared back at her, still as a statue.

Vera's field of vision narrowed. Her ears started ringing.

"There's another route we could . . ." Gawain was still saying something, but his words melted in with the ringing and became noise, and noise only. Vera's breath sped up, and her rage expanded with each moment Arthur held her stare and silently admitted his complicity.

"Are you going to say anything?" she said, interrupting an oblivious Gawain mid-sentence.

Arthur cast a fleeting glance at the mage. "It's complicated."

Vera was so angry she could hardly see straight. "Oh. It's complicated," she repeated, drawing out every syllable.

Gawain glanced warily between them as he shifted in his seat. "I am unsure what is happening."

"I will un-complicate it," Vera said as her muscles began to shake with tension. She wished that she could have screamed at him, but she'd never felt smaller. "Stay away from me."

She didn't want to be near him for another second. She stumbled out of her seat, nearly losing her footing as she rushed for the door. She was in the back courtyard before she realized her feet were taking her there. The water tower loomed ahead of her. Merlin's tower.

She wasn't even sure the mage was here. He'd wisely avoided her since the day with the procedure—and the potion. But the door to his study was open, so she stormed right in.

Merlin sat at his desk and looked up from the assortment of potion bottles in front of him, the shock at her entry shifting from a smile of greeting to concern as he saw her face. It all flickered through his features in the space of a second. "Guinevere?" He stood, keeping his fingertips on the desk below him.

"Is that it?" She pointed at the bottles on his desk.

"What?" Merlin's bewildered stare followed her eyes. "Oh, this," he said. He picked up the smallest bottle and walked toward her, holding it in front of him. "This is a brand-new potion I've developed for—"

Vera snatched the bottle that he cradled so delicately and threw it with all her might at the wall behind him. It shattered, the crash and Merlin's subsequent shock urging her on.

"For secretly drugging me and fucking with my feelings?" Vera asked. But it wasn't a question. Not really.

Merlin sighed before he, infuriatingly, smiled sadly. "No."

"Where is that one?"

"Guinevere—"

"I will smash every goddamn one if I need to." Her eyes shot to the shelves where Merlin's hundreds of colorful bottles blinked back at her in the orb light.

"That would be unwise," he said quietly. He crossed back to his desk and sat down, scooting the remaining bottles there to the corner farthest from Vera. "Many of those are rare, one of a kind. And I've no access to the necessary gifts to replicate them. Including the potion for traveling through time."

Vera's chest tightened as she turned back to the shards of glass sprinkling the floor beneath the remains of the potion that dripped down the wall. What had she done?

"That," Merlin said, "was a potion I made to help crops persist through poor conditions. I'd hoped it would help the kingdom in the coming season." He gestured to the seat near his desk. "Will you please . . . ?"

She stayed rooted to her spot. "Why didn't you tell me what that potion would do? I should have had a choice."

"I would have," he said. "But I thought it unwise in front of Sir Lancelot. And after the king forbade me from further work, I didn't have ample opportunity to speak to you."

"But you made time to get a fucking potion to Arthur," Vera shot back.

Merlin nodded slowly. "I did."

"Well, it didn't work. It's not going to work. There will be no connecting."

"I'm sorry to hear that," Merlin said. His calm was infuriating. "I thought I'd made it clear how important this work is."

Vera lifted her eyebrows. "Gawain said the memories might not be necessary."

"They are."

"As you have assured me," Vera snarled. There had to be more to this. More reason. "If connecting with me is all that's needed to save

The Once and Future Queen

Arthur's kingdom, why the hell is it so impossible for him? What aren't you telling me?"

Perhaps he saw in her eyes that she would not leave this room until he answered. Merlin gestured patiently at the seat near him. This time, Vera dropped into it.

"I've been surprised," Merlin began slowly, "that you never asked why Viviane cursed us—surprised, but grateful. I'd hoped you would remember on your own, and I wouldn't have to be the one to tell you." He didn't move. His expression hadn't changed, but goosebumps rose on Vera's arms and skittered up her neck.

"When the wars ended, and Arthur began to establish the kingdom, Viviane grew disenchanted," Merlin said. "She'd believed he would be a different sort of ruler than the power-hungry conquerors, and make no mistake, he is. But she wanted more. She dreamed of a rather idealistic economic structure, and when Arthur accepted money from the rich to build the kingdom and allowed them their titles of nobility, lands, and power, Viviane was dismayed that it was all the same. What was the point in fighting to build a country like every other? Her perspective wasn't without merit. In many ways, it was a fair critique, the kind of thing a ruler like Arthur wants in his advisors: someone to challenge him and hold him to a higher standard. But he's also pragmatic. He knew we needed to start somewhere.

Merlin rubbed at his temples and closed his eyes for a moment, like the words were draining him. "Viviane was an exploratory mage. She travelled to discover and develop new ways to use magic. She was away frequently. We did not know that Viviane used those travels to seek out another leader, one she deemed more worthy than Arthur. Her plot began when she found a Saxon ruler who shared her vision. Viviane intended to orchestrate the fall of Arthur and his kingdom."

Merlin's eyes lingered on her as if hoping she might remember the rest of the story so he wouldn't have to say it. "Viviane bewitched you. You were a key piece—the key piece of her plan against the throne."

Bewitched. It echoed in her mind, the subtle and persistent tap of a piece that didn't quite fit. "What do you mean by bewitched?"

Merlin didn't answer.

"Did she use a spell or a potion or something?" Vera pushed, dread rising in her gut.

Merlin glanced down at the desk before meeting her eyes. It all but confirmed her suspicion: the "bewitchment" had nothing to do with magic.

"Viviane was very powerful and very convincing. And you were uniquely situated to be swayed. You endured awful things. She saw how that weighed on you and capitalized on it. And there was no one better positioned than you to fill that role. You had the king's trust and access to all military information. It was easy for you to pass intelligence. Who better to help bring down the leader than the person closest to him?"

A new word now: betrayal.

"Bring him down? I wouldn't—she wouldn't—" In truth, Vera didn't know what Guinevere would have done. "But . . ." She thought of how Arthur loved his people and the magical pull that brought him to the throne. Of all the parts about this that were untenable, that may have been the most. "The people wouldn't stand for another ruler. She had to have known that! They would revolt."

Merlin steepled his fingers in front of his lips. If she hadn't known the conversation's context and had only walked in the room then, she'd have thought he was wrestling with a complicated maths problem. "The magic that calls Arthur to the throne would end upon his death. I don't know the specifics of Viviane's plan. I can't say whether she meant to kill Arthur or if she wanted that done by your hand."

"No," Vera breathed. She didn't know what she'd imagined, but it wasn't this. This was so much worse. An affair with Lancelot would have been child's play in comparison. And Arthur—she had seen the way his face had hardened last night. "Arthur knows, doesn't he?"

She needed no answer, but Merlin gave it. "Yes."

Ah. There it was.

She was a traitor. To Arthur, first and foremost. All the time he had been cold, had physically pulled away from Vera . . . He'd been exceedingly generous, all things considered. No wonder he stayed so deliberately distant. If Vera had anything more of Guinevere in her than memories, she was a danger to him and to everything he'd poured his life into.

Vera dropped her forehead into her hands. The fuel was sucked from the fire of her anger, suffocated by the truth. Her remaining feelings of disdain for Arthur melted into shame. "Why didn't you tell me before?"

"I thought we had time for you to remember on your own," Merlin said. "It used to be that my life force could sustain magic across the entire kingdom. Its reach has diminished. Now it won't even hold reliably to Exeter." Bitter frustration bubbled into his voice, and the pallor of his face looked greyer than before, as if merely thinking of his recent endeavors exhausted him. "And there are the attacks in the Frankish Kingdoms—another one quite recently. I'm not convinced it's unrelated to Viviane's ruler. The only chance we have of reversing the damage is if you remember what she did. If the magic continues to weaken this rapidly, the Saxons will seize upon that and invade even without Viviane. We'll need your memories then, too, to stand a tactical chance against whatever intelligence you gave them."

Vera tried to swallow and found her mouth dry. "And once I remember what Viviane did, you're not sure you'll be able to fix it, are you?"

Merlin held her eyes for a breath before he shook his head bitterly.

"That's not much of a hope," she said.

He clasped his fingers together and leaned toward her. "It's all we have. If we can't restore the magic, our society will crumble. The Saxons will invade, and they will win."

Though she didn't move, aware of the bite of her fingernails pressing into her palms and the way the front edge of her chair was becoming uncomfortable against the crook of her knees, Vera felt like she was falling forward or like the room was tumbling backward around her. She couldn't tell which. She only knew the sensation was in her mind because there was Merlin before her, an upright anchor to reality while her mind spiraled.

"But that—how do you know what should happen? That's the way my history books tell it. The Saxons do eventually conquer." Vera dragged words, leaden and heavy, from her depths and forced herself not to think of anyone, especially not of her friends—not of Lancelot, who would be the one leading the armies to their end. "Maybe this is the way things always were supposed to be. That magic dies, and Arthur's kingdom—" Her stomach churned. "That Arthur—" And Lancelot and Matilda and Percival... Vera clamped her mouth tightly closed, stifling the urge to throw up as a wave of nausea crested through her.

"Surely you don't hope for that," Merlin said softly, and there was no question in it. She willed herself to keep her face blank, to keep the intrusive vision of her friends bleeding on the battlefield from her mind.

"No," he said. "That's not the way it should be."

"But I've lived there. There's no magic in my time."

"How do you know that?" His lips ticked up at the corners, and his eyes glimmered. "Just because you haven't seen it doesn't mean it isn't there."

She had never considered that her own world might not be as it seemed. "Are you saying—?"

"It's complicated, Guinevere. All of it. And the future isn't fixed." Merlin held up a hand in anticipation of Vera's protest. "I know. You lived there. You came to be who you are there, but the only thing that tethers that reality into being is you."

"That can't be. I—I served food. I cleaned toilets," Vera protested weakly.

It brought a wry smile to Merlin's face. "Yes. And you held existence intact with every scrub. That's the rather tricky bit about the presence of magic in our world. It's a guiding force, much like the way it called Arthur to the throne and the way it makes me feel certain he should stay there, but it doesn't control us. We can break its call to our detriment."

"What can I do?" Her voice croaked. "Can you make me remember? Is there magic that can pull it out?"

Vera saw Merlin's eagerness, but a careworn determination quickly replaced it. "There is," he said. "It is invasive, and it will be painful."

"All right," Vera said. What choice was there? How could she choose her own comfort and damn the kingdom—damn the future? "How do we do this?"

"The procedure requires your consent, and you can end it at any time. I will enter your conscious memories and . . ." He paused, considering. "Add my memories of you from before. I'll use things that parallel emotional experiences of the life you know to help regenerate the life you don't recall. That's the part that hurts. And it's best we only do this once, so when you're ready, you should take this."

He held up a glass vial between his thumb and middle finger. The grey substance in it swirled of its own accord, only held in by the cork stopper. It was more than mist and less than liquid as it listlessly tapped at the cork like it knew that was the way out. Vera didn't have to breathe the question aloud. Merlin was already answering it.

"It does have an element that increases your attraction to Arthur. I'm sorry, but we can't proceed without it. That connection is the essential thread of your memory. Largely, though, this is a sensitivity potion. It won't help you recall anything from before, but it will make all that you experience today more vivid. You won't forget a single moment of what's to come. I do not wish to mislead you, Guinevere." He dropped his free hand to her arm. "This will not be pleasant. If we do it right, it could make all the difference."

It gave her pause. The first procedure had been frightening and debilitating enough.

"I'm surprised," Merlin said, pulling Vera from her anxiety. "You never asked me why Viviane turned on you."

She hadn't thought to. "Why?"

"Oh, dear girl." The wisp of a sad smile crossed his face. "You changed your mind. Your love for Arthur pulled you back. Call Viviane's hold on you bewitching, call it convincing . . . that you could break it was no small feat. You came to me, and you told me everything. I shouldn't have let you be unprotected for a moment after that. I will never forgive myself for that error. I was within seconds of being too late." He shook his head before looking at Vera with deep fondness, maybe even admiration. "The point is that you were willing to sacrifice your own life to try to fix what was broken."

Merlin spun the glass vial idly in his fingers. Guinevere had a part in creating the mess, but she'd given her existence in an effort to make things right. Vera felt no connection to the actions of her former self.

Nevertheless, she was riddled with a sense of responsibility. She could endure pain to complete the undoing of Guinevere's betrayal. Indeed, she was quite literally made for it.

Vera took the vial from Merlin's outstretched palm. She unstopped it and threw its contents back like a shot of liquor. The grey substance slid over her tongue, smooth and tasteless. It left a trail of warmth in its wake all the way down her throat.

As it all settled in her stomach, the warmth turned into a burn, and her impulsivity felt like a mistake. Vera gripped the desk in front of her, gasping helplessly. The stinging heat began to fade as soon as it started, replaced by something different than she'd ever known.

The tips of her fingers prickled with sensation. She felt not only the chair beneath her but the wood's grain through her clothing. The dim room now seemed bathed in light, and beyond the cellar's earthy aroma, Vera caught a whiff of baking bread from dinner preparations in the kitchen. She could hear the whirring mechanism of the well cranking above. Her senses had taken on all the fire of the potion. This must have been how Randall felt all the time.

Merlin stood and rounded the desk to stand right behind Vera. "Do I have your permission to enter your mind?" he asked. Vera was relieved that it was nearly a whisper.

"Yes," she breathed. Her heart pounded as loudly as the fire crackling in the hearth.

"If you need me to stop, say the word." Merlin raised his hands and carefully positioned them on Vera's head. His palms sealed over her ears firmly enough that they created a suction, making a surreal growling white noise. His middle and index fingers pressed into each of her temples, the next finger right on her cheekbones, his pinkies along her jaw, holding it tightly in place. Vera trembled under the pressure of the mage's surprising strength.

"Ready?" he murmured.

She tried to nod, but Merlin's hands held her skull in place.

"Close your eyes, Guinevere."

She took a deep breath and shut her eyes as she exhaled.

"Let's begin."

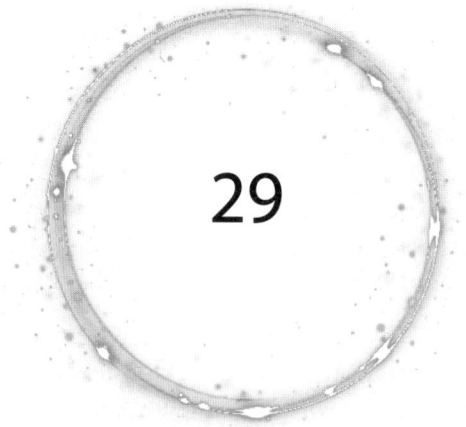

29

The dark behind Vera's eyelids swelled to an abnormal vastness that she intuitively understood to be some part of her mind. Everything beyond her mind, even her physical body, felt more like a dream.

"What are you looking for?" She asked it silently, testing her sense that Merlin couldn't hear her active thoughts. He didn't answer.

She felt his presence meandering through her memories, but there was no image of him, nothing to see. He wasn't in her active, thinking mind. His foreign presence was solely in her memories. Merlin moved like he knew where he was going. There was a distinct tug toward one sensation: affection.

He pulled it forth like taking a book from a shelf. Then, images flipped past in quick succession, slides of memory scrolling past until the Rolodex slowed. The first thing that came into focus replayed as Vera remembered it: Arthur holding her as they danced before the crowd and laughing as he called out the moves to her—God, how had that just been yesterday? She thought Merlin might stop there. That seemed a good place to begin, but he flipped past it.

Next was Lancelot. Short scenes in quick succession: him kissing her on the forehead in the throne room, nudging her with his shoulder on the hillside, laughing with her while on a run. Not all her memories with him went by, but there were so many: throwing his hands in the air in glee that first night, running toward the woods the day they went to the sacred grove ... Vera deliberately moved away from this one, realizing that she had some control if Merlin was aimlessly flipping through. Instead, she pulled forth one when they'd played tic-tac-toe and saw the adoration on his face in her memory.

"Guinevere," Merlin said disapprovingly. His physical voice sounded like it came from the farthest point of a jet-dark pit. "You need to be careful."

"It's not like that," she said, but he'd already moved on before she could offer more of a rebuttal. She chuckled despite her discomfort. What would he have said if he saw them half-naked in the cave together?

Merlin blazed onward, further back in her memories, back to university. This couldn't be right. This was too long ago. It was the beginning of Vera's third year, and she remembered this day in particular. The stormy day when she'd met Vincent in the library. It all played out as she remembered. It hurt to look at him in this memory, so full of life and light. He had no idea ... no trace of fear at what was to come for him and what would be his end.

Vera's immersion in the memory broke. It lay open in front of her, but the focus shifted. Darkness fell like the power to her mind was cut, and a loud ring in the obscurity of the black shook her as if she stood inside a church bell being struck. The tone made her seize up. Merlin had promised there'd be pain, and that was the first sign of it.

"Keep breathing," he said, his steady voice easing Vera some.

An incision sliced into the darkness, and a memory was born into her mind through it, but it wasn't hers. She was seeing it from someone else's perspective. The emotions that came with it were foreign. They had to be Merlin's. They had no home in her and experiencing them stung. The new memory shimmered into focus, and Vera saw Guinevere from Merlin's perspective.

Something of Merlin's context mystically transferred to Vera, and she knew she was watching Guinevere and Arthur's first meeting. She radiated nervous joy as she curtsied in front of him. There was her father not two steps behind Guinevere, severe even as he smiled, looking on as she passed Arthur a gift. She couldn't tell what the gift was from her vantage point—from Merlin's vantage point, she corrected herself. Guinevere and Arthur shifted, and Vera couldn't see her face well, only his. Beaming, he passed the gift straight to Lancelot and took both of Guinevere's hands in his. He kissed the top of one.

Merlin's emotions flooded Vera in full force. Relief and joy. Guinevere and Arthur—the hope for the kingdom.

It wasn't so bad now that she was used to this memory. Merlin maneuvered the whole of it to nestle against the one of Vincent. They fit nicely there together. A bit of what Vera felt that first day for Vincent leaked into the new memory, spilling over and recoloring her affection for Arthur.

Then, there were emotions that weren't Merlin's nor Vera's own, but they, too, came crashing into her mind. It was Merlin's understanding of what Guinevere felt: affection and attraction. He inserted it with the rest, making one misshapen package. That part hurt a little more. Vera gripped the arms of her seat and exhaled a stiff, shaking breath. The lumpy memory settled in with the rest, and Merlin backed away from it. She unclenched her muscles as the pain eased.

They were on the move again in Vera's memories, shuttling past them in a blur. They flashed by as the scenes with Lancelot had: Vincent's fingers on hers under the table at a bar—this one from right before they officially started dating, dancing at Vincent's sister's wedding, and finally one of her last memories of him. Merlin stopped.

Vera and Vincent lay in their bed in Bristol. His hand traced swirls across her bare stomach in a way that made her back arch, half tickled, half stirred into a gleeful lust. It was too intimate. She didn't want to remember this, and she sure as hell didn't want anyone else seeing it. And Vera couldn't forget that this was her last night with Vincent before he died—just last June. Barely half a year ago. She'd deliberately not thought of this, and while she could savor its goodness forever, it was tainted by the story's ending.

She tried to put it away the way she had with the sacred grove, but Merlin was laser-focused as if he'd been looking for it, and it didn't budge.

In the memory, she rolled into Vincent, and he buried his face into her neck. "I can't believe I get to love you," he'd murmured, raising goosebumps that raced over her skin.

She'd laughed. She'd gazed into his warm brown eyes, rich with earnestness and delight, and before she could say a word, his lips were on hers in no need of any verbal reply. The way Vera's hips curved into him, the depth of her kiss, and the joy that emanated from her movements were enough.

A tear squeezed past her closed eyelid and rolled down her cheek in the murky pit of the world outside Vera's mind. Merlin mercifully set the memory aside, present but no longer the focus.

Darkness fell before the sting of a new incision scorched through. Light shone in, unwelcome. The image shimmered like before and sharpened into focus. Guinevere and Arthur again, but it was wrong. Immediately, she could sense it was wrong. It was a private moment.

They stood atop the castle wall where Vera had only ever seen guards. She'd never thought to try to access it, but she saw it all through Merlin's eyes from where he stood, concealed in the nearest guard tower. Vera could feel his guilt at watching them in secret.

Guinevere's arms were spread wide along the wall's stone rail, her head bowed between them. Her hair hung loose and tangled. She was in an off-white shift dress, the kind Vera had been wearing as a nightgown. Arthur stood next to her. He reached a hesitant hand to her shoulder, and she yanked away at his touch.

Vera gasped at her expression: that of a cornered animal, knowing it's finished. There wasn't any fight in it. Arthur approached her accordingly, his hands out before him with his palms up.

"Please," he said, reaching out toward her but not closing the last six inches between them. "Please, let me help you."

It was Guinevere, her shoulders falling, who grabbed his hand like it was a life raft and pulled into him, stiff against his chest. Arthur closed his arms around her. He held her until she leaned back from him, the wild look replaced with something Merlin saw as being calmed but that Vera recognized more intimately as resignation.

Her stomach churned as Guinevere hooked her hand behind

Arthur's neck and kissed him, desperation in her taut limbs. She grabbed the front of his shirt and pulled for dear life. He yielded to the tug, sinking into her kiss as he stumbled forward.

Merlin's relief came in a flood. He believed it was a show of love. He saw devotion. He inserted his interpretation of Guinevere's feelings—love, gratitude, and yearning. But this woman who was so identical to Vera felt like she was a sister Vera had never met, and Vera knew better. It was wrong for Arthur, too. His eyes flickered open, and they were wrought with worry, not love. Not even arousal.

What Vera experienced in her body wasn't pain at first. Discomfort, certainly. Nausea, absolutely. It wasn't so bad, and if it worked to bring Guinevere's memories in union with her mind, it would all be worth it.

It hit like a boulder dropped on her head from above; sudden, unexpected, and with blinding pain. It set fire to Vera's lungs—every bit of her skin hurt. There wasn't a place on her body that wasn't in burning torment: eyes, scalp, even her tongue.

Then she understood why. Merlin was trying to combine this memory with the tender one of Vincent. He pressed them together as he'd done with the other. Maybe it was because the emotions of it weren't even close to being genuinely parallel or because there was so much pain in both memories. It was agony beyond anything Vera had ever known. This was what torture felt like.

It only got worse. The memory wouldn't stick. Merlin pushed harder.

"Stop!" she screamed, barely able to find the breath for it.

He paused but didn't release her. Merlin maneuvered his memory around hers, prowling the edges and searching for a way in.

"We're so close," he mumbled.

He pushed, and Vera whimpered. "Stop, stop, stop," she said frantically, expecting him to pull away as her tears flowed. He'd promised he would stop.

He began pulling the memory back. "Almost there," he said.

Vera realized too late that Merlin was only moving back to build momentum. The calm lasted two breaths before the foreign memory came hurtling toward her own, and there was nothing she could do to stop it. It smashed into Vera's memory with such force that she screamed in a way she hadn't done since she was a child, with all the power she could muster from her aching lungs. The new memory shoved so violently against the old one that she thought she would shatter from the pressure. There couldn't be a pain worse than this. In the midst of that unrelenting anguish, she would have been relieved to die.

But her chest continued to rise and fall. She tried to moan, but there was no air in her. Merlin relentlessly shoved against her memory.

And then it happened.

She didn't shatter, but the memory of Vincent did. The shards of it exploded and impaled her mind in all directions.

Vera gasped in one agonizing lungful of air and shouted with all the force of her body a snarling "No!" as she snapped her eyes open. She heard a thud and clatter on the floor behind her. She hadn't realized that she'd sprung to her feet in the same motion, freed from Merlin's grasp. She spun to find him on his back on the floor behind her, uninjured and rising to his elbows. She took ragged, furious, horrified breaths and glared at him.

The implications of her shattered memory seeped into her. She knew what it was, knew she'd been in her bed with Vincent. She could remember his name, but the memory itself—the image, the details, the feelings—they were all rapidly fading like a dream that slipped away on waking. Water already down the drain.

Most horrifying, Vincent's face was gone. Just gone. His image had been erased not only from this memory but from all of her memories. She knew who he was; she could even describe his features, but it was a poor rendition, a sketch an artist makes after a frantic witness describes the assailant. It was not him.

"Did you know?" Vera snarled. "Did you know what it would do to my memory?"

She hoped he'd say no. She silently begged him to, but he only stared at her. It was as good as a confession.

"Oh my God," she breathed, her hands flinging to her head, gripping her hair. She'd never asked him if the procedure was safe. Never thought to ask if there'd be loss. "You're a fucking psychopath!"

When Vera wheeled on him, he was rising to his feet and had the nerve to act disappointed. "I thought you understood how dire our situation—"

"I do! But all I had left of him was memory—" Her traitorous voice broke, and Vera clenched her teeth to steady her breath. "He was the only one outside of my parents who could slip through this fucking curse and know me." She'd never wanted to hit someone so badly, yet her whole body quaked. Her fury took all her energy. She had to drop one hand to the top of the desk to steady herself. "What happened to stopping if I said stop?"

"It needed to work," Merlin said without apology. "I didn't want you to have to do that again."

"Oh, I'm not doing it again. You want Arthur to connect with me? Fuck with his brain. I'm done." Vera stormed to the door, feeling emptier than ever.

"Guinevere—"

Vera turned to glare at him from the doorway. "I thought being brought back to bear a child would have been the worst thing you could have done to me. But you gave me a whole goddamn life to fatten me up with parents who loved me and with Vincent, who—" She stopped and swallowed heavily. "And for what? So I'd have more to sacrifice in exchange for Guinevere's memories?"

Merlin stared at her in silent sorrow.

"You should have let Viviane kill me." Vera slammed the door behind her and did not look back.

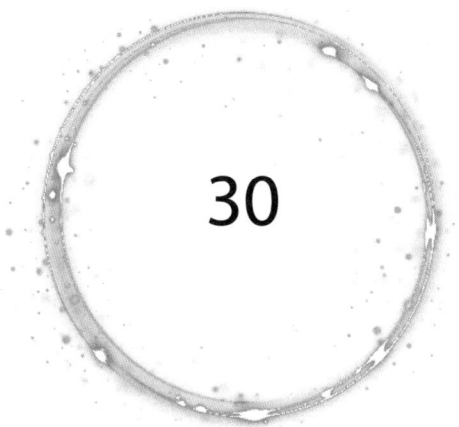

30

Vera didn't realize how long she'd been in Merlin's study until she emerged from the cellar expecting daylight and finding it was dusk. The sounds of dinner from the great hall drifted to her on the breeze. She hoped it meant she wouldn't run into anyone on her way to her room, but luck was against her. She'd been staring at the ground and looked up barely in time to avoid running head-on into Thomas. She stumbled backward and would have fallen if he'd not caught her at the elbow.

"I'm sorry," she said. Her vision swam as she tried to focus on him and pretend to be fine.

It didn't work. "What's happened, Your Majesty?" His voice pitched up with concern. "You look unwell."

She wished he'd let go of her arm. She tried to pull away, but he held fast. It was probably keeping her upright, though.

"You're near to swooning," Thomas said. She was close to passing out, but the way he said it added a flare to her anger. "I'll get the king."

"No, please don't—"

"You need your husband," he insisted.

"I don't," Vera said through gritted teeth.

"I—I can help you, my queen." Thomas's fingers dug painfully into her arm, and Vera wrenched away from his grasp.

"Don't fucking touch me," she snarled.

He recoiled, looking at her like she was a stranger. His mouth opened and closed like a fish before he swallowed heavily and took a hesitant step aside, allowing Vera to pass.

The pain and exhaustion only continued to mount as the initial shock faded. She was in such physical agony that she barely made it to her room, collapsing to the floor after she closed the door behind her. Vera had no idea if she stayed there minutes or hours before she realized she was drenched in sweat and crawled the length of her chamber to her window. Somehow, she fumbled the shutter open so she could lean her cheek against the cold dowels and let the evening wind lash at her face. For a while, she closed her eyes and tried to sleep sitting there by the window, but all she could see were Guinevere's hands clawing at Arthur's shirt, and all she felt was the void of the destroyed memory. The one truly born in love, replaced by fear and desperation.

She remembered every second of her time in Merlin's study and felt like she would melt into nothing. It was too much. She leaned her full body weight against the window's bars, eyes open and unfocused. It would have been all right if the bars didn't hold, and she fell. She knew she wouldn't feel that way in the morning, but the pain of right now ravaged her.

When the door opened, Vera didn't notice. The sound of conversation between friends, so out of place, brought her vision back into focus. She turned in time to watch the light dying in Arthur's eyes as they locked on her. Matilda was with him, and her face fell next.

He stepped toward Vera and stopped, looking helplessly at Matilda. She nodded and set right into action.

"Let's get you to bed," she said. It was a different tone than Vera had grown used to, the one quick to a smile or a joke. She spoke with the purpose of someone who'd dealt with such a crisis before.

"I'm fine," Vera mumbled.

"Yes, well, all the same." Matilda took her hand with a frightened smile. Vera allowed Matilda to help her down and to the bed without objection, if nothing else, because it seemed to make her friend feel better.

"I've got her," Matilda said over her shoulder. Vera turned her head, but it was more of a lolling roll of her neck. She didn't quite have control over her body.

Arthur stood there, fists clenched at his sides, frozen between staying or going. He met Vera's eyes and took one shaking breath before he turned and left, not to the side door but back into the corridor. She didn't bother to guess where he went from there. She couldn't focus. It still felt like shards were stabbing all through her brain.

As Matilda helped her change into her nightgown, her hand brushed Vera's face. She gasped. "You're burning up!"

Vera noticed a cold rag on her forehead as she drifted into unrestful oblivion.

She woke from what must have been a dozen nightmares before the sun rose, skin stinging like she had a sunburn, sick like she was hungover, but her mind was clearer, and she had an unbearable urge to move. She didn't even care if Lancelot showed up today. They hadn't confirmed their run, but Vera would go on her own if needed.

When she opened the door, she nearly tripped over him. Lancelot sat right outside her room, on the floor with his knees up.

"Hey," he breathed with a mix of relief and worry. Vera wondered what medieval greeting was translating via magic to "hey" even as a twinge of annoyance rang through her at his concern.

"Ready?" she said stiffly.

She didn't wait for an answer. She started toward the stairs and let him scramble to catch up. His eyes flitted to her every few steps. Vera ignored them.

"Is everything—"

"I don't want to talk. I just want to run," she said, even more frustrated because her voice shook, the words sounding like a plea.

Lancelot pressed his lips together. "All right. You set the pace. I'll follow."

It was the coldest winter day yet, but Vera was on fire. She ran harder than usual. They'd barely set out, and her shirt was drenched in sweat. She stopped at the clearing where they usually chatted after their runs, yanked her shirt over her head, and tossed it over a low tree branch.

Now clad in her sports bra and running trousers, Vera turned on

Lancelot, daring him to say a word—to laugh or make a joke, but he didn't. His even gaze met hers unflinchingly. "Better?" he asked.

She nodded bitterly, and they set off. Vera inwardly raged for the first few miles. Arthur must have run to tell Lancelot about the previous evening. Why else would he have been sitting there at her door, all fraught with worry? All along, Lancelot had known things about her life and kept them from her. Come to think of it, he'd probably been telling Arthur what she shared during their runs, too. The resentment pushed her pace.

She huffed angrily, wanting Lancelot to say anything so that she could have a reason to yell at him. He stayed silent, dutifully pounding the same pace as her, right at her side. As the miles wore on, endorphins began to dissolve Vera's wrath. The fog of her brain lifted enough for her to realize that being angry at Lancelot was simply easier than facing the potion-sharpened experience of the day before.

She called out a peace offering in the last kilometer before their clearing. "Lancelot?"

"Yes?"

"Tree root," she said, pointing down the trail.

His face broke into a half smile, and Vera gave a winded huff of a laugh. "There you are," he said with relief.

They came to the clearing and flopped down on the ground. Vera sat closer to him than she would on most days. When she lay on her back, he followed her lead and lay next to her. The sun rose so late in the morning now that it stayed dark their whole time together. Mostly, it was an inky blanket of clouds above them, with brief glimpses of a star twinkling through the gaps. After a stretch of silence, Lancelot spoke.

"I can't believe you aren't freezing."

She'd forgotten that she wasn't wearing a shirt. Her sweat had barely dried, and the air had only just started to feel cool. "I think I might have had a fever."

"Gods, Guinna. If that's how fast you run with a fever—" He stopped speaking abruptly, his face contorting with pain as his hands snapped to his calf. "Oh fuck, that hurts."

Vera sat up on her elbows, eyebrows raised. "Cramp?" she asked, totally unnecessarily. His calf muscle was visibly seizing into a tight ball under his skin.

He nodded, eyes clenched shut.

"Here." She rolled onto her side and pressed her thumb firmly on the knot. "You need more potassium."

"What the hell is that?" He strained to say through his writhing.

"It's a nutrient in bananas and potatoes—of course, neither of which you have yet," Vera said with a chuckle as she massaged the knot.

Lancelot moaned his pleasure as his muscle released under the pressure of Vera's thumb, only making her laugh harder. "It's a good thing there's no one around or—"

The leaves over Vera's shoulder rustled. She and Lancelot froze. They listened as something crashed through the trees, retreating away from them.

He was on his feet in a heartbeat. "Is someone there?" he shouted. The only answer was the whisper of the breeze, distinctly different from the other sound they'd heard. "Shit." Lancelot palmed his orb, considering it briefly before he heaved it in the direction of the sound. It hung above the undergrowth, alighting a bubble of space around it. "If that were a person, we'd probably be able to see them running off."

"Probably," Vera said, more a wish than an agreement. She hadn't moved from her place on the ground.

He nodded as he seemed to make a decision. "It must have been an animal—no doubt thinking my pathetic cramp noises were a dying rodent for an easy breakfast." Still, Lancelot grabbed Vera's shirt from the tree branch and tossed it over to her as he kept his eye on the light in the distance. He stretched his palm to the sky, and the orb zoomed back to him. Neither said aloud what else the noises might have sounded like to someone passing by.

Lancelot sighed, one hand on his hip and the other worrying at his brow. "We need to be more careful."

"Ugh. That's exactly what Merlin said." A flare of annoyance shot through Vera as she hastily pulled her shirt over her head.

"Why would Merlin say that?"

"It's nothing," she said quickly.

"No, it's not." He crossed his arms and frowned. "I'd say that's rather something. Since it involves me, I think I have a right to know."

Vera had a lot to say about everything she felt she had a right to know. Her raised eyebrows said as much, but she held her tongue. "Just all this time together between only the two of us . . . like Percival said and—and you did sort of look at me all swoony-eyed when I taught you tic-tac-toe." She tried to keep her voice playful, though she realized her error almost as soon as she'd said it.

Lancelot cocked his head to the side, the smile gone from his eyes. "Merlin wasn't there for that. Did you tell him?"

"I—well—"

"Because if you didn't, I'm not sure who did."

"No, I—"

"Then who did?" He wasn't giving her time to think.

"No one! He saw it when—" The mental fog from earlier was creeping back in. "I sort of showed him. I didn't mean to."

"All right." His eyes softened as he watched her struggle through it. He sat back down and patted the ground next to him. "Out with it, you."

Vera sank to the dirt beside him. She told him nearly everything: that she knew about Guinevere's betrayal with Viviane, her desperation to get her memory back, the potions, and the horrid procedure Merlin had tried. That he'd seen how close Vera and Lancelot had grown. She hesitated when she got to Vincent's part, but only for a second, making a gut decision to trust him with the whole story. He'd laid his free hand on her knee, drawing closer to her in the deepening of her hurt. When she told him how painful Merlin's procedure had been and how her body burned from it even now, he went rigid, his face darkening, especially as she relayed how her memory had shattered.

"So, if I seem broken, it might be that my mind stabbed itself in a thousand places. My brain could be actively bleeding for all I know." It was a feeble attempt at a joke.

"That was an awful thing he did to you." Lancelot rolled his jaw back and forth and stared at his feet. "Did you tell Arthur?"

Vera barked a cold laugh. "No. Last night, I couldn't even string a damn sentence together."

"He'd want to know. You have to tell him, Guinna."

"Did you not hear me about the 'betraying everything he stands for' bit?" she said, her spark of anger reigniting. "And the potion he had to have just to be able to be near me?"

Lancelot had the gall to look exasperated. "Come off it. I don't believe for a second that he drank that potion. And we all know what Guinevere did is not what you did." Vera started to protest, and Lancelot raised his voice. "Stop! You have to actually try to talk to him."

"Are you fucking kidding me? I have tried. I do try."

"No, you don't. You get weird and quiet. Why don't you talk to him like this? Why haven't you told him what an ass he's been? You're half a room away from him every night, and you've never railed at him like you would at me. What'd you say to him when you found out about that potion, hm? Did you tell him off or just bolt out of there?"

Vera scoffed but said nothing.

"That's not trying."

Her jaw hung slack. "I can't believe you're blaming me for this."

"You don't understand what he's been through—"

"You're right! I don't. That's the problem. You both know all these secrets about me and my life that I'm not entitled to. Fuck you. You deal with it."

She got up to leave, stumbling a few steps from the exhaustion of having pushed their run so hard. Vera heard Lancelot scrambling to stand and help her before she whirled on him.

"Don't," she said. She was confident he caught all her meanings with the one word. Don't touch me. Don't help me. Don't follow me.

She stormed back to the castle alone.

Losing Vincent's face was like having him die all over again. The shattering of that memory brought the day he died into sharper focus. It had been the worst day of Vera's life. And it would remain as such for some time to come.

But this day—the day that had barely begun, the sun coyly waiting to kiss the horizon with her warmth, would bring its own darkness.

Thus began the second worst day of Vera's life so far.

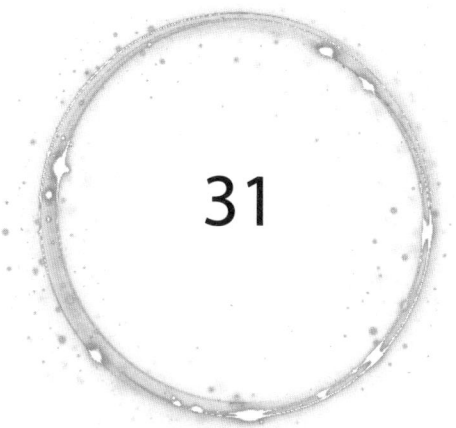

31

As the haze and stirring sick of the day before waned, Vera felt Merlin's magic at work. When her thoughts drifted to Arthur, albeit frazzled and nonsensical, she found an unwelcome sense of intimate fondness. This tug toward him had a pleasant aura tinged with the poison of its origin. It felt the way a funeral parlor smelled; overly sweet in an attempt to mask the odor of unstoppable decay.

Vera could begrudgingly acknowledge that Lancelot was right—Arthur had to know. And damn Lancelot. She would rage into Arthur's part of the chamber and shout him awake from his bed. She would do it.

But he wasn't there.

Vera looked for him all day, but her hours were far more occupied than usual. It was Christmas Eve. There was plenty to do to ready the castle for the evening's banquet guests. She thought she'd have time to search for him in earnest once she finished her tasks, but it was straight back to her chamber to get dressed in her green gown and moonstone circlet and then to the great hall without delay.

The hall was friendlier than usual. There was no table atop the dais. Instead, the space was occupied by a band of musicians playing lively background music. Hanging orb lights zigzagged from one side of the vaulted ceiling to the other. Guests milled about on the balcony, sipping from their goblets as they whispered about the growing crowd below.

Under different circumstances, Vera would have loved this, but her cursed fever burned on, as did her focus on finding Arthur.

She saw him across the hall, and her breath caught. He'd replaced his usual and much more casual attire with slim-fitting leather armor, dark like burned charcoal from shoulders to toes except for the cape of deep red clasped at his collarbone, the shine of his sword's hilt at his waist, and the simple crown of gold on his head. His hair was pulled into a tight knot at the nape of his neck.

He hadn't dressed this formally since Vera's arrival, yet it was as natural on him as anything and was very striking. His gaze met Vera's before he quickly turned away to greet a guest. A sudden flutter had thrummed in her chest. She felt the urge to cup her hand against his cheek. The thought of his skin against hers sent the warmth of desire spreading through her. With a start, she realized the feeling matched what had belonged to the memory that was gone ... that her dormant, tucked-away passion for the love she'd lost was now assigned to Arthur.

Something in what happened yesterday had threaded a cord from her destroyed memory of Vincent straight to Arthur. Even after the memory's disintegration, its emotions remained intact, questing out and latching on to the next face that came along. With the potion and ... everything else, Arthur was already the prime target. How could she feel furiously attracted to him and also want to scream wrath in his face and weep for days?

His conversation bore the marks of ending: nods and subtle leaning away from one another. If Vera didn't move now, she might lose her nerve. She plastered on the most relaxed smile she could muster.

Feigning confidence, Vera came to his side. Had his body stiffened at her arrival, even as his voice remained steady? She decided she'd imagined it and touched his arm. Arthur pulled away from her. No, he violently yanked his arm from her grasp like her touch burned him. Right in front of the nobleman, who was a stranger to Vera—and who absolutely noticed and shifted uncomfortably.

Vera did not try to hold her face pleasantly. She stared at Arthur with open ire. Fuck you fuck you fuck you, she said in her head and hoped he could feel it despite his refusal to look in her direction.

The Once and Future Queen

Her cheeks burned as she spotted others nearby whose eyes had widened and were whispering behind their hands. The hush swelled out from her and Arthur, the event's epicenter. One face in the crowd didn't match the discomfort of all the rest. She savagely glowered at Lancelot, straight ahead of her. His features churned with guilt. She tipped her shoulders up, her glaring shrug a question and a taunt. *See? What would you have me do?*

He had the decency to cast his eyes to the floor.

Fine. They could all have the satisfaction of believing Vera was the bane of the kingdom. It wasn't entirely untrue anyway. She turned without another word, snatched a goblet of wine from a passing server's tray, and sank into a chair right by the side door where the staff came in and out, as out of the way as she could be. She would not speak to anyone nor try to play the role of the good queen.

Vera saw Merlin from the corner of her eye. She deliberately avoided his gaze, but he was coming right toward her.

She loathed that she trembled at the prospect of talking to him. Lancelot, for his part, clocked Merlin's intent and cut him off at the pass, diverting him to a group of visitors eager for his attention. Vera was far too angry to acknowledge her gratitude for this kindness.

Arthur was back to greeting guests with his quick smile and easy laugh, as if he didn't have a care in the world. It pushed Vera near her boiling point, which seemed far more literal than she preferred as she still felt about a million degrees. She slouched in her seat and kept her head down.

"You don't have to do this."

Vera jumped. She wasn't sure how long Matilda had been standing at her shoulder. The ever-lovely woman bent at the waist so her face was near Vera's ear as she slid a bag onto her lap. Vera's embroidery supplies. She'd forgotten all about them after the nightmarish afternoon in Merlin's study.

"Do you want to slip away?" Matilda said. "I'll cover for you."

Vera clasped her friend's hand. "Thank you." Bless her, the only one among the lot who she didn't currently want to throttle. "If you see Arthur, tell him I've gone to bed."

Matilda's eyebrow quirked up.

"I don't want him to follow me. I mean it."

Matilda looked like she wanted to argue, but she nodded instead. She scooted in front of the table, giving Vera a discreet escape out the door behind her. A huddle of guests surrounded Merlin, enthralled by whatever stories of magic he told, but neither Arthur nor Lancelot was anywhere to be seen. Good.

The wintry wind in the courtyard was a sharp contrast to the oppressive heat in the great hall. It, and having escaped the banquet, lifted Vera's spirit some straightaway. She'd made it to the entry hall and was striding from the grand doors to cross the front courtyard to the chapel when her steps faltered at the sound of raised voices echoing from the corridor to her right.

She hesitated near the main doors, hoping to get a clearer idea of if the voices were coming toward her. It didn't matter, really. She should go on and hurry outside. Whoever it was would never know she'd been there. But she found her feet moving away from the entry and toward the other door, the one to the corridor.

They were distant enough that the sound didn't have enough shape to form coherent words. Vera crept closer as the voices picked up again, a sense of familiarity lifting goosebumps along her arms. She thought it might be Arthur—and words or no, it was clear from the volume and the clipped cadence of his speaking that he was angry. The door to the corridor was already open enough to slip through, and . . . yes, there was a nook in the hallway there that she could tuck into and keep unseen, as long as they didn't pass by her.

Vera weighed the risk, standing on the precipice, but chance decided for her. She saw the shadow halfway down the corridor, the warning alarm that Arthur and whoever was with him were about to come into view. Vera ducked into the nook. While the castle's main thoroughfares were well-lit, this corridor had only one torch lit over the whole length of it. No one was meant to be here.

Two sets of footsteps were coming Vera's way, and fast.

"I'm not doing this," Arthur said sharply.

The footsteps stopped, overtaken by scuffling. It sounded like something slammed against the wall. Vera leaned far enough forward to see and nearly stumbled from her hiding place as she saw that the slam had been Arthur's back as Lancelot shoved him. Lancelot held him pinned to the wall with his arm braced across Arthur's chest.

"You don't get to walk away from me!" Lancelot's shout ripped through the corridor. Vera would have cowered if he'd ever spoken to her that way. "You're so goddamn wrong. Do you know how long it took for me to know? One conversation with her the very first night in Glastonbury. That's it."

Vera covered her mouth to stifle her gasp. He was talking about her. He had shoved his friend, his king, and shouted at him in defense of her.

Arthur halfheartedly pushed Lancelot's arm away from him. "I am poison to her," he said.

"Oh, bullshit!" Lancelot threw his hands in the air. Vera had never seen him so angry. She thought he might punch Arthur as he wheeled on him. "Bullshit! You aren't protecting her. This isn't noble. What you're doing now—this is poison. Carry on like this, and we will lose her again. And this time," he added, his finger shaking as he pointed it at Arthur. "It will be your fault. You'll never forgive yourself." His last words were as good as a scathing slap. The two men stared at one another in fuming silence. Lancelot shook his head. "I'll never forgive you either." He turned and strode back in the direction he'd come from.

Vera had never had a best friend before and hadn't realized until she saw that look in Lancelot's eye that she had one now.

She backed into the nook and waited for the sound of Arthur's retreat but heard nothing. She began to wonder if he'd left, and somehow, she hadn't noticed. Vera peeked around the corner of her hiding spot as an exhaled whisper of "Fuck," echoed through the hall. With the word, he was in motion, pacing back and forth, his hands on his head. Vera held her breath when he stopped.

"Fuck!" Arthur roared it so loudly that Vera started. He stood motionless enough that the darkness seemed to swallow him until he, too, followed where Lancelot had gone.

Vera's anger at Lancelot melted away, and—Arthur? Well, she didn't know what to make of that.

She hurried to the chapel where her stitching was a balm, though she didn't sing or hum this evening and kept the lights dim. She was continually staggered by how comforted she was by the statue of Mary. Vera sat with her back against the wall, and her right shoulder leaned against the pedestal beneath the statue. She fished out her embroidery, a butterfly this time, and set in on a large wing section with bright blue thread. Vera must have been at it for some time because she'd made good progress when the main door to the chapel opened, jolting her from admiring her piece.

He was a silhouette against the night until he stepped into the room and pulled the door closed behind him.

"Thomas," Vera said, recognizing him quickly and relieved at first that it was a familiar face before something nagged at her. She'd run into him yesterday, hadn't she? While she was damn near out of her mind. What had she said to him? It hadn't been friendly.

Evidently, he wasn't angry because he spoke to her warmly. "I hoped you'd be here," he said as he leaned against the door behind him and closed his eyes.

"I'm sorry if I was harsh yesterday," Vera said, setting her embroidery in her lap. "I was unwell."

Thomas walked toward her, and Vera felt a tug of guttural warning. She couldn't identify right away what set it off, but as he drew near, his step hitched on its momentum, and he stumbled.

Vera stiffened as he sat beside her, a touch too close for comfort.

He leaned his head against the wall, chin raised, and eyes closed. "It might be fate—you being here right now."

Vera smelled the unmistakable stench of drink on his breath, and when his eyes lolled open, she saw the signs of it there, too. His pupils were too large. Staring into their unnatural darkness brought the sinking realization that what Vera took for warmth at a distance was more accurately inebriation. She pursed her lips, considering her options of what she could say or do, of how she could leave without causing a fuss. How many times had she been alone with Thomas? He'd never done anything untoward. It reassured the now screaming alarm within her. She was safe here.

"The festivities have interfered some with my chapel visits, but I'm not so sure about fate," she said as she resumed her stitching. She leaned away from him against the holy mother's pedestal. "I'm here many evenings." Vera's hands were shaking. She hoped he wouldn't notice the embroidery hoop shuddering.

"Not the mornings, though," Thomas said.

There was accusation in his tone. She trained her eyes on the quivering, partly formed butterfly in her hands and forced her hands to keep moving, for the needle to pierce the fabric. She had to grab at it twice before her fingers successfully pinched around it and was midway through her next shaking stitch when his voice bit into her.

"I saw you," he said. Vera's eyes flicked upward to meet his. "I saw you and Sir Lancelot together this morning."

Her breath stopped. He couldn't have. He couldn't have. It had been an animal.

"I saw you," Thomas's voice was eerily sing-songy, "and I heard you."

Vera shook her head quickly back and forth, the tiny negation was all she could manage. She instinctively knew she'd never been in more peril than she was right now.

"Thomas, that wasn't what you think, it—"

"I believed you were different. Loyal. But even those chosen by the Lord may fall to evil ways," he said as if she hadn't spoken. "I thought you were a gentle lady and I the lustful sinner."

Vera squeezed her embroidery more tightly. She couldn't believe what she was hearing.

"But I see it now," Thomas said. "Your temptations are ceaseless. You must be stopped."

The needle slipped and stabbed into her palm, lodging in her skin like an arrow buried in its target. She yelped as she wrenched her hand free from its point. A thick, shining drop of blood bloomed there and dropped from her palm onto a yet-white spot on her butterfly's wing, a steady trickle following behind it.

Thomas grabbed Vera's hand with both of his, and the startling swiftness of his movement froze her. His ravenous eyes fixed on the eruption of blood from her wound. Then he wrenched her hand to his mouth and sucked the blood off her palm.

Vera hadn't made any choice to act before she was in motion. Leveraging her free hand on the pedestal next to her, she pushed herself to her feet, intending to pull free from his grasp and run like hell, but Thomas's firm grip stayed her. He yanked her back with such startling force that the next thing she knew, she was face-down on the floor on Thomas's other side.

His breath was on her neck in a second. Vera pressed her hands beneath her and bucked her head and shoulders backward at him. He fell into the statue's pedestal. Vera heard the wobbling of the great stone and the crash that followed, knowing that the beautiful statue had shattered on the floor.

It did little to stop Thomas. Vera tried to scramble to her feet as he caught her ankle and pulled her back to the ground. This time, he flipped her over onto her back, held her shoulders down with his hands, and quieted her writhing legs by straddling her hips.

Every instinct in Vera's body told her to fight, and she did—like mad. With all the strength in her, she flailed against his hold. She wriggled and writhed; she snapped her teeth at his hands and even managed to free one hand and jab at his eye before he forced it back down. Thomas released both of her shoulders, and Vera thought she might have a chance. She thought he was giving up or coming to his senses, but he wasn't. He grabbed her head with both hands, picked it up, and slammed it against the floor.

Vera's eyes were open, but all she saw in front of her were stars. Her ears rang, and she moaned in pain. The seconds that it dazed her and shunted her movements were precious time when she couldn't afford to be incapacitated. When her vision cleared, she saw a short-bladed knife in Thomas's hand, not four inches long. He'd stopped straddling her, pulling both legs to one side, and he slashed a slit in Vera's dress from the waist down, revealing the top of her leg.

This was her opportunity. He wasn't on top of her. Vera's mind told her body to move, and her panic only rose as she found it wouldn't respond, addled from the blow to her head. Thomas was unrecognizable, his face now the contorted likes of a monster unparalleled to any horror Vera had ever seen close up, pupils consuming the entirety of his eyes. He hungrily brought the knife to her thigh, high on her leg on the outside. He relished in pressing it to her skin, so agonizingly slowly. She screamed out as it pierced her flesh, as he exercised such restraint in pushing it in, millimeter by millimeter, devastatingly slow until the hilt kissed her skin. This wasn't happening. This couldn't be happening.

Tears streamed down Vera's face. She didn't know when she'd begun to beg him to stop, but now all she heard were her own frenzied cries of "Please!" over and over.

He pulled the knife out at the same measured pace he'd shoved it in. Vera barely had time to regain her breath before Thomas raised his thumb and pressed it forcefully to the wound, smearing the blood and raising fresh screams from her. They were endless. Vera ceased being able to distinguish the sounds emerging from her mouth between "please" and "stop" and wordless cries of agony. She'd never felt this sort of pain in all her life.

She found new words when he released his thumb from her thigh, slick with her blood.

"Help! Please, help!" She screamed these loudly, praying that anyone might be passing near enough to hear.

Thomas leaned the weight of his body on top of hers. Vera shuddered, remembering that this man had once reminded her of her father. "I locked the door. No one is anywhere near here. Not tonight." His mouth was so close to Vera's ear that she could feel the heat of his breath on her skin.

"Why are you doing this?" Vera wailed through her sobs.

He didn't answer. He dragged the knife's edge up her bodice and across her breast as if spreading butter over bread, pressing hard enough to pick up bits of green fuzz from her dress as he scraped it to her shoulder, where he stopped, a fresh gleam of malice in his eye. Vera forced herself to face him, allowing all her fear to show, hoping against hope that it would help him see a person and not the temptress he'd conjured in his mind.

"Please, don't," she cried. It was the only play Vera had at the moment, and it was the wrong one.

Thomas smirked without mercy. He relished her terror. Again, he tipped the knife's hilt upward and pressed its point against her skin. He stabbed her shoulder to the hilt with the same tormenting pace as before.

Vera wished she would pass out, that the pain would end, but he seemed to be aiming to puncture her body carefully, causing as much agony as he could without rendering her unconscious. When he pulled the knife free and wiped it clean on her dress, she gathered her energy and surged against him. It was to no avail. He had too much of an advantage of size and position.

Thomas threw his leg back over her. He headbutted her against the stone floor to stop her flailing and screaming. The second blow to her head was enough. She wasn't entirely conscious anymore. Thomas pressed the knife to her throat with one hand and held both her hands pinned to the ground above her head with the other.

"Don't thrash about, or I might just slip," he said with startling calm as he slashed a tiny cut under Vera's chin as if to show her. She groaned and felt a pool forming beneath the back of her head. Some rational part of her mind wondered if it was blood.

She only half realized in her dazed stupor that he'd shifted, that her hands weren't pinned to the floor. He'd released them, instead groping down her body, grabbing her breast, and then toying at the top of her thigh. The knife was also gone from her throat. With that hand, he fumbled at the fastenings of his pants. He meant to take every morsel of her being.

Vera whimpered. As the sound left her lips, the last of her resolve to fight slipped away with it. She wasn't a brilliant strategist queen. She was nobody. And she had failed at the one purpose of her existence. She couldn't even be a vessel for Guinevere's memory. What did any of it matter? She went still. Her flood of pleas trickled to silence.

Vera was going to die here.

You are more than a vessel.

She heard the words in her shattered mind as clearly as if someone had said them in her ear. A current, potent and electric, surged from Vera's core to her fingertips. Her free fingertips. Thomas continued to struggle with his trousers. Where moments ago, she'd been ready to surrender, now her instincts screamed at her to act.

Vera groped wildly around her head, searching for anything she could grab, and her fingers closed on something that easily fit in her palm. Her hair splayed across her face, blocking her view.

Distantly, she heard a shout from the front of the chapel as she swung her arm at Thomas and made contact.

It was all so quick. He wasn't on top of her anymore. Vera was free. She lifted her head a fraction, and her hair fell away from her eyes. Arthur stood above her, having bodily thrown Thomas off her. Thomas had tumbled backward over the destroyed statue and now clung to the lifeless stone, trying to heft himself back up. Arthur's sword was drawn, and the last vestige of rage hadn't yet fallen from his face as he stared at Thomas in shock.

What had been a monster beyond reckoning was now replaced by a terrified man, barely clinging to life. In his attempt to rise, Thomas only made it to his knees. His eyes were clear and filled with fright. He clutched at his throat as blood gushed in horrible voluminous squirts between his fingers.

Vera rolled over onto her knees and pushed herself up, transfixed, as Thomas's breaths grew shallower, and his eyes bulged while he gurgled. He opened his mouth, and blood dumped from it as freely as if from an upended bucket.

It was perhaps only seconds of this sputtering, gasping, and squelching that felt an eternity. They echoed through the chapel's pristine acoustics, a chorus that was the song of death. As the stretches of silence between his breath lengthened, the color drained from Thomas's face before he collapsed, wide-eyed and blood-drenched and completely still on top of the broken statue.

Vera's eyes flashed to Arthur's sword, shining and clean, reflecting brilliantly in the dim light. She looked down at what her hand had found in desperation: Thomas's small knife. The knife he'd wiped clean on her dress that was now freshly bathed in ruby-red blood.

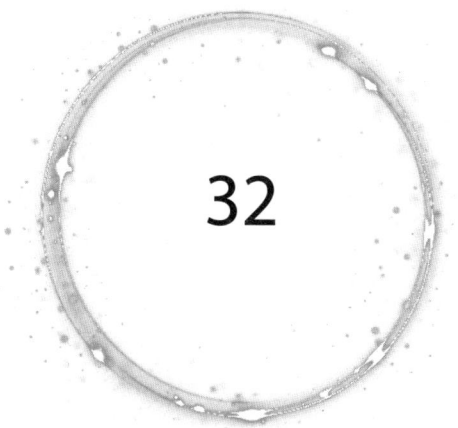

32

Vera stared at Thomas's body, not initially able to grasp that she now looked upon a corpse. His face was pressed against the statue's pregnant belly so that his cheek was mashed up next to his vacantly staring eyes, as lifeless as the stone beneath him. Blood trickled from a mouth hung slack.

As she waited for Thomas to draw a breath that would never come, her breathing accelerated. So fast, until it all lodged somewhere between mouth and lungs, useless air hanging in the void.

What the fuck just happened? And for Christ's sake, why?

Arthur's sword clattered to the floor as he knelt next to her. He lay a wary hand on her back. It was like Vera had forgotten how to use air. She gasped over and over, barely able to draw in a shallow sip. She hardly felt Arthur's second hand on her upper arm. Vera turned to him, trying to anchor herself in something breathing, something alive. His face was a blur, an abstract smudge against a backdrop of chaos.

"Guinevere." She thought he'd said her name. She couldn't be sure over a riotous ringing in her ears. When had that started?

Vera sat up, her panic rising with her. She'd survived Thomas. She'd killed Thomas, and now she could not breathe. Maybe his last blow to her head was killing her. What if she was bleeding as much as Thomas had, only all of hers was inside her head, causing her brain to swell and forget how to perform basic, life-sustaining tasks?

Vera felt Arthur behind her, his arm reaching under hers and across her torso as he helped her stand. She clutched his forearm to her chest, but she found right away that her legs couldn't hold her weight. Her knees buckled, and she fell back against him. Her attempts to draw in air grew louder and more frantic by the second.

"I—I can't breathe," she choked.

"You're safe. You're all right." Arthur's voice broke through her panic as he lowered with her to the floor. He leaned back against the wall, knees drawn up on either side of her as he held her to his chest.

"Breathe," he said, and as if to show her how, he took a deep breath, his chest rising against her back. She tried. She tried so desperately that her nails dug into his arm from the effort.

"I can't!" She managed to force the words from her.

"You can," he said as he continued his steady breaths. He spoke more quietly, right next to her ear. "You already are. Slow down. Come on, with me."

He took another deep breath, but Vera kept struggling. Darkness tugged at the corners of her vision. When Martin and Allison never heard from her again, she hoped they would assume she had found happiness. She prayed they'd never know what happened to her, couldn't bear the thought that—

"Breathe with me, Vera," Arthur said, his mouth a thumb's length from her ear.

Something snapped in place. The next time Arthur's chest rose, Vera's joined with it. One full breath of life to soothe her stinging lungs. Her exhale shuddered from her body. Soon, more of her breaths matched Arthur's rhythm than the discord of hyperventilation. Once she'd calmed to near quiet, Arthur let go of her.

She crawled forward on her hands and knees. Why, she did not know. Maybe the surge of grief and anger and confusion and relief was too much; she needed an island unto herself to release it. Her vision cleared, and the wreckage before her unearthed a guttural and inhuman scream, perhaps from her very soul. Vera curled into a ball on the floor and sobbed. The sounds she heard coming from her body were utterly foreign to her.

And then, she quieted.

"You're injured," she heard Arthur say. When Vera shifted to look up at him, the side of her head still against the nightmarishly wet stone floor, he was pulling his bloody fingertips away from the place on his shoulder where the back of her head had rested. He scooted along the floor next to her and tenderly touched the wound on her head. Although she didn't wince, he withdrew his hand quickly as if aware it hurt her.

"He stabbed me." Vera's voice sounded small in her ears.

Arthur shifted to cut off her view of the horrid corpse. He was so out of place here, despite his being the only body in the room dressed for battle. Vera and Thomas were the casualties of war, whereas Arthur's golden crown shone on his head. The smell of his pristine, unblemished leather armor was as good as potpourri amongst the rusty odor of blood and death.

"I need to get you to your room so we can dress your wounds," Arthur said.

"I can stand. I'd like to try to walk." She didn't want to be helpless, and he did not question her.

After the madness of what happened, she feared she'd find him awash with pity. But in his face, she found only the soldier. He was focused on what needed to be done next, on surviving the right now, and there was no room in his expression for extraneous things like pity. But it wasn't mechanical.

Arthur inadvertently pressed his fingers against the stab wound at her shoulder as he tried to help her stand, eliciting a pained cry from Vera. He pulled back, and she saw through the clenched squint of her eyes that his hands trembled. If she hadn't seen it, she wouldn't have known that he was afraid, too. Arthur rubbed the heels of his hands against his forehead as he took a slow breath before helping her to her feet with restored steadiness.

She leaned her uninjured shoulder into him, and he wrapped his arm around her waist. But Vera's good shoulder and leg were both on her left side, which made for poor hobbling. She didn't question Arthur as he led her away from the chapel's main doors and toward the altar. They turned left into an alcove, and there was a door there, different from the distinguished main entry, simple and small. A monk's door. She would have remarked on it another day. All that mattered now was that it got her out of here faster.

It led to a path right in the shadow of the castle wall. Arthur tried to quicken their pace once they were in the open air. Vera's breath hissed through her teeth as the pressure of every step pushed a fresh surge of blood from her thigh. Each footfall on her right side throbbed more than the last. Arthur stopped, casting a sidelong glance at her. She hadn't realized how much the wound was bleeding. The fabric of her dress was so soaked in blood that it was black. And the slit in her skirt that Thomas carved blew open to her waist in the night breeze. Her whole exposed leg down to the slipper on her foot was a scene from a horror movie.

"Can I carry you?" Arthur asked, his face tense with effort to keep his expression flat.

Vera nodded.

He bent to scoop his free arm beneath her knees. It was silly that she'd even tried to walk. The effort had only weakened her. Now, Vera was cradled in his arms, her blood soaking both of them, and his pace doubled. She tucked her chin, wedging her head in the crook of his neck. Despite the pain all through her body, despite her whole heart being wrecked at what she'd had to do to survive, despite now feeling on the edge of vomiting from the nausea of blood loss, a distracted satisfaction rumbled through Vera at being held by him, curled against his chest. She sobbed anew at it, cursing whatever Merlin had done to her.

Nothing . . . nothing about this should have felt good.

"I want to go home," she whispered between sobs.

"I know," he said.

Vera kept her eyes shut most of the way back as if doing so could shield them from anyone out on the grounds witnessing their passage. Neither she nor Arthur had said it, but instinct imparted a clear warning: they needed to remain unseen.

The Once and Future Queen

Matilda nearly always met Vera at her chamber in the evenings to help her get ready for bed, so it was no surprise to hear her shocked cry at Vera and Arthur's gruesome appearance. "Oh my God! What happened? Is she alive?" she asked, sounding as if she expected the answer to be no.

"Yes," Arthur said as he lowered Vera and lay her on something soft, presumably her bed, and she opened her eyes. Much of what had been making her feel so sick was the motion. She already felt better from lying still, or perhaps from being in a room with no stench of death.

"Should you call for Merlin?" Vera asked. She didn't mean to whisper. She intended to speak at a normal volume, but her voice was weak. Even so, Matilda's hand flew to her chest as if Vera speaking at all was a miracle.

Arthur did not answer. He gathered clean cloths, filled a pitcher with cool water from the sink, and knelt beside her, pressing one cloth to her shoulder.

"Can you hold this here?" he asked her. Vera nodded, invigorated by having something to do. "Matilda, I need you to get medical supplies." He peered down at her mess of a leg. "Where's the wound?"

Vera pointed at the precise spot on her upper thigh. Though it was actively bleeding, the blood was so thick across her whole thigh that it was hard to tell the origin.

He made to press the other cloth there but stopped, his hand hanging in the air between them. "Would you rather Matilda help you?"

"Arthur, it's not at all my expertise. I'm not—" Matilda silenced as he looked at her. One look, and she clamped her lips shut. Whatever unspoken language had passed between them flowed fluently.

Tears blurred Vera's eyes anew as she shook her head. Merlin's curse or not, she wanted Arthur there and dreaded the thought of anyone's hands near her but his. Matilda hurried out the door.

"All right," he said. His voice hadn't always been so tender, but then again, she hadn't always been bleeding from two different stab wounds and a head injury.

One hand on the wound at her thigh, his other worked quickly to clean the blood from the rest of her leg with a wet cloth. It looked more like a leg than a massacre by the time Matilda returned with supplies.

Arthur stepped away with her. Vera could hear tense whispers before Matilda left again. When he returned to Vera's side, he squatted nearer her head by the top of the bed. "Can you sit up so we can get your gown off?"

She nodded. Arthur gently helped her rise into a seated position. She hadn't realized he had a knife ready until he cut the laces at the back of her gown and helped her wiggle the dress over her head. Vera winced, especially as she pulled her shoulder free from the sleeve. The pain was remarkable. She had to remind herself to keep breathing.

He threw the ruined dress aside and began tending Vera's shoulder straightaway, cleaning the wound and pouring liquid that smelled of vinegar on it. She didn't think to feel exposed in her sports bra and knickers as she hissed at the sharp sting of acid burning into her shoulder. She would have recoiled through the mattress if she could have.

Arthur cringed with her. "I know," he said. "I'm sorry. I'm so sorry." He applied a sticky goo to bond the edges of her punctured skin together and wrapped her shoulder tightly with a strip of bandage, again drawing a groan through Vera's gritted teeth. Again, he apologized, his face matching the sound of her pain.

Arthur moved to do the same for the wound at her thigh, so careful not to look at her nearly naked body. "Neither of these are too deep," he muttered.

"It was a short knife," Vera said with a grimace as Arthur pulled the bandage tight around her thigh.

He looked at her as if he had a thousand things to say in response. "It was long enough," he said. "Long enough to do this to you. And long enough to end him."

Dread and regret in the first half, grim satisfaction in the latter.

"Can you hold this on the back of your head?" he asked.

Vera took another cloth from him and pressed it against her head wound. She had not realized before now that her circlet was gone, and she wondered where it lay in the chapel's upheaval. She wondered, too, where her ruined embroidery piece ended up and what the first person who stumbled upon the scene might think.

Arthur turned his attention to cleaning the blood from her body.

The Once and Future Queen

There was no telling what was hers and what had come from Thomas. He meticulously wiped it all away. Then he covered her with a blanket and moved on to her head.

His face was so near to hers and so controlled. Her eyes went to that muscle in front of his ear, and—yes, there it was: the bulge there, the only indication that he was clenching his teeth. For some reason, being this close to him made her cry again. She tried not to, but he'd already noticed. Of course he'd noticed. His brow furrowed as he picked up a clean cloth and swept it beneath her eyes. She didn't want him to wipe tears with the dirt and dust and blood. It was too much, too vulnerable. The effort to stop was fruitless, as good as opening a water spigot all the way when she'd meant to tighten it down.

Vera shuddered from her sobs and forced herself to breathe deeply. One breath (push it down, bury it), another (steadier now), and a final one. Her tears stopped.

"I'm fine," she said, her voice dull.

"Stop." Arthur practically growled it. "Stop doing that—making yourself go . . ." He shook his head as he searched for the word. "Empty."

A spark stirred in Vera as rage bubbled up, more powerful than how badly her injuries hurt. "What am I supposed to do? I can't exactly fall apart with the weight of existence resting on these memories. And you need a fucking potion to even be near me. You can't even stomach it to save your kingdom. There's something more than her betrayal, isn't there?" she asked through a clenched jaw as she fought the pain. "So what is it? What am I missing?"

"You're bleeding. This is not the time. Tomorrow—"

She leaned forward and grabbed his wrist, mastering the urge to cry out from the abrupt movement and instead pouring all she had, all her pain and fear and impotence, into her next words. "Now." Her voice shook. Her hands shook. "Right now. Either you tell me whatever the fuck it is that you've been keeping from me, or I absolutely will go on making myself be fine because I don't have any other way of surviving." The exertion left her gasping for breath.

"All right," he relented, and quickly moved his free hand to cradle the back of her neck. She was ready to berate him for it but nearly collapsed into his grasp. He eased her back down onto the pillow, his eyes holding hers with a strange glint of adoration. But she was dizzy and had to be mistaken.

"You're right," he said as he pulled his hands back and dropped his head between them. The logistics of caring for her left him in a posture of supplication, kneeling at her side, his hands clasped on the bed next to Vera with his head bowed. "I've been an utter fool." His face bore no trace of the mask of stone. Now, all she saw was sadness and regret. "I've been far worse than that, and I'm so sorry."

She nestled back into her pillows, unable to contain the groan that escaped her. But she didn't soften her glare. "How much have you kept from me?"

"Too much." He said it so quickly that it startled Vera out of her ire. "Everything that matters. It was wrong—"

"Tell me why you need a potion to be near me." There would be no resting when the offer of truth was on the table.

"I don't." Arthur took one shaking breath before he gave in and sat down on the bed next to her, heedless of where blood marred the sheets. "When Viviane attacked Guinevere, and Merlin restarted her essence, there was so much damage that—and I don't fully understand this—but he wasn't sure it would work. He was able to get three parts. Three separate pieces of her essence."

He stopped speaking and held Vera's stare. Her heart thundered in her chest. "What does that mean?"

"There were three of you," Arthur said. "Two other versions of Guinevere were restarted when you were. They came back before you."

All the physical pain, the feelings of dread, even her anger at Arthur—it all abruptly vanished as Vera absorbed his words.

"What—" she began, but all that came out was an unintelligible rasp. She cleared her throat. "What happened to them?"

Arthur looked at Vera with dread-soaked resolve. "They're dead."

Vera inhaled sharply.

"It was the same idea as with you," Arthur continued. "They were raised in another time. Merlin brought the first back a week after Viviane's attack."

"Did she remember?" Vera asked.

"She did. Not the attack. She had no recollection of that, but she remembered me after a while, who she was, about her life . . . And then, it was like something snapped. She became homicidal, almost rabidly so. She attacked me and the soldier who intervened, and she was killed."

The strange phrasing was not lost on Vera.

"By you?" she asked.

"No," he said. He forged on before Vera could question it further. "At that point, neither Merlin nor I wanted it to be in vain. He insisted we try again. So much about it had been right, and it was new magic. Complicated magic. We couldn't just give up. Merlin brought the second one back, and she seemed more like herself. She remembered about the same as the first, but she slipped into an even deeper melancholy than Guinevere—Guinevere from before. One morning, she woke . . ." Arthur's voice caught. He closed his eyes and swallowed. His cheeks went red as he fought down an onslaught of emotion. He dragged his gaze back to meet Vera's. "And there was nothing left of her. She was," he shook his head, "sorrow incarnate." His eyes flashed to the window. "She jumped."

It reminded Vera of Matilda, the horror in her eyes when she saw Vera leaning against the window the other night. "And Matilda saw," she said. She needed no confirmation, though Arthur nodded.

And the pain in his face made her ask, "Were you there, too?"

Arthur nodded.

"You saw it both times?"

"Yes." He paused. "And the first time, too. After Viviane's attack."

Arthur witnessed that horror three separate times. She felt like the wind was knocked out of her. She should have reached out to comfort him, but she sat there, frozen. She couldn't be sure if it was the story or if the shock was wearing off and leaving her empty, but a dull sick had started churning in her stomach.

"When she fell—jumped," Arthur amended. "It was more public.

People saw it, saw her body. Only from a distance, granted, but there was no denying that some sort of accident had happened. The word spread quickly, and it had to be addressed. That's where the story about healing at the monastery came from. Merlin wanted to try again right away, and I refused. He agreed to wait a year, which also fulfilled the need for an explanation. Anyone who saw it knew she couldn't possibly have been all right, not for a long while. Merlin spent that year trying to convince me to change my mind. The time came, and I still refused. I wanted to tell the people that Guinevere died from her injuries and leave you be where you were. Merlin went behind my back and brought you anyway. All I could think to do was to stay as far away from you as possible so that it didn't end as it had before." He looked at her apologetically, pleadingly.

"Why are you so convinced that you were the part that broke them?" Vera asked. "The magic went wrong, Arthur. You didn't do that."

He was in visible misery, and she knew he only forged on with his eyes locked onto her because he had committed to telling her everything.

"There was a turning point, and it was the same thing. Both times," he said, "it all went very badly very quickly after she and I were physically intimate. When I saw you last night after Merlin hurt you and you were so," he searched for the word, "destroyed, I thought it was because of me. I thought that what happened in Glastonbury had . . . well, it doesn't matter. I'd have known better if I'd asked or even listened when you tried to tell me."

"Oh," Vera said, stunned. "And . . ." Shit. She had to ask. "If we hadn't stopped that night, you think that what happened to the others would have happened to me?"

"I don't know," he said, shaking his head. "It's so clear in retrospect. Splitting one person into three was madness. Magic or not, there was no way it was going to work. Only one of you ever had a chance, and it's a miracle you did. You are your own person. I will never corner you into anything if I can help it. You shouldn't be with me because I'm here . . . because I'm the first person you've been shoved into close quarters with who can know you and remember you. Who can care for you. Your feelings have already been manipulated with magic against your will. You should be with anyone you want. I have no claim on you. You owe me nothing. If you want to be with Lancelot—"

"I don't," Vera said, unable to resist interrupting.

"I know," Arthur said with a certainty that surprised her. "Or Percival or . . . Gawain." Vera laughed, a meek sound in her present condition, but a laugh, nonetheless. He let one corner of his lips turn up in a half smile. "The point is that it's your choice. You will not be forced. Not by magic nor by circumstance."

"It's the only way I've remembered anything," she said. "I have to remember. I can't go home until I do. My dad—"

"You can't go back if the memory work kills you," Arthur said. "I will get you home. We'll find another way. Merlin said the next time the portal will be accessible is late spring. We have time. If the world starts to end or . . . well, we can cross that bridge if we get to it. But for now, we have time."

Far less than they would have if Vera had simply known the truth from the start. "Why didn't you just tell me?" she asked.

"Merlin thought it unwise, and before I knew you, I was afraid it would destroy you, too." He dropped his head into his hands. "And then I didn't know how to tell you. I thought if you could get your memories back, and we could get you home, then it wouldn't matter. But I was wrong. Keeping this from you was wrong."

Yet Merlin had insisted. She'd seen in Guinevere's memory how the woman had trusted him, how she'd adored him. And Vera had put all her faith in him, too. For him to do this, though? "Do you trust Merlin?" she asked.

Arthur tensed. "He's been backed into his own corner. Also of my doing." He was more riddled with guilt than anyone she had ever known, and Vera suspected she was only seeing the tip of it. "I trust him with the kingdom, but I do not trust him with you. He cares for you, but he will do what he believes is best for the kingdom, no matter the expense. That's where his first loyalty will always lay."

"And what about yours?" Vera said. "Aren't your loyalties to the kingdom?"

"Not at your expense," he said without hesitation. "Not anymore. I've made that mistake three times. I won't do it again. I will not destroy you to restore her."

"Is that why you didn't call for him?"

"I saw the way that first procedure left you scrambled. And what Merlin did the other day . . . when he well knows what happened to the ones who came before you," he said. "I'm sending him back to the Magesary at first light tomorrow. He is not to return to Camelot unless he finds an alternative to this torture. You—"

She thought he had more to say, though he swallowed it as he so often did.

"What is it?" Vera asked. "Please tell me."

"What you did a while ago when you went . . . blank? She used to do that near the end. More and more, actually, until it felt like that was all that remained."

It frightened Vera how much she related to the impulse to go numb, how close she'd come to it on the floor of the chapel. "It's more palatable than the alternative. Falling apart . . . hurting so badly I can't breathe."

"I don't know how to ease your pain," Arthur said, and she could see how desperately he wished he could. "But I promise I won't leave you to face it alone again. I am so sorry, Guinevere."

When he called her Guinevere, Vera's memory flashed to being on the floor of the chapel when she couldn't breathe, and then something had clicked, and she could.

"You said my name," she said.

It was Arthur's turn to look bewildered. "What do you—"

"In the chapel. You said my name. You called me Vera. How did you even know it?"

Arthur rubbed at the scruff on his chin. She knew this to be an anxious gesture from all the hours of watching him at court. "I heard you tell that little boy when you blessed his sister. I'm sorry. I was desperate. I thought it might help."

"It did," said Vera. As the truth of it settled in, she corrected herself. "It does."

"Is that better? If I call you Vera?"

"Yes." A shiver passed through her. She'd not thought of a name as having power before, but the breath of it, the act of someone saying it out loud and her hearing it . . . it made a difference.

"Vera," Arthur said as he gently laid his hand on top of hers. "I am so deeply sorry."

Vera had a choice to make right now. The truth had washed away her anger. She couldn't summon it now if she tried. She was hurt.

But so was Arthur.

"I forgive you," she said.

He looked at her like she'd slapped him. "An apology isn't enough. That shouldn't be enough for you."

"If you truly want me to be in control of my life, that's not your call," Vera said. "Do you promise not to keep anything from me going forward? I mean it. I mean nothing."

"Yes," he said solemnly.

"And . . ." If she was expecting honesty, she might as well give it. "After what happened between us in Glastonbury—"

"I'm sorry. I shouldn't have—"

"Don't be sorry," Vera said. Her hands shook and her heart thundered. "I'm not."

Arthur's lips parted as he stared at her, his eyes blazing. She had the distinct sensation that she'd shocked him into desire. That he wanted nothing more than to close the distance between them and finish what they'd started. It passed in a heartbeat, replaced by his resolute regret—probably owing, in part, to the freshly dressed wounds and the mess of blood surrounding her. And to the potion. Arthur carefully considered what he said next. "We can't pretend magic hasn't intervened between us. There are lines we cannot cross even should we want to."

His cheeks reddened as he paused and peered down at his hands. Vera nodded quickly. The shame of this was unbearable.

"You need rest," he said.

She could have asked him a hundred more questions, but he was right. She was holding onto consciousness by a thread. He helped her change into a nightgown and swapped out clean blankets for the bed.

He brought her a cup of water, which she gratefully downed, aware as the first drop touched her tongue how thirsty she was.

"May I clean the blood out of your hair?" he asked. Vera nodded. She'd forgotten that her hair was matted and bloody at the back of her head.

Arthur took one of many excess pillows and placed it on the side of the bed. He cautiously offered Vera his arm to help her shift to lie on it. His face, etched with doubt that she'd accept his help, almost made her smile. Almost. The only person who'd suffer from Vera's stubbornness was her.

She lay on her back, hair dangling over the side of the bed.

Arthur sat on a footstool behind her and poured warm water down the back of her head to help work the blood out in patches. His fingers were adept and gentle.

"Is this all right?" he asked.

"Yes." His touch brought more comfort than it had any right. "I don't want to be angry with you," said Vera, surprising herself that she'd decided to say it aloud.

His fingers halted. She wished she could see his reaction.

"All right," he eventually said as he resumed working through her hair. "But if you change your mind, I'll be ready."

She smiled, the breath of a laugh but one good night's sleep away.

They slipped into quiet. It was peaceful enough that Vera started to drift between wakefulness and sleep as he worked. She felt him towel-drying her hair and applying something to the abrasion on her head. He piled her hair on the pillow and pulled the blankets up around her, believing her asleep. She relished in the half-consciousness, aware enough to feel his presence but distant enough not to need to respond. He hadn't moved far. He sat back down on the footstool.

When Vera heard the door latch, she wasn't sure if it was a dream until she heard Matilda's voice. "Your Majesty, may I have a word?"

Vera's eyes shot open, and she grabbed Arthur's hand as he stood. "Don't leave me again."

She didn't care if he left the room for a moment. That wasn't what she meant, and he knew that. He knew what she meant. Arthur knelt back down and encased her hand in both of his.

"I won't." And there was so much unsaid behind his words. "I promise."

Vera held his gaze, expecting him to hurry to escape their closeness for the comfort of some critical task like ruling the country. He didn't. Vera was the one who eventually nodded and broke the moment.

"Let's turn you right-ways," Arthur said.

He helped reposition her in the bed, her right arm elevated on a folded blanket, a pillow under the crook of her knee. Her eyes drooped as she heard him say, "I'll be right back."

She believed him.

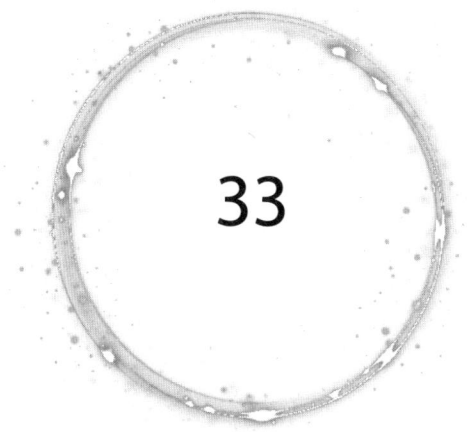

33

It must have been late in the morning for the way light streamed through the bars of her open window. Fresh white flowers adorned the table by the fire, which had burned down to smoldering embers. She liked that contrast when sleeping; a heated room with an open window to let a cold blast zip through when the wind saw fit.

And, as promised, she was not alone. Arthur sat in a chair next to her bed, reading. He looked different when he thought no one was paying attention to him. His brow pulled together slightly more than was natural as his eyes followed the page left to right and back quickly like a silent typewriter. There was one instance when his lips moved the slightest bit, half forming the words he read as the corners of his mouth ticked up. Whatever picture the passage painted must have pleased him.

She'd have liked to watch him longer, but his eyes flicked up to her. Arthur set the book down and leaned toward her. "How are you feeling?"

"Not nearly as poorly as I'd expect." She scooted to prop herself in a seated position. Her voice was raspy, and Arthur passed her a cup of water from the bedside table.

He stretched his neck from side to side, failing to stifle a yawn.

"Did you sleep?" she asked.

"A little." Before Vera could begin to feel bad about his discomfort of a night spent in a chair, he went on. "How do you feel about allowing Gawain to treat your wounds?"

The cup was halfway to Vera's mouth when his words stopped her. "But—Merlin will know. Gawain will tell him, won't he?"

"He might," Arthur relented. "But not any time soon. Merlin's already gone. I can tend a wound well enough on the battlefield, but it would be better for Gawain to examine and heal them. It might sound foolish, but Lancelot thinks he's trustworthy, and that is enough for me." He shrugged with a sheepish smile. "Speaking of, he's eager to see you. When you're ready."

"Who is?" Vera sat up straighter. "Lancelot?"

Arthur nodded. "He doesn't mind waiting until your wounds—"

"I'm fine. It doesn't hurt badly," Vera insisted. "I'm ready." The last words she'd shared with Lancelot were horrid. She was eager to say new ones.

She assumed he would have to send for Lancelot, but Arthur had barely opened the door to their chamber before he charged right in.

"Were you sleeping in the corridor?" Vera asked through a disbelieving laugh.

He didn't answer. He rushed to her side, pulled the chair Arthur had slept in as close to the bed as he could, and sank into it.

"Vera?" Arthur said, drawing her attention and causing her heart to somersault. "I'll return soon."

She nodded and held her breath as she watched him go, like she could hold in how it felt to hear him say her name.

"You're . . . you're still here," Lancelot said. His eyes searched her face and landed on the bandage on her shoulder, peeking out from the neck of her nightgown. Trancelike, his hand drifted up to touch it—so gently. She could barely feel the brush of his fingertips through the bandaging.

"I'm here," Vera reassured him.

"I—I was an ass yesterday morning. I'm so sorry."

"Stop. You don't even need to apologize—"

"Yes, Guinna," he snapped back, grimacing, and she knew it was only at himself. "Yes, I do. You had endured a sort of torture I can only imagine—and that was before what happened last night."

Unbidden, her eyes shifted to his throat, where his Adam's apple bobbed as he swallowed. She knew the way it would look if he were stabbed in the neck, how it would heave and stutter. Knew the way blood spurted from an artery with force at each slowing beat of a heart. She met his eyes again. He'd seen the way her face changed. Two lines carved down the middle of his brow.

"I saw the chapel," he said. "And the body."

"I killed him." It was the confession she'd been bearing like a leaden weight. She'd killed Thomas. It didn't matter that it had been born of self-defense. All she could remember was the fear in his eyes as his life left him.

Lancelot lay a hand on her knee. "I know."

The way he said it . . . like he understood in a way no human should. But it was the gentleness in his voice that undid her. Vera's tears came quickly after that, tumbling into racking sobs that shook her sore body.

"Oh, love," he whispered. Lancelot climbed onto the bed next to her and gingerly wrapped his arms around her. "I know. I know."

Vera clung to his shirt and cried into his shoulder.

"Do you want to tell me about it?" he asked.

She did. And when she tried to apologize for struggling to say it through tears, he hushed her, insisting she take all the time she needed. He held her closer as she explained how Thomas pulled her to the floor when she finally (stupidly, belatedly) tried to run away. He rubbed her arm as she finished the story with the bloodied knife in her hand.

"Why did he do it?" Vera asked as her breathing steadied. "Even if he was right about you and me, was that enough for him to try to kill me or control me or—I don't understand. He was only ever kind to me before that. A friend, even."

Lancelot's chin had been atop her head. She pulled back and craned her neck to look up at him, hoping he could explain it. But he didn't.

"I don't know. People can be awful, and sometimes there's no reason for it."

Vera curled back into his shoulder, as comfortable with him as she'd ever been with anyone and absolutely certain that there was no intention in it beyond care. But she wasn't a fool. She knew what even the appearance of their affections had wrought and was grateful for the privacy that allowed it now. For the privacy Arthur had given them. A mad huff of a chuckle escaped her.

"What?" Lancelot said.

"Last night, when Arthur told me about everything, he suggested I take up with you."

"Did he now?" His pitch lifted with his amusement.

"Mmhmm. And when I insisted I wasn't interested," Lancelot scoffed in mock offense, "he suggested Gawain."

He laughed loudly at that. "What an impeccable pairing." He untangled his arms from Vera and got her settled, propped against her pillows. But he didn't move to the chair. He nestled back to sit against the pillows beside her. "It will be interesting to see how Gawain handles the lead mage role while Merlin is away."

Merlin. Shit. Vera regretted disappointing him the way she would her own parents, yet she couldn't believe the pain he'd inflicted on her.

"Do you think Merlin regrets what he did?" she asked.

"I certainly hope so," Lancelot said with a grimace. "I've never been his biggest admirer, but I admit he was very good to you—to Guinevere—before. He was her closest confidant, often the only one who could lift her from melancholy."

"They were that close?" Vera asked. Though she'd felt the truth of it in Guinevere's memory, it was hard to reckon with now.

"They were," Lancelot said. "I think that's part of the reason Arthur trusts him—because of how Merlin cared for her. He wants to fix things so badly . . ." He shook his head. "The mages are an especially fucked up bunch, usually with some savior complex. Have I ever told you that my mother was a mage?"

Vera's eyebrows shot up. "No, you did not."

He knew he hadn't. She would remember that, and he would remember telling her.

"It's a lonely life. I think that's why I get under Merlin's skin so much," he said with a grin. "I've got his number better than most. When I was little, I always tried to get my mum to play some stupid games with me to divert her from her work and studies. I usually failed miserably, mind you, but when she'd play—Gods, she was so much fun. And she was creative and silly. She came up with the best stories. I wish she'd have used her gifts to be a great storyteller rather than . . ." he shook his head.

"Did she die?" Vera asked.

He smiled sadly. "Yes. Some time ago."

"I'm so sorry."

"Thank you. I miss her."

"What about your father?" Vera asked. "Is he alive?"

"No idea. Never met the man. I am fully a bastard. Most mages end up alone, I'm told. It was rather extraordinary for my mother to have a child at all. Tell me about your innkeeper parents," he said much more brightly. And it was Vera's turn to be uncomfortable.

"They're . . . they're the best. My mum, well, you'd have a difficult time finding anybody kinder than her. She's the sort who's never met a stranger. We have people who stayed at the hotel for two nights a decade ago who still call around Christmas. And Dad . . ." Vera laughed. "I don't think the word 'shame' is a part of my father's vocabulary. He's never once worried about what somebody else thinks. Not for a second. He'd love you."

Lancelot smiled wistfully with her. "I wish I could meet them. You must miss them."

"I do. And," her breath hitched, "my dad is quite ill, which makes it, er—" She didn't know how to put it into words, but she didn't need to.

"That makes it harder," he said softly.

"I have deliberately avoided thinking about them as much as possible since I got here," Vera said. "I thought I'd fall apart if I let myself dwell on them too much." It wasn't untrue. The sting of speaking a word of their stories and letting herself sink into their memory was immediate.

"You can fall apart with me." He had a deep crease between his eyebrows as he watched her. "Why are you looking at me like that?" he asked.

"We've never talked about serious things." Vera picked at the blanket's seam, embarrassed to say the next bit. "I was afraid you'd decide I wasn't any fun."

"Not any fun?" He clicked his tongue. "I don't love you because you're fun. I love you because I love you."

Her heart was so full that it felt on the edge of bursting. "It's that simple, hm?"

"Yes," he said. He leaned back into the pillows. "And for your power and clout, obviously."

She snorted.

"But I did abandon you, Guinna." Something minuscule shifted in his voice, and his eyes glazed as if his mind were someplace else before he shook himself from whatever memory had taken him. "You never should have been left alone last night. I'll do whatever I must to keep you safe. I will be your personal bodyguard every minute of every day."

Vera's heart sank. "I know you're trying to help, but that sounds horrible. Needing constant protection is the last thing I want."

"I'm sorry." His eyes searched her face. "What can I do?"

"I'd rather learn to protect myself."

Lancelot's lips quirked into a lopsided grin as he tipped his head to the side. "I can teach you that. I'm actually really good at that."

"All right," Vera said. "That settles it."

She hadn't meant for him to begin that very moment, but he launched into brainstorming aloud how he might structure Vera's training plan with the king's guard. That was how Arthur found them when he came in: sitting in bed, shoulder to shoulder, engrossed in conversation.

"I'm sorry to interrupt," he said, sounding like he earnestly meant it. Even after last night's revelations, Vera was astonished by how unfazed Arthur was at seeing them together. But the thought stumbled to a screeching halt as she saw Gawain trailing behind him.

"Goodness," Lancelot said. "Someone should invite Percival and Matilda, and we'll have ourselves a proper party!"

"Please refrain," Gawain said. "I am here to heal the queen, which should be a private matter. I would prefer if you left as well."

Lancelot grinned. "Understood. I should go join training, anyway." He kissed the top of Vera's head before he slid off the bed, nodded to Arthur, and clapped Gawain on the shoulder on his way out. The mage rolled his eyes, but Vera caught the start of his smile.

Arthur sat at the bedside with Gawain standing next to him, ready to start the healing at Vera's thigh. But the moment Gawain's hand touched her nightgown's hem, she felt like she was on the chapel floor. She could see Thomas's ravenous eyes, could hear the tearing of her dress from hem to waist, could smell his sweat as if he was on top of her.

"No." She gasped the word as she pinned the nightgown down to her sides with shaking fingers. All at once, Vera's throat tightened, and her heart pounded.

Gawain took a step back.

Her breath rattled in. "I'm sorry. I don't know why I—" She reached for Arthur, and he was there, taking her hand. "I was fine when Arthur bandaged them."

"That's understandable," Gawain said in his deadpan way, though he spoke quieter. "The body's memory is more powerful than the mind. Your body remembers His Majesty, even if your mind does not."

She bit the inside of her cheeks and avoided looking at Arthur.

"I don't have any other obligations," Gawain said. "We need not hurry. Move your nightclothes how you need to, and His Majesty can help remove the bandages. Tell me when you're ready." He looked at her with something akin to softness before he turned his back and took a few steps away.

Arthur's hands brought only comfort. He helped remove the bandage dressings, and his eyebrows shot up as he inspected her wounds. Both incision points were raw and open, but neither bled. "These aren't as bad as I expected. I must have been more panicked last night than I realized."

Vera called Gawain back.

"I'll start at your thigh first and will need to touch the edges of your wound," he said, waiting until she nodded to proceed. He did all of it that way, telling her precisely what he was doing as he went. She'd not expected his sensitive bedside manner. But it did help.

"The shoulder and leg are both stab wounds?" he asked as he ran his thumb over the open cut just under her collarbone.

"Yes," Vera said.

"Hm." Gawain frowned as he folded his hands in front of him and stared at a spot on the blanket next to Vera's knee.

The silence lengthened. Vera and Arthur shared a glance. "Is there a problem?" Arthur said, but Gawain looked up at the same time.

"No. I can heal these." He reached toward her thigh more slowly. "It will be uncomfortable, but it should not hurt."

The healing itself was . . . strange. Gawain ran his fingers over the cut at her thigh, and then Vera felt very lightheaded. She thought he had said something. There was the sound of a breeze, and a prickling tingle rose on her neck.

As her head stopped swimming and her vision cleared, the skin at her thigh was whole, only a faint pink line remaining where the stab wound had been.

He moved on to next one at her shoulder and it was much the same. Finally, Gawain addressed the abrasion on the back of her head. She sat further forward so Gawain could easily touch the spot. This time, sweat beaded over the surface of Vera's body as the energy of all the healing crackled under her skin. Her thoughts went sluggish like before. But this time, she was sure she heard a voice.

"What were those words?" she asked as if through the fog of sleep.

Arthur gave her a quizzical look. He obviously hadn't heard anything.

"You—you heard words?" Gawain said.

She nodded. He took a step back to stare down at her, his brow furrowed and lips parted, but he didn't address it again. "Your wounds were further in the healing process than they should have been. I'm not typically able to heal stab wounds." He sank into the chair like the effort had drained him. "But yours had already begun to mend."

"How?" Arthur asked. He sat on the bed next to Vera, and her stomach did an infuriating somersault.

Gawain was statue still with a vacant expression. He swallowed and gave one stiff nod as if he'd made a decision. "Before the procedure that did such damage the other day, you took a potion."

Vera was too stunned to confirm or deny it. Had Arthur told Gawain about the procedure, too?

But Arthur's bewildered face made clear he hadn't.

Merlin, who'd emphasized the danger in others knowing the truth, wouldn't have . . . would he?

"Since my arrival, I've been stocking the castle stores with healing potions. I would guess," Gawain paused with a hard look at Vera, "that Merlin included that in your potion, anticipating the way his memory work might damage your mind. There's no evidence that healing potions work when administered preemptively, but that is the only explanation—" He stayed silent a moment. "It's the only feasible explanation I can think of."

"Merlin told you about the procedure?" Arthur asked.

"He did not. I knew there were secrets, so I have been listening where I should not. I heard the procedure. I've heard a great deal more than that, too." He fixed Vera with a meaningful stare. "There are some gaps in the story for me. But . . . I know."

"You need to start explaining what you mean, and you'd best do it very quickly," Arthur said quietly, which was somehow more unnerving than if he'd shouted.

Gawain sighed. He stood and crossed to the corner of the bed nearest the door, reached beneath it, and procured a thin wooden disk, smaller than his palm. He moved to Arthur's side (a brave choice, Vera thought) and handed it to him. "This picks up sound, and this," he pulled a wooden block from his pocket—the one Vera had seen him with before Yule that she'd thought looked like a phone, "is the receiver. The disk was hidden in our study before, and—I hid it here yesterday."

"You did what?" Arthur all but growled at him.

To his credit, Gawain didn't cower. But Vera's mind was on the conversations—the ones during the procedure with Merlin about her time travel. And about Vincent. And here with Arthur about the two versions of Guinevere that came before her.

Vera's mouth hung slack. "You know everything."

"More or less," Gawain said. "I won't try to justify my actions. All I can do is assure you and show you, if you'll let me, that I am worthy of your trust. I will not report this to the council of mages. I can help you."

Arthur stood, and he rather towered over Gawain. "If you think—"

"Why?" Vera asked.

Arthur went silent. They both looked at her.

"Why should you trust me?" Gawain asked.

"No—well, yes. But . . . why do you want to help us?"

"I don't want you to suffer," he said bluntly, his sallow stare boring into Vera. It was not the first time he'd surprised her today. "And I do not want magic to die. You—both of you," he amended as he turned to Arthur, "are the best chance we have. I know my demeanor does not inspire confidence, but I am loyal to my king. I am." Gawain said it with such ardent fervor. Arthur held his gaze in silence before he exhaled a long breath and sat down.

"I have never known Merlin to have healing gifts," Gawain continued, now addressing Vera. "Whatever he did to save you is a power he has concealed completely. There is no mechanism for magic that can restart someone's life essence in the realm of known gifts. It's unheard of. And when he entered your mind . . ." His breath shuddered. "Your Majesty, that you survived that is nothing short of miraculous. Whatever moved your healing along was powerful. You may even—" he took a deep breath and frowned. "All I can say is that your existence is a precarious balance and," he shook his head in disbelief, "delicate. So terribly delicate. It's far more shocking that you remain than it is that the other two perished. The commonality when the other two were lost was physical intimacy, correct?" He said it clinically, and Vera couldn't decide whether that was worse.

"Yes," Arthur said. His hand slid over the blanket to Vera's.

"Before, with the original Guinevere, was there trauma with that experience?" Gawain asked.

Vera inhaled sharply. Arthur started, too.

"I—none." He looked at Vera like he was being freshly crushed. "Not that you ever told me, at least. If . . . if I hurt you, you never told me."

"Whatever it is, the body's memory is deeper than the mind," Gawain said, repeating the phrase he'd uttered only minutes ago. "There is something vitally important in your mind. And your intimacy may well trigger your memory to come back, but . . . I may be wrong, but I believe you've been wise to refrain from intercourse." Dear God. There was the Gawain Vera expected, clueless that this made her want to melt into a puddle. "At least until we understand the magic playing into it. And you also should not engage in any more memory procedures."

"Then what are we supposed to do?" Vera asked.

"If Merlin's right—if it is a curse laid by Viviane, there is more than one way to break it. Magic work loses strength over time. Viviane's curse would naturally weaken, especially after her death. We can hasten its end by fortifying the powers already in existence all around Camelot. One gift is good. Multiple gifts used together are better. People don't tend to try combining gifts often. I can help the gifted of Camelot with that aspect.

"And you can build up the kingdom diplomatically. We must do everything we can to bolster the country—the people's connection with you, with one another. Empower them; build the kingdom up to its fullest. That can break the curse if a curse is truly what's at play."

The "if" stayed with Vera. Because if it wasn't a curse, then what in God's name was it?

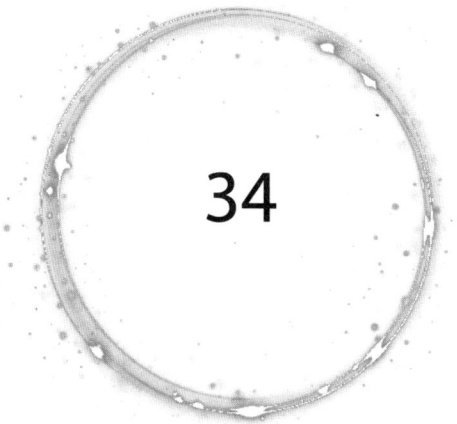

34

The story of Vera's attack would not be publicly shared. They'd made some progress with the people of Camelot; they didn't need news getting out of another attack on the queen. It would be a small circle who knew even a version of the truth: the king's guard and the priest who'd already seen the carnage. The whole next day was spent crafting and sharing the narrative that Vera and Arthur together were attacked by a Saxon spy. That Arthur had been the one to kill him. No one would be informed of Vera's injuries. It was the falsehood Arthur had told Merlin before he departed, too.

The lie felt wrong, especially when it came to Percival, who'd supported Arthur—and Vera, for that matter—with all his energy. But Gawain had been insistent. They couldn't take a chance that word would get out and begin to unspool the story. One lie had born another. How had the queen healed so quickly from stab wounds that the mage shouldn't have been able to heal?

Because she'd taken a preemptive healing potion.
Why had she taken it?
Because Merlin was doing dangerous magic on her mind.
Why?
Because she had no memory. Because of what Viviane had done.
One truth led to all the truths. They were too deeply entangled in lies.

Arthur hated it. "We should have trusted the people with the truth the day Viviane attacked," he said, his face taut with regret as Percival headed back to the training field, having been told the latest fabrication.

"No," Gawain said. "The high council of mages is suspicious of the queen's entire story—as I was. Naiam is our leader, and she is well-known for being just, but the lower council listens to Ratamun more readily. I fear his lust for power would blind him. This magic is too tempting a force. For the council alone, you never could have been truthful."

"Because they could learn to use that magic?" Vera turned to him.

He pursed his lips. "In a manner of speaking."

"What does that mean?"

"There are some things about mages and magic that I could not tell you even if I wanted to." He eyed her keenly. "You needn't worry. Focus on your work with the king."

Gawain was right. She and Arthur would continue what they'd started before Yule: being seen together through Camelot as a loving couple. This time, Vera was determined to do it right, determined to play the part of the proper queen. She would be serious at meals and reserve demure smiles only for when the men laughed. She wouldn't make the mistake of avoiding conversation and appearing standoffish like before but would speak sparingly like a well-bred lady might. What she didn't know about courtly customs, she'd learn. And she and Arthur would convince the people that they were soulmates. That the kingdom was everything the subjects dreamed of during the years of war, and the people could rest safe in their benevolent leader and his dutiful, loving queen.

It was the seventh century, and Vera had already allowed for too much selfish distraction. Her moment of clarity during Thomas's attack rang true: she wasn't just a vessel for Guinevere's memories. Of course. She was a vessel for everyone else's memory of Queen Guinevere as well.

She had to do better.

And she'd have her first opportunity later in the morning when she and Arthur were to meet in the town square and visit the market together. First, Lancelot was taking her to the armory to try out various swords and chain mail to ready her for training. He was rather giddy, but she couldn't enjoy it for her laser focus on what was to come next.

It was at the forefront of her mind as he accompanied her back through Camelot, and a raucous cheer sliced through her anxious reverie. She and Lancelot simultaneously snapped their heads toward the sound: the keep-away pit, which was surrounded by the largest crowd Vera had seen there and was the source of the uproar.

"What in the Gods' names . . . ?" Lancelot murmured. His feet seemed to drift of their own accord, the pit's crowd drawing him in like a moth to the flame.

The crowd parted easily as he touched a shoulder here or gave his charming and crooked smile there, Vera merely riding his draft up to the front.

He laughed loudly as he reached the crowded wall. "I'll be damned."

Vera squeezed through a gap, edging around Lancelot's shoulder so she could see what was happening. At first glance, nothing was strange aside from the considerable crowd. Then her eyes found him. How she could have missed his form, commanding and graceful, for even a second amongst the half-dozen players was beyond her. There were four men left in the game on one side of the pit, and on the other, there was a tiny girl who looked like she belonged in nursery school and who was hiding behind the last player.

Arthur.

"Has he ever played before?" Vera asked.

Lancelot smiled broadly without taking his eyes off Arthur. "Not to my knowledge."

Arthur bodily shielded the girl, his arms spread, sleeves rolled to the elbow, and pants scuffed with dirt. Sweat beaded on his brow despite the chilly morning. He was fighting tooth and nail to keep both himself and his little shadow in the game. She shouted orders from behind Arthur, to both his and the crowd's delight.

"King, get him! Get HIM!" she shrieked, pointing at the man who'd pelted the ball in their direction. She addressed him that way every time. "Smack it, King!" or "Not like that, King. Kick it better."

Arthur made a great effort to keep his face serious and focused, but his smile broke through frequently. The crowd roared with laughter as Arthur's teammate chided him to play tougher.

Somehow, either by the other players laughing too hard to carry on or perhaps by their generosity, it was soon only Arthur and the child left. He crossed the pit to make space between them and turned to face her, the ball sitting directly between them. The girl's eyes were the size of saucers.

"What do I do?" she asked Arthur.

"Kick it, Flora," he said. "Go on—see if you can get me!"

Flora licked her lips and tossed her golden hair behind her shoulders. She ran her fastest at the ball and gave it a clumsy kick that Arthur made no effort to dodge. It bounced along the ground and rolled slowly into his foot. As soon as it made contact, he dropped to the dirt as if knocked unconscious. Flora screamed her glee while the crowd erupted. Arthur grinned from his place on the ground before he got to his feet and was all but tackled by Flora as she threw her arms around his neck, yelling, "We won! We won!"

"You won!" He gave her a jubilant spin, letting his gaze land on Vera. Arthur's eyes glimmered as he spoke quietly to the child. She glanced at Vera, too, then gave a beaming smile before he set her on the ground.

Flora wasted no time in dashing over to Vera, pulling Arthur with her with one hand and grabbing Vera's hand with the other. "Come on!" she said. "It's your turn!"

Vera looked from Flora's sweet face with her big, pleading eyes up to Arthur and the others preparing for the game.

"Go on." Lancelot nudged her with his elbow.

"I—" This was not a part of Vera's plan. "I shouldn't . . ."

"I insist," Arthur said. "Let's play."

So she played, and that was merely the beginning of it. As often as weather permitted, dinners with performers were moved into the town square. There was dancing, initiated by Arthur, no less, on more than one occasion. Vera didn't have to become more formal because Arthur became less so, and all of Camelot seemed to fall in stride.

In the midst of it all, her training with the king's guard had begun in earnest. It was grueling and absolutely humbling, but it was something of a treat, too. She often stayed after to watch their faster, much more intense sparring that left her slack-jawed at their prowess. But today, Randall was helping Percival into full, plated armor and helmet while Lancelot set up the strangest rig on the far end of the field, a pole with a wooden arm extending from it and a chest plate dangling beneath. He gave it a smack, and the arm spun about the pole. Lancelot caught it on its way back around and nodded, satisfied.

At the other end of the field, Percival was on horseback, and Randall passed him a hefty spear at least two meters long. Her jaw went slack. Surely not...

Percival tucked the lance beneath his arm and set his horse galloping toward the dangling chest plate. The tip of his lance slammed into it, sending the hinged arm spinning about the pole.

"Is he...jousting?" Vera asked. "You lot have jousting?"

Arthur nodded. "We have a tournament in Camelot every spring. It's the only time of the year all the knights gather in one place. Largest tourney in the kingdom," he said with no small measure of pride.

"That..." Percival looped back around to make another pass. "I'm a poor historian, but I am almost certain this should not exist yet. Not for several hundred years." Plenty of Camelot had advancements beyond what she expected, all owing to magic. But things like having the orb lights and magically heated water made sense. Of all things, why would magic advance the advent of jousting?

Arthur nodded to Randall in the distance, who raised his hand and gave a stiff wave. "It came about during the wars. I think it was a soldier from the Frankish Kingdom who introduced us to it...but we started playing at it between battles to ease the tension, and it became rather popular."

Maybe that explained it, and jousting had some earlier origin in France.

Percival dropped the shattered remnants of one lance, rode close to Randall to take a fresh one from him, and started his next charge.

"Just watching him practice is rather thrilling," she said.

Arthur leaned against the fence next to her and eyed her.

"What?" she asked defensively, but Vera lived for moments like this. Tiny, private gestures that proved his promise of friendship wasn't merely for show.

He grinned. "Do you want to try it?"

"Me?" Vera laughed, though Arthur didn't. "I—oh God, I could never. I'd be a wreck . . . If I didn't fall or die, I'd probably lose control and kill someone."

"No, you wouldn't," Arthur said in his quiet way. "You should give it a go."

"And pray tell, who's going to teach me?"

"I can," he said.

Not two days later, Grady saddled their horses, and Vera and Arthur rode into the woods where she and Lancelot often ran. She followed him to a clearing, fully outfitted the same as the jousting practice arena in town.

He'd thought of everything and prepared accordingly, having at the ready armor that was likely made for a teenage boy, her running clothing to wear under, and three sizes of lances. After turning away to give her privacy as she changed from her gown to trousers and top, he helped her dress in the armor. First, a thicker pair of breeches to go over her own. On top, a long-sleeve padded shirt.

"This is called a gambeson," Arthur said helpfully as he held it aloft, ready for her to dive her head and arms into it, followed by chest plate with metal skirting that hung down over the tops of each of her legs, then shoulder and arm pieces strapped on somewhat like a harness.

He knelt down to secure the full leg pieces, each one tying at the back just beneath her bottom. Her skin tingled as the backs of his fingers brushed against her thighs. She needed it over immediately—and wanted it to never end.

He armored up as well. They started by working on simply riding a horse in armor, which was challenging enough. She practiced with the lightest lance next, and he took her through the motions with the practice plate at an absolute snail's pace. She still missed twice. But this was their first of a handful of sessions over the following weeks. Session by session, Arthur added more elements of the joust.

All along, he told her how well she was doing and how quickly she was learning. Vera gave a perfectly adequate performance, but he treated her like God's gift to medieval sport. And she charged into practice runs shouting quotes from films that would be pure nonsense to Arthur, but it made him laugh, which was a lovely sound, so she kept at it.

He made the other part of their act, the feigning love, easy . . . far too easy.

He needed only to catch her eye while his face was bright with laughter for Vera's insides to dance. When he took her hand, when his arm casually snaked around her waist at the market, or, worse, when they shared even a quick, chaste kiss in public for show, any notion of pretense evaporated. Her mind was utterly addled for him. The potion had done its work well, and it hurt every time Vera remembered the truth: that her feelings weren't really hers.

But she didn't want it to stop—and it was effective. The more affectionately Arthur behaved toward her, the more people sought her attention nearly as much as his. And he was either a practiced diplomat aware of the impacts of their act, or he was still magic-addled into adoring her, too.

Perhaps both, because he behaved that way when it was just the two of them as well. Before Arthur retreated to the side chamber to sleep, they spent most evenings together. They'd sat down to finish the last chapter of The Hobbit when a knock came at the door. It was a letter for Arthur. A shadow passed over his expression as he read it.

"What is it?" Vera asked from where she sat on the bed with her legs crossed beneath her.

"The Northern Lords." He sighed as he tossed the letter on the desk. "They're threatening to secede from the kingdom."

Hearing it was like being punched in the stomach. Vera pressed her hands to her face. "It's my fault. Guinevere's father. Wulfstan . . . they were fine until I showed up."

Arthur began shaking his head before she finished speaking. He sat down in the chair next to the bed. "They've had different notions of how to structure a kingdom all along. There wouldn't even be an alliance without this marriage. The lords were hesitant about how unification diminished their power, but with the threat of invasion and the need for protection so high, they had little choice." He chuckled ruefully as he leaned forward in his seat and rested his elbows on his knees. "But their people want to be a part of Britain. How do we capitalize on that? Come to that, how do we help the whole nation remember that we're trying to build something different?"

"By doing it," Vera said without thinking. "You have to actually build something different and not just say you're different."

The corners of his lips ticked upward.

"I'm sorry," she said. "That was—"

"No. You're right." He rubbed at his chin as his other hand tapped one finger against his knee. "I can't simply say that I want a governance that shares power while the lords remain the only ones with meaningful say. But how do we build that without power being stretched so thin that it collapses in on itself?"

Vera waited for Arthur to continue. He didn't.

"Sorry, are you wanting me to answer?" she asked.

"Yes."

"Arthur, I'm not—" She huffed a laugh. "The entire purpose of my existence is recovering Guinevere's memories. If you don't need them, the best I can do until the kingdom can break the curse on its own is to not cause any more harm. I'm not anybody. I'm a vessel for a woman who is . . . gone." They were words she'd said before. Words she believed. She'd never said them to Arthur, though. It felt a little more like a recitation and less like the truth than it once had.

His face had gone rigid as she spoke. Vera tensed at the thought that he might go distant from her again. But he got up and knelt on the bed next to her, looking her squarely in the eyes. "You don't see it, do you?"

"See what?"

"We are better because you are here. You don't have to be Guinevere to matter. You, Vera, matter very much to this kingdom."

She dropped her chin to her chest and squeezed her eyes shut. "Yes, I have brought it to the brink of war—"

She felt his hand on her shoulder and the other gently lifting her chin. His lips were so close to hers. She yearned to close the gap. "You matter to me. I don't want to do this without you. I want to know what you think."

She wished she could have fallen into him. Instead, she scooted over to make room for him to properly sit next to her. They wouldn't solve all the kingdom's problems that night, but it was the beginning of something. The weight they each bore, with no secrets left between them, became a shared burden.

And with a quiet voice in Vera whispering that perhaps she could do something good here—something good with him—they put ruling to bed for the night to finish the final chapter of The Hobbit.

"It's a wonderful story, isn't it?" Arthur laid the book aside. "Going on a life-changing adventure and then coming back home? Maybe you'll have your own There and Back Again to write soon."

"Maybe," she said, hoping he couldn't hear her uncertainty. It was only January, after all. The end of spring was a long way off. There was no sense in worrying about that now. "This book is actually the story's beginning."

"Really? Does Bilbo have more adventures?"

Vera listed her head to the side. "Hm, not exactly. It's more about the ring he found. It turns out to be, like, the most powerful thing in Middle Earth made by this dark lord Sauron to rule the world or what-have-you." She sat up more in her excitement. "Anyway, Bilbo's nephew has to go on a quest to destroy it. That one's a trilogy called The Lord of the Rings. It's amazing. They even made them into these fantastic films."

Arthur's smile warmed as he listened. "Do you know them well enough to tell me the story?"

"No!" Vera said, scandalized. "I mean, yes, I know them well enough, but I can't do that. I don't want to spoil them for you!"

He laughed. "How would it—" His expression softened. "Vera, I'm never going to read those books in my lifetime. And I'm certainly never going to watch those films."

He was right, of course. She knew that, but still. "I can't," she insisted. "What if we can convince Merlin to bring them back . . ."

When he takes me home.

She couldn't finish the sentence. She didn't need to. Arthur understood.

"I'd like that," he said, his eyes glinting. He seemed happy. Vera wished she could join in his joy. Arthur belonged in another world, and there were some things—many things—they would never share. It didn't matter that her feelings for him were magic's fabrication; she decided she would not waste a moment of it.

He stood to leave, as he always did when they finished reading.

"Will you stay?" Vera asked before she had time to change her mind.

When he hesitated and looked back at her with a flicker of longing, it urged her on.

"I know you slept in the chair a few nights. And that you come in during the night to make sure I'm all right." She'd been awake a few of the times, though she pretended not to be. "You're running a young country that's in a bit of a shitstorm. Good sleep is the least of what you need right now." She tried to smile reassuringly, but it did nothing to unknit the furrow of his brow.

"I don't want you to feel . . ."

"I feel safe with you," she said.

Vera saw it again: a flicker of shame as brief as a spark's life. "All right," he said.

She scooted to the side that she'd been sleeping on, and Arthur settled in on the other side.

They did not touch that night, but he never went back to sleeping in the chair or even the other chamber, and it was not long before the guise of sleep became a refuge for what they would not allow in the light of day.

Under the cover of unconsciousness, Vera and Arthur's arms found one another. It started innocently when she rolled over in the space inches before sleep, and her hand landed on his chest. A reflex from a love that was gone—it was how she'd slept with Vincent almost nightly, but she froze as she realized where she was and who her arm was draped across. His eyes didn't open, but his breathing changed. He was awake. He didn't pull away. He covered her hand with his and held it.

But she always instigated it. One night, when she was determined not to indulge her need for his touch, Vera lay on her side facing away from Arthur. It surprised her when he rolled close behind her, slid his arm around her torso, and held her, gently rubbing his thumb back and forth across her collarbone.

It elated and frightened her in equal measure to realize that, in his arms, Vera felt like she was home.

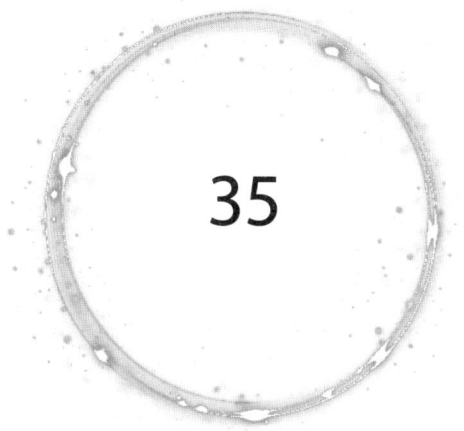

35

Her nights with Arthur had them staying up late, reading and dreaming. And, come morning, Vera didn't want to get out of bed when he was next to her. She felt a little guilty because she and Lancelot were running markedly less, though he hadn't seemed to mind. Vera suspected there'd been something else—someone else—occupying his hours. Perhaps the lady he'd snuck off with in Glastonbury was a Camelot local?

He didn't pry about the status of her and Arthur's ... whatever this was, so she abided by the same courtesy. And he'd found quite a friend in Gawain, of all people. Their pairing actually worked astoundingly well. Lancelot acted as Gawain's social interpreter as the mage got to know the gifted of the town and started training them.

Vera and Arthur arrived at the stables one morning to fetch their horses and found Grady seated with Gawain in the grass outside, a single log hovering between them, rotating slowly. Grady's forehead crinkled in concentration, though Vera had seen him juggle about eight sticks of wood at a time, all far larger than this one that hung low in the air. Sweat beaded on his brow despite the ground beneath him harboring a silvery kiss of frost.

"That's it," Gawain said. "Very good, Grady!" It was a low bar, but

Vera felt a surge of affection for the mage at the kindness in his voice and for the simple fact that he used Grady's name.

"Do you know what he's doing?" Arthur murmured to Vera, but the noise was enough to draw Grady's attention. The log froze in midair before it tumbled to the ground.

"Your Majesties! I—I'm sorry. I lost track of time." He glanced eastward at a beam of shining pearl running up the length of the castle wall like an iridescent stripe of paint. Only it wasn't paint, it was the same material as all the orbs and lights throughout Camelot. And beside it were distinct markings: the first one a third of the way up signaling daybreak, another third for midday, and at the top, sunset. It was a clock—one of Gawain's many additions to Camelot over the past four weeks in collaboration with none other than the castle priest, Father John.

Vera hadn't thought to wonder how Father John could time chapel services perfectly with the sunrise each week, but it so happened that was his gift. He knew the sun's position in the sky at all times—how many hours it would be visible overhead and how long before it returned overnight. The pearly strip was lit from the ground up to between the first two notches, signaling it was midmorning. There was a magic clock down in the village and two at the castle.

The boy scurried into the stables, shouting apologies over his shoulder. Gawain held the log in front of him with one hand as he stood and examined it.

"What were you doing?" Vera asked.

He handed her the log as if that was an answer. It was lighter than it should have been and felt hollow. She passed it to Arthur as Gawain said, "Grady removed almost all the moisture from that log."

"Grady did that?" she asked. "Did you give him that power? I thought he just had the power to move wood."

Gawain eyed her with scathing suspicion, extending his hand to reclaim the log. "I didn't give him anything. Most gifts are more complex than they seem and can be used in far broader ways than their recipients appreciate. People haven't been taught to explore the boundaries of what their gift can do, and seldom few figure that out on their own.

You look at Grady now and think he has multiple gifts when he's simply learned to use his one power to greater benefit. Outside of studying at the Magesary where we mages are trained, there've not been opportunities for anyone to learn about that. The select few young people who are identified as having multiple gifts and sent to train as mages usually only have one power to start . . . but those few happen to have a more thorough innate understanding of their single gift's breadth—not because they truly have more than one. That comes later."

Vera had so many questions to ask, but Gawain carried on, hardly pausing for a breath.

"Grady can now control the amount of moisture in the wood: he can ring it out like a wet cloth. He can also increase its porousness and absorption, compress any piece of wood, split it in two . . . If he continues to practice and hone the skill, I don't see any reason why he won't be able to shape and sculpt any wooden material as finely as a carver with a sharp knife."

"That could be an impressive weapon," Arthur said with a frown. "Shaping spearheads and having the power to send them flying through the air . . ."

"Hm," Gawain said. "I hadn't thought of that, Your Majesty."

"What did you have in mind?" Vera asked.

He blushed and swallowed heavily. "Erm . . . very fine flutes."

Collaborative creation guided Gawain's every move, and the ripples from it crested into a tide that swept through Camelot. The town had never been a stronger community. And Vera and Arthur followed suit in ruling, which they very much did together.

Arthur held to the ideals he'd had since they formed the kingdom. His ultimate aim was for the power that came with lordship to not be based on riches and instead on merit. But the structure had already been built atop a foundation when the lords were made such because they had the money to fund building a kingdom. Altering course would be a slow process. Through many hours of idea sharing and discussion—even bringing in the other members of court and trusted townsfolk, they came up with a first step. They would create a new position of power. Akin to knighting a soldier who has performed beyond the highest standard of expectation, they would do something similar for citizens who served their local communities especially well, bestowing upon them the honor of town steward.

They wouldn't rule their town. Instead, they would oversee the popular election of a local council. The lords could maintain their position of oversight while the crown discreetly dispersed more power to non "noble" folk.

Between ruling, jousting lessons, running with Lancelot (albeit less frequently), and training with the king's guard, Vera grew stronger by the day. None of it happened as quickly as she would have hoped. She liked to arrive early to her sessions so she could catch the end of the proper king's guard drills. She learned loads just from watching these men who had been fighting and training all their lives.

Arthur usually came to escort Vera to the training field, so he was never a part of the sparring matches. Today, though, Vera met with Randall before her lessons to be sized for her own armor. He worked especially quickly as she gushed about the perfect Yule gown he'd made her, and the attention made the armorer visibly uncomfortable. He hurried her out and led the way over to the training field, leaving her more time than usual to watch the king's guard.

Each knight was recognizable by their armor's variations or the small ways they'd personalized it. There were two soldiers locked into an intense sparring match. Vera recognized Lancelot's form and shining helmet straight away, even from a distance, but it took her a second to realize that the fighter in the darker armor opposite was Arthur. She hurried to close the distance and stood next to Percival.

She'd only seen Arthur teaching before today, his pace slowed, but this was different. Damn, he was good at this: faster than his bulkier frame would indicate, strong, and very skilled. When both must have been exhausted after minutes of carrying on at top speed with heavy swords and cumbersome armor, there was an opening, and Arthur lunged a shoulder into Lancelot, sending him toppling onto his back. He pinned Lancelot's sword arm to the ground with his knee and simultaneously thrust his sword into the dirt directly next to Lancelot's face before rising without any fanfare and offering a hand down to his friend. Lancelot yelled a growl of frustration from the ground. He accepted Arthur's hand to help him hop up and pulled his helmet off, already shaking his head as he grinned.

"Dammit!" he yelled, dropping his hands to his knees while he caught his breath. The rest of the king's guard, who'd spent plenty of time being bested by Lancelot, were quick to pile on in good-natured ribbing. Arthur said nothing as he set his helmet aside, wiping sweat from his brow.

"Yes, well . . ." Lancelot tugged at his gloves, plucking them from his hands a finger at a time. "When you've watched a person fight their whole life like Arthur has with me, you've got a bit of a leg up." He fixed them with a smug smile.

"Haven't you watched him fight his whole life, too?" Vera asked slowly.

Wyatt, the oldest and also most enthusiastic member of the king's guard, positively howled. Lancelot stared at her in stunned silence as Percival clapped him on the shoulder. Even Randall let out a full-bellied laugh.

Arthur looked at Vera appreciatively. "What's that thing you and Lancelot do?" He took a few steps toward her and held up his hand for a high five.

"Now that is some horseshit!" Lancelot scrambled between them, grabbing Arthur by his upraised wrist and holding an arm out stiffly behind him to bodily keep Vera back. "That's our thing, Arthur, and you can't have it!"

The next two months were, unquestionably, some of the best days of Vera's life. She had never been in a situation where she so constantly ran into people who knew her and wanted to talk with her. Whether it was Margaret from the kitchen, who was thrilled by Vera's interest in available ingredients; Father John, who checked on her with somewhat regular frequency; townsfolk enjoying their queen's attention; or one of her many friends.

Many friends . . . and more by the day as she grew closer with the members of the king's guard. She wasn't used to it and expected that any moment, she'd pass Percival, Wyatt, or any of the others on the road, and they'd see her as a stranger.

And then there were the evenings. One night, Arthur came back to their room after meetings to Vera and Matilda rolling with laughter amid a game of Never Have I Ever. He started making an excuse to give them privacy, only to have both shouting so emphatically that he couldn't possibly understand a single word of what they were saying—and only by their excitement and gesticulation knew that they wanted him to stay. Two became three.

This lasted approximately two nights' worth of gatherings before Lancelot got wind of it and showed up at the next one. It wasn't long before they decided to move to the mostly unused chamber downstairs with a fireplace the size of a washroom and ample chairs and sofas for a proper party. At least once a week, all the local king's guard and even Gawain with his lute in tow gathered in the big room (Vera's name for it—but it stuck) to . . . hang out.

New buds adorned the trees every morning. The spring tournament was less than a week away, and the joust was all anyone in Camelot could think about.

"And all of our knights will be here," Percival said one evening as they lounged in the big room in the comfiest seats pulled close to the fireplace in a semicircle. "The jousting tournament will be the largest it's ever been."

Gawain sat in the circle, strumming his lute and trying fruitlessly to teach Lancelot how to play. Even Randall stayed this evening, his head bent close to Matilda's, listening intently with a dreamy smile as she told him a story. Vera grinned before she turned her attention back to Arthur and Percival, still on about the joust.

"You have a title to defend, don't you?" Arthur asked. "Have you been preparing?"

Percival shrugged modestly. "I may not take the prize, but I'm confident I'll put in a good showing."

Arthur gave Vera a look as if he was considering something. He slid his hand onto hers as he said, "Guinevere's been learning to joust."

She wasn't bothered by Arthur calling her Guinevere in company with others who didn't know her story, but she was taken aback to hear him proudly sharing this trivia.

Percival's interest was thoroughly piqued. He leaned toward her. "Are you really? How's that going?"

"Mm, it's a mixed bag." She laughed nervously. "But I can consistently hold up a full-sized lance now, so that's something."

"You're being modest," Arthur said to her before he turned back to Percival. "She doesn't believe me when I say it, but she's doing incredibly well. I think she's ready for an opponent."

It was the second time he'd said that aloud this week. The first was at their most recent training session, and Vera brushed it off as a bit of hyperbole for the sake of encouragement. As Arthur looked pointedly at Percival, she started to realize his comment this evening wasn't simply for the sake of conversation. Percival tilted his head in question. Arthur nodded.

"I could do it," Percival said, his eyes gleaming as he leaned forward.

"You have the best aim," Arthur said.

Percival beamed. "It's the one thing I can actually best Arthur and Lancelot at. His Majesty is stronger, Lancelot's better at . . . well, every single other thing. But I've mastered the lance. Bit useless in anything that matters, but I'll take it. Do you want to?" he asked her.

Vera straightened in her seat. "Seriously?"

Their rising voices drew Lancelot's attention. "What are we serious about?"

"Arthur's been teaching Guinevere to joust," Percival said. "And I'm going to be her first opponent."

The smile hadn't fallen from Lancelot's face, but it darkened significantly as he looked each of them in the eye, landing on Arthur, who he fixed with a scathing scowl. "Are you out of your mind? That is so dangerous. No. Absolutely not."

Vera's eyebrows shot up.

"All right, all right," Percival conceded, raising his hands apologetically in front of him.

Lancelot nodded, apparently mollified. As soon as he'd turned his attention back to the lute, Percival leaned across Arthur to Vera. "He doesn't have to know."

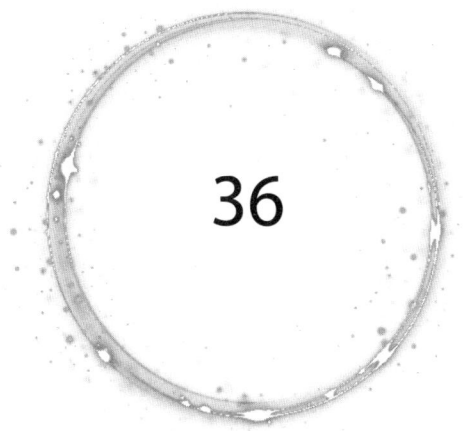

36

Before their run in the morning, Vera had decided that she wasn't going to tell Lancelot that she, Arthur, and Percival had made plans for her first official jousting bout a few short hours later. But the damn man read her face like a children's book. He knew she was hiding something less than a mile in. And after he chipped away at her resolve for the better part of an hour, peppering her with annoyingly earnest concern, Vera's guilt won out, and she came clean.

He went silent for a few tense minutes.

"You're angry with me," Vera said, surprised to realize it.

"I'm not—" He stopped. "All right. Yes, I am. This is foolish. I'm angry with all three of you. I'm not going to allow it to happen."

But it wasn't up to him, and he ultimately knew that.

He was methodical in his attempt to peck away at the jousting plan as they walked to the practice arena in the woods. "You can't use that ill-fitted armor she's been wearing for an actual match. It will have to wait at least until she has her armor," he said reasonably.

Vera pursed her lips as Arthur said, "That's true, but Randall's already finished it. She's been using her new armor for two weeks now."

Lancelot huffed and turned on Vera. "And what do you intend to do if Percival misses his mark, and you are seriously injured?"

"Well," she began calmly, only serving to make Lancelot's brow furrow deeper. "Thankfully, you had the good sense to bring Gawain. He can fix us right up if either of us gets injured."

"But not extensively," Gawain piped in unhelpfully. "If either of you is impaled, that's far beyond the scope of my magic. You'd be fucked."

Percival turned slowly to glare at Gawain as Lancelot threw a similar but more pointed look at Arthur.

"She's not going to be impaled," Arthur said patiently. "That's why I'm not doing it and why I didn't ask you." He didn't mean it as a jab; it was the truth. "Percival's aim is as steady and true as they come."

They arrived at the clearing, and Arthur and Percival started helping Vera get her armor on. She loved how it fit and the way it made her feel like a proper warrior. But despite her feigned confidence as she argued with Lancelot, Vera privately had many of the same misgivings.

She and Percival mounted their horses, and with the imminent joust now seeming inevitable, Lancelot turned his rage on Percival. "This is an awful idea," he said, the vein in his forehead pulsing as he snatched the reins of Percival's horse to force him to listen. "If you tip your lance and hurt her, as your commanding officer, I will have you executed."

Was this really Lancelot speaking? The same Lancelot who told Wyatt not to help Vera when she struggled in training, who goaded her into swinging from a rope into a dark pond, who—for God's sake—the same Lancelot who brought Vera to a roadside shakedown of teenage thieves the first night she'd met him. And now, when she was adequately trained and armored and her opponent steady and trustworthy, Lancelot was out of his mind. Percival looked cowed by his threat because he sounded like he meant it.

"Lancelot," Vera said, "if I happen to accidentally be injured by Percival, I order you not to execute him. And," she added, having only recently gotten a good grasp of hierarchical statuses, "in the matter of ordering executions, I'm fairly certain I outrank you."

"She does," Arthur called from behind them.

Lancelot wheeled on him and yelled a wordless roar before marching over to stand next to Gawain, his arms crossed as he mumbled and shook his head. With a sigh and an apologetic smile at Vera, Gawain patted Lancelot's back. The role reversal might have been comical had Lancelot's fervor not rankled her deeper than it ought to.

Vera and Percival were nearly ready. They met in the middle, approximately where they would soon collide in the joust.

"Don't you dare pull your lance," she told him sternly, worrying that Lancelot's threat may have shaken him too much.

But Percival flipped his visor up, and his eyes glinted. "I wouldn't dream of it, Your Majesty." She couldn't see his mouth but knew from his cheeks bunched up against his eyes that his smile matched her own.

Arthur met Vera at her starting point to help her get her lance situated.

"Are you frightened?" he asked.

"A little bit," she admitted.

"That's good. Keep some fear, but don't let it be in charge. You are well-trained, capable, and ready. Tuck your lance tight." He mimed the motion, pulling his elbow into his side. "Head down a fraction to keep your helmet steady and do your best to stay horsed." As he instructed her, Arthur patted her horse's neck. If he was nervous for her, he wasn't showing it. "Ready?"

Vera nodded and flipped her visor down, making much of her vision go dark and leaving a slim slit through which to see.

"I'll wave the flag, and that's your signal." He brushed his fingers along the one unarmored place on the back of Vera's leg. She held her breath at the touch—and the way he smiled at her. "You're ready."

Every so often, Vera had experienced moments of existence when time went extraordinarily fast and simultaneously moved at a snail's pace. She felt Arthur would never reach the center point where he was to wave the flag. He seemed to be walking in slow motion. And then, her heart thundering in her chest and her legs shaking enough that she could hear the faint rattle of her armor quivering at its joints, the flag was high in the air and rushing toward the ground. Time overcorrected in the other direction, and everything began happening too quickly to take note of it all.

Vera set her horse to a full run, her weight in her feet in the stirrups to steady her body. She was intent on keeping her lance aimed right at the breastplate of Percival's armor as her horse thundered across the clearing. She would never be able to say if anyone cheered or yelled encouragement, or if there was any noise other than the pounding of hooves and her breath echoing strangely in the narrow cavern of her helmet.

She had a split second of appreciation for Percival, who, as he neared, she could see was a man of his word. His lance was tipped toward her, and he leaned forward in his saddle. This was not someone about to lose his nerve or decide his opponent couldn't handle the blow.

There was no more time to think. When she felt the distinct impact of her lance on Percival's chest (she thought it was his chest but couldn't be sure), a millisecond's worth of euphoria rushed her extremities.

And, dear God, as his lance slammed into the center of her chest, a burst of splinters exploded in all directions. Some distant part of her marveled at the satisfying crunch and shatter of the massive weapons.

The rush transformed into being bodily jarred as Vera felt more things at once than she might have recognized as possible. Adrenaline thrummed through her and drove her determination to, above all, stay on her horse. The blow sent her whole upper body reeling backward. Vera clinched her legs on her horse's flanks as her torso flattened back against the rump. It took everything in her to keep her legs from flying over her head and sending her tumbling off her horse, but somehow, when the world went back to its normal speed and control and calm were restored, she was still on her horse.

Vera sat up and whipped her helmet off. She realized she clung to what remained of her lance (scarcely more than a jagged handle now) and dropped it. She turned to see how she'd done.

Percival practically jumped from his horse and tore his helmet from his head as he sprinted to her, whooping excitedly, his fist in the air.

She dismounted, and a stabbing pain surged through her wrist, making her wince, but she ignored it.

"That was good!" Percival said, staring at her in awe. Arthur tore past him, his face all pride and excitement. He hugged Vera so enthusiastically that he lifted her from the ground, armor and all.

"You were incredible," he said.

"Thank you," she said breathlessly. "I barely stayed on my horse."

"Well, me too, Guinna!" Percival exclaimed. "That was bloody good!"

Not knowing what to do, Vera looked at her hands, her cheeks hot from the attention. There was a wooden shard sticking out of her metal glove. Right where it disappeared into the gauntlet was where her hand now throbbed. To make matters more complicated, the tingling sensation all across her skin was creeping toward a burn.

Lancelot and Gawain approached from the middle of the field. Surely Lancelot wouldn't panic over such a minor injury. Still, Vera hastily yanked the sizable shard out and dropped it before crushing it into the dirt with her foot. No one seemed to notice. Gawain was his ordinary sullen-faced self, which was something of a comfort. Lancelot, however, was pale as he exhaled a long breath and only managed a thin smile at her.

"You're bleeding," Arthur said.

Vera opened her mouth to respond, but he was speaking to Percival, not her, who had a trickle of what was unmistakably blood dripping down the silver armor on his chest. She'd injured him.

Percival glanced down with an appreciative frown. He hadn't even noticed. Vera held her breath as his chest plate was removed, revealing only a minor cut at his shoulder where the edge of his armor must have dug in and broken the skin under the force of the lance's impact. Percival shrugged, and Vera exhaled a low laugh.

Then, very suddenly, it was like she'd been plunged into boiling water. It was the hottest her skin had ever burned. She doubled over and braced her hands on her knees.

"Are you hurt?" Arthur asked. She couldn't see him. The pain had her clenching her eyes shut.

As quickly as the sensation started, it was gone.

"No," Vera said, standing upright. Gawain still had a hand on Percival's wound, but he watched her with narrowed eyes. Lancelot raised a white-knuckled fist to his mouth.

"I'm fine." She didn't understand why her skin sometimes burned like that. It started after her first memory session and had happened with increasing frequency since, even after the memory work stopped.

It passed quickly today, as it always had, and Vera tried to brush it off as nothing. "Just—" She chuckled uneasily, searching for the lie. "Overwhelmed. Percival, I'm sorry—"

"Don't be!" He waved her off. His broad smile had yet to fall from his face. "You're not quite ready this year, but keep training, and you could compete in the joust next spring!"

Lancelot groaned, bringing a full, heaving laugh from Percival. Vera and Arthur shared a glance. Neither's smile faltered, though she saw the recognition in his eyes, too. She wouldn't be here next spring.

She went back to her horse's side to remove her armor. When she heard the movement behind her, Vera assumed it was Arthur, so she was surprised when it was Gawain who spoke. "Guinna?"

Some of the others had picked up Lancelot's nickname for her, but it sounded bizarre coming from Gawain. "May I check you for injuries?" he asked.

Vera looked past him, noticing Lancelot ten steps behind him, chewing at his thumbnail and pretending not to notice them. "Is this Lancelot's idea?"

"Yes," Gawain said, very matter of fact.

"Oh, all right," she relented. "I might have a cut on my hand." Vera worked the metal glove free, and sure enough, a rivulet of blood ran out of it. The cut on the back of her hand smarted, but the gauntlet must have helped the blood coagulate and slow the bleeding. It wasn't gushing the way she'd expect from being impaled by a six-inch splinter.

Gawain ran his fingers over the cut, back and forth, with increasing pressure as he examined it. The last time, he pressed so hard that Vera yelped in pain.

"Sorry." Gawain's fingers stopped, but his brow remained furrowed. "This is shallower than I anticipated."

Vera expected the dreamy fog to come as he lay his right hand over the injury and closed his eyes in concentration. But her mind stayed clear. "Ishau mar domibaru," he mumbled.

Her body hummed with a sense of release. Gawain inhaled deeply, audibly, and exhaled the same way. It was akin to how she'd been instructed to breathe by a doctor holding a cold stethoscope to her back, but Gawain did it with control and intention—as if it were the most valuable breath in his body.

"I know those words," Vera breathed as Gawain's hand lifted from hers.

He drew back, fixing her with his piercing stare. "You do?"

"I think I've dreamed them." Already, though, Vera couldn't remember what he'd said. She couldn't find the words in her mind either. "Can you repeat them?"

He shook his head. "Some secrets of the mages are so important to keep that we are bound to them by magic. Most people forget those words immediately." He surveyed Vera carefully. "But I'm sure Merlin would have used them when he saved you."

"What are they?"

"Words of power. Passed down to the mages over generations. Most often spoken aloud when doing magic that pertains to lifeforce. There's power in words," he told her. "I can't repeat them, but I can tell you about the end." Gawain patted her hand in a funny, grandmotherly sort of way. He paused before he breathed in that audible, intentional way once more.

"The breath of life," he explained. "It is the name for the source of all things."

It reminded Vera of something she thought came from Hebrew scripture. "God?" she asked. Was that right? That the name of God was the breath of life?

Gawain shrugged. "That's what some will say. Creator. God. It's all the same, but the mages simply say 'Source.'"

"The mages are religious?"

"Oh yes. The Magesary is its own religious order. We believe our power, our gifts, come from our Source. Whether that is a sentient being is up for personal interpretation. In any case, we all agree that magic is a gift to humanity, and it is our highest duty to continue the ongoing work of creation."

"I can tell you take that seriously," Vera said. If there was anyone who embodied that, it was Gawain. He alone had trained the gifted folks of town and had used magic to help revitalize Camelot in countless ways.

She peered over his shoulder and found Lancelot looking up at her at the exact same moment. He averted his eyes quickly. Vera scoffed.

"I'm fine," she yelled at him. She expected him to relax and laugh, to come jogging over with some smart remark. Instead, he turned on his heel and joined Arthur and Percival.

"What is wrong with him?" Vera mused in exasperation.

"He couldn't protect you. And it's driving him mad."

"What? That's not it. We've done loads of dangerous things together. In fact, he's usually the one encouraging it."

Gawain raised his eyebrows. "Yes, but I'd guess he was also directly involved in those things. If something went wrong, he could intervene. That's not the case in a joust. You were on your own."

"I—" Shit. He was right. She glanced at Arthur, who carried on in his conversation. He seemed fine. Pleased even. She felt a pang. "You would think that's how the king would react."

"Of course not," Gawain said, as if it were obvious.

"Why would you say that?"

Of the hundreds of ways Vera might have guessed the mage would respond, she'd have never gotten it right.

"Because he knew you didn't need protecting."

Vera had never believed that falling in love happened in an instant. It came about over time, as bonds were formed like a thread between two souls, a simple tether with affection that slowly thickened into a golden cable with love.

But it was in this exact moment when Gawain's simple proclamation lodged in Vera as truth, and as Arthur smiled over at her (pride and ease and care—how was it she could see all that in one expression?) that Vera knew.

She loved him.

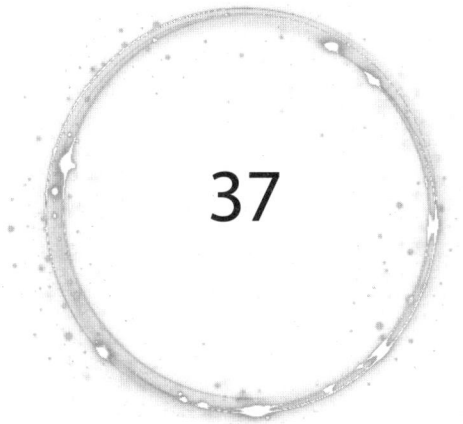

37

She'd done it.

She'd forgotten to shove her feelings out of reach. Instead, Vera had crowded in on them and ended up cradling her love until she couldn't deny it. And now? Now, it was inescapable. In the days leading up to the festival, the words were right there, tempting her tongue every time she looked at Arthur.

But she kept swallowing them.

There was the rancid uncertainty of the love's origin. Was it what she'd had for Vincent, mapped via magic onto a new source?

And if the whole kingdom was thriving like Camelot, they had to be close to breaking the curse. They had to. Which brought her to the simpler matter of reality: there and back again. Vera's tale. She'd be leaving in late spring. That left . . . what? Two months? Maybe less?

So she wouldn't breathe the words, but she would spend every possible moment with him. On the day of the festival's welcome feast, Vera's morning was chock-filled with helping ready the castle while Arthur took audiences with travelers and knights who had been pouring into town all week.

But they were both to have a midday break, and when the clock's chime tolled, Vera made a beeline across the castle grounds, nearly charging in when she reached the throne room—the door was left ajar, after all, but she stopped short at the sound of voices. Arthur must not have been finished yet.

She inclined her ear toward the opening, trying to make out whether the conversation had the polite sounds of ending, but nearly jumped out of her skin when the next sound wasn't that of a voice but of something (a fist?) slamming down on the table.

"It will work, Your Majesty." She recognized that voice with a jolt. It was Merlin. Vera hadn't realized he'd returned from his travels.

"I won't allow it!"

She recoiled from the door. Arthur had . . . shouted. He was furious.

"You haven't traveled since Yule." Merlin countered Arthur's volume with an agitated whisper. "You haven't seen the ways infrastructure is failing. We have over one hundred mages, and magic is breaking down at a rate we cannot keep up with. Your kingdom is suffering. If you think word of our weakness has not reached the Saxon—"

"Can you guarantee that she will not be harmed?"

Oh shit. They were talking about Vera. She leaned close enough to look into the room and found the two men separated by a table. Arthur leaned over it, braced with his hands wide on its surface. If he sounded angry, it was nothing to how enraged he looked.

There was silence before Merlin answered. "I can guarantee that I'll be able to retrieve her memories—"

"I won't hear it." Arthur's tone was measured and even again. It was as much of a peace offering as Merlin could hope for.

"You must!" The mage rounded the table to Arthur's side. "When the Saxons attack and you have no plan, no one's survival will be guaranteed. This is your duty!"

That was the wrong thing to say. Arthur leveled Merlin with a cold stare. "And what of your duty? So far, the mages have made promises about magic that they cannot keep." His voice was rising again. "What of your responsibility? That you would ask me for a human sacrifice for the magic you don't understand is appalling. But that it's Guinevere? You said she was like a daughter to you."

"She was. She is!" Merlin cried. "Which should convey nothing but the importance of—"

Arthur slammed his fist on the table again. "I told you not to return without a safe solution. You do not rule this kingdom. You do not rule me. And you will not touch her."

Vera was careful not to move in the silence that followed, aware that even the softest noise would be audible.

"If you do not wish to serve under me," Arthur said quietly. Merlin huffed. "I will release you back to the council of mages. Is that what you want?"

"Of course it isn't," Merlin said. "Your Majesty, is that what you want?"

Arthur cast a glance toward the door, and Vera jolted backward and out of view before she heard him say, "Prove to me that you can unlock her memories and keep her safe."

She couldn't stay here. In a daze, with her head buzzing, Vera left. She knew where she needed to go.

The door to the mages' study was closed. Merlin could be coming back any moment, but she'd decided the chance of a word in private with Gawain was worth taking. He might not even be there, but . . . she knocked.

"Not now," Gawain's voice scolded from beyond the shut door. "I already told you that I will meet you at the festival set up—" he'd flung the door open midsentence and stopped as he saw Vera there. "Oh. Sorry."

"Is this a bad time?" she asked, curious who he'd been expecting to find.

He opened the door further in invitation, and Vera obligingly stepped in. "I'm just finishing . . ." he gestured vaguely toward his desk as he closed the door.

There was a glass instrument on the desk—a round globe with a tube as wide as the tip of Vera's pinky stemming from its bottom and running beside the bulbous main container up to the top.

"What is that?" she asked. She was stalling.

But Gawain's expression brightened. "It's . . . well, magic creates a sort of pressure. Its presence impacts the atmosphere of a space, particularly an enclosed space." He picked it up. It fit comfortably in his palm as he held it between them. "This device is able to measure that pressure. I've just done my first successful test." He beamed at her.

"Brilliant," Vera said, bewildered by what it meant. "Congratulations."

"Thank you. It is rather brilliant." He laughed like he held the key to the world in his palm. "It's actually revolutionary." When he met her gaze again, his excitement faltered, and his head tilted. "But that's not why you're here. Is there something wrong?"

"How is the kingdom outside Camelot?" she asked, endeavoring to sound casual. "Is magic doing better out there, too?"

Gawain set the device down. "Why do you ask?"

She'd come to believe that any time Gawain shirked from answering a question, there was a reason. Vera's heart fell, afraid she'd already gotten her answer. "I overheard Merlin and Arthur arguing about it."

He sighed and moved the chair that sat beside Merlin's desk closer. Then he sat on the edge of his desk across from Vera. "Conditions have worsened. Especially in the eastern part of the kingdom."

"They don't have a Gawain," she said, trying to make light of it while a pit gnawed at her insides. She was shaking a little and sank into the seat.

He smiled briefly. "They don't have yourself and His Majesty."

"You're getting better at jokes."

But Gawain didn't so much as chuckle.

Vera needed to be brave now. "It sounded like Merlin's figured out how to break through my locked memories."

"That's my understanding as well," he said slowly.

"Arthur wouldn't hear it because Merlin can't guarantee my safety."

He nodded. "A prudent choice."

"I was relieved at first . . . to not have to do it." But the relief had hit a wall. She was terrified to let magic in her mind. But if the kingdom was suffering, and they weren't any closer to breaking Viviane's curse outside the walls of this city, what choice did that leave? She didn't want to do it.

What if Merlin was right, and it was the only way? Late spring was no longer a distant imagining. The kingdom was running out of time—and so was Vera. "I can never go home if I don't remember," she said. "Do you know how Merlin would get through my mind?"

"Yes," he said. "It's not so different from what he did before."

She tried to hide the way an involuntary shiver pulsed through her, but she was sure Gawain had seen it. His deep-set eyes were fixed on her.

"Would it be like before with the pain and . . ." The pain. She could feel that searing, shattering horror just thinking of it. And there was the hole left in her memory, gaping where Vincent's face should have been. "And the loss," she added.

"I don't know," Gawain said.

"What if . . . could you try?"

Surprise made him look younger. "I only know the theory. I've never put it to practice."

"Well, neither has Merlin," Vera said. "Could you?"

Gawain frowned. She had spent enough time with him to know that he did this occasionally—went silent mid-conversation to think. So she waited.

"I could try," he said. "I won't pretend that my motives are entirely altruistic. I am curious. I'd like to study this block better for myself. I have the potion for it. And . . ." At this, he leaned forward and said through a tight jaw, "I will not proceed without your permission."

If someone had told Vera three months ago that she'd choose Gawain to meddle inside her brain over Merlin, she'd have laughed. Merlin was the one Guinevere had trusted. Even Vera's childhood dream memories included him making Guinevere smile on her dark days. And Merlin—the one the queen confided in when she came to her senses. Merlin, who had saved Guinevere's life.

Not entirely out of kindness, though. He'd saved her to fulfill a task, one he believed vital to their survival. She'd heard it said more than once: Merlin would always put the kingdom first. Ahead of everything. Everyone. Vera should be half as selfless as him. This was her purpose, dammit.

But . . . what did it hurt for Vera to have some foreknowledge of what she'd be getting into this time? And Gawain, the rude and insufferable young mage who'd spied on her most private moments, who none of them really knew, was the one she chose to trust. Gawain, the secretly tender soul who thrived when teaching others how to use magic and dreamed of gifts being used to make musical instruments rather than weapons.

Yes. It was selfish, maybe even foolish. But she chose Gawain.

She took the potion and felt all her senses awaken as she sat in the chair. He stood behind her as Merlin had, his hands in the same position over her ears, fingers on her temples. Vera's heart raced, pounding at her chest as if it wanted to escape her body.

Yet as soon as he breached the space where her mind began, it was different. He moved gently. As he roamed through the corridors of Vera's mind, she could sense his care in avoiding things that weren't pertinent. He inspected her memories from a safe distance like a child with his hands in his pocket at a museum, scrolling quickly past her moments alone with Arthur. Paying no heed to Lancelot at all. He didn't tug anything to the forefront, though he lingered near the spots where Merlin had interfered before.

Those sections felt like . . . like torn paper. A page ripped from where it belonged.

She knew—she didn't know how, she just knew—that if he'd gone any closer to those jagged places, it would have hurt. But he didn't. Vera began to relax.

Then, Gawain reached a spot where he outright stopped.

"Oh," he said, stunned, and it echoed through the cavern of her mind. "Can you feel this?"

She shook her head beneath his fingers. There wasn't anything where he stopped. It was . . . blank.

Wait.

It was blank. No other part of her mind had been empty.

"I think if I . . ." His presence moved closer to the dark void, drawing a perimeter around it, bringing it into focus for Vera. It had a feeling to it, too. A dull throb that was quite at home in her, like a toothache she'd had for so long that she'd forgotten about it.

It was a barrier.

"Holy shit," Vera said. It was expansive and—this was it. She was entirely certain. This was everything she couldn't access. It was in there. Gawain traced along it, back, back, back into the recesses of her memory.

"I would guess that the front, where I started, are your most recent memories. It's ironclad. I believe this part," he said of the space farthest into her mind, "is early in your life as Guinevere. It feels more porous. We could probably find some openings there, though it will hurt if I apply pressure."

They were close, though. Now, having sensed it and knowing that it truly was there, Vera couldn't stand the thought of walking away. "Can you try?"

Gawain's presence went still. "Are you sure?"

"I am."

She braced herself for it to begin. When he started to apply pressure, the pain came with it. She gasped, and he hesitated, but she'd felt it. The barrier had given a tiny shiver.

"Keep going," she said. But he didn't move. She'd lose her nerve if he didn't go now. "Do it!"

He did, with renewed vigor. The agony swelled like her head was being slowly crushed. Vera had a death grip on the arms of the chair, her teeth grinding together with such force they might crack. It hurt so badly that she couldn't breathe. That explosions of light appeared on the backs of her eyelids. That awareness and reason drifted far from her grasp.

Then it all stopped.

Gawain's careful presence was gone inside and out, his fingers having released her. Vera was left gasping as the pressure abated into sweet, blissful relief.

"I was fine," she barely managed to mumble as her chin lolled onto her chest, which only served to emphasize that, indeed, she wasn't.

She rubbed at her temples—they were shockingly hot to her own touch. Vera opened her eyes and blinked. She couldn't see straight. She heard a loud scraping that didn't make sense before something cool and solid was pressed into her hand.

"Drink," Gawain said. It was a cup filled with water.

She drained it all before her vision swam into focus. Gawain had dragged his chair over and was sitting in front of her. A blessedly cool blast of air blew over her skin. He'd opened the door and extinguished the fire, too.

Vera willed herself to speak and found she couldn't.

"I could have broken that barrier," Gawain said quietly, his low volume a gift to her throbbing skull. "It's the same way Merlin would do it." He swallowed and shook his head. "You would not be all right. It would sever many of the connections in your brain, leaving you permanently changed."

It sounded like a lobotomy. Well . . . plenty of people had gotten those. It wasn't ideal, but some had good lives after, didn't they? Different, but . . . maybe good.

Gawain made sure she was looking at him before he continued. "But that is the best outcome you could hope for, and it's highly likely there would be far worse impacts. My best guess is that you would succumb to the trauma of your injuries before you could share those memories. The sort of magic that would be required to save you only exists in myth. Merlin should know that." He stared at the smoldering embers in the hearth. "You would be dead, and all that you contained gone with you."

It was a strange notion to consider her life like a question in an ethics class: should you take the chance of finding the key to fixing a whole world at the expense of one life?

It would have been an easy choice to make—if it had a decent shot of working. "Shit," Vera said.

Gawain hummed a rueful chuckle. "Indeed."

"And you're beginning to agree with Merlin . . . You think my memories are needed, don't you?" she asked.

The Once and Future Queen

"There's something important within you," he said carefully, just as he'd told her before. "But the king is right: this is not an option."

"What am I going to do?" Vera dropped her head into her hands. "I have to fix this, Gawain."

"If I break the barrier by force, that's what would cause the damage. But did you feel the way it moved a bit under pressure?"

"Yes," she said.

"With healing intervention, we could keep doing this. I push enough to chip away at the barrier but give you potion and time to heal in between sessions, and then we try again. It won't be as fast as Merlin hopes, and it's certainly not ideal for your well-being, but after some time, I believe it may work to dismantle the barrier. It's likely our best option."

He fished out a healing potion for her, but other than running hot, she already felt fine by the time she drank it.

"You're busy. I don't want to take any more of your time," Vera said, thinking of whoever he'd thought he was scolding when she came in. Whether she acknowledged it or not, she was the queen, and Gawain had been beholden to drop what he was doing for her.

She was halfway to the door when he said, "Guinna?"

She turned as he carefully tucked his glass-bulbed instrument into a box beneath his desk.

"Would you like to walk with me to the festival grounds?" he asked.

She smiled as she nodded, and they left the tower in silence. Vera never felt a need to fill the quiet with Gawain.

Tables and chairs were already set for the welcome feast in the open space behind the training field. Workers rushed to and fro, stacking a buffet table with trays and plates. Five men were positioning a massive and ornate marble sculpture in the middle of it. The impressive piece had to be at least as tall as Vera, depicting a soldier with his sword raised. It was unwieldy to manage, taking all the men's strength to keep it steady.

Gawain set to work right away, and Vera scanned the field until her eyes landed on Arthur. He stood next to Percival and Lancelot, who were seated at a table on the outskirts.

Arthur's gaze was pulled up to her as if compelled by an unseeable force, and his face brightened, lips lifting at the corners. Butterflies exploded in her stomach. How had she ever been unsure if he was handsome?

The instant she was within reach of him, her hand was on his cheek. And when she could press her body close to his, she did. These were the yearned-for moments when she could let it all show. They were in public. Affection was good for the kingdom. Vera bowed to her adoration and kissed him, quivering with the bliss that he sank into it and slid his arm around her waist to hold her tightly.

It could have lasted for hours, and Vera would have been perfectly happy. But it should appear like any other kiss a married couple might share and decidedly not one of a desperately pining woman who thought of this man's touch more than she'd ever care to admit. Her lips lingered on his for as long as she dared before pulling away.

He smiled at her, caressing her cheek with his thumb and laying another kiss on her forehead. "Is everything—"

"Oy!" Lancelot called. "Pardon my interruption, but we were in the middle of important business." His effort at sounding scandalized was thwarted by the colossal grin on his face—like a kid who'd been hoping for ages that his estranged mum and dad would get back together. He gestured across the field. "Poor Merlin and Gawain are painstakingly hanging lights one by one—and you're snogging."

"By important business," Arthur said conspiratorially to Vera, "he means planning the jousting tournament's after-celebrations."

"And," Percival added, holding up a square of linen, "we've made a deal with Margaret. She'll set aside some of her immaculate sweet cake for us if we fold napkins for her."

"As I said," Lancelot waved his own napkin and gestured to the pile of waiting linens on the table, "important business."

Percival and Arthur laughed, but Vera's smile was merely polite as she shifted to watch Gawain and Merlin raising orbs and positioning them. Both, remarkably, acted like nothing was the matter, that the one wasn't angry and the other hadn't plumbed the depths of her memory half an hour ago. They were good pretenders. They focused only on their task, each orb taking a few minutes to hang just right in the air.

"Why are they doing it like that?" Vera asked.

The three of them stared at her.

"What do you mean?" Lancelot asked.

"Can't they just toss an orb, and it'll hang where they want it to?"

He chuckled and shook his head. "No, they don't do that."

She turned to him. "Yours does that."

Lancelot's lips pressed into a line. "Mine's a little different."

Arthur tilted his head to the side.

"The council knights have arrived," Lancelot said casually.

"All of them?" Arthur asked, his brow furrowed as Percival simultaneously said, "Is Elaine here?"

Lancelot laughed. "Yes. To both questions. I forgot that you carry a torch for—"

He didn't have a chance to finish that thought as a commotion arose opposite them from the men setting the sculpture on the buffet table. The whole marble thing was wobbling dangerously, and then the enormous piece began to fall backward. There was nothing any of the workers could do about it except shout and scramble clear from where it would crash to the ground.

But the crash never came. The sculpture stopped mid-fall, dangling at a forty-five-degree angle like a dancer held low in a dip. Then, it was as if someone tossed a rope around it and began to pull it upright. It steadily rose to standing, where it wobbled back and forth on its base three times and came to a stop. Gawain stood, hand still aloft, toward the saved statue. Many spectators clapped.

But Percival's face snapped to recognition. "That's how it looked when magic saved me." His voice was quiet, reverent. "That's exactly how it looked." He exhaled a laugh. "If Gawain had ever served with the soldiers, I'd think I'd solved the mystery of my miracle."

Lancelot stopped folding his napkin. "He did serve with the soldiers."

Percival snorted. "No he didn't."

"All the mages did," Arthur said.

"But not with our brigade. I'd have seen him."

Arthur and Lancelot shared a look.

"Perce," Lancelot said, "we were four thousand in number with nearly a hundred mages. D'you honestly think you could have met all of them?"

Percival had stopped folding the napkin in his fingers. He stared at Gawain with an expression of disbelief until he suddenly rose from his seat.

"Mage Gawain!" he shouted as he strode toward him, drawing the attention of everyone who'd just finished celebrating the statue's salvation. "Were you at the Battle of Kent?"

Gawain didn't answer. He dropped his arm, and he shifted uncomfortably under the attention.

"Were you?" Percival pressed, his voice cracking beneath the force of his eagerness. The workers didn't even pretend to carry on. They outright stopped to follow this exchange.

Gawain swallowed. "Yes."

"Holy shit," Lancelot breathed.

Percival staggered a step backward like he'd been struck. "It was you, wasn't it?"

Gawain didn't have to say anything. He held Percival's stare and did not feign ignorance, which was confirmation enough.

"You saved my life. And all this time, I thought you were an ass. I treated you like you're an ass." Percival shook his head, exasperated by Gawain even in this moment of reverence.

Gawain shrugged. "A good man was about to die, and you decided to give your life to save him. And from where I stood on the battlefield, you, another good man, were about to die for your king—and it cost me nothing to intervene."

Percival let out a brief, amused breath and shook his head as he muttered, "Dammit, Gawain." He glanced over at Arthur, asking an unspoken question with a raised eyebrow.

Vera and Lancelot looked at him, too. One side of his lips turned upward. His hand shifted to his sword's pommel, and he nodded.

The Once and Future Queen

"How many witnesses do we need?" Percival asked.

"Two." Arthur tipped his head toward Vera and Lancelot.

"Are you ready to be a part of something amazing?" Lancelot murmured as he rose. Vera scrambled to follow them.

Arthur stepped forward, drawing his sword. "Gawain, take a knee."

Gawain's eyes darted from Arthur to further across the field, where Merlin ran toward them. "What are you doing?" Merlin called, rather frantically.

"Making Gawain a knight." Lancelot's voice was thick with emotion. He cleared his throat and mastered himself with a proud smile.

Merlin cast a sharp frown of warning at Arthur. "Mages can't be knights."

"They haven't been knights," Arthur corrected. He turned back to Gawain as he continued. "There is no law stating they can't. Gawain," Arthur repeated.

Gawain hesitantly stepped forward and dropped to one knee.

Arthur held his sword at his waist. "Ready?" he asked them all.

Gawain looked like he was about to speak before clamping his mouth shut.

"What is it?" Arthur said.

"Does the sword need to be held by the king, or can it be done by any knight?"

Arthur smiled knowingly. "Any knight would suffice with my approval."

"If it's acceptable to you, I would be honored if Sir Percival performed the ceremony." Gawain's eyes flicked back to the ground.

Arthur beamed as he extended his sword to Percival, whose cheeks went a deep shade of crimson. He stepped forward, his expression that of a man who'd won an award he didn't feel he deserved.

"Gawain," Arthur said, "for your acts of selfless heroism on the battlefield, for your dedication to the betterment of magic in the kingdom, and for your valiant service with no expectation of reward or recognition, I, Arthur, King of the Britons, name you a knight of our great kingdom."

Arthur nodded at Percival.

"I, Sir Percival, charge you to serve your king and your people justly, with honor and generosity." Percival held the flat of Arthur's blade on the tops of each of Gawain's shoulders. "Arise, Sir Gawain."

Vera blinked, and the first tear rolled down her cheek, which ached from how broadly she smiled, but there was no escaping the quiet nag at the back of her mind.

Sir Gawain.

Even for her, for someone who didn't know a fraction of the nuances of Arthurian lore, there was no way that the stories should have gotten so many parts right. She reflexively looked to Merlin. He knew it, too. Beneath the veneer of his anger, she saw fear.

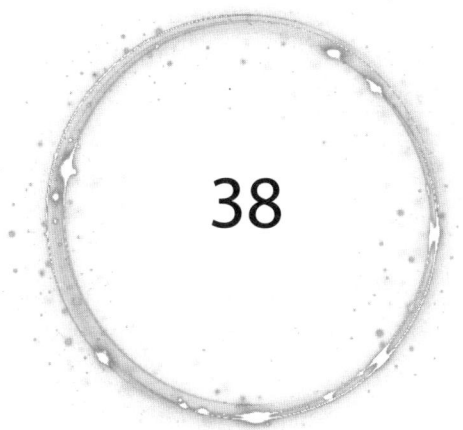

38

As it happened, nobody had been knighted since the end of the war, and it was big news. Vera was bowled over by the number of townsfolk who wanted to personally come and congratulate Gawain as the word spread. She knew he'd taken his gifts for teaching magic into the village but hadn't grasped the number of lives he'd touched. His off-putting demeanor hardly seemed an obstacle. In fact, it might have endeared them to him even more.

When the sun sank low and drew near to kissing the horizon, all the orbs through town flickered to life, signaling that it was time to gather for the evening banquet. It was customary that a crier announced the arrival of guests or performers, and tonight, Arthur's visiting council of knights were the guests of honor. There were five of them, and as their names were called out, they each entered with varying degrees of comfort at the attention.

Vera and Arthur stood together at the front for the procession. She recognized right away that these knights were the ones from Guinevere's memory in the great hall—the memory from before the final battle. She had incorrectly assumed that the two women at the table were wives of knights. They weren't—they were knights.

First was Elaine, who had the air of a cowboy in an American western. It was a small tragedy that she didn't have a revolver strapped at her hip, but one hand snapped to her sword as the other gave a flick of her wrist, more a salute than a wave. She stalked through the scattered tables to bow to Arthur and Vera (followed by a far less formal hug initiated by Arthur) and sat at the table with the local king's guard.

Next came Tristan, with his bright green eyes striking as new grass in the springtime and soft brown hair that curled and stuck out at awkward angles but somehow made him look ruggedly handsome. He followed in the same way, not displeased by the attention but uncomfortable with it. He let out a prolonged exhale through puffed-out cheeks when he reached the front.

Edwin had grey hair cropped short, and he had a wise and steady way about him. Then Lionel, who was built like a tank that could steamroll any opponent but who had deep smile lines and a boisterous laugh as he egged the crowd on, like a footballer soliciting louder cheers after an exceptional play. Marian brought up the end, gracious and relaxed, her dark, long hair in a single braid. Her lithe legs and lean, muscular body drew the enamored stares of more than a few as she passed. She was resplendent in her flowing black gown, though the short sword dangling from her waist sent a clear message that she was far from defenseless. Marian beamed, squeezing the shoulder of someone she recognized on her way to the front.

When Arthur hugged her, she kissed his cheek and framed his face between her hands with a fond gaze. Vera made sure her smile didn't twitch—though a deep part of her inwardly roared.

Vera's jealousy melted when Arthur's hand slid around her waist, holding her back as the others went to fill their plates. He leaned close to her ear. "There's something I should tell you about Tristan."

"The young one?" Vera glanced at Tristan in time to see his head tip back, laughing at whatever Elaine had said. He had dimples when he laughed. She somehow knew they would be there before they appeared.

"Yes." Arthur paused as Lionel and Edwin passed by and took their seats at the farthest end of the table. "The two of you grew up together. Your fathers intended for you to marry."

"Oh," she said. "Fuck."

He laughed. "And that changed when I expressed interest in your father's partnership. And in you."

"So, I dumped Tristan for you. Do I have that right?"

"Something like that," Arthur said with a fleeting smirk. "He's a good man. I'm honored to have him as a member of my council."

She didn't know why he told her that, and the opportunity to ask vanished as the rest of the knights descended upon the table. They were a rowdy bunch. Their table was the loudest by far as they told story after story.

When dinner finished, the night was still young, and the council knights and king's guard had plans for the evening. They could have asked castle staff to prepare the big room for their after-dinner merry-making, but a unit of soldiers who hadn't had any need for a mission in recent years acted as though this was their own covert operation.

Lionel swiped platters of food, and Elaine and Wyatt made off with pitchers of drinks in each hand. Arthur stepped in to advise against Edwin and Percival's plot, goading Gawain to bring the giant marble statue as Marian stood nearby, happily watching the shenanigans unfold.

Lancelot attempted to use Randall as a silverware mule by dropping spoons in his pocket every time he passed. Randall noticed each attempt, perhaps owing to his sensory gift but more likely due to Lancelot's inability to be discreet. Randall removed the utensils without so much as a glance in his direction.

After his failed flatware mischief, Lancelot caught Vera's eye and gestured for her to follow him.

"Come with me to the kitchens to get the sweet cakes?" he said as she fell in step with him.

She doubted he needed any help, but that all his dearest friends were in one place, and he wanted time with her brought Vera a sort of happiness she didn't know how to hold.

Margaret had the cakes sliced and ready on a tray.

"You are too good to us," Lancelot gushed.

"Of course I am." She squeezed his cheek and gave him a crinkly-eyed smile, reserving a pat on the arm for Vera. "Now, off with you so I can catch a wink of sleep before we cook for half the kingdom tomorrow!"

They grinned like schoolchildren, ready to make off with their prize.

"Oh! One moment," Margaret said as she held up a finger. She bustled over to the cabinets and rifled through until she procured what looked like a large milk carton—except that it was made of leather. "You'll see Merlin before me, I'm sure. I used the last of your tonic tonight, Your Majesty. Good timing that he's back to make more!"

The smile hadn't yet fallen from Vera's face, but her insides lurched. "My tonic?"

"Well, yours and the king's," she amended as she pressed the jug into Vera's hands. "I hadn't thought to use the mage gifts to keep your health up through the winter months, but it seems to have fortified the both of you well."

"How, er, how long have you been using the tonic?" Lancelot asked with a glance at Vera.

"Merlin gave me the first batch after Yule. Be a dear and have him refill it?"

Vera wasn't sure if she'd answered or acknowledged Margaret's words at all. She distantly heard Lancelot and Margaret's voices saying some sort of pleasantries to one another—which were mercifully short. She had to get out of this room.

She left the kitchen as fast as she could without running and made it halfway through the courtyard before she stopped to let Lancelot catch up.

"I'd thought at least Arthur was safe from magic's influence by now." She wanted to fling the damn jug over the castle wall. "I never thought to worry about what comes from the fucking kitchens. Why would Merlin—"

"Stop it," Lancelot said gently. "Maybe it is a health tonic."

Vera leveled him with a scathing glare.

"All right," he relented. "It doesn't look good, but were you having fun tonight?"

"What?" He had lost his mind. "No! This isn't my idea of—"

"Before," he said. "Were you having fun before you knew?"

"Yes, of course—"

"Nothing has changed." He nodded at the jug in Vera's hands. "That's empty. There's nothing we can do about what's already been done. Don't let this ruin a perfectly fine evening."

Vera scoffed. "That is idiotic."

"Is it?" He chuckled. "You're right. How foolish to let yourself enjoy a party with the greatest knights you'll ever meet when you could spend the whole time miserable about something you can't do a damn thing about."

He had a point.

"And if you can set the weight of the world down for a few hours of dreaded fun," Lancelot added, "I promise that we'll talk with Gawain about it before the night's over and see if he can give us some answers."

She had to admit that sticking her head in the sand for a bit had its appeal. "Fine." She sighed. "Lead the way."

The group, with all their contraband in tow, had made it to the big room by the time Vera and Lancelot got there. She tucked the jug from the kitchen under a table near the door. Tristan lumbered in a few minutes later, weighed down with a bulging drawstring bag slung over one shoulder and a sheathed sword in his opposite hand.

"What'd you steal?" Lionel called as he arranged his bounty of lifted platters on the table with pride.

"Nothing!" Tristan said indignantly. There were two open tables, one on each side of the enormous fireplace. He slung the bag onto the smaller of the two as the other was already occupied by some of the knights. "These are for the king and Guinevere from my travels."

"You brought gifts?" Lionel huffed. "You're making the rest of us look bad."

Tristan grinned. "They're gifts from Tang Gaozu."

"I'm fairly certain you made those words up," Wyatt said, though he and Marian crossed the room to get a good look at the sword. Its sheath was a dark and shining wood and was ramrod straight. Wyatt pulled the blade free by its jade-encrusted handle. It was sharpened to a fine point along its edge with a slanted tip. He frowned appreciatively as he balanced the weapon in his hands.

"He's the emperor in the Far East, nitwit," Marian said as she, too, took in its craftsmanship. "Arthur will love that."

Arthur was the only one yet to arrive. This was normal, though, especially when guests filled the castle. He would be the earliest to arrive at meals and meetings and the last to depart.

Vera stayed at the table with Tristan and the gifts as the others meandered to their seats by the fire. This was a gold mine. Nobody from her time had touched artifacts like this, items scarcely few had even seen beneath thick glass at museums. She ran her fingers across the sword as Tristan unpacked more treasures. Vera still carried her instinct to touch the ancient things, the way she'd touched St. Michael's Tower on the Tor or the abbey's walls. But these items weren't so ancient just yet. They were gleaming and new.

"I don't know what the hell—sorry." Tristan gave her a look. Guinevere must not have had the mouth that Vera had. He corrected himself and went on. "I don't know what any of it is or what to do with it." He pulled items out one at a time. There were at least half a dozen small statues wrapped in brightly dyed silks (their protective wrappings prizes in themselves), and then came a wooden box tied neatly with brown string.

"What were you doing in China?" Vera asked. Was it even called China at this point in history? She had no idea, but Tristan understood her.

He shrugged as he leaned against the table. "I enjoy travel. When the king asked for a representative to visit, I was happy to volunteer. I got to study their battle strategies and learn some fascinating combat tactics. Their emperor has done many things like your husband—uniting tribes, building a nation—all that."

His eyes were unreadable and trained on the door as Arthur entered and joined the others by the fire. Tristan picked up the palm-sized box and shook a hefty stack of rectangular sheets free from it, turning them in his hands.

"Do you know what these are?" he asked.

"No," Vera said with a quick glance. But then she did a double take, and her brow furrowed. Tristan had five thin plates in hand, and he fanned them out so that they overlapped one another. She cocked her head to the side.

"May I—?" She reached toward them, and Tristan passed them to her. They had little pictures on them. One was a sketchy painting of a person's face, and the others had delicate flowers. One with two blooms, one with four, another with eight. She flipped them over. They all had the same intricate geometric pattern covering the reverse side. Her mouth dropped open.

"It can't be." With the five cards in one hand, she began to flip through the rest, confirming her theory. Vera laughed. "I think . . . I think they're playing cards."

Tristan scooted halfway behind her to stand close with his chin over her shoulder, his cheek nearly brushing her skin. His history with Guinevere was readily apparent. He was clearly comfortable with her. "What are playing cards?"

"Well, I don't exactly recognize these symbols, but that's an easy fix," Vera said, an idea taking shape. "You can play loads of games with them."

"How do you know all this?" Tristan asked in wonder. He reached to touch the cards, but his pinky also grazed the side of Vera's hand. Her fingers twitched, but she didn't pull away as she should have. She looked at Tristan out of the corner of her eyes.

He was behaving normally except for how he gazed at her with tenderness.

"Guinna stayed at an interesting monastery during her recovery."

Vera jumped at Lancelot's voice, foolishly feeling like she'd been caught doing something wrong. He stood a few steps away, his stare fixed on Tristan.

"Did you?" Tristan asked, nonchalantly stepping back.

"Yes." She cleared her throat in an effort to break the tension that probably only existed in her mind. Vera spread the cards out on the table, flipping them so their unique sides with the blossoms or faces pointed upward. There were well over a hundred, with enough repeats among the patterns and the pictures. She organized them into piles and looked up at Lancelot as the idea solidified. "Will you get a quill?"

Setting aside the sacrilege of graffiti-ing an artifact that would be priceless in her time, Vera added notations to the cards. She made two fifty-two-card decks, with some left over and laid aside as spares. Lancelot watched while she worked. After a while, Tristan wandered to join the others.

"What's this game?" Lancelot stood just as close to her as Tristan had. His arm brushed hers, and he even rested his chin on her shoulder. The knot in Vera's stomach eased. See? Friends, especially dear friends, could be affectionate. Vera conveniently chose to ignore the whole arranged betrothal bit.

"I think we should play poker," she said. "Texas hold'em."

"Excellent." Lancelot pulled over a chair and sat down. She loved that he didn't question it. "Teach me."

They spent the better part of the next twenty minutes going over the game: what the hands meant, how to understand them, and the finer points of how to play. She made a cheat sheet of which hands beat what. Lancelot was excellent with games, so he caught on quickly.

"This is grand. Let's do it." He wheeled around to the others. "Who wants to learn a game?" Lancelot said, clapping his hands together.

Matilda yawned pointedly. "I'm exhausted. Next time."

"I'll turn in, too," Randall said, looking anywhere but at Matilda.

Vera contained her suspicions about what the two leaving together meant to a short, clipped giggle as Matilda bid her goodnight, sighing in mock annoyance as her cheeks flushed.

Everyone else wanted to play except Marian, who adamantly said she'd rather observe.

"Too competitive," Elaine murmured. "Afraid she's going to lose and show us she isn't graceful every second of every day."

"That is absolutely correct," Marian said as she sank into a seat, lounging back with each hand draped over an armrest. She looked like a pristine painting in motion.

Edwin scoffed as he scooted his chair closer to the table. "No sense in that. We've seen her piss on the front lines, same as the rest of us."

"Yes," Marian said, "but that wasn't a contest. And if it had been, I'd have won. This will be more fun for all of you if I spectate."

Vera pulled a chair next to the empty one Arthur had occupied only minutes ago. But when he sat back down, it was across the table from her. Tristan slid into the chair by her side. They all scooted in close together for the ten of them to fit at the table. Vera and Lancelot gave the instructions, collected enough varied coins to use as chips, and, after a few questions and practice rounds, they were ready to begin.

It wasn't without bumps. After winning the first hand, Wyatt was a self-deemed savant and spent the rest of the game telling everyone what to do—in what turned out to be terrible advice. Twice, Tristan tried to play a flush using two different suits. Vera laughed so hard, correcting him the second time, that she could barely sit up straight.

They started to get the hang of it after a while, and it was a brilliant way to thaw the ice between her and the visiting knights. Vera liked Elaine very much. She was wickedly funny and had the most unreadable bluff of anyone at the table.

Unlike Wyatt, Marian roved around and offered sound advice until Lancelot called her out. "Oy! You can't peek at all our hands and then meddle in the game."

One corner of her mouth quirked up. That was exactly what she'd been doing. She settled into a seat at Arthur's shoulder, becoming an advisor solely to him, often leaning forward to murmur in his ear. He inclined his head toward her when she spoke, and Vera tried not to bristle. She realized with a jolt that she'd been staring at them for the entirety of this hand and determinedly pulled her attention back to Tristan.

He was great fun, excited like a puppy when he won a hand, but he didn't care enough about the game to be upset when he lost. It drove the more competitive players mad as he carelessly called when he shouldn't have or raised on a pair of threes that turned into a four-of-a-kind on the flop. He felt familiar to her, similar to how Lancelot had, and he didn't find it suspicious that she loved hearing him recollect their childhood adventures. Percival was on Tristan's other side and encouraged him to tell the most embarrassing ones. This packed table was the happiest family Vera could imagine.

Tristan and Percival's laughter dimmed in her ears as Vera's eyes found Arthur. He'd pulled them all together. The kingdom was practically a paradise, more peaceful and prosperous even than the life of comforts from the future that Vera grew up with. It didn't seem possible—but here they were.

Arthur's eyes flicked up from his cards and met hers. Butterflies thrummed through her as he smiled at her. She returned it, embarrassed because she knew her adoration glowed plainly on her face.

Lancelot shouted and pulled her from her reverie.

"Dammit, Gawain!" He slammed his cards down on the table. "That's so stupid. How did you know I didn't have the ace?" Gawain had successfully called out Lancelot's attempts at a bluff every time. The last one cleaned out his paltry stack of chips, and he was the first to be eliminated from the game.

"Nicely played, Sir Gawain," Vera said, keeping her eyes locked on Lancelot as she high-fived Gawain.

Lancelot scowled and pointed at each of them. "Fuck you both," he said.

The table burst into laughter, any notion that Vera might be offended by their language long forgotten.

On the next hand, Percival went out and erupted in frustration because Elaine, seated next to him, had peeked at his cards.

"Well, hold them closer if you don't want me to see. You've got them all the way out here." She mimed holding her cards with her arm fully extended. "What am I supposed to do?"

"I am not doing that," he snapped. "You're right next to me; it doesn't matter how I hold them. Guinna, how did they keep people from being unrighteous cheaters at the monastery?"

It was Vera's turn, so she was busy studying her hand as she responded. "Poker tables are usually circular. I think that helps."

"That's what we need." Percival rapped the table sharply with his knuckles. "A round table."

She heard it.

A round table. She looked up from her cards and around at the knights, Arthur's most trusted council of knights. The round table. Vera did the only thing that made a lick of sense to her: she laughed. Really laughed. Laughed until tears wet her cheeks. With no way to explain it, she'd simply have to accept their cocked eyebrows and bewildered stares.

"Probably a monastery thing," Gawain said as he pushed more coins to the center.

The game pulled them back from Vera's hysterics. She lost shortly after that and stayed for a while, leaning toward Tristan to offer him quiet advice or to explain the difference in suits when she could sense he was about to mess up. Lionel took to yell-singing made-up sea shanties to roast everyone around the table, but even amid the raging ruckus, Vera's eyes grew heavy, and she nodded off where she sat.

"Hey." Lancelot's whisper at her ear jolted her. Vera lifted her head from Tristan's shoulder, where it had lolled as she dozed. "Ready to turn in?"

She nodded in a haze. "Sorry," she mumbled to Tristan, who wasn't bothered at all. Vera wasn't so groggy that she missed Arthur looking up at her from his cards every few seconds as he pretended not to watch.

"I'll walk you," Lancelot said with a glance at Gawain.

He rose quickly. "I'll come, too."

"Why not?" Lancelot said. He played it off perfectly, as if he'd not orchestrated it all ahead of time. "Let's make it a proper escort."

Vera scooped up the jug on their way out. She waited until they reached the tower stairwell before she stopped and passed it to Gawain, explaining what Margaret had said. "Is there any way you can test it?" she asked. "To know what it is for certain?"

"Yes." Gawain frowned as he ran his fingers around its base. "If there's enough residual liquid." He didn't unstop the cork to check; rather, he closed his eyes and mumbled beneath his breath. The jug glowed green as it had when he tested Percival's liquor on the way to Yule. As the glow faded, his eyes shot to Vera. "I'm sorry, Guinna. It is what you expected."

Her heart plummeted. She wordlessly turned and started up the stairs. She knew Gawain and Lancelot followed as their steps echoed behind her. When they reached the landing, Gawain broke the silence.

"Do you want me to tell the king?" he asked.

"Yes—No," she said, changing her mind as she spoke. This wasn't fair. "Wait until after the tournament tomorrow. It will only be a distraction that we can't talk about until the day is done anyway."

"And we can't have him punching Merlin," Lancelot added, and Vera knew it was only half a joke.

"Thank you, Gawain," she said, determined to push it away. In the end, nothing had changed since this morning. It was all as it always had been. "Can you give Lancelot and me a minute, please? And no listening devices."

Gawain nodded, eyes darting between them.

"Wait for me here on the landing," Lancelot said, giving Gawain's elbow a squeeze.

"Am I wrong to wait to tell Arthur about the potion?" she asked once they were halfway down the corridor.

"Honestly, I don't think it matters. I have known him all my life. He's never looked at anybody the way he looks at you."

She wanted to believe that, too. When Arthur held her in his gaze, she could nearly believe she was the most important, most lovely human alive. Nearly—because it was tainted. "He's never been under a potion to adore someone either."

Lancelot sighed dramatically. "There's not a mage alive who could make a potion with those results." He leaned on the doorframe as they stopped outside Vera and Arthur's chamber. "And why does it even matter? What's so bad about two married people being disgustingly in love?"

"What if I'm playing right into some awful destiny that I can't stop?" The words were tumbling from Vera now. "Merlin was adamant that the stories about Arthur from my time didn't get any of it right, but there've been a number of suspicious coincidences."

"What do you mean?"

"Well, first, there's the two of us. And I know it's not an affair, and we're not in love or any of that . . ."

"Speak for yourself." He raised his eyebrow suggestively.

"Oh, shut up," she shot back, grateful for a reason to smile. "But Gawain's in the legends, too. At first, I didn't think much of it because I knew the Gawain in those stories was a knight and ours wasn't, but then—"

"Ah. I see."

"And," Vera went on, feeling rather silly, "there's a whole part in the story about how Arthur's knights are the knights of the round table. Did you hear what Percival said today?"

"Yes, but he was talking about poker."

"I know. It's ridiculous. But," she said, realizing it as she spoke, "history has little evidence from this time period. To even get Arthur's name right, let alone so many others, and their roles, and you, and me . . . It's strange."

"Huh." He tilted his head back and stared into space as he considered it. "You said there are a lot of different stories written about it. Is there a primary one? One that's better than the rest?"

"I think Le Morte d'Arthur was the first that told the whole story."

Lancelot pulled a worried face. "The Death of Arthur? That sounds pleasant. Is that what it's all about?"

"I don't know. I haven't actually read it."

He snorted. "Shit. That's unfortunate. I wish you had."

"You and me both."

"The amount of time you are spending alone at the queen's room has now crossed the boundary from acceptable to suspicious," Gawain called from the stairwell.

Vera and Lancelot laughed. "Thank you, Sir Gawain. I'm coming." Lancelot rolled his eyes, but his face lit as he said, "It's always an adventure with Gawain. Look, I'm sure it's nothing. They're . . . oddities—and they aren't quite bang-on right, are they?"

She supposed not. She'd never heard anything about Gawain being a mage. And certainly, the round table wasn't in reference to poker.

Lancelot kissed Vera's cheek. "Night, darling. Lock your door. Arthur has a key."

"I know. Thank you, Mother. See you tomorrow." But she watched Lancelot's back as he left. Her intuition hummed that there was something odd in her interaction with him, but she couldn't place what.

Vera didn't need help changing, but she wanted to talk to Matilda. She crept over to her door and listened carefully for a minute, not wanting to interrupt if Randall was there. After a stretch of quiet that reassured her, she knocked. No answer.

If Matilda wasn't here and she and Randall left at the same time . . . Vera giggled alone in the hallway. What a conversation that would be tomorrow. She couldn't wait to tell Arthur.

She changed and got into bed. It had been a splendid evening, the kind that led to things like pining lovers finding one another's arms.

The unbidden image of beautiful Marian with her lips inches from Arthur's ear came to Vera's mind. Her eyes shot open. What if he didn't come back at all tonight? Maybe he'd go to Marian's bed. He was allowed to, after all. Vera had no claim on him. He made it clear that she could pursue whoever she wanted, and he had the same right.

They were friends, and she was leaving soon. In fact, it would be better if he ripped off that bandage tonight and found intimacy elsewhere. As much as he emphasized not wanting Vera backed into a corner, he was stuck, too. She wasn't the only one being fed a potion to manipulate her feelings.

Something could have already happened between Marian and Arthur. She acted awfully comfortable with him. There was that year-long gap after Arthur had already witnessed three versions of Guinevere perish. He didn't even want Merlin to bring Vera. Why shouldn't he have found pleasure or even love in that time?

Vera wanted to throw up.

She lay in bed, trying not to think about it and finding that she seemed to have no other thoughts. After at least an hour, she was nearly asleep when the faint sound of metal clinking came from the lock. She opened her eyes just enough to see Arthur's distinct silhouette in the door. He took care to shut and secure it quietly. He didn't even change his clothes. He took off his shirt and crawled into bed.

Vera was infuriated to notice that she was so relieved she was nearly in tears. She rolled over toward him and laid a hand on his bare chest, surprised by her own bold familiarity. He didn't wait to pretend to be asleep. He reached up and covered her hand with his own.

She shivered. Vera wanted to lay her whole body on top of him, and her heart heaved at the thought of it.

He traced his thumb over the back of her hand. "Goodnight, Vera."

"Goodnight," she said.

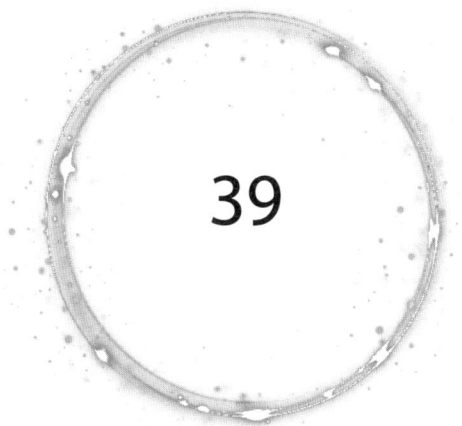

39

The only jousting tournament Vera had attended was at the Glastonbury Abbey's Medieval Faire, where there was also a man dressed as a jester who juggled one-handed while playing a plastic recorder through his nostrils. Camelot's festival was short a juggling nose musician, and the jousting was a far cry from the staged reenactments at the Faire. Those entailed graceful unhorsings that ended up in choreographed sword fights on the ground.

Sitting on the sidelines with Arthur in the raised suite for royalty and nobility and watching bout after bout of real jousting had Vera alternately clenching her eyes shut or with them shocked wide, unable to look away. Lances exploded into splinters, collisions sent riders flying from their horses, and there were plenty of injuries. In Wyatt's first bout, he took a lance right to the face shield of his helmet. While there wouldn't be any lasting damage, he was far worse for the wear. Vera gripped the arms of her seat tightly as each run began, shrinking and cringing like she could sink through her chair if she pushed back hard enough.

Arthur noticed her tension and kept a firm hold on her hand. He distracted her with trivia and jokes. It was barely mid-morning when a server appeared at Vera's side with a glass of wine. She took it out of politeness but was confused because she hadn't asked for it.

"I thought it might help to take the edge off." Arthur winked. The playful gesture was so handsome on his often-serious features.

There was no doubt to be had: Percival was the best jouster in the tournament. Barring an accident, he would win. He unhorsed his current opponent in one pass.

Tristan and Lionel fared well, too. Wyatt struggled after his unfortunate start to the day. He'd lost two matches now. Vera was sweating by the time Lancelot showed up near the lunch break.

"You aren't jousting," she said.

"No," Lancelot said with distaste. "Jousting is stupid."

"He's not very good at it," Arthur said. Lancelot rolled his eyes but otherwise ignored Arthur.

"I have an idea." He drummed her chair's arm with his fingertips, his eyes glinting. "An activity for all the folks who aren't soldiers to do after the lunch break. Can you help?"

Vera grinned. What could he possibly have in mind?

She had none of Guinevere's memories of Lancelot during the war, but Arthur had once said something that stuck with her. "If it seems like I carry a heavy burden now, that's how it was for Lancelot throughout the war. He was a different man then. I wasn't sure the person I grew up with would ever return."

But Lancelot's appreciation for peace only served to bolster his spirit. When it wasn't war, much of life was a game to him, from annoying Merlin to taking Vera to the pit after her first morning run to roping in a new knight to their party. So, Vera should have had some inkling of what to expect.

She and Lancelot set out to start the first ever rock, paper, scissors tournament in the history of the world. They built a single-elimination bracket and spread the word that the people should gather. Camelot liked games, evidenced by the pit's popularity, and that was where they held their tournament. It was conveniently close to the training-field-turned-jousting-stadium for the festival.

How often did the beloved king's general, the war hero, Sir Lancelot, serve as emcee and referee for a brand-new tournament specifically for non-royals, non-nobility, and non-knights—a tournament for regular, ordinary villagers and travelers?

"Never," Lancelot told Vera when she'd asked. "We've never done anything like this, which, obviously, was madness." He gestured at the growing crowd. Nearly everyone not actively watching nor participating in the joust had gathered for the inaugural Tournament of the People (that's what Lancelot called it). He hopped up on the pit wall and shouted with impressive bravado. "Gather 'round, good people of Camelot and travelers from hill and valley of our great kingdom!"

"Ooh, very nice," Vera murmured from his side.

He glanced down at her in satisfaction. "Good, right?" he said quietly.

"Hear ye, now! I present to you a game not for the likes of those skilled on a horse nor with a sword: a game for all. A game that will test the skill of your eye at reading the face in front of you, a game that will tire your hands and excite your hearts." He lowered his voice dramatically. "A game that, ultimately, can only be determined by fate."

"All right, get on with it," Vera said.

Obligingly, he did. In the same dramatic manner, he told the game's rules: that they'd play "matches" of three games for each opponent, and he added rules that Vera hadn't taught him. "You must show your selection on the fourth slap of your hand. You'll receive one in-good-faith warning, but after that," he pointed emphatically in the air and paused for a breath, "your opponent wins that game." As he wrapped up, he reviewed the rules with the crowd's help. "Is this paper?" Lancelot cried, holding his flat hand turned on its side with the fingers atop one another.

"No!" the crowd shouted in unison. Vera chortled into her hands.

"Is this paper?" He corrected his hand, flattening it out in front of him.

"Yes!" they cried.

Lancelot thrust his fist into the air and pronounced the tournament's official start.

"Uh oh." He hopped down from the wall.

"What?"

"Merlin," he said, looking pointedly over Vera's shoulder.

She heard him before she turned around to see him.

"What are you doing?" He held his face carefully taut, though a vein pulsed in his forehead.

"Playing a game," Lancelot said, as if it were obvious. "Guinna taught me."

Merlin pointed stiffly at the match playing out behind them. "That is not a game from our time, and you've taught everyone. You cannot do that. You can't make up your own rules!"

"Oh, I see," Vera said. "You're the only one allowed to do that."

He glowered at her as Lancelot, without so much as a glance in her direction, held his hand up to the side for a high five. Vera grinned and slapped it. Merlin visibly seethed.

"Aw, come now, Merlin. There's no harm in it." Lancelot gave Merlin's shoulder a companionable squeeze. "I've actually got you slotted to play in the tournament, and you get a pass this round. What do you say? Automatically compete in round two?"

He huffed, fixing Vera with a disappointed shake of his head, but he gave up on arguing.

"Poor Merlin." Lancelot sighed as the mage strode away. "Between the two of us, we'll be the death of him. I'm sure of it."

Vera might have felt guilty that they'd ganged up on him if she hadn't just learned of his damn potions. He deserved more than a little social discomfort. But Merlin surprised her and actually showed up to play his round. When he won the first two games of three, taking the match, Vera thought she saw the flicker of a smile as the spectators cheered their mage on with pride.

Lancelot intervened during match disputes when someone threw their pick at the wrong time or hesitated too long. He kept it light and kept Vera laughing.

"Now, now, now, wait a minute!" He charged in as some folks in the crowd grew heated at perceived cheating. "We, the convened, have a duty, nay—a responsibility to uphold the honor of this prestigious tournament. Are we without compassion?"

The Once and Future Queen

They all chorused a resounding no.

"Nay! We are not. As was discussed, we will give one warning." Lancelot turned to the accused party. "All right, a reminder, lad: rock, paper, scissors, and then show your choice."

The jousting finished before the rock, paper, scissors tournament, and all the knights and soldiers came to cheer on whoever remained in the game, throwing their support behind who was most local to their towns. They cheered loudly at victory and groaned when defeat came.

Merlin was the clear crowd favorite and progressed all the way to the final match before he was beaten in the third bout by a sweet elderly woman from out of town. He laughed, something Vera had never seen, and hugged the woman in congratulations. Percival, the joust's winner, rushed to Vera's side and pushed his prize, a golden peacock statue, into her hands with a glance at the woman.

"Are you sure?" she had to yell to be heard over the roar of the crowd. He nodded.

Lancelot announced the winner as she presented the woman with her prize. Vera caught Arthur's eye in the crowd, clapping with the rest. She saw pure, untarnished joy—certainly, for the day's goodness, for the sense of community among his people—but this, what she saw right now, she knew to her core it came because of her.

Vera had never been happier in her entire life than she was right now, staring at Arthur through the crowd. He started toward her, and she tore her eyes away to congratulate the woman once more before turning back to him.

Vera knew what she wanted to say and felt a thrill of nerves course through her. "Arthur, I—" she said as he got close enough to hear, but he didn't stop. Without breaking his stride, Arthur slid one hand around her waist, pulling Vera to him and kissing her without hesitation.

Her hands went to his chest, grabbing his shirt and clutching him to her as if afraid he might change his mind at any second. When Vera felt the tip of his tongue tease a caress across her own, she gasped only to keep herself from moaning in pleasure. She pulled back from him and pressed her lips together.

"I don't know how I'm going to leave," she said as soon as she trusted her voice, letting her selfish thoughts win out and feeling the heavy sting of guilt that followed. She had to get home to her parents—to her father. And she wasn't Guinevere; she didn't belong here.

Arthur was a master of his emotions, and Vera had become nearly as masterful at reading him. She saw him try to tamp down his elation with a heavy swallow. "I don't want you to leave," was all he said. Her heart would have leapt were it not all fouled by magic's intervention and Vera's inevitable, necessary departure.

He kissed her—tenderly this time. Slowly. As he pulled away, he thought better of it, instead resting his forehead against hers. Such untamed desire in his eyes—ah, of course. The potion to make him want her. Arthur didn't know he'd been drinking it. She had to tell him.

They had not even broken their embrace when a sound echoed through Camelot. It was the multi-toned dissonance, its quality the contrast of rich and shrill, and its unnaturally loud volume planted a sense of dread in all who heard it. It was a horn's blast, but different from the one the day the boar got loose. Arthur had told her of this horn, that it was made to be a siren. That was the purpose of it, never to be blown except under the gravest of circumstances.

When it blared its torturous call, it was met with more terror than it would have received had it not come at a time when it could crush such brazen bliss. The cries were more panicked. Many people ducked as if the horn was a dragon in the sky, swooping down to set them aflame. Frenzy erupted.

Arthur tensed, but he did not immediately let go of Vera. He held her a fraction of a second into the turmoil, a frozen pool in the roiling waters, and kissed her once more—for Arthur knew what the horn meant. Whatever was coming, whatever reason the alarm was raised, it all came back to one thing.

Camelot . . . life, as they knew it, had ended.

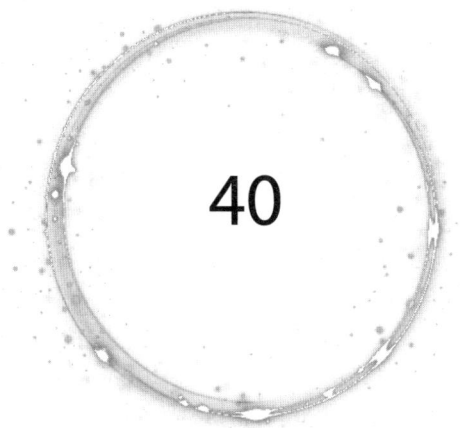

40

The heavy quiet in the throne room offered a reprieve from the shattering chaos outside, but it was not better. It was the stillness of waiting for awful news and praying it was the least sort of awful rather than the most.

When Arthur had released Vera from his embrace, he kept hold of her hand, pulling her to tail behind him as he entered the cacophony. She bore witness as a remarkable order unfurled among the knights and Arthur. Foreign to her, for them it was as natural as breathing. She hadn't seen Elaine all day, but now she was there, right next to Vera with a protective hand on her back, her eyes hard, and the lines of her square face set. All of them—all the king's guard and his knights, save for Randall and Lancelot, found Arthur as if summoned by some invisible force. Arthur climbed atop a barrel one-handed, for he hadn't let go of Vera.

His eyes searched the knights, falling on Edwin. Vera watched their silent exchange in awe as Edwin wove through the others and climbed up next to Arthur. He closed his eyes, his face drawn in concentration, as he cupped one hand around the front of the king's throat. It would have looked like a threat were it not for Arthur's calm, which spread from him like a rush of warmth on a cold day.

When he spoke, his voice was amplified by a gift flowing through

Edwin's fingertips. The people quieted at his call, and not only because of its volume. That wave of consolation came through his voice, too. It felt like the taste of caramel; just as it slowed the tongue in eating, Arthur's voice slowed the swelling panic.

He announced that the people would be welcomed to the keep and set Percival to lead, reminding them of all the protections in place, assuring that he would give more information as soon as he could, and above all, that he would exhaust every resource to protect them. Vera felt so small in his presence that she was embarrassed to be touching him, like he was too great a force to be lassoed to the ground by her.

When Lancelot and Randall dashed through the throngs with a soldier between them that Vera recognized from the wall, everything rushed back into motion.

"Tell me," Arthur said without any formalities as he stepped back down.

"Two thousand by my estimation," Randall said. "They're a day's ride out, but one rode ahead. We're apprehending him."

Now, in the throne room, they waited for the messenger. Two thousand was small for an invasion, making that an unlikely explanation. Vera naively thought this was good news, that it saved them from the weight of dread closing in, but it did not ease the tensions. Two thousand was too large a force for anything that wasn't sinister.

They were all gathered: the whole king's guard, Matilda, and both of Camelot's mages. Vera was frightened. They were all in hushed conversations with one another or staring at the door expectantly, except Tristan. Her eyes found his, and a memory bloomed in her mind.

Vera stood on a vast and smoldering field dotted with dirt hillocks for a crop she couldn't guess at, smoke rising in curling tendrils in unnatural jewel colors, shades hinting at magic. It might have been beautiful if she'd not been able to taste the acrid odor of roasted flesh and something grossly metallic. The hillocks' uneven spacing, the awkward sizes . . . her eyes focused through the smoke's haze and the expanding light of sunrise. Bodies. Body parts, not dirt. The sharp slap of the smell of blood, the beginnings of decay, and the looming understanding that this was her doing.

The Once and Future Queen

Vera—Guinevere—Vera turned in place, her face a careful mask of calm. She was the architect of this bloodshed. All the lives wiped clean from existence on this battlefield were on her hands.

When she turned, she nearly bumped into Tristan at her shoulder, strong, muddied and bloodied. He wasn't to be fooled by her façade. He saw the truth; Guinevere was destroyed. For a fraction of a second, his chin quivered. He gripped her elbow and surveyed the wreckage.

That was it.

Vera blinked the memory away.

Tristan offered a thin smile across the throne room that she couldn't return. The gravity of what had just happened—a memory, a real memory—pressed down on her. That had been different. That wasn't like Merlin's memories or the things that felt like a dream in the sensory tub. Vera remembered. Her own memories. Did that mean that she—

The doors flung open. The messenger was rushed in, supported on either side by two of Camelot's soldiers. He wasn't bound nor flanked from behind by any additional guards. He wore no armor and was only held beneath the arms by the soldiers because he'd collapse on his own. Arthur was on his feet first. The guards got the man a chair as Lancelot brought water. Arthur knelt before the man, peering up into his face with intensity, an impressive amalgamation of scrutiny and compassion.

The man's breaths came in ragged, unsteady heaves. He wouldn't be ready to speak for some time. Arthur turned to the soldier at his right. The soldier cast about himself uncertainly and only spoke after Lancelot gave him a curt nod.

"It—it was a Saxon invasion on Crayford, sire. The ones to come are refugees. Survivors. The entire city's been destroyed. This is Robert, their town steward."

It set the room humming with murmurs. There'd been no invasions since the final battle of the wars. When the exhausted messenger from Crayford began to speak, his voice was so quiet that Vera almost didn't hear him at first. Arthur leaned closer to him.

"Quiet," Lancelot barked as he sat down next to Vera.

"Every person with a gift was killed." Robert's voice broke, but he valiantly continued after a pause. "There was a light, bright and fierce. Everyone with a gift in the reach of the light fell immediately. The gifted who escaped its reach were tracked down and slaughtered—" He cleared his throat heavily. "Impaled by spikes the size of my arm."

"How did they know who had gifts?" Gawain asked, his face markedly emotionless.

"We celebrate our gifted more than any other city in this kingdom," the man said, his eyes pleading with the mage for a forgiveness and peace that no one could give. "Their names are on a celebrated roll. We paraded them. It was no secret."

"How many were among the Saxon force?" Arthur asked.

Robert recoiled, his surprise enough to stave off his grief. "You misunderstand me, Your Majesty. It wasn't an army. It was one Saxon."

"One man did this?" Merlin said sharply.

"Yes. A king. A mage. There is nothing left of Crayford."

"The village was burned?" Arthur asked.

"No. Most homes and shops are fine." Robert shook his head, and his eyes drifted out of focus, back to Crayford. "The land. The land has died. Every blade of grass. Not burned." His voice rose, nearing hysterics. "Dead. The life was sucked out of it."

Robert gave in to the heaving sobs. Arthur lay a hand on his shuddering shoulder as he spoke to the soldiers. "Take him to rest."

"I need to ask you all to leave while I speak to our mages," Arthur said as he stood, his eyes following Robert and the soldiers out the door. "Percival, tell the people what we know, and then come find me. Anyone from the festival who wants to stay in the safety of Camelot may do so. Tristan, go with him. The rest of you, we need to ready the troops and send word to prepare the kingdom's forces. Pray they won't be needed."

They left without question. Lancelot didn't move.

"Should I go?" Vera whispered.

"You stay," he said. "You always stay." Evidently, so did he.

The second the room was clear, Arthur turned to Merlin. "Do you think this is the leader Viviane had in mind?"

"I believe it is," Merlin said gravely.

Oh my God. Vera's heart sank. They'd waited too long. They'd played it too slowly. What were they thinking?

Merlin's next words were a life preserver, the one escape from the disaster she'd thrown them into. "We need to get Guinevere's memories back. The procedure will work, and we must do it now. I would not suggest it if it were not necessary. I'll be as careful as I can."

He was right. Of course. How could she have ever put herself above this kingdom? It was so much more real now, with an entire town's gifted exterminated. How many would that be? If there were two thousand remaining, what did that mean? Five hundred dead? Five hundred lives traded for Vera's life, for her comfort and happiness.

"I'll do it," she said.

Arthur's face had gone pale. He knew they were out of options.

"We should not push the queen's mind," Gawain said. Merlin went unnaturally still. "Your Majesty, we must go to the council of mages. Viviane has been in the grave for nearly two years. The Saxon mage brought the doom. It wasn't a curse of magic fading. It was a deliberate act perpetrated by a dark mage and an aggressor against this kingdom. He destroyed the magic in that village and corrupted the land. We don't know what else he has done, and we can't afford to wait to seek help."

"We also don't know where he is," Merlin bit back. "Traveling with a large enough party to stay protected makes us a target, and it makes us vulnerable. What if this dark mage kills us all, Gawain? What then?"

Lancelot sat up straighter. "Then let's not travel with a large party."

They all looked at him.

"It need not be public information," he explained, seeming to build on the idea as he said it. "We travel small, and we move quickly."

Merlin shifted in his seat. "Your Majesty, you must consider the uncertainties. The mages may not be able to help. We can retrieve Guinevere's memories."

"If you don't kill her first," Lancelot spat. And he didn't even know what Gawain and Vera knew, that there was no outcome where she emerged unscathed.

"It doesn't make sense to start with the queen. The risk is high. It's far too high." Gawain appealed directly to Arthur. "There is the likelihood, perhaps the certainty—"

"Gawain," Merlin warned.

Gawain didn't stop. He spoke louder. "That further intervention will cause her mind to break. She might survive but wouldn't have enough brain function left to swallow food."

"Enough!" Merlin slammed his fist down on the arm of his chair.

Gawain's characteristic scowl was nothing to the wrath that marred his features. "What good would it do if she dies before she can tell us what happened? It's prudent we go to the mages first and only push Guinevere's mind as a last resort."

Merlin began arguing, but Arthur held up a hand. "We're going to the mages."

It was decided. Merlin and Gawain, Arthur, Lancelot, Vera, and two other soldiers.

"I think we should also bring one more knight with Guinevere coming," Lancelot said. "Percival would be best."

"No. Percival will stay as king regent," Arthur said. "We'll bring Tristan."

Lancelot nearly hid the glimmer of a scowl, but Vera saw it. "Why not Randall? Or Marian?"

Arthur shook his head. "I want them in Camelot. Tristan is the right choice." He didn't elaborate; it was not up for discussion. Lancelot stiffly crossed his arms over his chest, displeased.

They would leave this evening under the cover of darkness.

Arthur and Vera went straight to their quarters to pack. She shoved her running trainers and socks into a rucksack, deliberating what to say to him. The memories were right there. She'd had a real memory. The rest couldn't be far behind. But that brought up another issue entirely that Vera hadn't had time to reckon with: she truly was Guinevere.

Before she could work up the nerve to speak, Percival and Tristan were at the door. Percival dutifully reported the city's status: calmer than before but fortifying itself in preparations for the barrage of refugees.

"They responded to Percival well," Tristan added, clearly impressed. "Almost how they'd respond to you."

Percival shrugged off the compliment. "What news from the mages?" he asked.

Arthur was honest. There was plenty he couldn't say, which Percival readily accepted. He only balked when Arthur relayed their travel plans. "You'll stay in Camelot," he told the young knight. "I need you to serve as king regent."

Percival drew back before his brow furrowed, making his scar the dominant feature of his handsome face. "The queen should be in charge," he said.

Arthur shook his head. "She's coming with us."

"Why?" Percival asked. It was a fair question, and there were plenty of reasons. Because she wanted to, for one. Because Arthur knew the safest place would be with him and Lancelot. And because if something happened with her mind, they needed mages there.

Instead, Vera said, "I want to go," at the same time that Arthur said, "I will not leave her."

To her surprise, that was justification enough for Percival.

"Tristan," Arthur looked to him, and he dutifully stepped forward, "I need you to come on the road as the queen's guard."

Vera jolted. She hadn't realized that was the additional knight's purpose.

"I'd be honored, Your Majesty," he said, his eyes lighting up.

"Arthur, I don't know how to act as king," Percival said.

"Of course you do." Arthur crossed the room to the desk. He collected a stack of parchments and handed them to a stunned Percival before he paused thoughtfully. "I'll show you a few things. Come on." Vera began following him to the door. Arthur stopped her. His eyes flicked to Tristan for the length of a blink before resting on her. "Stay. Finish packing."

"I—" she stammered. "All right."

"Should Tristan—?" Percival began.

"No," Arthur said. "He can stay."

Their footsteps echoed down the hall, leaving her and Tristan alone. Unsure what else to do, she resumed packing while he wandered over to the window. Its shutter was latched open, and a pleasant breeze slipped through the rods. Tristan grabbed one of the bars and gave it a sturdy shake. Vera hadn't realized she'd stopped, a travel cloak mid-fold between her hands, to watch him. There was something she was missing about Tristan. She was right on the edge of it and couldn't break through, couldn't clear the last cobweb obscuring the memory. Vera clamped her eyes shut in an effort to focus. She dropped to sit on the bed behind her.

"Gwen?" Tristan said warily. Vera let her eyes flutter open. He was already closing the space between them. "Are you frightened?"

"I'm—" She cast about for the right words, but her head spun. She was so close to it.

Tristan pulled a chair over and sat, facing her. He smiled grimly. "I know. It hasn't felt like this since the wars. It'll be all right." He rubbed her arm above the elbow, and there it was.

Vera remembered.

There was no dramatic moment of recollection, no reliving the scenes like in the sensory tub. One second, she'd have never thought to touch this dusty corner of her mind, and the next, Tristan and so many things about him were just . . . there as if they always had been. There was a whole childhood of memories with the man in front of her. Their parents had one tutor who taught both of them. Tristan had shown Vera how to hang upside down from a tree branch by her knees, and she'd gotten him into a world of trouble when they started a midsummer bonfire that nearly set his neighbor's barley field aflame. Between two lifetimes of growing up, Tristan was the dearest childhood friend she'd ever had.

So many years ago, on a rainy summer day in Tristan's father's barn, he had been her first kiss. Sour, salty, or sweet. It was a game they played when one's eyes were closed, and the other was meant to surprise with a bite of food, and they'd laugh together when it shocked the tastebuds. They took it in turns, and it was Tristan's turn to keep his eyes shut. Vera was fourteen, and the tension had been rising between them for months. Years, really. She had decided hours before that today would be the day. When Vera had filled his lips with her own rather than the sweet cake between her fingers, Tristan's lips joined the dance.

But it didn't end there. And their fathers' plans that they should marry weren't merely advantageous; they were kind. Tristan and Vera had been in love. The missing years she hadn't been able to reach before flooded in. Flashes of joy, brushing hands beneath tablecloths at banquets, dances when he held her a little too tightly, stolen kisses when they thought they were being sneaky behind their parents' or the servants' backs, but everyone had known.

And she remembered the day it all ended when she met him in that same barn. This time, it was a perfect sunny day. The light found each chink and crack in the wood-slatted wall and lit Tristan and Vera in uneven stripes. She cried as she told him she'd chosen to marry the king. He'd begged her not to and painted the story of the life that Tristan and Guinevere could have together. It would have been a good life, a great one. She'd known what she was giving up, but she also knew it was best for the kingdom . . . that bringing her father's lands and troops (Tristan among them) would make it all possible to build the new dream of a nation.

Tristan had even ridden with their party the whole journey to Camelot, not yet having given up that Guinevere might change her mind after she met Arthur and that he could whisk her away. But then he met Arthur, and Tristan came to her that night.

That time, it was him who told Vera through tears that she was right, because Tristan had seen the light in Arthur that everyone else saw, too.

He'd even traveled the distance from his home in the north after the wars. Arthur had sent for him when the original Guinevere was at her lowest, barely able to rise from the bed. Tristan sat by her side for days, but it made no difference to her.

"I regret ever leaving," Tristan said. It brought Vera out of her remembering. His gaze darted to the window. "I left, and then you fell." Sorrow marred his handsome face.

"That wasn't your fault," Vera said. That wasn't what had happened to the Guinevere he'd known and loved. But she couldn't tell him that.

"Are you . . . happy with him?" Tristan asked, not daring to look at her.

"Yes," Vera said, and it wasn't a lie.

"I'm glad for you. I mean it," he said as he stood. "It is my honor to serve as your guard."

"Thank you," she managed to murmur once he was halfway to the door.

By the time Arthur came back, Vera knew that she should tell him, but she couldn't find the words.

They left as soon as the horizon devoured the sun's last light, and they rode through the night, taking only short breaks. The Magesary was in Oxford, well over a hundred kilometers away. They'd ride the next two days as well.

Dawn was a solid two hours off and the sky an inky void when they arrived at their destination, an unassuming nunnery north of Bristol. The prioress was a woman Arthur knew and trusted. She discreetly put them up in their guest rooms.

Vera collapsed gratefully on the bed and would have fallen asleep sitting up if Arthur had not taken her hand. She blinked at him through her stupor.

"Can you stay awake a bit longer?" he whispered.

She nodded, intrigued enough that her brain roused from its fog. Arthur led her through a door opposite the one they'd used to enter the chamber and into a modest chapel. Vera stumbled over her own feet. "Our room backs up to a chapel?" she said.

It was a small space: two benches in front of a wooden altar. Arthur sat on the front bench, so Vera followed suit, waiting for an explanation.

She turned at the main door opening behind her. Lancelot came first, followed by Gawain.

"We only have a few minutes," Lancelot said.

Arthur nodded at Gawain to begin. So this was why they were here, but why so secretive?

"I believe that the Saxon mage who terrorized Crayford is the same as the one who committed the massacre in Dorchester," Gawain said. Arthur, Lancelot, and Vera all shared expressions of shock. "The way their messenger described those deaths, both by magic and traditional violence, that's how it was there."

Arthur leaned forward, bracing his elbows on his knees. "In Dorchester, it was all those without magic who were killed. This time, he slaughtered everyone with a gift. That doesn't make sense."

Lancelot was looking at Gawain with a strange, drawn expression. "You were there? In Dorchester?"

"Yes," Gawain said to the air between Vera and Arthur rather than facing Lancelot. Nonetheless, Lancelot's hand flinched as if to reach out in comfort. He balled it into a fist on his own thigh instead.

"I was born there," Gawain continued. "My family was killed in the attack. Merlin was the first mage to respond after the massacre. He offered me a place at the Magesary. He's the closest person to family that I have."

Vera hadn't realized. It brought a surge of affection for Merlin, complicated by his actions of late. "Do you trust him?" she asked.

Gawain hesitated before saying, "I do. I always have."

"Then why are we having a secret meeting?" she said.

"Because of the real reason that we must see the mages." Gawain took a deep breath. "I believe they can help with the Saxon, but there is another aspect to magic's dwindling that needs to be addressed with the mages. Merlin would stop me if he knew."

"Why would he do that?" Arthur asked.

"Because it has to do with how the mages expand our powers."

Vera sat up straighter. She'd long wondered about that. It had been lodged in the back of her mind since the day Gawain told her that most mages start with only one power. "How do mages amass more gifts?"

Lancelot answered automatically, "Study and innovation."

Arthur nodded along with him.

Gawain held Vera's stare.

She leaned toward him and asked again. "How?"

He licked his top lip and swallowed heavily.

"You can't say," she breathed.

"Now you are asking the right question." Gawain said, smiling weakly at her. He turned to Arthur. "Mages can speak freely only at the Magesary during a convened council gathering. After you have asked the mages for help, you must stay in the room. They will ask you to leave. They will pressure you to leave. As the ruler of this kingdom and thus of the mages, it is your right to stay. Tell them that. Do not leave that room." His voice was stern. He rubbed anxiously at his temple with his thumb, his hand trembling. Whatever he meant for Arthur to understand, it frightened him.

"I won't," Arthur said.

"What did the mage in Dorchester look like?" Lancelot asked.

"He was obscured by magic like a shadow made flesh. Horrible and somehow unseeable."

Vera shivered. Something . . . there was something else. It flitted around the edges of her thoughts, evading her. She kept coming back to the stories of Arthurian legend from her future. Vera tried to swat it out of her thoughts, but she could not stop its buzz.

Le Morte d'Arthur.

The tome's name rose up in her mind, and she froze. The Death of Arthur.

She remembered a character from the legends that she had yet to meet. He had to be fiction. And yet . . . so many other pieces had come to fruition. A jolt of fear seared through her.

"Did the mage have a name?" she asked, hopeful that the truth would free her from her dread.

It did not.

Gawain nodded. "He called himself Mordred."

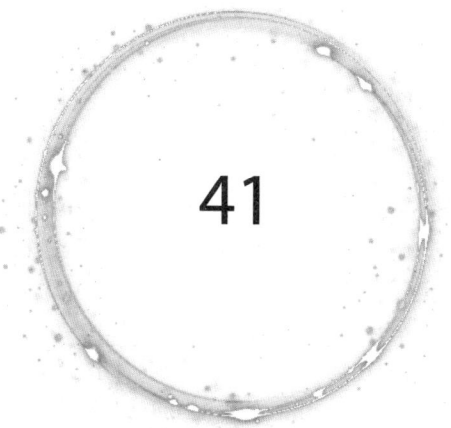

41

Arthur and Lancelot had no reaction to hearing the name Mordred. Arthur asked another question, but Vera couldn't hear it. She heard only a muted ringing inside her head.

Gawain didn't answer Arthur's question and kept his gaze steadily on Vera. "You're familiar with that name," he said. It was not a question.

There were names from the legend of King Arthur that she recognized, but she wasn't sure of their role in the story. Not Mordred. She knew that name, and in any snippet of the myth Vera had heard, Mordred was the one who killed Arthur.

"He's—a villain in our stories," she said.

She had no more words. She couldn't even follow the conversation that continued in murmurs around her. Her thoughts were dominated by fear and, above all, the determination to make sure that version of events never came to fruition. She went back and forth at war with herself over what to do with this information until she landed on a decision: she would tell Arthur when they got to their room. There would be no secrets between them. She had to tell him everything—including about Tristan.

By the time they went their separate ways from the chapel, Vera was itching to say it. She launched in as soon as the door closed behind them.

"Arthur, something happened earlier." She anxiously twisted her fingers as she sat on the foot of the bed. "I looked across the throne room and saw Tristan, and then I—"

Arthur came and sat next to her, stilling her fingers by covering them with the comfort of his own. Vera's heart raced, but this time, trepidation and not attraction drove it.

"I remembered him," she blurted. "A whole childhood of friendship and, erm, growing up together." She wouldn't breathe aloud the feelings that came with those memories, but they weren't the point anyway. "They were my memories. My childhood, even though it feels like they're from so long ago. I—I am Guinevere. I'm sure of it."

His face remained determinedly passive. "Do you remember what happened with Viviane?" he asked in a quiet way that raised goosebumps on Vera's neck.

"No."

He nodded, and she saw the muscle in his jaw begin its flex-relax cycle.

"I'm so sorry," she said. This was what she needed to say most, the part that had her stomach in knots. "This means that I am the one who betrayed you. That was me. I did it."

"It's all right," Arthur said half a moment too quickly. "I don't blame you for any of it." His face was the mask again, and it made her want to cry.

"Do you mean that?" she managed to ask without her voice quaking.

"Yes." He gave her hand a squeeze before he stood and crossed to his bag. "And we both need sleep."

They were fine. She decided to trust his word because soon, mere minutes from now, she could crawl into bed with him and rest in the solace of his arms for a blessed few hours.

But Arthur wasn't fishing in his bag for a change of clothes. He'd picked up his saddle bag and slung it over his shoulder.

"Are you going somewhere?" she asked.

"There's an open room at the end of the corridor. I'm going to sleep there."

Her heart plummeted. "Arthur—"

"Gawain told me about the potion we've both been receiving. I think..." He pushed his jaw forward and addressed Vera's shoulder, not meeting her eye. "We've been fooling ourselves into wanting what's between us to be more than magic, but it wasn't like this before she was—you were—gone."

Vera gaped at him, the only expression she could manage that didn't involve yielding to the prickling ache of tears and the rising lump in her throat.

"Tristan can stay with you if you want," Arthur said. "I'm fairly certain he's still in love with you."

At first, his words landed as gibberish. "What?"

"You like him. I can tell." Arthur shrugged. How was he saying this so casually, as if talking to her about the weather? "Those feelings are untouched by magic. You haven't remembered with me—"

"I remembered the dance steps," Vera interrupted, knowing she was grasping at straws. "And during the procedure—"

"The procedure was magical intervention," he said. "And the other was body memory. Not conscious. You remember Tristan. Real memories."

His determined, even voice incensed her. "Let me get this straight. You don't want me to feel cornered with you. But it's all right for me to be cornered into having sex with Tristan?"

It stung him as she'd intended. He avoided looking at her. "You don't have to, but you can. You'll be leaving soon, so you're running out of opportunities. You've always liked him. Maybe loved him." She heard the underbelly of bitterness. "Do whatever you want. And if that includes being with Tristan, all the better. You might remember. I'd sure as hell love to know what drove you to betray our people."

And there it was.

"You've been biting that one back for a long time, haven't you?" Vera said.

Arthur grimaced. "That was unfair. I'm sorry. I'm tired. I'm going to go."

"No. Go on. Say it. Say all of it. Tell me what you think of what I did."

"Vera," he said with forced patience. "You didn't do anything—"

"I did. I'm her. I did all of it, whether I remember it or not. Say it."

He stared at her with that cold mask from their early days together. It stoked her fearful rage to erupt.

"Say it!" she demanded.

Arthur breathed heavily through his nose. He was almost there. She could tell. One good shove . . .

"What kind of a king shares his bed with a woman who tried to destroy his kingdom? I was meant to be the one who killed you. And you knew that before Yule. Merlin told you that. What do you want, Arthur? What's the fucking end game here? To let me finish the job?"

Arthur's breath came faster. "I had no idea how much you hated me. The depths of betrayal that you went to are unthinkable. To bring war on our people? To give up the secrets of our security? How could you do this? Why didn't you talk to me?"

Vera laughed. It was thick with scorn. "Talk to you! You think you could have fixed that kind of broken through conversation? Imagine how well that would have gone if you'd given me the same statue-faced bullshit you pull with everyone else. Do you wish it had been like this? Screaming at each other?"

The control of his face shattered into unbridled fury. "It was never once at all like this." He spat each word like it was venom. She hadn't expected that to be what enraged him the most. "I would have done anything to make it better for you. I was ready to let another man take my place in our bed, and it wasn't enough for you!"

"Then nothing's changed," Vera said savagely. Oh, God. Why was she doing this? It was pouring poison on the pain of his rejection. It soothed at the moment to hurl words she knew would hurt but would rot her later. Shocked, Arthur took a step back. "You're still putting my comfort ahead of your kingdom. You're still the fool sending another man to your wife. That's what you're doing right now, isn't it?"

"Jesus, Vera," Arthur said. "Nice." He looked at her like he was seeing her for the first time, and he'd found an enemy. She'd done it. She'd effectively severed whatever affection he had for her.

"I thought you were leaving. Go on, then. Glad it's at the other end of the hall. Don't want to hear him fucking me, do you?"

His eyes went wide. For a moment, it seemed he might pull the mask back into place, but he stared at her with abject, open disgust.

"What is wrong with you?" he snarled as he crossed the room and ripped the door open.

Vera threw her hands in the air, a mad laugh jumping from her lips. "That's the question, isn't it?" she shouted as Arthur slammed the door behind him.

She stared at the door, waiting for him to come back for a full minute before she crumbled to the floor, landing hard on her knees. She'd have wailed if she wasn't afraid that Arthur might be in the corridor to hear it. Vera sobbed; her mouth contorted in the shape of a scream with no sound. He was done with her, and it was probably best. Arthur was right. She remembered more with Tristan in a few days than she had with anyone in nearly half a year. Maybe she should go find him.

But not tonight. It was the last thing Vera wanted.

When she was out of tears and felt like an empty shell on the floor, she dragged herself into the bed and slept fitfully until there was a hand gently shaking her shoulder after far too few hours. She forgot not to hope it was Arthur waking her. It was Lancelot. If he knew what had transpired between Arthur and Vera, he didn't let on.

The morning was young as they set out. They'd only stayed to sleep for four hours. It worked in Vera's favor; no one was especially talkative, so the stiff silence between Vera and Arthur fit right in. She actively avoided him, riding on the opposite side of their travel party, opting to stay near Gawain, who didn't expect any conversation from her.

As they settled into the steady rhythm of bouncing along in their saddles, Vera hissed at the harsh rub of leather against her sore thighs. She wasn't used to riding all day and then hopping back on to ride some more. Gawain reached one hand in her direction and mumbled quiet words. Then, Vera's saddle felt like it was covered with an invisible soft blanket. She blinked up at him. He offered a flash of a smile and rode ahead.

Tristan found Vera around lunch when they were all more awake. She cast furtive glances toward Arthur. When their eyes met once, they both quickly looked away. She tried not to think about him because the longer she spent in Tristan's company, the more she realized Arthur had been right about more than just her memories.

She did like Tristan. He had an easy way about him and a levity of spirit that distracted her from the overwhelming obstacles ahead. Vera shivered as the rain began to fall. Gawain and Merlin could shield them from getting drenched with an invisible cover traveling above them, but the air went unseasonably cold. She couldn't easily get to her cloak, so Tristan unfastened his and passed it over to her without pausing his story. He didn't mean for it to be a noble act worthy of praise, simply a gesture a decent knight guarding his queen might do, which made it that much more endearing.

And he loved making her laugh. She could tell by the giddy way his eyes glimmered and his smile broadened when she found his comments particularly funny. Lancelot, oddly enough, spent most of the day sequestered at the rear with Merlin. A pity, as Vera was hoping to get a word with the older mage.

She had her chance when they stopped midafternoon to water the horses. It seemed he'd been waiting for the opportune moment as well. When Arthur and Lancelot bent their heads close in conversation, Merlin sidled beside Vera at the river's edge.

"In the end, it is your choice, Guinevere," he said, moving his lips so little that she wasn't sure he'd spoken. When she looked at him with surprise, he went on. "If you're willing, I will try the procedure." He studied a nearby tree as if he and Guinevere were talking about a bird perched on its branches and not a dangerous magical procedure.

Vera smiled idly at the tree, though her heart gave a flutter. "Can you do it on the road? If I meet you tonight . . . ?"

Merlin nodded. He let his casual pretense drop enough to meet Vera's gaze with heavy, sorrowful gratitude.

She thought of nothing else for the rest of the day. If there was any chance that Mordred was going to kill Arthur, Vera had to stop it. It was better that they weren't speaking and that he'd drawn the line of distance from her. If she disappeared into nothing, being on poor terms would make it easier.

They bunked down at an inn in Faringdon, not far from Oxford. After a few hours' ride in the morning, the journey would be done. Arthur had separate quarters again, and Vera's decision was made. She would not wait. She had noted the location of Merlin's room as they entered, and, as soon as she was sure everyone was asleep, she rose from her bed, took two quick shots for liquid courage from a bottle Percival had given her a while back, and tiptoed to the door, determined not to lose her nerve—for she was afraid.

Vera dragged the metal bolt free from its lock. There was no quieting the rake of steel against wood, though she did try. She waited in the following silence for a breath and, hearing nothing, opened the door enough to slip out. Instead, she saw the unmistakable glow of two eyes and the dark, hulking shape of a man not three steps from her. Vera gasped and stumbled backward.

"It's me! It's all right!" Tristan rushed into her room after her. "I'm sorry. I didn't mean to scare you."

"Jesus!" Vera lay a steadying hand on his arm. "What were you doing out there?"

"I'm on guard," he said. "What were you doing?"

"Oh . . ." Vera thought quickly. He didn't know about the memory situation. "I, er, wanted to speak with Merlin about tomorrow. And get a potion to help me sleep. I'm . . . anxious," she said and was struck with an idea, albeit a weak one. "You could walk me, and then no need to stand guard because I'll be with a mage. I'm sure you'd like to get some uninterrupted sleep."

Tristan shifted. "I can't do that."

"Why?" Vera asked, eyes narrowing.

He scrunched his face awkwardly. It might have made her laugh another time. "You're going to be angry. I'm—not allowed to let you leave your room. It's an order," he added, as if that made it any better. He at least had the decency to look embarrassed as he told her.

"Fucking Lancelot," Vera growled. It was exactly the sort of overprotective bullshit he would pull. "Go get him. I'm going to throttle him with a fire poker."

"It wasn't him."

She stared blankly at Tristan, though she knew who that left.

"The king told me directly," he said.

Vera was tired. She was already furious with Arthur and more hurt than she could put into words. Her ass hurt from riding in a saddle all day. Her plan to help was thwarted, and now the liquor for bravery left her aimlessly tipsy. Otherwise, she might not have let out the profanity-laced string of insults that followed. They began at a mumble, but as her anger rose, her voice did, too. Tristan, his eyes wide and hands rising defensively, hurriedly shut the door as he shushed Vera.

"Did you shush me?" She ripped her elbow from his attempt to soothe her.

"Do you want me to go get him?" he asked, eager to divert her fury.

Vera huffed. "No."

"Why, er," Tristan began warily, "why isn't he with you?"

She didn't answer.

"Why did he know you'd try to see the mage? And why doesn't he want you to?"

"You're full of questions." Vera turned abruptly back to the bottle of liquor on her bedside table. "I have one. Do you want a drink? Is that allowed?" she added with no small measure of disdain, already pouring one for him.

When she turned back to him, Tristan's face stopped her mid-step. It wasn't the hopeless horror she'd seen from Arthur the night after her broken memory, but it was in that family.

"Why did you want to see Merlin?" Tristan asked more pointedly.

"I can't tell you that," Vera said, the only honest answer she was prepared to give.

Tristan sighed and sat down on the foot of her bed. He fidgeted to get his sword situated beside him, got frustrated, and took his sword belt off in a huff. Vera sat beside him and passed him a cup half filled with liquor.

"Were you about to do something self-destructive?" he asked quietly.

Vera started. It took her a second to cover the flash of guilt at how close to the mark it hit. "What's that supposed to mean?"

Having not missed any shadow of her expression, Tristan nodded.

He turned his goblet in his fingers as Vera threw hers back like a shot and let it sting down her throat.

"You tend to do that," he said. "I don't know how many times you took the blame for things we did as children. Falling on the sword has taken on higher stakes as queen, though."

"Well, in this case," Vera murmured, her words running together at the edges, "I forged the sword that will destroy all of you. Do you think someone else should fall on it?"

"That doesn't make any sense." Tristan shook his head and downed his shot, too. "I hope you know I would give my life for Arthur a hundred times over," he said. "I don't think there's a better ruler in the world, and I've met a fair few, but . . . he's a fucking idiot when it comes to you." He set his goblet aside, and as he put his hand back down, he laid it on Vera's thigh.

Her eyes shot to his face. Tristan stared straight ahead while he traced circles on her leg with his thumb. He turned to her, eyes filled with longing. He tentatively reached up and stroked her hair. His throat bobbed as he swallowed heavily. Tristan's smooth face, less lined with the weight of years and responsibility than his king's, was a perfect mixture of trepidation and yearning.

Maybe this was best. Maybe Arthur was right, and this was what was needed. Vera's heart was so broken—by Arthur's rejection, and by the choices she'd made in the life she hardly remembered that put those she now loved in peril. With disaster looming, it might be best to put an end to this magically driven obsession with Arthur once and for all. And maybe being with Tristan could achieve that. Maybe it could help her avoid this procedure that was probably—likely—going to destroy her.

"I love you, Gwen," he said. Vera held her breath as he leaned toward her, his eyes fixed on her mouth.

She had loved him once.

But not anymore.

Vera turned from him with a sharp inhale before his lips could find hers.

"I can't do this," she said.

Tristan closed his eyes and pulled away.

"Understood," he said. Without another word, he rose and left the room. He didn't storm away or slam the door. That might have been easier to bear.

Fuck. Poor Tristan was the one who suffered in all this.

Vera nearly tripped over his sword when she got up. She scooped it up and hurried to the door, expecting he'd be halfway down the hallway. She wouldn't have blamed him for bailing on his guard duty, and at least then her plan to find Merlin could progress. But Tristan stood just outside the door, his hand instinctively moving to where his sword should have been at the sound.

"Here." Vera thrust it toward him. He silently took it, and her stomach fell. "I'm sorry, Tristan. I'm so—"

"Stop it," he said. She clamped her mouth closed, and his face softened at her reaction. "Are you going to be all right?"

She was about to respond when a noise down the hall caused them both to start. It sounded like a door closing. They both looked, but it was too dark to see more than shadows. Well. If anyone saw this, Vera in her nightgown as Tristan refastened his belt . . . it looked worse than she and Lancelot stretching in a field after their run.

But all stayed quiet. Tristan fixed Vera with an appraising stare.

"Do you see what Arthur's doing?" he asked in a scornful whisper. "He's so convinced he can't love you well enough that he is trying to let you go."

He was wrong. She knew so many parts to it that he was missing.

"That's not what it is," she managed to say.

"Then what is it?" Tristan asked skeptically. When she didn't answer, he scoffed. "I admire everything about him except that he has you, and he keeps fucking it up. This one massive thing. It's a laugh to love the man who stole my future and is making a mess of it."

"I'm sorry." There was nothing more to say.

"Me, too." Tristan sighed. He swept a stray hair back behind her ear. She knew he wanted to kiss her. Instead, he said, "If you change your mind . . ." He grimaced self-consciously and shook his head. "Get some sleep, Your Majesty."

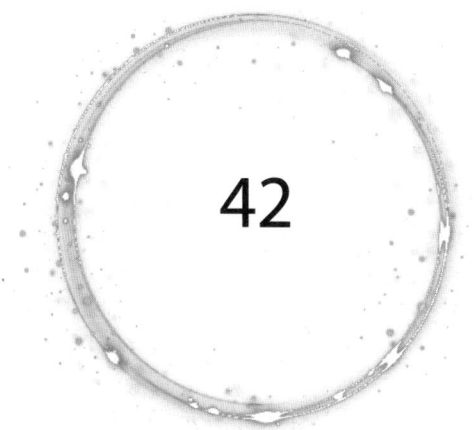

42

The room was still dim, and she wasn't sure what woke her. Vera sat up and saw right away that someone was asleep in the chair across from her, next to the window. She thought for a minute that it was Arthur, like the days after Thomas when he wouldn't leave her side. What a strange time to be nostalgic for. But it was Lancelot, and it became clear what had roused her. He was snoring. Loudly. Vera exhaled a laugh as she gathered a blanket in her arms and crept over to cover her friend.

Movement outside drew her to the window, where she saw Merlin in the courtyard, dismounting his horse and passing the reins to a stable hand. What on earth had he been doing at this hour?

Vera glanced back at Lancelot. If he was in here, did that mean he was on guard, and now no one stood outside the door? She went to check, timing the heavy lock's scrape with a snore and managing not to wake him.

The corridor was empty.

She could go. Nothing stood between her and Merlin. Vera took a shuddering breath and slipped into the hall. She got to the door of his room as he did. He seemed relieved to see her there.

"Where were you?" she asked.

"There've been reports of sinister happenings in the neighboring town. It's a short ride from here. Their steward got word that we were in the area, so I suppose our secret travel isn't so secret anymore." He offered a faint smile, an ineffective disguise for his concern. "They're having an issue with plots of land dying like in Crayford. We went with the king to see what could be done. The others are still there."

"Why aren't you?"

He looked a little ashamed. "I was hoping to find you. They will be gone a few more hours. We have time to do the procedure if you're willing."

Vera's breath was coming faster than normal. "We're so close to the mages and—and I did remember Tristan. It's coming back. I know it. Can we wait until after the mages?"

"Tristan . . ." He frowned. "I didn't expect that. But you haven't remembered anything else?"

She shook her head.

"He's here, Guinevere," Merlin said, his eyes trained on the end of the corridor as if Mordred might appear there. "The Saxon is on our soil, and he could be anywhere. We are out of time."

"But couldn't the mages help us? What does it hurt to wait one more day?"

"I have suspected for some time that Viviane was not working alone." He spoke patiently, as if to a child. "I fear we are walking directly into a trap. And if we are, there may never be another opportunity."

"You said I could go home." Vera stared down at her feet. "I want to go home."

"I know," Merlin said. "And I hope you'll be able to. I am confident you'll fare better than Gawain expects."

But even if she wouldn't, she couldn't keep being selfish. She could not stack the priority of seeing her father again above the entirety of Arthur's kingdom. Of Arthur. This—remembering—was her entire purpose.

"I'll go get dressed." She could at least lose herself (or her life—whatever it came to) with the dignity of not being in a nightgown.

"Vera?" Merlin said as she started to walk away. He hadn't called her that since Glastonbury. She glanced back, and he smiled sadly. "Thank you."

She tried to be quiet. She even managed to get in the room and get changed before she stumbled into the bedside table, the sound of it stirring Lancelot.

He looked at her with groggy eyes. "Morning, Guinna," he croaked. "Was I snoring?"

"A bit," she said with an unbidden smile. Part of her was relieved she'd get to talk to him one last time, but it would make this harder. She needed to get him to leave. "What are you doing here?"

As he explained what Merlin had just told her about the nearby trouble, Vera feigned ignorance. "It's just you and me until they return later this morning," he added.

"I thought Tristan was my guard. You shouldn't be the one babysitting me," she said. "Go have a lie-in in your room where you can be comfortable." Go. Please, go.

"Tristan is your guard." Lancelot busied his hands, folding the blanket on his lap. "But he's better at tracking, and I wanted to stay with you. Is that a problem?" He said it casually, but his eyes were dark. Vera knew her cheeks had gone red. She took the blanket from him and turned to toss it on her bed.

"I think this shit's idiotic," he said. "The whole 'giving you space to decide if you want to take up with Tris'?" She whirled to face him, her eyes wide. "It's fucking stupid."

"You don't need to be an ass about it," Vera shot back to hide her shock that he knew. "I didn't ask for any of this."

Lancelot was relentless with his grim, knowing smile. "No, but you did bring him into your room last night."

Shame threatened to smother her, but indignation was easier to sink her teeth into. "You're one to talk." She gestured at him. "Sleeping in here without my even knowing—"

"It's different with you and me, and you know it's different."

"If you're angry, be angry at Arthur," Vera said.

Lancelot petulantly crossed his arms on his chest. "All of this would be a lot easier if you and Arthur could just admit you're in love with each other."

Hearing it was like swallowing a stone. "We aren't," she said weakly.

He scoffed. "I know you, and I know him even more. You're in love."

"Stop it," Vera said. "We aren't. Everything between us is false, and it isn't fair to me or Arthur. He's a good man and a good friend." She stumbled on the words. Despite her anger, it was all true. "We're both under the influence of some fucking potion and calling it love is cruel and humiliating."

Lancelot leaned back in his seat with his legs splayed in front of him in an irksome display of easy confidence. "All right. Sure," he said, rubbing wearily at his forehead.

Vera mechanically turned away from him. It would be easy to shuttle him out the door, but that smug disbelief left her hands shaking.

"Have you always meddled like this?" she said, turning back to him. "Acted like you know what's best for everyone around you? Is that why I couldn't stand you before?"

He stiffened. His brow furrowed slightly. Sensing the tender spot and fueled by his reaction, Vera pounced, just as she had with Arthur.

"Oh, that's not it," she said with saccharine sweetness. She hated herself right now. "So, what was it? Why is it that my only memory of you from before is looking at you and being disgusted?"

Lancelot recoiled like she'd slapped him. The line of his mouth went thin. He wasn't going to answer.

"Un-fucking-believable!" Vera shouted, throwing her hands up in the air. "You're still keeping secrets from me. This isn't friendship! You don't get to sit there high and mighty and try to tell me about who I am and who I love when you can't even be honest about yourself. Too terrible to name, is it? What rotten thing did you do that you'd rather I forget forever?"

He trained his stare across the room, away from her, as red blotches bloomed on his neck. There was nothing Vera could dream up that might make her hate Lancelot, but her words struck a nerve, and she would not yield.

"If you can't tell me the truth, then get the fuck out," she said.

Vera's brutal façade nearly broke at the hurt she found in his expression.

He rose and walked to the door. She only had to last a few more seconds, and then she could collapse into the puddle of her agony. But the sound of the door's latch never came. She chanced a look. Lancelot's hand was poised above the knob.

"I'm not leaving," he said, swiftly turning to her. "I know what this is."

There was that cocky sense of knowing. "Fuck off," Vera said.

"No." He shook his head and strode back to her. "I'm not going to fuck off."

"Why? Want to come back for more insult hurling—"

"Shut up," Lancelot said.

"Excuse me, did you just—"

"Yes, I did." He came very close to her, so Vera had nowhere to look but at him as he said emphatically, "Shut. Up. You're not going to push me away. You're my best mate."

Vera snorted. "Arthur's your best mate." It sounded childish.

"Shut up," he said for the third time in half a minute. "I see what you're doing—trying to make it easier when you're gone, that it? Pushing us away to soften the blow? Make yourself less worthy of existing?" Vera clenched her teeth to keep from reacting. "Well, guess what, Guinna? You are fucking worthy."

It broke her. Her breath hitched as the rage disrobed for what it truly was: fear. "I'm not. I betrayed him. I betrayed all of you. I was saved to remember so that I can make this right. If my life continuing is at the expense of all of you—"

"You don't know that it will be!"

"I can't risk that. I am not worth risking that! How can you not understand this? This is my purpose. Remembering is all that I'm good for."

"No," he said, taking her hands and holding them to his chest. "It is not."

There was a knock at the door with barely time to register it had happened before Merlin's muffled voice said, "Guinevere? Are you ready yet?"

Lancelot gaped at her. "You have got to be kidding." He stalked over to the door and flung it open. "Fuck you, Merlin," he said with the deepest, most ardent sincerity. He slammed the door shut and turned back to Vera. "I will not allow this."

"It's not your choice!" she said. She made for the door, but Lancelot stepped in front of her and blocked her way. Vera shoved him hard in the chest. It didn't even cause him to stumble. The sound of the door opening drew her attention as Merlin entered.

Lancelot hadn't looked away from her, hadn't so much as blinked. "If you were in my place," she said more gently, appealing to his sense of duty, "if the answer to all this suffering was in your mind, you would do it in a heartbeat."

"No. I wouldn't," he said stubbornly.

A scornful laugh burst from Vera. "This is my life—my body. This is not your choice!"

"You're right," Merlin interjected. "And it is a courageous one that you are making."

Lancelot gritted his teeth and breathed heavily through his nose. "Fine," he said as he turned to face the mage. "And here's my choice." He drew his sword. "You want to do this? Fine. But not while there's breath in my body."

Oh fuck.

"Lancelot, don't—" Vera grabbed his arm, but he shook her off, eyes fixed on Merlin.

"That is unwise," Merlin said coolly.

Lancelot laughed far louder than was appropriate. "Unwise? You saved your queen's life so that you could bend it for your own designs. And I'm unwise to stand in your way? And what would happen if Arthur comes back and finds his wife dead on the floor? Then what?"

"I don't know." Merlin's calm slipped as he said it, a glimmer of loathing flashing in his eyes. "I was not there, nor was I responsible the last time he found his wife dead on the floor."

What did that mean? Lancelot's eyes darkened. He raised his sword and reached back to lay a protective hand on Vera.

Merlin's mastery over himself collapsed. "I would end you without even taking a breath."

The Once and Future Queen

Lancelot's lips twisted into a wry smile. "Ah. There it is," he said. "You've been holding that in for a long time."

"Stop it!" Vera cried.

Merlin blinked, his gaze flitting to her as if he only just remembered she was an important part of this conversation.

"I—I was wrong to say that," he said. "I would never . . . Guinevere, he loves you. I can see that. I'm glad for it, but Lancelot does not understand what I do."

Vera stepped forward, gently pushing Lancelot's sword arm down. This time, he yielded and let her pass him without a word, only a plea in his eyes.

"He doesn't understand that I gave you all the life I possibly could," Merlin said. "There was a reason you were the last one I brought back. I wanted it to be one of the others so that you could go on and never bear this burden." He tilted his head thoughtfully to the side. "I'll forsake humility and tell you how proud I am that I chose Martin and Allison to be your parents. They were perfect. And you. You, child, were special. The way you persisted in finding beauty and light even in the limitations of your life . . . I gave you all I could."

He had. He really had. Vera'd had more than she ever deserved. How many children had ever been so loved, had seen so many glorious sunrises with full bellies and safe arms to run to, had gotten to fill the shoes of a queen and live in a legend even for a short while?

"Guinna, please," Lancelot moaned from behind her.

"I know you've had hard days," Merlin continued as Vera took another step toward him. "And I didn't leave you to suffer then, either. When I let Vincent remember you—"

"What?" Vera stopped.

"Yes," he said with a benevolent smile. "An intentional lapse in the magic that kept you unnoticeable for—"

"You controlled who could remember me?"

The smile faltered. Vera saw Merlin begin to realize that what he had thought was shocked gratitude was nothing of the sort. Her world was spinning, but his words had turned a key, and pieces began clicking into place. In her former life, when she was Guinevere, she'd clearly suffered from depression. And with the two who came after, intent on their own destruction...

"You were afraid I'd end my life before I was ready to come back here, weren't you?" Vera asked. Merlin inhaled sharply but did not speak. "So you gave me Vincent when I was at my most miserable."

Had any of her life been her own?

It's your choice. Merlin had first said it that evening in the pub in Glastonbury, right on the heels of telling her existence would crumble if she didn't abide by his wishes.

That was how it had been every time. Every "choice" came after Merlin offered no other feasible option.

"You have never given me a choice. You painted me into corners. You controlled my entire life." She only realized the breadth of her statement's truth as she said it out loud.

"You exist because of my actions," Merlin said, all softness gone. "The things that you carry within you are the entire reason you matter—"

"I am more than a vessel," Vera said with such force that it silenced him. She'd voiced Merlin's exact sentiment countless times, but the conviction of it as falsehood now reverberated in her bones.

And it wasn't because Lancelot or Arthur said so, nor Matilda, or Gawain, or even her parents. Vera had breath in her body, a heart slamming against the inside of her chest, and a mind that, yes, might contain secrets, but that was hers, and she would not forfeit it. She'd spent her life wanting to matter to the people around her, to fill their empty spaces, expecting that would make her whole.

But it wasn't about being whole. She was broken and messy and utterly, wondrously human, and the weight of that mattered. She mattered.

"I will do the procedure," she said, breath heaving like she'd just finished running a marathon. Still, Vera's voice was steady as she held Merlin's stunned gaze. "But only after we go to the mages. And Gawain will perform it, not you."

"Do not be ridiculous," he said, stepping toward her. He foolishly believed the argument wasn't over. "Gawain can't see all of that. And he only thinks the procedure would destroy you because he's probably not capable of safely performing it—"

"He already has." She relished the way the revelation made Merlin gasp and stumble a step backward. "Gawain has been in my mind. He knows all about me."

Fear flashed across his face. "That wasn't yours to tell," he said.

"Right. Because it's only my choice when it benefits you?" She knew he wouldn't answer, but she let the silence hang between them before she continued. "Go out and get the rest of our party. We'll leave for the Magesary as soon as they're back. You can tell Arthur what happened here, or you can wait and let me. I'll leave that up to you."

Merlin looked at her like she was mad. "I'm not leaving you here—"

"I am your queen," Vera said, "and I command you to go."

Merlin took a long, rattling inhale. He touched his fingers to his forehead, his eyes wrought with disbelief. "You will doom us all."

He left without so much as a glance back.

Vera watched the closed door for a long moment before she looked at Lancelot. "Have I made a terrible mistake?"

"No," he said adamantly. He swept her tightly to his chest and held her, kissing the top of her head. "I'm so proud of you." She felt his body trembling.

Vera pulled back, really seeing him, taking in the depth of his panic, and hearing Merlin's words echo in her mind. *I was not responsible the last time he found his wife dead.* At that moment, she understood, and her heart ached. "When Merlin brought Guinevere back, and she went mad, you were the one who killed her, weren't you?"

He closed his eyes and breathed deeply before he quietly said, "Yes. A version of you died at my hands. I won't let you die again."

She took his hand and kissed his knuckles. "We're all going to die someday."

Lancelot opened his eyes and fixed her with a stern look. "You are not allowed to die."

Vera laughed, and he smiled, too. "I promise not to die if you promise not to," she said.

"Deal. No dying allowed."

43

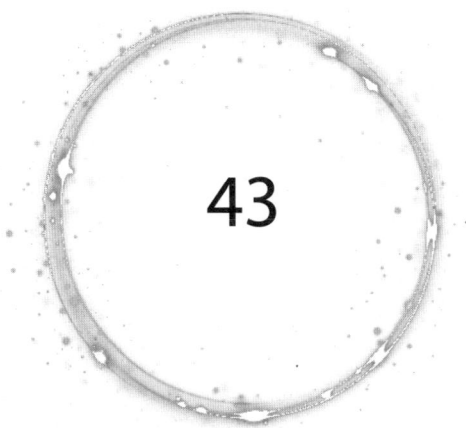

The rest of the travel party wouldn't be gone much longer, but Vera buzzed with adrenaline. She felt . . . different. There was dread about her decision's gravity, but there was elation, too.

"Do we have time to run?" she asked as she paced the room.

Lancelot had been nearly as eager for it as her, though he insisted that Vera wear her armor and sword. "We should have been doing this more. It's good training."

Vera groaned. She'd only run with her armor and the sword Randall made her once before. It was cumbersome how the sword, strapped to her back, clanged about and threatened to trip her every step when she didn't actively think about its presence.

"All the more reason to do it now and get used to it," Lancelot said. "Sort of the whole point of training, Guinna."

She argued for no helmets or leg guards, just a chainmail shirt over her running clothes with her sword and shield strapped on her back. Lancelot, presumably softened from his close brush with losing her, rolled his eyes and relented.

Vera took the back stairs down past the kitchen, where she nearly ran head-on into a tank of a man hefting giant sacks of grain from the back of a cart into the inn's kitchen.

"Morning!" she squeaked as she darted past him. His eyes landed on her, and they didn't leave. She thought he might have recognized her, but then his expression went vacant and unreadable. It unnerved Vera, but she quickly forgot about it when she rounded the corner and found Lancelot waiting for her in his chainmail shirt with his much heavier sword strapped in a sheath on his back.

Lancelot reached into his pocket and pulled out what, at first glance, she thought was a rodent. She jumped back from the fuzzy grey ball dancing in his palm. But it wasn't fur. Vera stepped closer. The baseball-sized lump was made of swirling grey smoke that whirled contentedly in his hand. It had no face nor any kind of features, yet somehow, it felt happy.

"I wanted you to know about this in case I bump my head on a branch and get knocked out or otherwise incapacitated. It's another Gawain invention," he said, his mouth lifting in a crooked smile. "He has one, and I have one. If shit goes sideways for them, his will come flying and find us—and then it can lead us back to his location. Likewise, if one of us gives this a good chuck, it'll find Gawain."

Vera poked the wisp and had the distinct sense that it giggled, though she heard no sound. "How is it . . . cute?"

Lancelot laughed. "I don't know. Gawain is the most extraordinary weirdo," he said fondly.

It only took ten minutes of running for days of mounting stress to feel lighter. Vera and Lancelot slid back into their usual banter. She teased him about how many times he'd told her to "shut up" earlier before they moved on to gossiping about whether Randall and Matilda had taken up together.

It was never to be more than a few miles out into the woods next to town before they turned around. They'd looped around a tree to head back and had run past a burly man with an axe just off the lane. After a few minutes, Lancelot went quiet. He only responded to Vera with one or two-word responses. Then his smile dropped, and his features went taut.

Vera's skin prickled as she said, "What's going—"

"Keep running." Lancelot dove his hand into his pocket without breaking his stride and pulled out the friendly wisp, giving it a toss. It darted away from them through the trees at an impossible speed.

"We need to get out of the woods," he whispered. Vera matched his faster gait. They didn't have far to go until they cleared the trees into the expansive open field. She sighed and slowed when the morning sun hit her full-on in the face, but her sense of safety was short-lived. Lancelot grabbed her arm.

"Keep going."

They were at least twenty minutes out from the inn or any building, for that matter. The road stretched before them, and when Vera followed it with her gaze, she saw it. Three figures—coming toward them.

"Shit," Lancelot hissed. He glanced over his shoulder. Vera chanced a look, too. There were yet two more men behind them, slower under the bulk of sheer body size, but they were running. The shorter made up for his height in width—and the Viking axe in his hand. It was the man Vera had seen in the woods. Assuming he was a woodcutter, she hadn't thought anything of him, but that was a battle axe. She didn't know where the man at his side came from. He was taller, with an impressive beard and wild hair, and he ran with an unsheathed sword. The blade was so large Vera would have hardly been able to swing it once. He wielded it as easily as a plastic toy.

The other figures, the ones approaching from town, were much closer now. Three men, and not young either: two looked like grizzled farmers in their simple dirt-worn clothing, armed with swords and daggers. She nearly stumbled when she recognized the third as none other than the giant of a man she'd seen behind the inn.

Vera and Lancelot could have outrun the two behind them, but with three in front of them? They were trapped.

"They can't be coming for us," Vera said, a desperate plea. She knew the answer.

"I've fucked up." Lancelot slowed to a stop. She followed his lead, stopping next to him as her eyes darted from one armed group to the other, far too close now. "I'm sorry," he said as he drew his sword. "We're going to pull off the road here, and if they follow, you're going to have to fight, Guinna. Stay close. Keep your focus. I'll get you through this." He took her elbow and led Vera off the road so no one was behind them. All five men approached, making a beeline for them.

"Sword drawn, shield up," Lancelot said hurriedly. "Now Guinna. Get your sword. Stay behind me."

It was all he had time to say as the first two, the ones who'd followed them in the woods, reached them. The one with the enormous longsword came first. He fought with it in two hands. Lancelot held his sword one-handed, his shield in the other, giving him more reach but less power. It was all deliberate. He drew the man out, feigning vulnerability and enticing the attacker into swinging his sword with all his might. Lancelot raised his shield just in time to take a blow that was so powerful Vera was convinced it would crack the shield in two. She cried out on the impact, but Lancelot held strong and seized on the man's vulnerable stance to slice deep into his belly and rip the blade free, entrails and blood following in its wake.

One down.

Vera pulled her gaping jaw shut and forced herself to breathe deeply. This was no time to panic. No time to process the horror she'd seen at her friend's hands.

The wide man with the battle axe was already on Lancelot, and the other three were close behind. Lancelot was a great warrior, but four men were too many to fight on his own. Vera inched closer. She didn't want to make it worse with her ineptitude, but she didn't want to leave him stranded. Lancelot fought the man with the axe and the first farmer to join the fray from the other group, too. He was locked in with both when the giant from the inn lumbered in with a blow aimed at Lancelot's vulnerable side. Vera lurched forward with her shield out and blocked him. The force of it sent her tumbling backward, feet over her head.

"Up, Guinna!" Lancelot shouted without breaking from his fight.

It was the first thing she'd learned in their training: to stay on her feet at all costs. She scrambled up, nearly slicing her leg with her own blade, and stumbled backward.

The giant fixed on her with ravenous eyes, his black pupils so large they filled his whole iris.

"Guard up!" Lancelot cried over his shoulder. She raised her shield, having not even realized she'd lowered it. The giant man skirted around

Lancelot and the other two (soon to be three as the final farmer joined the fray). Lancelot tried to maneuver to stop him, but there was nothing for it. Vera had to fight.

When she used her shield to deflect his sword's first swing, it rattled her, reverberating from the spot on her forearm behind the shield all the way to her teeth, clenched together in effort. Vera blocked blow after blow. The man was relentless—and gaining speed as he attacked. She knew she should counter-strike when he came off balance but was terrified to chance it. She channeled all her focus into one task: trying not to die.

Lancelot fought his three back enough to steal a second and rush to help Vera. With his sword, he stopped a swift swing aimed at Vera's collarbone and yelled to her, "Run!"

She needed no more telling.

Sweat drenched her skin as she sprinted further into the field, Lancelot on her heels. This was different from distance running, though. It was a mad sprint following exhausting sword fighting. They couldn't sustain it and used it only to gain better footing before their assailants caught up, and the fight resumed.

Vera couldn't imagine holding off three attackers the way Lancelot did. Her arms drooped from trying to keep them up to block the non-stop attacks, and her breath came in rattling gasps. She wasn't going to be able to carry on much longer.

"Stay in it, Guinna!" Lancelot called, sensing her weariness as he shot a hopeful look down the path toward town. No one was coming. Who knew how far away Gawain had been? Vera couldn't keep taking the blows on her shield. The pain burned in her wrist. She reluctantly started parrying with her sword. She had to drop the shield to wield her weapon with two hands; she needed all her strength to steady her sword.

Her assailant leered as he scooped up the discarded shield. She tried to take advantage of his movement, swinging her sword hard, and he barely got the shield in place. Vera's sword bit into the wooden shield and wedged there. It wouldn't yank free. It had been the wrong choice. It left her too close to this man, his inky black eyes lapping at her soul.

This was bad. If she stayed close enough to try to leverage her sword free, he could swing up and stab her in the side. It was too high a risk. She let go of her sword and scrambled back. Vera grabbed a rock from the ground, the only thing near her feet remotely resembling a weapon. His advance was fast. How was he not exhausted? Vera swayed where she stood, fighting to stay alert with the rock cocked back, ready to throw.

Lancelot was fully entangled. He wouldn't even know what happened to her. Vera stared defiantly up into the hateful face of her assailant and—

She heard the thunder of horse hooves growing steadily louder. She and the attacker looked up in its direction together, and the giant was promptly sliced into oblivion by a horsed warrior and his great upward-arcing swing. Vera staggered back.

The rider glanced back at her as he rode toward Lancelot. It was Arthur. Vera stomped on the discarded shield with one foot, wrenched her stuck sword free with aching arms, and ran behind him. Neither he nor his horse wore any armor. He swung down from his saddle and ran to join the fray as he yelled without turning back, "Ride, Vera!"

She didn't want to leave them but knew she'd be no help fighting. Vera sprinted to Arthur's horse.

"Where is Gawain?" she heard Lancelot shout.

Vera was struggling to get her foot in the stirrup when she looked back at the fight as Arthur reached the three remaining men. He had only reeled his arm back to swing when he faltered. For a split second, panic gripped her heart. Was he hurt?

And then she saw.

The oldest farmer in front of Arthur sprouted a gaping hole in the center of his chest. His skin, his organs—all that had once filled that space was removed in a perfect circle, evaporated into nothing. He crumbled to the earth before the light could leave his eyes. The same happened to the man in front of Lancelot, too. From where she stood, clutching the saddle of Arthur's horse, foot suspended in the stirrup, Vera saw straight through the man's body to the unstained grass beneath him. He didn't even bleed. The third man jolted. His black pupils shrank in a flash. His eyes cleared and registered surprise as Lancelot delivered a clean and fatal blow.

Vera looked to the road like a magnet had drawn her attention.

Merlin, still horsed, had both hands raised before him. There was a fire in his eyes, and power pulsed from him. For all the times Vera had stood toe-to-toe with him and shouted him down, she'd never once thought to fear him.

Relief and exhaustion collided, and she dropped to her knees, panting and dizzy. Then, there were hands on her shoulders, and Arthur knelt in front of her.

"Are you all right?" he asked, his eyes searching over her for injury and settling on her face. Expectant foreboding etched his brow with lines.

Vera thought of how her body had forgotten how to draw breath after she killed Thomas. But that was different. She nodded.

"She was brilliant," Lancelot said, panting with his hands on his knees. "Held her own better than I could have hoped."

"I had to fight," Vera said through heaving breaths. "I couldn't— I'm so sorry." She hoped he heard all that was unsaid behind her apology. But as he stroked her hair, she could see in his eyes that he understood.

"I know." Arthur kissed her forehead, clutching her shoulders, and she leaned her head into him, still catching her breath but not shaking. Not in pieces. And relieved. He didn't hate her.

Merlin caught up to them with Gawain on his heels. "What were you doing out here?" he demanded, his smoldering eyes locking onto Lancelot.

"Training. Running," he said. "I thought the risk was where you lot were. Those men were bewitched and set on the queen."

Vera sat bolt upright, ignoring the sweat that threatened to drip into her eyes. "They were?"

Lancelot nodded. "They were hell-bent on getting to you. I was just in the way and—" He gestured at the dead men littering the ground around them. "Did you see their eyes?"

She had. The unnaturally ravenous, black eyes.

Lancelot knelt down and wiped his bloodied blade clean in the grass as he spoke. "The Saxon?" His eyes darted between Merlin and Gawain. "Does that mean he's here?"

Gawain climbed down from his horse. He didn't answer. Instead, he strode purposefully from dead body to dead body, pulling their shirts aside at their chests and moving on after only a few seconds.

"What are you doing?" Lancelot asked, voicing the question for all of them.

Gawain ignored him. He went to the next man, the one Vera had seen behind the inn, the one she spent all her energy to keep from killing her. Gawain stayed at his side longer. He mumbled quiet words with his eyes closed and his hand hovering above the man's bare skin. A breeze rustled the nearby trees, and Arthur's horse stamped uneasily in the dirt—and then an unnatural squelch came from the man's body like a stuck boot being pulled from the mud. A bloody clump zoomed into Gawain's hand. He wiped it on his trousers, turned it, and held it up to Merlin. "A trigger hex."

"What is that?" Vera asked.

"It's a multi-layer bewitchment," Gawain said. "This man was the trigger, embedded with a vial of your blood. It bound him to you. Once the embedded person sees their target, they have the scent and track the target like hunting dogs. He infected the others."

"That's possible?" Lancelot asked in disbelief. "Mages can do that?"

"It's mostly theoretical," Merlin said. "And it's strictly forbidden. I've never seen it used so effectively in practice. They are imprecise and terribly dangerous."

"How did he get her blood?" Arthur asked.

Merlin shook his head. "I'd guess it was some sort of arrangement with Viviane. Collateral, maybe?"

"Does that mean the Saxon has been here recently?" Vera asked.

"There's no way to know." Merlin reached for the vial, and Gawain readily handed it to him. He incinerated it right there in his palm. "After a trigger hex is set, it will last until it's cleansed by a mage or the embedded one dies. Now that we know he's used them, Gawain and I can scan for more."

The fallen men here weren't evil. Just bewitched. Lancelot stared at the last farmer he'd cut down, the one whose eyes cleared and who was left in confusion as his life ended. He sighed heavily and rubbed at his brow. Blood trickled from a cut above his elbow.

Aided by Gawain's magic, they moved the bodies to the edge of the wood while Merlin prepared to ride ahead to the town. He'd check for more hexes and go on to Oxford to prepare the mages for their arrival.

He looked at Vera from astride his horse, his expression resolved with dread. "There's no turning back now."

Vera wasn't sure what she could say to him. "Thank you for saving us."

He breathed a sigh. "I would never abandon you, Your Majesty."

She expected shame to rise at his loyalty and more so at the path that Vera had condemned them to with her choice, but it did not.

As Merlin disappeared down the road, Arthur walked his horse in a wide loop to help calm the beast and Gawain hovered near Lancelot.

Lancelot's expression broke from the drawn anguish that had been fixed there since the fight ended. He chuckled. "You want to heal that, don't you?" he said, glancing at the cut on his arm.

"Very much," Gawain said. He launched into it immediately.

Lancelot grinned over his head at Vera. "We're lucky. Healing gifts are extremely rare."

Gawain's face reddened in the midst of his focus. "Mine aren't good for much more than cuts and scrapes," he said as he rubbed the wound the way he had with Vera's. But he glanced up at her for a breath before he added, "There are greater healing gifts out there, but I am fortunate."

"It's the gift he was born with," Lancelot said as Gawain shut his eyes in concentration and hissed, "Shh!"

Lancelot's grin broadened. He tilted his head down and touched his forehead to Gawain's, as close to a hug as he could manage with his arm occupied by healing magic. Gawain's cheeks reddened. He fought not to smile and lost the battle, staring up at Lancelot with an intimate sort of adoration.

And in that instant, Vera understood what she'd been missing all along. That wasn't just friendship. The night at the Yule festival when Vera thought Lancelot had been off in the field with a girl, hadn't

Gawain been right there on the edge of the light, too? The way she and Lancelot ran less after that. The way Gawain and Lancelot were nearly always together.

Holy shit. Now that she'd seen it, it was obvious. And a selfish pang followed. Lancelot was her best mate. She wished he'd told her.

Vera rode back to town with Arthur on his horse, and Lancelot rode with Gawain. She made herself resist looking over at them every few minutes. It was the least she could do; this wasn't a story she was meant to know.

The soldiers were ready when they arrived. Tristan took it in turns to bear hug them on their return. Vera pulled away from the embrace quickly.

They needed to get moving. Arthur wanted an audience with the mages as soon as they arrived in Oxford, the sense of peril more imminent a threat than ever before. Gawain hung back with Vera while she mounted her horse. She could never tell if he wanted to talk or had simply chosen the area near her to stand.

"There's more to what you know of Mordred, isn't there?" he asked.

"He kills Arthur." She said the words so quietly that, at first, she thought Gawain hadn't heard her.

He stared away at the others and said, "I'm glad we're taking action to thwart him."

"What if it's the wrong action?" Vera asked.

"Because Mordred may have set hexes to come after you?"

"Whatever I know, it must be vital. It was selfish not to do Merlin's spell work if it would have given you that advantage. That has to be the most strategic course of action."

"I disagree. Lancelot told me what happened with Merlin this morning," he said. "Merlin is far too intent on what is locked within you, Guinevere." He fixed her with a piercing stare. "There is more in you than memory."

The skin on the back of her neck prickled. "What do you mean?"

Gawain stared into the distance for a long time before speaking. "I'm glad you refused and that you're safe."

"That doesn't answer my question," Vera said. "You do that a lot, you know. And I am well aware that it is deliberate."

He gave a quiet chuckle and then a long sigh. "Don't underestimate what you might have to offer." His words were slow as if he was choosing them carefully.

Vera thought back to how he'd referred to Grady as an inhuman specimen, yet here he was, facing a dire situation and answering it with compassion.

"Why are you protecting me?" she asked.

Gawain looked Vera squarely in the eyes. She'd always been so distracted by how deeply set they were, how he often looked up at people with that unnerving scowl. But he had very kind eyes.

"Because the mages have a part in this, and we must be accountable for it," he said. "And because you are my queen."

Vera stared down at her toes, touched by his loyalty. She was stunned when he spoke again.

"But most of all, because you are my friend."

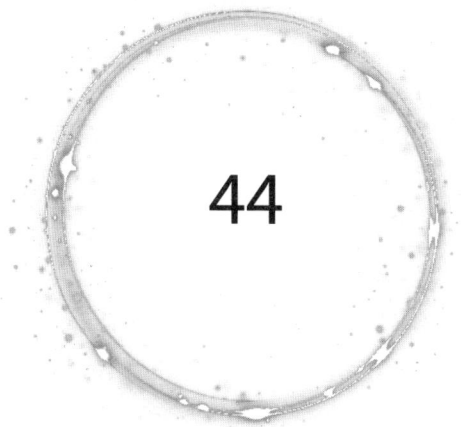

44

Vera shifted in her saddle, unaccustomed to how armor stiffened her movements while riding. Lancelot was right: she should have worn it more to practice before it was necessary. After the ambush this morning, they were all in armor, even Gawain. It strangely suited him. Save for Vera, their entire traveling party had been on the front lines of war. She was the only one out of place.

Tristan drew even with her. His dark silver armor shone, and when the morning light hit it from certain angles, the dents and nicks revealed themselves, things he certainly could have fixed. He'd chosen to wear the marks of battle. He looked at Vera sidelong, trying not to let her catch him.

She smirked. "What?" she said, like she would any other day. In an unspoken agreement, they were pretending as if boundaries had not been crossed last night.

"I never thought I'd see you in armor," he said. "You look incredible."

She couldn't keep from glancing in Arthur's direction. He rode with the younger of the two soldiers, a man with a severe yet boyish face and a nose that had clearly been broken before. He glowed under Arthur's undivided attention, though Arthur glanced away just long enough to catch Vera's eye, inclining his head to her with a smile before he returned to the conversation.

He wasn't avoiding her, but after she and Lancelot gave him the full story of what happened with Merlin, he kept his distance. Tristan, however, stayed close. He rode at Vera's side, as charming as ever. When he made particularly affectionate comments, he'd cast furtive glances in Arthur's direction, checking for the king's responses. Vera chuckled as she realized Tristan was still trying to woo her. She couldn't imagine she would change her mind about being with him, but she admired his persistence.

There was no definitive delineation between where one town stopped and the next began. But an hour and a half after they left Faringdon, they crossed a wooden bridge (just broad planks bound together) over a trickling creek, and midway, everything in sight visibly shivered like the air above boiling water. Vera whipped around to Gawain in alarm.

He nodded once, his calm an immediate reassurance. "We've entered the Mages' Cloak," he said. He pulled his horse even with Vera and murmured, "Oxford is shielded by a network of mage craft in a ten-mile radius surrounding the city. If attackers come, this will stop them. There's no army here, no lord or lesser king. But there are a lot of mages," Gawain's eyes glinted, "and it's a great treasure to protect."

Nothing could have prepared Vera for Oxford. She could see from a distance that it wasn't the Oxford she knew. Where she'd expect dramatic gothic spires pointing to the sky, instead, Vera found the skyline dotted with peaked domes, like clouds specked above the city. As they rounded the bend onto the High Street, her eyes went wide. Most of the buildings were round ("It's the most magically conductive shape," Gawain had whispered in her ear) and made of polished cream stones that gleamed in the light of enormous orbs glowing even in the daytime. They floated above the cobbled lanes like centerpiece chandeliers every thirty steps. No matter what direction Vera turned, she saw magic at work.

They passed an open-air amphitheater where a team rehearsed their telling of an epic adventure complete with flying performers, precise and colorful explosions of pyrotechnics, and perfectly amplified sound. On the opposite side of the road walked a full-sized elephant crafted of shimmering stone—for what practical purpose, Vera couldn't divine. She nearly cried out when a woman with wild hair and her face bent low, poring over the parchment in hand, walked right into the elephant. But she wasn't bowled over. She passed through the beast's belly, only a puff of mist disturbed from where she reemerged.

As they traveled the High Street, Vera tried not to blink. She peered in any open door she could as they passed, spotting a round room splattered all over with vibrantly colored paint and two people in the center standing back-to-back. There were no features, gender, or clothing to be recognized because they, too, were covered in paint and were only distinguishable as humans because of the way they waved their arms like orchestra conductors, color spraying out at every gesture.

Further on, she craned her neck to watch a wizened woman laden with scrolls in her arms kick open another door. Magnificent indigo smoke seeped out and swirled overhead, dissipating into oblivion. Bright sparks crackled in the laboratory beyond before the door was promptly closed.

Reaching the end of the lane was almost a disappointment, but Merlin waited there, tense and his expression unreadable. He stood before the most prominent building yet; the round structure behind him had tubed corridors jutting from its base on both sides, extending farther out and back than the eye could see. It towered above them. Vera counted five stories of vaulting windows beneath the dome at the top. In lettering no taller than her index finger (useless compared to the vast building it adorned) were simple block letters stamped above the arched doorway: MAGESARY.

"The council is convened and awaiting your arrival," Merlin said. He arranged for their horses and bags to be taken to the inn, where their party would stay for the night. The soldiers remained at the ready outside the Magesary, with Tristan joining them. Vera didn't know if that had been discussed before, but he didn't act surprised nor affronted by his exclusion. The attack this morning had done at least one helpful thing: there was no doubt as to the urgency of this meeting. Gawain took his place next to Merlin, his movements stiff and face pale. Merlin gestured them toward the arched doorway.

There was no door, no visible barrier there at all. Arthur walked through first with Vera on his heels, but as her body crossed the threshold, she felt a sensation of many hands passing over every bit of her skin, whether exposed to the air or beneath her clothing—even the most concealed and intimate parts of her. She jumped at it and turned in time to see Lancelot raise his eyebrow and give a shudder. He'd felt it, too.

The happy cacophony of sound had gone silent on this side of the door. Merlin and Gawain stepped through the entry, unfazed by the experience.

"What is that?" Vera asked.

"It's an unmasking," Merlin said, striding past them to resume his place at the front and lead them across the echoing rotunda. "Any enchantments on a person are stripped away when they cross the threshold."

Their footsteps echoed on the flagstone floor of the vaulted entry until they passed into a long corridor directly opposite where the sound deadened. There were many doors on either side, but they passed them all, walking until the corridor ended at another door, this one made of granite and reminding Vera of the entry to a mausoleum.

Merlin laid his palm against the center of it. It lit up at his fingertips, and veins of light spiderwebbed like cracking glass. When the network of glowing tributaries reached the edges on all sides, the weight of it evaporated, and as the granite slab slid backward, it didn't groan against the floor. Its movement sounded like a breeze against tall grass. The door slowly slid to the side, leaving a gap only large enough for them to pass through single file.

The room they entered was unsurprisingly round, with three rows of tiered seating in a semi-circle. Each row sat behind narrow desks.

It was a stone auditorium, and where they entered was the stage, with an audience of mages observing them. Vera's eyes were drawn to the front row, where four of six seats were occupied. The man who sat right of center held command of the space and these people in an unnamable way that Vera thought must be magic. His energy drew her, and when he made eye contact with her down his hooked nose, he smiled in satisfaction. There was no kindness in it. She averted her gaze quickly and felt his pleasure at her intimidation.

On the hooked-nose mage's left side sat a man who looked much closer to how Vera had imagined Merlin to look. His silver beard hung down to his navel, and his eyes were clouded with grey pools of cataracts. The backs of his hands had golf ball-sized knots on them. On the hooked-nose mage's right was a woman who wore a silk turban. There weren't any lines on her face, though she bore the wisdom of centuries. And beside her, Vera had to focus on seeing the fourth mage in the front in order to notice her. She was a petite wisp who looked quite comfortable with not being noticed.

The rows behind them were in shadow. Vera couldn't see any of those mages' faces, but they all rose at Arthur's entry, an impressive wave of identical cream silk robes winking in the darkness.

"Welcome, Your Majesty." The woman in the turban spread her arms wide. Her voice effortlessly filled the room. "We are honored by your presence."

Arthur stepped forward. "Thank you, Naiam. I wish it were under different circumstances."

She smiled, her head tilted. "You are always welcome, sire. It need not take a disaster for you to visit. Please, sit." Naiam gestured at where they stood. A row of chairs appeared behind them.

They sat down. With a wave of their arms, Merlin and Gawain changed into their cream-colored robes to match the rest. They stood in the front row. Vera assumed these six were the high council. Following Naiam's lead, all the mages performed the breath of life in unison before they sat. "I call this special assembly of the full council to order on the matter of a magical crisis."

Vera caught Gawain releasing a long-held breath and saw his shoulders relax.

The mages had heard the story of Crayford but asked Arthur to recount it—and the attack against them that very morning.

"You're certain it was a trigger hex?" Naiam asked Merlin.

"Absolutely. Gawain extracted the vial of blood, and I destroyed it."

"That was unwise." The hooked-nose mage glowered at him. "There could have been information to be gleaned from it, and you destroyed it without running any tests."

"The hex lay in the blood itself, Ratamun," Merlin said. "Do you think there's any test worth the risk of an untamable spell's spread? There are maybe three of us in this room who could even theoretically perform such a hex. I was not willing to risk the queen in such a way."

Vera didn't chance half a second's look at Lancelot, who, in Camelot, would have audibly scoffed or shifted in his seat. She imagined he'd like to pummel Merlin for claiming the moral high ground about Vera's safety after being ready to risk her mind hours prior.

Ratamun snorted. "The queen risked herself when she took ranks with the traitor, Viviane." Her name snarled from his lips. "A crime which we have continually been denied the right to try or call to account."

Of course they couldn't call her to account. Viviane was dead.

Then Vera realized they meant her.

"Queen Guinevere should be questioned and tried," Ratamun said. A murmur rose from the other rows of mages at his proclamation. Some in protest, others in agreement.

Ratamun had a talent for holding a room, but so did Arthur. He leaned forward in his chair, eyes darkening as he set them on the mage.

"Ratamun," he said with dangerous quiet. It called silence over the assembly as sure as if he'd shouted them down at sword point. "You sent a mage to my court who undermined the kingdom. The kingdom, I might add, that we built and would have called an impossibility before it was the reality we now live in. Guinevere was bewitched by Viviane, your trusted high council mage, and Guinevere ultimately had the fortitude to stand against her at her own peril. Her crime was against the kingdom and against me. I am satisfied by the resolution, and she has been pardoned. If you need evidence of Guinevere's loyalty, search no further than the attack on her this morning. I did not call the council of mages to trial for raising up and sending forth the traitor Viviane, and you will not call the queen. Do I make myself clear?"

Ratamun's snarl was twisting to form an argument.

"Enough," Naiam said, but she eyed Vera like she had questions of her own.

The small woman spoke up next, with a soft voice that matched her stature. "And you believe it is the dark mage Mordred?"

"Yes," Arthur said, "and I believe it to be tied to the declining magic within the kingdom, too."

There was a stirring amongst the mages. Merlin pursed his lips and stared at his feet, displeased.

"Why?" the quiet mage pressed.

"I call on Mage Gawain," Arthur said.

"Gawain, this theory comes from you?" Naiam asked, surprised yet kind. The way she looked at Gawain, her junior by at least thirty years... Others among them looked at him the same way; the only mage to ever be raised in the Magesary from childhood. He was their collective child.

Not all of them, though. Notably, Ratamun glowered as Gawain straightened in his seat.

"It does. The description of Crayford matches my own experience in Dorchester. But there is more. And—and I first must apologize to the convened council," but he addressed Arthur as he said it, "because I have concealed much of what needs to be said. There is a bigger matter than Mordred to address regarding the disappearance of magic." He didn't allow anyone the time to interject, forging on after barely a breath amidst a titter of discomfort.

"We know that magic isn't infinite; it's a type of energy that recycles itself. For the six hundred years of its recorded history, the birthrate and regeneration of magic remained steady." Many among the council nodded their confirmation. "It changed when the mages began amassing power, especially during the wars."

The room had been quiet, but all fidgeting, all movement, and most breathing altogether stopped with a palpable gasp. Even Merlin turned to Gawain in horrified shock.

Ratamun broke the stillness. "Any magical deficit should only have been felt among the Saxons."

A brief flash of triumph crossed Gawain's eyes, replaced in a blink by his regular sullen expression. "We all know that's not how the gift works. It doesn't discriminate against one nation's people over the others. And then there's the advent of the Retention Spell. How many mages have died, and their powers destroyed with them? How many were lost with Viviane alone?"

Arthur and Lancelot looked as confused as Vera felt.

Gawain went on. "Crayford is a microcosm of what we're doing at large. In Crayford, the mage took all the gifts of those he felled. Every known bit of magic in an entire town was sucked dry by one man, and what happened? The earth itself shriveled and died. We are draining the earth of its powers."

"We should discuss this matter in a closed assembly," Naiam said, a clear warning, the delicate chimes of her voice now sounding shrill.

"As your ruler," Arthur said at a nod from Gawain, "I insist on being present for a conversation of this gravity. By the first order laid out in establishing the council of mages, I am entitled to bear witness to your proceedings when it pertains to a direct impact upon this kingdom." It sounded like he was quoting the order word-for-word, and, Vera suspected, that was precisely the case. Nevertheless, they were shocked to hear it invoked. "Proceed, Mage Gawain," he said, without turning away from Naiam. Her smile no longer reached her eyes.

"The king must know," Gawain said. "We're on the edge of the destruction of all we've worked for. He has to know. We can't persist in claiming that we keep this secret for the kingdom's safety. We're protecting our own power at the expense of magic itself."

"Do I correctly understand that mages get their power from another source beyond training and study?" Arthur directed his question at Naiam, who was clearly hesitant to answer.

"I—it's complicated."

Arthur held her stare.

"Yes, Your Majesty," she said, finding no way out of it.

"How?" One word that rocked everything. Tilted it sideways. No one answered. "Do I need to command an answer from you?" Arthur asked, scanning their ranks with a hard stare.

The ancient and bent mage with a beard down to his middle was the one who answered. "Study and training teach us how to broadly utilize our gifts. There are two ways we might acquire new powers. A gift may be given from one magic being who has some mastery over their skill to another. The second way is . . . on the battlefield. When an enemy with a gift is killed, if they are stabbed by a mage's weapon directly to the heart while any life remains there, the mage can absorb their gift with the dying one's last breath. It was a closely held secret that only the council knew until now, and it was our greatest advantage during the wars. No one we fought understood how our mages were so powerful."

"The wars were long," Gawain cut in. "To my count, we have over ten thousand known gifts among the high council alone. That's just between the six of us. It doesn't include the other mages in this room, not to mention any of the lesser mages not on the council. I believe this accumulation is causing magic to dissipate. It's dying because we are hoarding it. And it's hiding, too."

"Do you mean the boy from your first report out of Camelot?" It was the mage with the quiet voice again.

Gawain nodded. "Grady. His gift only appeared when he would have perished without it. Magic is wiser than all of us. It's actively hiding, so we can't take it. But for every Grady whose gift could manifest, how many have gifts that appear too late or that cannot save them? I'd guess many of you saw instances of it during the war as I did—bursts of power as a soldier was in peril, snuffed out before the gift could manifest. How many are lost in a state of traumatic duress?"

"As interesting as your stories are, what do you propose we do?" Ratamun said in annoyance.

Gawain unhunched his shoulders, pressing them back. "We should conduct a sample study of what happens when mages release their power back to the earth."

The mages on the high council shared stunned expressions.

"Are you volunteering?" Ratamun drawled.

"If I need to do so, then yes, I am," Gawain said.

Ratamun's rehearsed disinterest slipped. He hadn't expected that. "Did you concoct this with him, Merlin?" he asked after a moment.

"No—" Merlin began before Gawain interrupted him.

"I kept my theory from Merlin. This is my work, my specialty. I'm prepared to take on the consequences of it."

Vera realized that she was witnessing a quiet act of extraordinary courage.

"Let's not be rash, Gawain," Merlin said. "What good does dumping power do? It would take years to meaningfully survey and measure any change. There's no way to know if it has an impact on such a small scale."

"Yes, there is." Gawain carefully pulled a bundle of cloth from his pocket and unwrapped it. Vera craned her neck to see. It was his glass instrument, the one he'd shown her in his study. The mages shifted in their seats for a better look.

"It measures the balance between assigned gifts and ones that have become available at any given moment in close enough proximity to this instrument. When someone with a gift perishes without a Retention Spell in place, a liquid-like substance will appear in the tube. If the gifts are distributed by the birth of a new magical child, they will transfer to the bulb. When mages accumulate masses of gifts and die with a Retention Spell in place, the magic doesn't go back into circulation. Magical births cannot occur. While we live with thousands of gifts locked up within us, those gifts cannot be circulated either. I believe that if we release some of our many gifts—not all, but some—those will be recirculated. My instrument can test that."

"The magical birth rate first noticeably dipped twenty-three years ago," the oldest mage said thoughtfully. "And the Magesary was founded four years prior. I don't know why none of us recognized the alignment before."

"It's been slow enough that it was easy to blame other things," Gawain said.

Vera wasn't following. Was this the secret she had known? Was this Mordred's aim? To steal enough magic that Arthur's kingdom began to collapse on itself?

Naiam stood and said sharply, "We don't know that this is correct. Hearing it and thinking it makes some logical sense doesn't make it so. The kingdom wouldn't even exist without the power of our mages. We protect the magic. Mage Gawain is not old enough to remember. But many of us well recall when our grandparents hid their gifts because they were deemed unholy and could land them a death sentence before the order was founded. I respect Gawain's ability to remove his self-interests from his studies, but I will remind you: it does not mean he is right."

"Let me perform the experiment," Gawain said. "By our best guesses and records, there are twenty births a day in our kingdom. I will release twenty of my own gifts tonight. If my theory is correct, releasing gifts will also put powers back into circulation, the same way a death would. We would be able to read if that part were effective immediately. And then, if we take a reading tomorrow, there should be fluid in the larger bowl."

The tiny mage shifted in her seat before she spoke. "If all that happens as you theorize, it means—"

"Yes." Gawain nodded. "It means this crisis is no one's fault but our own."

"And your device. You've made that using your gifts, have you?" Ratamun said, his anger gone, hunger replacing it. "There's never been anything that could track power before. Does it work?"

Gawain hesitated. "I believe so." He didn't answer the first question and quickly wrapped the device back up, tucking it away.

Ratamun's chin jutted forward, and he called out louder than the murmurs around him, "I think we should do it."

The room erupted. Gawain wasn't bolstered. He clasped his hands tightly, knuckles going white. Naiam tapped her hand on the table, the thick gold ring she wore echoing like a gavel with each strike.

"We will take a vote," she said as the room quieted. Her eyes were dark, and all the lilting of her voice had gone. "Will you excuse yourself?" she asked Gawain.

Gawain, shoulders tight, stiffly nodded as he rose and left the room, not through the main entry stone that entombed them but into a side chamber directly behind him.

Lancelot's chair scraped against the floor as he stood abruptly. "I would like to excuse myself as well." He moved before anyone acknowledged him.

Vera started to follow, remembered that they were already suspicious of her, and settled back in her chair.

Arthur gave her hand a soft squeeze. "Go on," he whispered.

She darted to follow, noting Naiam's tight-lipped disapproval and feeling it on her back the whole way. Vera didn't care. She slipped into the side chamber and closed the door. It was little more than a closet, a stone dungeon with no windows.

Gawain pressed himself into the corner. "I've signed my death warrant," he said dully, though his eyes were wide and skin pale. "It would have been enough to tell our secret, but suggesting we sacrifice our gifts . . . I'll be executed."

"You won't." Lancelot took Gawain's face between his hands, giving the mage's roving eyes a focal point. "We aren't going to let that happen."

Gawain looked like he felt sorry for Lancelot. "The authority you have does not carry the power you think it does," he said in a monotone.

Lancelot sighed, patting him on the cheek with an exasperated laugh. It set Gawain off. He pushed Lancelot's hands away. "Did you not hear what I told you in there? About how we get our gifts? Stabbing in the heart. Lancelot, I have more than a thousand powers."

"You've killed that many people?" Vera said quietly.

"No." The animalistic urgency cleared from him, bringing back the Gawain they knew as he thought about the numbers. "More were—" His mouth twisted, moving soundlessly as his face reddened. "Shit. I'm not in the room. I can't say it. I should have said it before." He groaned and shook his head. "Over two hundred and fifty human beings have met their end looking into the whites of my eyes. Do you understand?" His voice rose frantically.

Lancelot reached for him. "You were only—"

"No," he snarled, reeling away. "I am a monster. Look at me like I'm a monster." Lancelot didn't. Vera knew she didn't either. Gawain stumbled back against the wall. "Fuck." He crushed his hands against his face.

"What's a Retention Spell?" Lancelot asked abruptly.

Gawain sighed. "It makes a gift impossible to steal on death, disincentivizing killing amongst mages. Viviane invented it. She had more gifts than most mages combined." Had they known that alone . . . that those gifts weren't won by her brilliance in the laboratory but by her willingness to end life, would they have ever trusted her? Would they have trusted any of the mages?

The door opened, and they all tensed at the combination of movement and noise, relaxing some when it was Arthur who entered the already crowded room. Gawain moved like he was about to kneel, but he wasn't fast enough.

Arthur hugged him, muttering, "Thank you." As he released Gawain, he said, "That was selfless and courageous to stand against all of your upbringing—"

"My upbringing but also my choice, Arthur. No one forced me to keep being a mage."

"How old were you when you became a mage?" Arthur asked. "Did you have to kill to receive your earliest gifts?"

Gawain shook his head. "We're all given our second power, marking the start of life as a mage. I was seven when Merlin gave me mine."

"On receiving that, you were also inducted into the secrets you were magically bound to keep. Then there was war, and you did what we all did in battle."

Gawain's voice chirruped in the start of a protest that Arthur would not hear as he continued. "And you were made the youngest member on the high council of mages. And today, you stood against them as no one has ever done, and it just might save the kingdom and save magic for all of us. I'd knight you for a second time if I could."

Gawain dared to look hopeful, searching Arthur's gleaming eyes. "Did they approve—"

"Yes. They've approved the test."

It was evident that the vote had not been unanimous, but it passed, and enough mages shared Gawain's spirit of selflessness that they offered some of their own gifts to the cause. The ancient man and the quiet woman who had asked the best questions offered three gifts apiece, and, surprising to Vera, Ratamun offered up five of his own, so Gawain only needed to release nine to meet the agreed-upon number.

They gathered in the open space, the rest of the council and the royal party watching. Gawain passed his instrument to Arthur to hold.

"How do we do it?" the quiet mage, who Vera learned was called Phoebe, asked in her tiny voice.

"It's exactly like when you would give a gift to another person, but focus on the earth . . . dirt or grass or trees," Gawain said. "Whatever part of nature you need to call to mind, and then . . ."

"Release," Phoebe finished for him.

Ratamun smirked as he rolled the sleeves of his robe up. "What if one of us lies and gives fewer gifts than we vowed?"

"If the instrument works, we should be able to count, and we would know," said Gawain. "If it doesn't work? Nothing will happen."

Gawain went first. He steadied himself, closed his eyes in a silence that stretched on for long seconds, and then breathed the deliberate and sacred breath as he extended his hand, palm down before him. Nothing notably changed, but Arthur made a hum of approval beside Vera, and all eyes pooled on him.

A swirl of gel-like liquid bubbled up from nothingness into the tube. At first glance, it was all the same silvery sheen. But from another angle, there were sharp delineations and, indeed, nine separate and countable sections, each a slightly different color.

At that, the mages stirred. Naiam sucked in a sharp breath. One by one, the three mages who'd volunteered also released their gifts, and the tube slowly filled.

"The gifts are in circulation?" Ratamun said, moving closer to Arthur and the instrument.

Gawain's hand flinched toward Ratamun as if to stop him, but the mage was out of his reach. "Yes," he said.

Naiam did not look pleased. "So it appears." She drummed her fingers on the desk as she scanned the room. "We will reconvene at first light to see what comes of this experiment."

Merlin's lips parted. He watched the instrument in Arthur's hands in disbelief. Ratamun bent low over the globe, shifting his head back and forth between two angles.

"They're all a different color," he mumbled, eyes glinting. "Can you tell what each power is?"

Gawain shifted uncomfortably. "No," he said sharply. "Only the number. There is no way to know anything more."

The smirk never left Ratamun's face. "As you say."

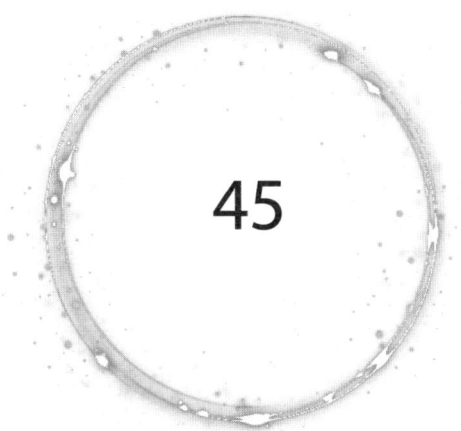

45

It felt like a victory—until they got out of the Magesary and into the quiet of Vera's chamber at the inn where she, Arthur, Lancelot, and Merlin convened. Merlin's tight expression betrayed the anger simmering under the surface of his calm.

"Why didn't you tell me this was your plan?" he said through gritted teeth.

"Because I knew you'd stop me," Gawain said.

Merlin huffed. "Of course I would have. Even if you're correct, this was an ambush. It was not the way. You're going to be expelled from the Magesary at the least."

"I know," Gawain said. "But you know as well as I that if it hadn't been an ambush—if the king hadn't been sitting in that room, they would not even have entertained it."

Merlin's face filled with sorrow as he looked at Gawain. It frightened Vera.

"And Ratamun's suspicion about your instrument?" Merlin said.

Gawain nodded. "He knows how it might be used."

"How might it be used?" Arthur asked. He held the instrument cupped in his lap where he sat.

"Ratamun correctly guessed that this tool is the foundation to sense what gifts someone has and how many," Gawain said. "I knew that was a risk in revealing it."

"Not a risk," Merlin corrected. "An inevitability." He directed the next at Arthur. "Ratamun is one among us who believes in the great gifts. Immortality and invincibility are the two most sought-after. He, and others for that matter, would want nothing more than the ability to sense and track those gifts. And take them, no matter the cost: enemy, friend, family..."

Vera could imagine the danger of such a power, but not in Gawain's hands. He would never use the gift that way.

"Why is that a problem?" she said, eager to pull them all away from fear and back into the hope they'd felt mere minutes ago. "The device is made with your magic, Gawain. They can't use it without you. Isn't it your living magic that powers it?"

Merlin's frown deepened.

Lancelot sat with knees spread wide and elbows on his thighs, leaning forward to listen. It wasn't a strange posture for him, and he looked at ease, except for his hands, clasped tightly. "That puts you at risk, doesn't it? They'd need the device, and they'd need you to be able to use it."

Gawain's eyes were full of a thousand words he didn't say as he met Lancelot's gaze.

"Or they'd want him dead," Merlin said, dropping into the seat next to Vera. "All of this is precisely why no one can know the truth about you, Guinevere. The draw of the power I used—time travel, restarting a human life—is irresistible. Some would stop at nothing for it, and if they couldn't have it, they'd want to be sure no one did."

Vera blinked. She turned to Gawain, who smiled sadly at her.

"Goddammit, Gawain," Lancelot mumbled at the floor. "You altruistic son of a—"

"Look!" Arthur cut him off, his voice hushed with awe. He held the instrument up for them to see. A paper-thin swirl of silvery liquid covered the base of the glass bulb. It hadn't been there before.

Gawain nearly knocked over his chair, scrambling to Arthur to take the instrument. His mouth went slack, and his eyes glimmered as he stared at the tiny pool with reverence.

"A child was just born," he said, hardly more than a whisper, "and one of my gifts is now theirs."

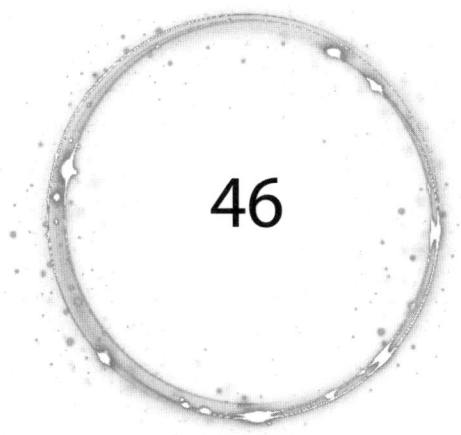

46

No one slept well that night. They already knew the experiment's outcome. Vera's chamber was the most spacious, so the knights dragged extra mattresses from nearby rooms. While the others took turns standing guard, Vera and Gawain attempted to sleep—but mostly, they watched the instrument. Watched as magic was born into brand-new souls.

By the time they gathered at the Magesary, only the visible signs of two gifts remained in the tube. The visual of it was powerful. Even the mages who had expressed doubt the evening prior, Naiam included, were transfixed by the pool gathered in the bulb, filling it past the half-way point. It didn't hurt that, as they looked on, the instrument vibrated in Arthur's hands, and one more bit from the tube bubbled into the larger dome.

Before their eyes, magic transferred. Phoebe, the quiet mage, blushed, and her eyes clouded with tears. That had been one of her gifts. Gawain explained that to Vera last night. He could feel it when a transferred gift had been his. Evidently, so could the others. Ratamun's conceited smile fell. His gifts had been reassigned, too.

Merlin did most of the talking. He convinced the council that the liquid in Gawain's instrument had been accidentally discovered. There was no formula for it, no replicating it. And that the instrument itself would only work one time. It would be useless after this.

Gawain had argued against this tactic, afraid that without the instrument to hold them accountable, the work of releasing a considerable number of gifts wouldn't be done.

"But you will have the instrument," Merlin reasoned, "and plenty of ability to monitor it. We can address logistics later. For now, we need to get you safely back to Camelot, and that means they have to believe that it can't be replicated."

The mages had ever presented themselves as a religious order seeking peace and the protection of magic. The nature of their powers was disconcerting. Arthur was especially dismayed that the threat within the mages' own ranks was so dire. The council had transformed from a shining beacon of hope for the kingdom to its biggest liability overnight—and they knew it.

Vera was sure it was a driving factor as the mages charted a road map for proceeding with this new information. Their immediate priority was to track Mordred and either kill him or, preferably, bring him in to face justice. Naiam assigned ten pockets of mages, one from the council with five lesser mages, to go on the hunt for him. And on the matter of magic, each mage on the council was asked to release ten gifts. Gawain would have preferred a more aggressive approach, plainly written in his furrowed brow, but Merlin silenced him with a sharp glare.

They were on the right track.

Naiam officially adjourned the mages, and Arthur's party did not linger. Their horses were ready just outside. They bid polite but terse farewells and made for the road, even though it was nearly dark when they set out. Neither Merlin nor Gawain wanted to linger in Oxford for questions that might get closer to the truth. They'd travel ten miles to stay within the Mages' Cloak of Oxford, where Naiam arranged for a secure camp with extra magical protection.

Vera steered her horse next to Gawain's. "Did Viviane know about this?" she asked him as they rode west, chasing the setting sun toward Camelot.

He frowned. "If anyone could have figured it out, it would have been her. She was the most brilliant mage I ever met." It shook Vera that his voice shone with admiration for Viviane. "She didn't have to lay any curse on the kingdom—just steal enough magic and convince us to do the same until it all began to run dry," he mused. "We cursed ourselves into vulnerability."

"How did you know?"

"I wouldn't have without Mordred's last attack. I suppose that's the silver lining to it. There was no other way we could have seen a concentration of magic theft and its immediate impacts on the earth. He did us a favor in that way."

"And that was what I knew?" Vera asked.

Gawain pursed his lips. He shook his head like he didn't believe it, though he said, "It must have been."

It was over. Gawain had figured it out, and her memories weren't even needed.

Her memories weren't even needed.

Merlin need not have saved her. Lancelot need not have some broken version of Guinevere's blood on his hands. Arthur need not have witnessed Guinevere die three times over. She turned her head to watch Arthur riding behind them.

She'd known she loved him since the day of her jousting bout, but Lancelot's saying the words aloud had uncaged her feelings. And in the tumult since then, it had become an inner roar. Vera was and would remain completely and entirely Arthur's.

His feelings, on the other hand, did not reach so deep. He was a loyal man. He'd promised to be Vera's friend, and he'd honor that, but it was magic and magic alone that enchanted him to desire her. The sooner she could accept their feelings' disparity and start dismantling her own, the better.

Gawain lay his hand on Vera's shoulder, pulling her from the spiral she'd tumbled into. "When we get back to Camelot, I'll focus on figuring out this hold magic has on you. We'll get the barrier dismantled, and we can take our time."

"Thank you," she whispered.

"Will you go back to your other home after that?"

"I—Yes." That was another piece she hadn't been able to process. This meant she could go home and be with her parents. She could help her father get better, and she did want that. But . . . she was Guinevere. She didn't belong in the future. But Vera didn't exactly belong here, either.

She must have been quiet for some time, lost in her thoughts, before Gawain eventually asked, "Are you done talking to me now?"

Vera shot him a look, only to find Gawain grinning.

It was well after dark when they bumbled into their rather luxurious camp. Five tents were laid out like a circle of wagons around a crackling campfire—only these were fantastic, brightly colored silk tents three meters tall. The mages each had their own. Then, there was one tent for the soldiers and the two knights and one each for Vera and Arthur. She'd heard Arthur discreetly make the request to Naiam. She hated it. She'd have given anything for the comfort of his arms tonight.

Lancelot stood outside the soldiers' tent, painstakingly suspending his orb with Merlin's magical aid as Vera eyed him with a cocked eyebrow.

She laughed. "He can do that himself, Merlin."

But Merlin glanced up from his work, bewildered. "What do you mean?"

"The orb—" Vera said, then she stooped. Lancelot shook his head minutely behind him. "Erm. I thought you were—never mind. I was confused." She was eager for Merlin to clear off so she could ask Lancelot what the hell that was about when a hand on her elbow turned out to be Tristan's.

"May I visit you this evening?" he asked quickly.

"Oh, erm." Vera tossed a glance at Lancelot, who was pretending not to listen as he tied his tent flaps back. "I can't tell you about what happened with the mages," she said apologetically, steering him farther from Lancelot.

"I know," Tristan said. "I'm used to this job: here to be chivalrous muscle, and they'll tell me more if it's pertinent for me to know." He laughed. "I wanted to give you some company. Only if you want it." He squeezed her elbow, trailing his thumb in a circle there as he had on her thigh the other night.

"All right," Vera heard herself say.

"All right," Tristan echoed. "I'm going to get cleaned up a bit, and then I'll come by."

He trotted off, leaving Vera with Lancelot's disapproving stare. He was quickly distracted by Gawain, who crawled out from behind the tent nearest them.

"Gawain, what on earth are you doing?" Lancelot asked.

The mage lowered his face to the dirt, examining it closely. "Checking the boundary line of our camp to be sure it's safe."

Lancelot sighed and shook his head, chuckling with Vera, his judgment apparently forgotten. He strode over to Gawain and offered him a hand up. "Come on, sir mage, I'll bunk up with you tonight. Your own private security detail."

Gawain stared at his hand disdainfully. "You are helpless against magic," he grumbled.

Lancelot lay his hand over his heart and frowned. "That hurts my feelings. Hey!" He said more brightly. "Nobody's ever died in battle next to me, remember? Didn't you and Percival think that was my magic? There you have it. That's that sorted. Now . . ." He shook his offered hand at Gawain, who glowered and reluctantly accepted it.

"Aw, there he is! That's the Gawain we love!" Lancelot slung an arm around his shoulder and steered Gawain toward his tent, calling to Vera over his shoulder, "Let's run tomorrow, Guinna. How often will we get the privilege of running under the Mages' Cloak?"

She marveled at the nonsensical yet also somehow perfectly logical fit of them.

Vera went to her tent, on the other side of the soldiers'. Merlin's was beside hers and then Arthur's, directly across the circle. His tent flaps didn't stir.

At least she could overthink things in comfort, Vera thought as she pushed through the entry. The camp set by Naiam put the finest glamping to shame. Lavish rugs carpeted the floor from one end to the other beneath furnishings as fine as any inn could offer. The bed (and it was a bed, not a cot, with a frame and ornately carved wooden headboard) only took a fraction of the space. There was a sitting area with wide-armed chairs and even a fireplace (did the tent have a chimney? She'd have to check in the morning), a desk like back in Camelot—and both hers and Arthur's bags had been neatly piled by an armoire made from the same cherry oak as the bed's headboard.

Arthur's bags. Damn. Whoever delivered them hadn't gotten the memo that the king and queen kept separate quarters. Vera sighed as she hefted his two saddlebags over her shoulders, partly glad for a reason to go to him, partly dreading another perfectly friendly and all-business encounter.

When she turned around, Arthur was already standing in her entry, framed in the light of the orb.

"Looking for these?" she said, with a cheeriness she didn't feel. Arthur hurried to her side, taking the bags from her shoulders. Warmth rushed through Vera when he set the bags down rather than leaving immediately.

She seized the opening. "Would you like to sit for a minute?" Vera gestured awkwardly to the sitting area.

Arthur smiled. "I'd love to sit."

He took the chair across from her, resting his elbows on his knees as Lancelot had done last night. It was funny to know them both so well now. One didn't bear any resemblance to the other, but they were so similar in mannerisms, kin in a hundred tiny ways.

"How are you?" he asked.

She exhaled a laugh. "I don't know where to start. Thank God for Gawain."

Arthur nodded emphatically, his face serious. "Without him, I'm afraid you would have gone ahead with the memory procedure." He smiled fleetingly and seemed to take an interest in the rug between his feet. "I'm glad it's not on your shoulders anymore, and we can get you back home soon."

"Oh," Vera said. "Right. Yes, that's good." Her throat tightened. She willed her chin not to quiver as tears threatened from the back of her eyes.

"I should go . . . let you enjoy your evening how you wish." He stood and collected his bags. His words were perfectly cordial, but Vera felt the meaning. Arthur meant Tristan.

"Stop," she said before he'd made it more than a step. "I don't—" Her voice caught and broke.

Arthur settled back into his seat and leaned toward her. "What's wrong?"

Vera shook her head, questing for what to say, for how to cover this moment. A strange clarity took her. Arthur saw it and sat up straight, bracing himself. The stone mask slid into place across his features. Her tears cleared from her throat, and she began speaking before she had a chance to think better of it.

"I don't want to do this anymore. I don't want Tristan. I want you, and it is driving me mad that you can be not fifty feet away and believe that I'm fucking him and be—" she gestured frantically at him, "and be fine with it!"

He listened to her, keeping his eyes trained on her and his face unreadable, barely moving a muscle. She had to watch closely to see his chest rise with his breath.

"Is that what you think?" Arthur asked in a whisper.

Vera nodded.

"Do you want to know what I think?" he asked.

"Yes," she said. A tear found the corner of her eye and slid down her cheek. She flinched toward brushing it away or trying to hide it but stopped herself.

Arthur rose and pivoted away from Vera, his hand rubbing hard over his mouth. He turned back to her abruptly, and his face had transformed. No longer were his features the pool of calm. His face grew dark, clouded with an intensity of rage and passion.

"I am not fine with it," he growled. "I did not sleep the night I thought you might be with him. I paced the room, and it took every ounce of control within me not to burn all that kept me from you to the ground.

"And the next day, I smiled at him when I wanted to rip his throat out for even daring to think of being with you. I promised never to trap you, but I'm a selfish fool, and I cannot let you go."

Arthur knelt in front of Vera and pinned her forearms to the chair's arms with his hands. "I want you with every breath that enters my body. I want—"

He stopped, tilting his chin down. Vera turned her arms underneath his hands so that her palms faced upward and clasped his wrists.

"Tell me," she whispered, hope igniting a spark in the depths of her belly that she hadn't dared to let herself entertain.

There was fire in his eyes. "I want to untie your dress without pulling my hands away when they touch your skin. I want to rip your gown from your body without looking away. I want to hold you without pretending to be asleep. I want," he paused and leaned closer, his eyes boring into her, "to please you and to hear your pleasure on your lips. I want to take you right now and throw you on that bed and make love to you until the sun rises."

Vera's insides leapt, though she hardly had a thought to spare for her elation. It all crushed together in a swell of desire. She freed one of her hands, sliding her fingers up his arm and further along his neck into his hair, delighting in how the bit of curl at its ends twisted around her fingertips. He closed his eyes at her touch and turned to catch her palm with his lips. This kiss sent a ripple through Vera's body.

"Why don't you?" she asked.

It nicked the tension enough for Arthur to exhale a laugh which, on his features, burning with passion, made him look so young. "We've made it this far and kept your mind intact. I won't risk that." Arthur slid his hands to her waist, dropping his forehead into Vera's lap. Her fingers roved back into his hair, massaging his scalp as she pulled him tighter to her legs.

She could just barely feel his hot breath on her thigh through her skirt and swallowed to keep herself from sighing with pleasure. It was Arthur whose sigh emerged as more of a moan. He lifted his head. "Though don't misunderstand me, Vera. I want to. Very badly."

A bell chimed from Vera's tent door. She and Arthur's eyes both snapped in that direction. She hadn't realized the tents had doorbells. Who could possibly be coming at this time of—

"Oh. Shit," Vera said as she remembered the plans they'd made. "It's Tristan."

Arthur dropped back onto his heels, creating space between himself and Vera. His eyes flicked from the doorway to her. "It doesn't matter, and it's not important," he said. "And I have no right to ask—"

"I didn't sleep with him," Vera said, and she knew from the way he had to work to suppress his relieved smile that she'd correctly assumed what the question would be. "I'll . . . tell him to go, shall I?" She squirmed free from her chair to go to the entry.

"No," Arthur said from behind her. "I'd like to speak to him."

She glanced back. Vera recognized that blasé tone. She pursed her lips as she held the tent flap back for Tristan to duck inside. He greeted her warmly with a squeeze of her elbow. His head flinched back slightly as he raised an eyebrow. "Were you running? You look flushed."

Vera must have blushed three shades of red. "Erm, no." She glanced at Arthur, who, she realized, matched her appearance with his hair mussed and eyes alight. Tristan followed Vera's gaze and had the decency to look embarrassed as he took a quick step away from her. He wanted to be anywhere except for in this tent right now.

Tristan stared down at the ground. "I'm sorry," he said. "I'll—"

"Tristan," Arthur cut in. He crossed the tent to stand next to Vera. "You're a good knight. And I need you to go back to Camelot at once."

Vera and Tristan both gaped at Arthur.

"Sire?" he said.

"I need a trustworthy messenger to ride fast ahead of us and bring word that we're coming," Arthur said. Vera released a relieved breath. But then he continued. "But truthfully, it's because you haven't done anything wrong, and I might kill you."

Tristan's eyes went wide.

"You're in love with my wife, and you actively want to bed her," he said with a calm that somehow made it that much more alarming. "So I might end up killing you if you stay."

Vera's eyes darted back and forth between Arthur and Tristan in silent shock. She should not find this hot, but she absolutely did.

Tristan retreated another step. "Your Majesty—"

Arthur stopped him with a raised hand. "There's no need. And we won't speak of it again."

Tristan opened and closed his mouth twice before looking at Arthur as if he'd spent the whole time interpreting a language he barely knew and only just understood. Arthur nodded curtly.

Tristan bowed, avoided Vera's eye, and left quickly.

"Arthur," she said, letting her mouth hang slack with a laugh barely contained.

His dangerous calm slipped into a sheepish grin. "Would you like to get ready for bed?" he asked.

"I would," she said, butterflies exploding in her chest. She turned to let him untie the laces of her dress.

"It seems like it's the body memory of our intimacy that's been a trigger for whatever curse is on you," Arthur mused as he worked his fingers through the laces. He didn't pull away when he got to the base of her back. He slipped his hand between the fabric and her skin, wiggling his fingers around her torso to loosen the bodice, and bent his head low, so close to her neck that his breath raised goosebumps down her spine. He kissed her neck, dragging the inside of his lip across her skin.

Vera closed her eyes and tilted her head back.

"What if there was something your body can't remember?" he whispered in her ear.

She shivered as a warm ache of need awoke between her thighs. Vera looked at Arthur over her shoulder.

His eyes glowed with hunger. "There is one thing we never did."

Vera could have cried out as he slid his hands off the skin at her middle, but Arthur took her hand and led her to sit on the edge of the bed. For the second time tonight, he knelt in front of her. This time, he lay a hand on each of her ankles and slowly ran them up the length of Vera's legs, pushing her skirt up until all of it gathered above her waist. Having helped her change out of gowns countless times, it was no surprise to

Arthur that she wore knickers. He made eye contact with Vera and asked the question without breathing a word. She nodded.

Arthur hooked his fingers beneath the elastic waistband and pulled them down in a fluid motion. He took Vera's hips and pulled her with ease, dragging her closer to the edge of the bed.

Her heart thundered, eager but trembling in her vulnerability. Arthur kissed her knee as he slid one hand into hers and held it tightly. With his mouth, he traced the line of the muscle up her thigh, working slower the closer he came to the top. Vera's head dropped back.

He paused just shy, the scruff of his chin biting at the tender skin of Vera's upper thigh. "Shall I stop?"

"No." She'd barely said the word before his lips plunged onto her, and she fell back onto her elbows with a moan.

Arthur released her hand and held her thighs apart as his tongue dipped inside Vera. Her back arched, pulsing her hips toward him, her mind going blissfully blank as everything save for this disappeared from existence. His lips closed around Vera's most tender point, and she yelped.

"Is this all right?" Arthur asked, pausing only long enough to utter the phrase.

"A little more pressure," Vera managed to gasp, anxious he might mistake her direction for displeasure.

But he obliged. "Like this?"

Vera reeled backward. "Yes," she gasped.

Reality narrowed to only this bed, her body writhing and Arthur's mouth exploring her. Vera's muscles tightened with the building ecstasy. Her elbows gave out beneath her, and she gripped the blankets in clenched fists as the sensation pulsed at her base, building until even sound dulled in her ears, and the frenzy peaked in the most sensational pinnacle of physical joy. All her tensed muscles released.

"Oh my God," she panted, covering her face with her hand. Arthur climbed up to lay next to her and kissed her hand. She rolled onto her side to face him, ready to reciprocate, tracing her fingers down his torso, finding the ties of his waistband—but he caught her fingers.

"No," he said. "It's not a transaction." He kissed her softly on the lips, and Vera's every insecurity melted away.

They fell asleep, enfolded together in bliss. She heard the ethereal words; this time, they were the drumbeat of her dreams through the whole night. One perfect and quiet night.

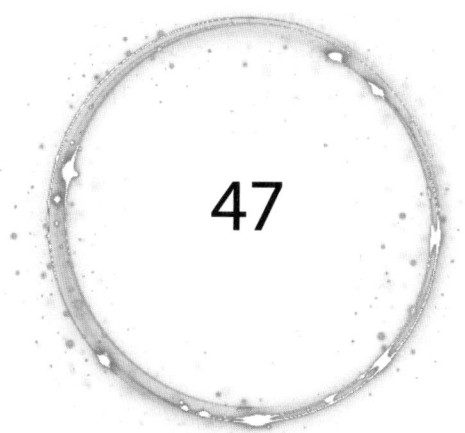

47

Vera nestled against Arthur's side, relishing the heat of his skin through her nightgown. Though he'd held her through the dark hours of many nights before, this was different. This time, there'd been no pretense, no tension or wondering. She felt his steady breath on her neck and knew he was still sleeping.

She carefully slid out of bed and changed into her running clothes in the dark as she had so many mornings. She was three steps from the door when he called out in a groggy voice, "Where are you going?"

She glanced back. He was propped up on an elbow with bleary, half-awake eyes.

She went back and sat on the bed beside him, smoothing the hair away from his forehead.

"Running with Lancelot," she whispered, pausing to kiss his brow. A hum of contentment rumbled low from his throat. "Keep sleeping."

He laid back down, and she stayed there, admiring his handsome features freely: the sharp line of his jaw and his perfect lips, eyelashes splayed delicately onto his cheeks. She stroked his hair, and he opened one eye, accompanied by a raised brow.

"Having second thoughts?" he murmured.

She was. She'd loved the hours lying next to him. But Vera laughed as she stood and threw a pillow on his face. Arthur smiled and hugged it to his chest as he rolled back over.

There was only a faint hint of a glow on the horizon's easternmost point. Lancelot hadn't yet emerged from Gawain's tent, so Vera sat on the ground and stretched, debating whether or not she should wake him. She didn't want to disturb Gawain, but she sure as hell wasn't going to let Lancelot keep sleeping. This run had been his idea.

He came out not a minute later. She started getting up to go to him, but Gawain followed. She had no place in this moment.

Vera couldn't hear what Gawain said. She only heard Lancelot's laugh in reply, an uninhibited sound as he turned back to Gawain and lay a hand on his cheek, gazing tenderly at him. Lancelot tipped his forehead to rest on Gawain's and then kissed him. It was as natural as if they'd shared such a kiss hundreds of times before—because they certainly had.

But it wasn't for her to see. She wished she could sink into the earth. Hiding wasn't an option. If she got up, the movement would only draw attention to her. Gawain went back into the tent. He hadn't seen her.

As Lancelot turned toward the soldiers' tent, his eyes landed directly on Vera. She froze. The easy joy melted from his features. His shoulders slumped as he tucked his chin to his chest and ducked into the tent.

Vera scrambled to her feet. She was still trying to decide what to say when he reemerged. His hard, blank expression stopped her. He didn't look at her as he said coolly, "Ready?" sounding nothing like himself.

They ran in stiff silence. Vera let it simmer for a few miles until they reached a grassy hill, and her steps stuttered to a stop. Lancelot ran a few paces further and reluctantly stopped, turning to face her.

"Let's take a break." She didn't wait for him to agree. She stepped off the path and plopped down on the ground. For a minute, it seemed Lancelot would stand there, staring into the distance by himself. But he dropped to the ground next to her, leaving more space between them than he usually would.

She couldn't let this stand. "Can I just say that you are both a great and a good man?" Vera said. "Has anyone told you that lately?"

His eyes were cast determinedly at the ground between his feet. "There's something wrong with me."

"Huh." Vera shook her head. "There are so many things about this time that aren't as I thought they'd be . . . but of all the things to be exactly as backward as I expected, this has to be the one." She sighed. "I disagree. I don't think there's a damn thing wrong with you."

Lancelot looked at her, a glimmer of hope in his eyes that snuffed itself out within a heartbeat. "Well, you are in the minority."

"It won't always be this way, you know. In a lot of the world in my time, it's not this way. You get to be who you are. You could get married if you wanted."

He scoffed at that. After a stretch of quiet, he abruptly said, "Do you think Arthur will hate me if he finds out?"

Vera inhaled deeply, her nostrils flaring at the idea that knowing this about Lancelot could impact how Arthur felt about him.

"I love you," Vera said firmly. "I don't love who you're supposed to be, or some idea of you. I love you. And if Arthur doesn't or can't, then I'm sorry, but he's the one who's broken and doesn't deserve your friendship. Not the other way around."

Lancelot's chin quivered ever so slightly as a tear fell from the corner of his eye that he hurriedly wiped away. Vera felt a surge of loyalty.

"I wouldn't want to have a thing to do with him, either," she added.

She was surprised when that comment cracked the shell of Lancelot's pain. He chuckled. "Those are harsh words from the woman who loves him."

She crossed her arms stubbornly across her raised knees. "Well, I very much mean it."

Lancelot reached to affectionately squeeze her ankle. Then her words sank in, and he jolted, his mouth falling slightly open in a lopsided grin as his whole posture perked up. "You didn't deny it."

"No, I didn't."

"So, you do love him?" Even in this vulnerable moment, Lancelot's eyes twinkled. Vera thought he might have been relieved that the focus had moved away from him.

She sighed, and he wiggled his shoulders with a gleeful giggle.

"You don't have to be so fucking smug about it," Vera said, but she laughed, too.

The sun had broken the horizon. Lancelot reached out his hand to call in his orb, hanging readily over their heads. It zipped into his hand.

Vera nodded toward the pocket where he tucked it. "Why the bloody hell don't you want Merlin to know what your light does? Wasn't he the one who made it for you?"

"Ah, erm. No. Sorry." Lancelot grimaced. "I lied before. I didn't ever anticipate telling you my mother was a mage when we met in Glastonbury. She made my light. And she was rather cleverer than Merlin, not unlike our Sir-Mage Gawain." Lancelot looked off into the distance toward their campsite with love in his eyes. It wasn't just a casual fling between them.

His brow furrowed, and he stiffened.

"What is it?" Vera asked.

"I don't know," he murmured. "Something. Something's wrong."

She looked, too. Back toward camp, though it was too far to see the tents. Vera wasn't sure what they were looking for.

"It's just a feeling, and I'm probably being paranoid." Lancelot tried to shake it off. "I—"

A flash brighter than the newly born sun on the horizon mushroomed from their camp. If there was any doubt that it was an explosion, the sound of the blast that followed, carried slower on the wind than the light, confirmed it.

Vera and Lancelot sprang to their feet. They were running before either acknowledged out loud what they'd seen. Vera felt ill. The creeping nausea of instinct whispered quietly that this would end her world. She saw Arthur's peaceful, barely awake face in her mind. She could almost feel the surprising softness of his cheek, the sensation of her fingers twining in his hair. That interaction this morning could have been their last.

Arthur might already be gone. The thought rose, unbidden, and Vera stamped it out. They were in the Mages' Cloak. Merlin was there.

Gawain was there. Maybe . . . maybe it was an accident, and everything was fine. It could have been nothing.

Vera was lying to herself.

She and Lancelot ran harder than they'd ever run. He was a few steps ahead of her, constantly glancing over his shoulder. She was holding him back. "I can't keep up with you," Vera said between ragged breaths.

"Do you want me to slow—"

"No!" she cried. "Go! Go as fast as you can."

"I can't leave you," he said.

"I'm fine. Just get there!"

Lancelot slowed to look at her. He hesitated for two breaths, calculating the risk. With one last glance at Vera, he took off at nearly double their pace. Good. He'd get there. He had to get there. And if he was there, it would all be okay.

Vera ran as fast as she could. These would be the fastest miles of her life if she'd been timing them, but they were also the longest. Her mind was a cloud of fear and dread, only worsening as she got closer.

It hadn't just been one smoldering explosion. Fires burned in its wake. She was close enough to see flames consuming two of the tents, lapping at the silk now blackened by heat. The other three were already reduced to rubble. She couldn't make out distinct faces from this distance, but through the smoke and her tears, she was nearly certain that some of the lumps on the ground were bodies. Vera's world spun. Her feet pounded the ground so hard and fast that her lungs screamed for relief. She couldn't stop, though.

She expected battle cries, sounds of clashing swords and commands being shouted . . . even wails of pain from the injured. But there was nothing, and it drove the spike of fear deeper into Vera's heart. The crackle of fire might have been the merry sound of Bonfire Night, but today it was accompanied by the distinct stink of charred flesh. The air of camp was so clouded with dark plumes of smoke that she tripped and landed splayed out on her front, sucking in air. Her skin scorched, and some distant and reasonable part of her mind told her to move, that she must have landed on some debris that had burned down to hot coals. Vera rolled over. It was only grass next to her, but her skin blazed. In a daze, she lifted her head to see what she'd tripped over, and her heart stopped.

It was a body.

Her mind demanded precious seconds to determine that the face didn't belong to Arthur, nor Merlin or Gawain. It was one of the soldiers, the younger of the two. His vacant and unseeing eyes stared back at her.

She was ashamed that relief flooded her first—that it wasn't one of her friends. She'd never even learned his name. And now, he was gone. This wasn't how it was supposed to be.

This was a nightmare.

Oh God. Where was Lancelot? At the thought of him, her adrenaline surged. And where was Arthur?

The other soldier (why had she never even learned their names?) was dead in the grass not ten feet away. She didn't see Lancelot or Gawain, but there was Merlin, standing and surveying the wreckage, blood up to his elbows on both arms, smeared across his cheek, dripping from a gash on his forehead, and splashed across the bottom half of his robe. A sword hung limply from one shaking hand as his mortified gaze fell on Vera.

"Where's Arthur?" she demanded.

"Guinevere." Merlin stumbled toward her. His hand shook as he bent to touch the soldier's head, swallowing heavily. "I—he—"

"Where is he?" She screamed it.

Then she heard Lancelot. "Guinna!"

She spun around. Across what remained of their camp, Lancelot knelt on the ground next to another lump, another body. But it couldn't be. It could not be Arthur. She tore toward him, forgetting to be frightened if enemies were among them because the impossible was materializing before her eyes.

Arthur, on his back on the ground. Lancelot pressed a cloth against his abdomen. Next to him, there was a pile of red fabric—Vera realized in horror that those hadn't started red. They were used compresses. So many. So much blood.

Arthur's eyes were only half-open.

"He's—he's asking for you," Lancelot said, his face pale and shell-shocked.

Vera dropped to her knees. They flanked Arthur now, Lancelot on one side, Vera on his other.

"I'm here, I'm here," she said, smoothing his hair back from his face. For the briefest moment, she was relieved to touch him and feel the force of his life humming through him. But it was short-lived, because this was very bad.

Arthur revived some at her touch and her voice, blinking up at her.

"It's all right," she soothed. "I'm here."

He turned his face into her hand, and she thought he tried to kiss her palm, but he only had the energy to press his lips to her skin. Vera wept quietly. "It's—it's fine. It's going to be fine."

She looked up at Lancelot. He held the compress in place, but his face was awash with defeat. He met Vera's hopeful, pleading gaze and shook his head minutely. Uneven trails streaked through the dirt and ash covering his face. He was crying, too, and Vera crumbled.

She heard Merlin approach from behind, frantically explaining. "It had to be—it couldn't have been anyone else. It had to be a mage. I can't believe they would—"

"Where's Gawain?" Vera demanded, not a question. He could help. His healing could help.

"I—I don't know." Merlin's eyes were wild. He was terrified.

Vera's heart jumped. Merlin could fix Arthur. He'd fixed her, hadn't he? "Save him," she cried.

He stared at her blankly. "I can't."

Why didn't he understand? "Do what you did to me." She scrambled to her feet, grabbing at Merlin's arms. "Save his essence. Do whatever you have to do!"

Merlin stumbled as if struck. "Guinevere!" He grabbed her wrists. "I cannot do it."

"What do you mean? You did it to me. You saved me!"

"I didn't!" he said. "It is not my power!"

Vera reeled back. What the fuck? He meant it. She wailed wordlessly, ripping her hands free and slamming her fists against his chest. "What are you good for!" she screamed. "Go back to the mages. Get someone who can help." Her voice faltered into desperation. "Please!" she begged through a sob.

Merlin reached out a hand to comfort her, but she saw the pity in his eyes and wrenched away. "Go!" she screamed.

Vera didn't watch to make sure he'd gone, but she heard the thunder of hooves fading as she spun back to Arthur and dropped down at his side. She was dizzy, nauseous, and in such physical agony from the pulsing fire on her skin.

Lancelot clutched Arthur's hand and knelt with his face close to his.

"Get Vera to safety," Arthur said in a strangled voice. "If you can get her home, do it. If you can't—just . . ." He sucked in shallow breaths from the effort.

"I will," Lancelot assured him through tears. "You know I will."

Lancelot gripped Vera's arm over Arthur's chest, binding himself to her. She clung to him, too. Vera cupped Arthur's face with her other hand like if she held it just right, his life wouldn't slip away . . . water between her fingers.

She wanted to beg him not to die and let all the pain and burning and fear explode from her in desperate screams, but those could not be the last sounds Arthur heard. Vera wondered if he was afraid as he struggled to breathe and fought against the pain, his beautiful face drawn and clenching when the waves of it hit. She wanted him to know he was surrounded and loved.

It was all she could give him.

"You're going to be okay," Vera said. A lie and a prayer. She didn't know what she was going to say until it was already out of her mouth. "We'll go back to my Glastonbury together. I want you to meet my parents. My dad will love you." Lancelot let out a strangled sob. She squeezed his arm more tightly. Tears streamed down her face.

Vera imagined cradling Arthur in her words, and his eyes fixed on her, held by her voice. "We'll read the Lord of the Rings together at night, and we can run the Tor at sunrise if you want. Or walk." Arthur's lips turned up at the corners, and Vera managed a strangled laugh before her tears choked her. She'd painted the life she dreamed of because this one was ending, and she wanted to keep it from being a nightmare for him.

Arthur blinked his eyes clear and took great effort to lift his hand to Vera's cheek. It shook. He couldn't hold it up, so she held it there for him. The blood from his wound soaked all of his body, even his hands, running down his fingers in delicate rivers on the current of Vera's tears.

"Vera," he said, more a breath. "You have given me everything." His fingertips trembled violently against her cheek. He smiled faintly and with extraordinary effort. Blood began to trickle from the corner of his mouth. Arthur was about to die. This couldn't be real. "I wouldn't trade the time with you for any long life. I love—"

His voice failed as blood gurgled in his throat.

"No," Vera said forcefully.

Lancelot launched forward, trying to clear Arthur's airway with his fingers.

Arthur was about to say he loved her. She somehow knew that meant it was done, and he would be gone. Yet Vera could hardly keep her eyes on him through the screaming pain in her skin. She was uninjured and unblemished, but she would have sworn that she was burning alive, about to explode from a pent-up force with nowhere to go.

Ishau mar domibaru.

It echoed within her from someplace untouchable.

And she knew.

Vera had a certainty that she didn't understand, and it came through foreign words that her tongue craved to cry.

"You need to move," she hurriedly said to Lancelot. Now that she knew the words, it took all her effort to keep from saying them.

"What?" He looked at her like she was insane. But she couldn't explain, and they were running out of time.

"MOVE!" Vera bellowed with a voice that would carry for acres.

Lancelot scrambled to his feet and stumbled backward.

Vera rose to the full height of her knees, and the words tumbled off her tongue. "Ishau mar domibaru."

There was power in her voice that she didn't recognize. And she knew what to do next. A deep inhale and exhale, the name of the origin of all things, the breath of life itself. As the last wisp of breath parted from her lips, an unnatural silence filled her ears for microseconds. Then a surge of power rocked through Vera, up from her toes and down from the top of her head, meeting and exploding at her chest, down her arms and out her palms, too. It was a light so bright, radiating out from her with a blinding blast.

Instantly after, there was something alive inside Vera. She knew it like her oldest friend. Now that it was here, she understood that it always had been. She and Lancelot shared one wide-eyed look.

"Go," he breathed.

Vera dropped back down and pressed her hands to Arthur's wound. The effect was immediate. Please don't let it be too late, she silently pleaded. Let it be enough.

His skin started to knit itself together at her touch. As the force flowed through her hands and into his body, Vera began to learn more. Closing the wound wasn't enough. She could sense the blood loss and instinctively regenerated his blood supply. She knew the organs that had been pierced even though she didn't know their names. Vera bound them shut.

He would not die on this patch of earth today. His life force intensified. The closer he came to wholeness, the weaker Vera became. Her fears of whether she could give him enough renewed. She kept at it, pushing the power from her, drawing from what felt like the bottom of the well of her gift until every wound in his body had been healed and his blood was restored. Vera was terrified to release the grip of her power, but there was nothing more she could do.

She fell back, panting and terrified.

His eyes were open, and the haze was gone. Arthur sat up and tore back his blood-soaked tunic, revealing a mess of blood on his skin.

But there was no wound.

"You're still alive," Vera said in disbelief.

"Yes I am." Arthur's voice was thick with awe. One of the burning tents collapsed in on itself with a crash, jolting them from their reverie. He blinked and surveyed the wreckage. From somewhere not far off, a horse's whinny cut through the quiet.

"We can't stay here." He looked to Lancelot. "Are you all right?"

Lancelot nodded. He was, and he wasn't.

Oh God. "Where's Gawain?" Vera asked. She was afraid of the answer.

"He's gone. There's no sign of him." Lancelot's jaw jutted forward as he shook his head. "I'll find the horses."

"Can you stand?" Vera asked Arthur, offering her hand and helping him up. He was fine. He was healed.

But Vera's vision swam in front of her. She grabbed Arthur's arm to steady herself. "I don't feel good," she mumbled before promptly doubling over and vomiting.

She stood back up and swayed. Arthur held her upright. The world spun around her. "I think I'm about to lose consciousness," she mused. It was her last waking thought.

As she faded, she felt Arthur's arms around her. She heard his and Lancelot's voices, but they sounded far off. Vera felt the bump of movement and vaguely recognized that she was on a horse with Arthur's arms holding her fast, but she did not know where they were going.

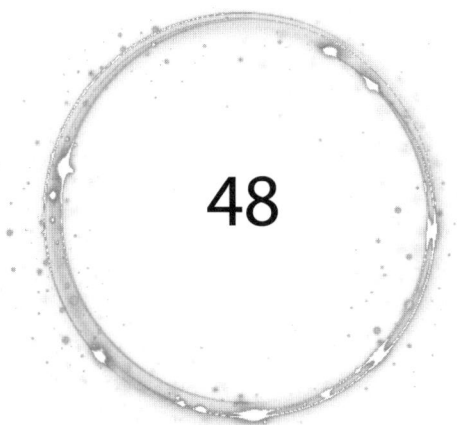

48

Vera swam in and out of awareness so fluidly that reality became an obscured confusion. She thought she felt rain, but she opened her eyes to the bright sun and waving long-stemmed flowers in the breeze, like the ones from the dream she had in the memory procedure. Maybe she dreamt this, too. She saw a farmhouse with a thatched roof. At some point, she was off the horse, and perhaps Arthur had carried her inside. There was another voice, familiar and simultaneously a stranger.

There was a hand on her forehead, the stroke of loving fingers over her cheek in a dark room. Night had fallen.

When she woke, it was to the bright light of day shining through a window. She was in a bed, and as Vera sat up, two blankets fell from her shoulders. Her head throbbed like she had a horrible hangover. Her running clothes were gone, replaced by a clean, oversized tunic she recognized as Arthur's. She glanced around. This wasn't the castle at Camelot, that was for sure. Nor was it an inn.

This was a home. There was a fireplace in one corner. The chamber was simply but comfortably appointed, and just one chair sat near the bed. The book lying on it betrayed that Arthur had sat there beside her.

Arthur. Still alive. The joy that came was muted by the rising memory of the soldier's lifeless stare, of Gawain missing, of all that was lost and ruined. Vera rubbed her face, trying to sweep together the mess of all that had happened.

She heard quiet voices and could not resist going to them. She didn't want to be alone, but she couldn't exactly walk out in the equivalent of an oversized T-shirt. Vera noticed a simple dark blue dress draped on the end of the bed and decided it must be for her.

She changed into it before she tiptoed barefoot to the door, opened it a crack, and listened.

"—not sure what you're asking," said the nearly familiar deep voice of a man.

"Do you know anything about the extent to which emotions can be manipulated by magic?" Vera closed her eyes, gratitude sweeping over her. That voice, she knew. Hearing Arthur speak easily, unencumbered by the strain of injury, lifted a weight she didn't realize she carried. She slipped through the door and into the main room of a farmhouse.

There was a wooden table next to the hearth. Arthur sat nearest her, facing away. The man opposite him, facing her, was the stranger. His dark hair, streaked with grey, fell to his shoulders. He listened to Arthur with a furrowed brow, emphasizing natural lines of years and worry that wizened his face. But he saw Vera as she entered and smiled warmly. She recognized that smile. Arthur turned and had no sooner seen Vera than was out of his seat and rushing to her. He hugged her and then held her by both elbows, searching her face.

"I'm fine," she said. And it was true, but the mystery of what happened in the space of an hour when she and Lancelot were on their run ate at her. "What happened?"

"I'm not sure," Arthur said. "I never quite fell back asleep when you left. Things went too quiet—no breeze nor crickets . . . nothing. I couldn't even hear my own breathing, and I knew something wasn't right." He shook his head. "I should have gone out to check, but I thought I was just on edge. Then there was a blast that lit blue, and I knew it was magic. It was pitch dark and then so bright it was blinding. It was all focused on Gawain.

"I tried to help him, but when he saw me, he threw out a hand at the same time I was hit with a spike." Arthur's hand went to where the wound had been on his abdomen, touching the ghost of his fatal injury. "Gawain sent me flying backward with one hand, and he had his device in the other. I think he was trying to destroy it, but he was . . . bound right then. Wrapped up in a rope that looked like it was on fire. He yelled one word. Mordred." Vera's stomach churned. It was another chess piece sliding into play from the legend. How could this end well? "And the rope tightened of its own accord and—" Arthur grimaced. "God, he screamed like a tortured man."

It ached to imagine their soft-souled Gawain in that sort of agony, and at the hands of a villain whose name would survive the next millennium. "Is Gawain dead?" she whispered.

"I don't think so. They took him," he said slowly. "Mordred and whoever helped him. No one came for me after that. They weren't interested in me. It got very foggy for a while. And then you showed up."

Arthur's mouth lifted in a smile, his fingers rubbing the back of her neck. They hadn't reckoned with the tenderness of what they thought would be his final moments, of the honest adoration that spilt from them before Vera . . . well, before Vera found her power.

But the way she'd pushed it so hard until there was nothing left to give . . . she suspected she'd scraped her depths and given it all to him, and that would have been fine. But as soon as the fear rose, she knew the gift was there, humming in her blood. Vera wouldn't be able to use it right now, not on an injury like Arthur's. She felt like she'd carried a heavy weight as far as she could before being forced to drop it. Her strength was sapped. She'd need more rest before she could use the gift again.

The sound of a chair's leg scraping against the stone floor reminded Vera that there was someone else in the room, blocked by Arthur. She peeked around his shoulder at the man who was politely absorbed in whittling a palm-sized block of wood with a short knife.

Arthur turned to open the conversation with the man. "This is my father."

"Otto," the man supplied, rising to join them with that same warm smile. Of course, she'd recognized it. He'd passed that expression on to his son, a perfect match of effusiveness. Otto was a full head shorter than Arthur.

"I'm so glad to meet you. I'm . . ." She paused, unsure how to introduce herself. Should she say Vera or Guinevere?

"Vera, love, it's my pleasure," he said. Her eyes flashed to Arthur, who looked down as he smiled.

Vera defaulted to greeting Otto as she would have in the twenty-first century. She shook his hand and was already releasing it before she realized the gesture would be eccentric to him. But he wasn't fazed. He smiled with crinkling eyes that reminded Vera of Martin.

"He knew Guinevere. He knew you before," Arthur corrected himself. "I told him everything."

"I owe you the world, Vera. You brought my son back to me." She blushed at his kindness. "I was mighty worried when you lot showed up drenched in blood yesterday afternoon and you sleeping as soundly as the dead."

That had all happened yesterday. "What time is it?" Vera asked.

"Midafternoon," Arthur said. "You've been out for more than a day."

As if on cue, her stomach growled.

"Let's get you something to eat." Otto turned back and pulled a seat out for her at the table. "You must be starving."

She was. Arthur and Otto sat with her while she ate. She was on her second bowl of soup when Lancelot charged in, loudly complaining before his foot crossed the threshold.

"Do you know your barn door is half off its hinges?" He was sweaty enough that his shirt clung to him, and dirt streaked his arms and down his cheek. He knocked the dirt from his boots, completely at home here, and started to pull them off his feet. His eyes finally fell on Vera with a shoe half off. Lancelot forgot the bawdy show he'd been putting on as he was swept with relief.

"Oh, Guinna," he said. He stumbled over and fell into the chair next to her, wrapping her in a sweaty hug that was much more than relief. She could feel the pain that he was barely keeping at bay. Her darling friend who was terrified, who was enraged, whose heart was shattered because there wasn't a damn thing he could do to help the one he loved.

She didn't say anything. She didn't need to. They clutched one another, his face tucked into her neck. When he pulled away, he'd wrangled his expression to one of wonder. "You've got quite a power."

It had been nagging at Vera, too. She could feel now that it wasn't a new part of her, but had Guinevere known about it before? And...

"Do you think Viviane knew about my power?" She asked it aloud.

A drawn hesitance came over Lancelot's expression.

"I think," Arthur said, staring intently at Lancelot, "that we should ask her."

"What?" Vera reeled back in her seat.

Lancelot nodded grimly. "How long have you known?"

"Since last week," Arthur said. "When they were hanging lights for the festival, and Vera asked about yours. I don't know why I didn't realize it before. Have you known all the while?" There was an edge in his voice, a hint of accusation.

Lancelot didn't directly answer. He pulled his orb from his pocket and lit it in his hand. "I kept waiting for it to go out. She was so powerful, though. If anyone's magic could sustain beyond the grave, it would have been hers. But, for about a month now, it's been getting brighter. I'm sorry I didn't tell you sooner. I didn't know what to make of it."

Vera gawped at the both of them. She spared a glance at Otto, too, who seemed keenly interested but not at all confused.

"But you said your mother made your light," she said.

"Yes." Lancelot looked at her. Understanding crashed down on Vera, and it must have shown on her face. He nodded as he said, "Viviane's my mother."

"What?" she cried. "That's a massive fucking thing to not tell me!"

Otto casually wiped at his mouth, though Vera saw the mirth in his eyes and knew he was trying to conceal a laugh at her outburst. Lancelot looked guilty, but Arthur didn't, and it incensed Vera.

"Who all knows?" she demanded.

"Only the people in this room," Arthur said. "That's it."

She turned to Lancelot. "So, you were in Camelot together, and no one knew? You—"

"Pretended to be strangers," Lancelot said. "No one could know. It's the same sort of secretive mage bullshit we're reckoning with now." He rolled his eyes and tapped his fingers irritably against the wooden tabletop.

"To protect you and her both," Otto said pointedly, inclining his head toward Lancelot, whose expression softened at the reminder. Otto turned to Vera. "That's how Viviane found Arthur. She and Lancelot lived down the road, and these two grew up wreaking havoc together. Viviane was the one who recognized Arthur's call to the throne—at far too young an age, I might add. I was none too pleased with that." Though his words hinted at annoyance, Otto's eyes glimmered as he remembered.

Vera's fire faded as the whole truth of it hit her. "Your mother is alive," she said, turning to Lancelot.

He smiled sadly. "Yes. My mother, the mage who tried to kill you, is alive." He turned to Arthur. "Even though she was supposedly executed by the mages. That's clearly not the case. We've got more than a bit of a problem with our mages, sire. And now there's this Mordred. He has Gawain's instrument, and he has Gawain. That damn fool will never give them the power to use it. Do you know the kind of torture Mordred will put him through?"

He looked at Vera, lost for a moment in his turmoil. She reached for his hand beneath the table. "We'll find him," she said. "You'll find him."

"How?" Lancelot asked. Hopelessness mired his face.

"There must be something we can do! We have to tell Merlin," Vera said, her voice rising. "He'll think you're dead, Arthur. And he has to know that Mordred has Gawain."

She stopped. It was all wrong. "But . . . how could Mordred know about Gawain's instrument? Gawain only told the council of mages and—"

Oh no. A mage on the council working with Mordred. It was the only explanation. Could the betrayal really run that deep? It was what Merlin had tried to warn her of, wasn't it?

"Who performed Viviane's execution?" Otto asked. "Do you know?"

"Merlin," Arthur said darkly. "It was his duty as her closest collaborator."

"He would have had a witness with him. Another mage," Lancelot added. "Which means there is one more of our mages who know the truth of it."

"And—and they're the one working with Mordred?" Vera asked.

"I don't know." Arthur shook his head. "We have to get back to Camelot. There are refugees there, and if Mordred figures out how to use that instrument against our people, I can't be sitting by in the countryside."

Lancelot heaved a sigh. "I knew you were going to say that. We can't, Arthur."

"Convince me why we shouldn't," Arthur growled.

"Because I know you think Merlin's not in on this, and you might just be wrong." Arthur started to protest, but Lancelot raised his voice and spoke over him. "We can conjecture about it all we want, but he lied to you and not about something insignificant. It's treason, Arthur. Even if you're not wrong, even if there is some noble secret bullshit reason for sparing my mother, we can't trust him. I don't know why I'm saying it. You already know this. Plus, there's another matter." Lancelot looked at Vera and squeezed her hand. "By all rights, you should be dead. When you're not, we're going to have to explain how. I've never seen a gift like Guinna's. They will want it. Our mages. Mordred. All of them."

Arthur nodded grimly. "I never should have relied so heavily on the mages. I thought I was building a better world, not positioning myself as a high-stakes puppet."

If Merlin and his witness kept Viviane alive, there must be a reason for it. They all agreed on one action they could take: they needed to find Viviane, to get answers and reclaim some power in the game. The kingdom was not fine, and they didn't know who they could trust outside of one another.

"What now?" Vera asked. "How do we find her?"

It left them at a dead end. Lancelot angrily flung his orb on the table. He glared at it as it rolled to a stop, wobbling in place before changing direction. It spun one-half turn to the left and was still again. Lancelot dropped his forehead onto the table. They sat in defeated silence for a few moments before Lancelot jolted upright with wide eyes and snatched his orb in both hands.

Vera put a hand on his arm. "What are you—"

"Shut up," Lancelot snapped as he jerked away. "Sorry. But shut up a second." He closed his eyes. He spun the light in his hands, stopped, and held it in the new position. He repeated the action two more times.

He laughed. "Holy shit," Lancelot said as he opened his eyes. "There's more energy on one side of the orb. No matter how I spin it, it . . . hums on my left hand. Westward."

"Do you think it will take us to her?" Arthur asked.

"I think it will do exactly that," Lancelot said with a smug rap on the table.

Vera was ready to leave then and there. It wasn't much of a plan, but doing something felt right. After Arthur, Lancelot, and even Otto insisted that she should rest for the remainder of the day, she grudgingly agreed. They'd leave in the morning.

Lancelot hassled Otto into heading to the barn with him so he could fix the door. Arthur tried to get Vera to lie back down but, seeing that she was stubbornly refusing, offered to go for a walk with her and show her around. She was eager to know more about his life.

"Your mother?" she asked as they walked out the back door.

"Died when I was young," Arthur said. He offered Vera his hand to help her step over the knee-high garden wall behind the house. "That's actually one of her dresses you're wearing. I can tell it makes my dad happy to see you wearing it."

He led her to a fenced pen with half a dozen goats grazing inside. She laughed at the smallest kid as it hopped around like a wind-up toy. They also watched Lancelot in the distance, jovially laughing with Otto as he clapped him on the back.

"He's not okay, you know," Vera said.

Arthur nodded. "Your passing out was the only thing that kept him from riding off in search of Gawain that very moment." He was silent for a long stretch, his eyes still on Lancelot. "You know about him and Gawain." It was a statement, not a question, and Vera held her breath to keep from reacting. "Did Lancelot tell you?"

"Oh. Erm, no. I . . ." She looked at her feet, Lancelot's worry about what Arthur would think springing to the front of her mind. "I saw them together, but I didn't think you knew—"

"Vera," Arthur said sharply, "I need to be clear before you say anything else. I'm not sure how you feel about Lancelot's proclivity or if that changes your opinion of him. I realized this about him when we were young and decided that it did not matter. You may feel how you want, and I won't try to change you, but I will not hear a word against Lancelot on this matter." His confidence fell as soon as he finished speaking. He glanced at her worriedly from the corner of his eye.

She'd thought she couldn't possibly adore Arthur more, and there he'd gone and proven her wrong.

"What did you want to say?" he asked more gently.

Vera stared at him. As long as they were being boldly honest, there was only one thing left to say. She shook her head. "I love you," she said. "I'm in love with you."

He hadn't been expecting that. His smile lit every part of his face as he moved his mouth soundlessly, looking like a man drunk on goodness itself. He bent his head and rested his forehead on hers. He was happy and also . . . relieved.

"I love you, Vera," he managed to say through the obstacle of his joy.

When his lips found hers, they moved deliberately. There was no rush to their embrace, no sense that it could be stolen away. They said nothing else to mar this perfect bliss for quite a while.

"I heard you asking your father about how magic might manipulate emotions," she finally said, hearing her voice quiver and willing it to be strong. "The way Merlin transferred my feelings for Vincent onto you frightens me. And I knew the potions have had a hand in desiring one another, but I've been wondering about how deep it's taken us." He gazed at her with so much yearning that she could hardly breathe. "Because," and this part was difficult to say, "it's also more than what it was with Vincent. I haven't felt anything like what I feel for you in my whole life."

He nodded. "I feel that, too. And what if it comes from magic?"

What if. Vera let all the questions hang there: what if it was puppetry? What if nothing they felt was real?

Arthur took her hand.

"Even if it's all magic," he said, "knowing right now that you feel the same is more than I could hope for." Goosebumps raised all over Vera's body. He lifted her hand to his mouth and kissed her fingers.

There was no telling what tomorrow might bring. For all that they'd lost—for Gawain, who was likely enduring horrors, for their dear friend, the protector who could not protect his beloved, for a kingdom which teetered on the edge of disaster—and for a love that might fall apart and betray them both as pawns in the mages' game. It all hung in a horrible balance.

But today, tiny dots of yellow flowers waved in the tall grass under a clear sky. The sun shone. The three of them were safe. Arthur and Vera loved one another.

They were alive.

And for now, that was enough.

Meeting Vera

A Bonus Scene from Arthur's POV

When Guinevere left for her respite in the countryside, Arthur had been relieved—accompanied by a wash of guilt. He was used to being able to fix things. If he showed up to a task with integrity, with humility, with the inevitable power that once only came from his gift and was now magnified by his throne, he could find a way to win the unwinnable.

Except with Guinevere.

It all started so well. She arrived in Camelot (with her awful father) and right away it was clear that she and Arthur were a well-suited pair. She every bit the poised and noble queen to help establish their new kingdom, he with his raw gift for the leading of a nation—and both sharing the vision to build something new, something better than what had been.

It was all but decided before she'd arrived, and it solidified with Guinevere and Arthur's meeting: they'd be married. But the wars were not all won yet. They didn't know it, but there was a year yet to go of battle—and the fiercest they'd face. On the precipice of losing it all, when all truly seemed hopeless, Guinevere had been the one to find a way to win.

And then she stood on the smoldering battlefield and saw the wreckage of her designs.

And slowly (so slowly at first that Arthur could convince himself it was her ordinary poise), she grew sad. It was the beginning of the melancholy. If he'd not ignored it then . . . if he'd stopped everything then to care for her, he still wondered: would it have made a difference?

She was the one to finally tell him. On a rainy morning when Arthur had been awake since before sunrise preparing for audiences with lords and then having the audiences with said lords, he returned to their quarters for a treaty draft he'd left lying on his desk and hardly noticed her sitting there.

He'd done a double take when he realized she was there—perched on the edge of the bed with her feet on the floor and eyes cast down between them. It was only when she looked up that he could see her eyes were red-rimmed from a good long while of crying. She insisted there was no direct cause of her sadness, that it was just a general feeling, though he knew the devastation she'd wrought to end the wars had ignited it—and it took off like a wildfire within her, sadness devouring everything it could reach.

For a while, Arthur dropped many of his duties. Delegated tasks and audiences and kingdom responsibilities to others so he could try to help Guinevere—with the full expectation that he could help her. That care would be enough.

It was not, no matter what Arthur did, said, or offered. She assured him she just needed time. Slowly, he slipped back to the things he could make better, back to the kingdom building.

And then her sadness changed. She stopped sharing it with him, instead becoming hyper critical and angry about . . . about everything. That was harder. Like the sadness, he couldn't fix it. Unlike the sadness, she seemed to come to abhor his very presence.

Then it changed again. She retreated into herself. He'd thought (hoped, really) that it was the beginning of her getting better, but it was worse. She stayed in bed for days at a time. Merlin was able to cheer her some . . . she'd rouse herself for regular sessions with him. But he travelled often, especially in those early days. So it was back to bed for Guinevere.

The alarms screamed within Arthur, a very correct instinct that something terrible was on the horizon (though he never in a million years would have guessed what was coming). He cared for Guinevere very much. He loved her—not in any sort of nonsense way, but grounded and real care.

And it went far deeper than any sense of possession. Arthur knew that she'd loved someone before . . . in all the ways. Grounded and real—and the stunning nonsense of great stories. He'd taken her from Tristan. Of course, she'd come willingly. But maybe that was it. Maybe she was sinking into sorrow for the love she'd lost.

She could have him.

Arthur would turn a blind eye to an affair at this point. Hell, he sent for the man across the far reaches of the damn nation, put Tristan in his room with his wife, offered the plea, "Help her. However you can, please help her," and left. That wasn't turning a blind eye, that was facilitating an affair. It didn't matter if it would work to help her.

It didn't, though. And Tristan went back to the north.

Arthur couldn't remember how the plan came about that Guinevere should spend some time in the countryside, only that he learned of it and immediately felt like a weight was lifting. She could go, be away, get whatever it was she needed—and he, without seeing her daily deepening despair, would feel like less of a failure. And he could do the thing he was actually decent at. He could work.

God, what sort of a man had he become?

So, yes. He was relieved when she was gone to the country, and he could believe it would all be well soon.

She was gone for nearly a month before she returned. Arthur hadn't even known that Guinevere was back in Camelot until it all went wrong. He hadn't so much heard the scream as he . . . felt something. Like a shockwave blasting through his blood.

He began running without direction, just a guttural pull. Down the stairs from his chamber—their chamber—through the room with the enormous fireplace, out into the back courtyard that they hardly used, and there was Guinevere, decimated on the flag-stoned ground at the center.

Decimated.

Hers wasn't the only body there. Viviane lay nearby with her hands in front of her, cuffed with beams of glowing cord, eyes open and frozen—magically still—on her side facing the horror. There was no time. No time to wonder at what the fuck was happening.

The only movement came from Merlin, who knelt at Guinevere's side, his hands working feverishly around her body, centered at her chest where her blood was spurting—where the wound must have been.

Guinevere was hardly recognizable, but in the same way Arthur had been pulled here, he was certain it was her. And he had caught sight of the light blue and gold of her dress's hem—the same one she'd worn on the very day they met. He thought it might be her favorite and realized now that he'd never asked her. Now . . . now, most of the gown was ruined by her blood, drenching the entirety of the bodice and midway down the skirt. And she lay in a pool of it. More blood lost than could possibly be survivable. And her face—oh God.

It was like her features were . . . were melting away, blurring before Arthur's eyes. But that couldn't be. It was all wrong, and surely his mind just couldn't handle what he was seeing. He must have cried out though he didn't hear any sound, just a heavy thrumming in his own ears. But Merlin jolted and turned toward Arthur barely long enough to see him there.

"Stay back, Your Majesty!" he shouted with an edge to his voice that Arthur had never heard before.

The words had no sooner cleared his lips than Guinevere's body began to change beneath Merlin's hands. She gave a shiver, and Arthur gasped, lapping up the tiniest drop of hope into his lungs. She was moving. She could be all right. She might—

And then it happened.

In the snap of an instant, her body lost all shape as it melted entirely into dark pink goo, a perfect mixture of the color of flesh and bone and blood. Arthur had seen so much in years of war, but not this. Never this.

He dropped to his knees, all emotion fleeing from him because how—how could a human possibly feel the entirety of what he was witnessing happening to the single person in this world he'd vowed to protect with his very soul? Arthur was left with a dull, encompassing sickness in his gut and a hearty sense of denial as he watched Merlin continue his feverish movement.

She wasn't even a human body anymore. He couldn't imagine what the mage possibly hoped to accomplish. Arthur's eyes stayed transfixed on the gruesome scene as the goo that was once Guinevere started separating into parts, forming into three clumps. There was a strangled yell—it took Arthur a moment to realize it had come from Viviane who, evidently, couldn't quite wrangle a scream from her captive state.

Merlin explained it all to Arthur. Viviane had attacked Guinevere. He was restarting Guinevere. She was going to live. She'd be a baby. She'd regrow to herself in—in another time. It was insanity. It was nonsense, but it was nonsense that he clung to.

Guinevere was still goo, though slightly, disgustingly, strangely more solid (like soft lumps of unshaped clay), when Merlin left with her pieces.

So.

When Merlin returned one week later with Guinevere—alive. Walking. Breathing. Real. It was a miracle.

This time, Arthur would love her well. Everything he'd done wrong before, he would do right.

It started well. Her memories were returning. Merlin's work was effective, and affection was blossoming between she and Arthur—before it promptly fell off a cliff. And then she was dead by Lancelot's hand as Arthur watched and Merlin carted the body away before Arthur even touched her.

The day directly following that disaster, Merlin arrived with yet another alive and fully formed Guinevere. This time, Arthur led with fear, though a sense of hope had taken him. And Merlin. And Lancelot. He could tell they all felt like maybe they'd made it through the worst of it. Guinevere's daily sessions with Merlin had been progressing well, with her memory steadily returning. Arthur and

Guinevere had been ... progressing well. It made him a little bit sick. There was a lot of duty tied up in all of this. But there had been tenderness too. They could be dutiful and tender.

Ugh. She'd been ... eager, even, when they eventually were intimate. That had actually been their best day. She insisted on skipping her session with Merlin, and Arthur cleared his morning to be with her. The time together made Arthur believe that it might all be all right.

But overnight, it shifted. She came back from her next session with a headache. Around midday, it made a subtle turn. It hadn't been so bad, just a little melancholy.

By night, the creeping sadness was so swollen it filled the room.

"Talk to me," Arthur had pleaded. It was all too familiar. And, like before, she'd not given him anything. She'd rolled onto her side, and he listened to her sob as he stared at the ceiling.

Merlin reassured him. He could help. She'd gone to her session with him the next day, like she always did. Arthur came back to their chamber, feeling hopeful, Matilda at his side.

And they opened the door in time to see her standing in the window.

Her eyes were closed as a ray of sun split through the clouds and bathed her face in its glow. There was probably a rainbow out there. Arthur would always remember the way the sun hit her face that morning. She looked beautiful, mostly from the relief he saw in her features as tears rolled down her cheeks. She turned at the noise of their entrance, and the relief fell.

Arthur saw the danger and moved toward her, his hand raised. "Guinevere—"

Without ceremony, she looked away and stepped out the open window. Matilda screamed and fell to the floor. Arthur ran to the window, hearing the crushing thwunk of her body hitting the ground as he mounted the three stairs up to it in one bound. He barely glanced down at her body below the tower, left leg at a strange angle, before he turned and tore out of the room, down the tower stairs, sensation gone from his fingers.

The Once and Future Queen

There were two people standing outside beneath the tower looking on in horror—close enough to see but dumbstruck as Arthur rushed by them. He got to her, ready to check for her pulse, ready to carry her to Merlin, ready to try to save her—

But she was unmoving, and her eyes were open, a tear still clinging to her cheek. She'd landed on her side where blood pooled around her head—she'd hit a rock. He tried not to notice that her head was misshapen, slightly caved in on that side.

He scooped her into his arms and cradled her body close. This was the third time that he'd witnessed her die (well, all but die), and it was the first time he'd been able to hold her body. He sobbed as he clumsily ran with her to Merlin's tower. "I'm sorry. I'm so sorry. I'm so sorry," he whispered into her hair all the way.

Maybe she wasn't so far gone. Maybe. Maybe Merlin could fix it.

He could not.

This time, like the last with Lancelot, she was not far gone, she was dead. But there'd been three lumps of goo that first day. And there was one more Guinevere to be retrieved. Merlin laid his hand on Arthur's shoulder. "The next one will work," he'd said.

"No." Arthur's voice came out in a broken croak. "Leave her be." This was doomed.

Merlin had argued, but Arthur wouldn't hear it. Couldn't hear it. He just kept saying, "No" over and over again.

Merlin finally ended it with a defeated, "We'll talk later."

Arthur left the study. Shivering, which was strange. It wasn't cold. He started up the stairs to their chamber—his chamber—his body quaking so much he found he couldn't move another step forward.

He let his knees fall to the stone beneath him and dropped his hands and head on the stair in front of him. The sound careening from his throat was the keening wail of absolute self-loathing.

They'd all followed him—everyone, all the tribes—into war, into peace, into this kingdom. Being their king had never felt normal even though it had, bafflingly, felt right. He'd led them to becoming a nation. He'd protected people he would never meet.

But he could not protect her, and in his desperation, he'd fled to Merlin once more.

He would regret that decision forever. He should have let those onlookers by the tower see that she was dead. He should have let them know that Guinevere was gone.

If he had, this final version of her could have stayed right where she was and lived a life free from all of this, free from him. Instead, Merlin left this morning and by the time Arthur knew the mage had gone, it was all in motion and entirely unstoppable. He'd had his first cup of wine in his chamber then.

Merlin was retrieving this girl from her life in the future at the last moment before time travel would become impossible again for nearly six months. There'd be no stopping her arrival, and Arthur was to meet them—Merlin and her—in Glastonbury.

Hands trembling, he'd made his way to the Great Hall. Lancelot was there waiting for him (bless him) in his riding clothes.

"Ready?" Lancelot said.

But Arthur couldn't do it. Lancelot went instead, and Arthur stayed in the hall, not in his throne on the dais but on one of the long benches by the lower tables, where he'd drunk more wine than he meant to and kept drinking it out of shame and nerves and defeat. With each cup, the edges dulled, more like being crushed by a smooth boulder than a jagged one. He very rarely drank to excess but found it was birthing a physical ache, a dull sick in his gut—physical pain felt like one tiny morsel of punishment for all he'd set in motion. And physical pain was better than the terror. Horror. Fury. Sorrow of what he knew was coming: he would take her life, too.

She'd be the same as the others.

He should have expressly forbid Merlin from retrieving her rather than what he'd done: perpetually saying, "not yet," leaving a window for exactly what happened today. Having not done that, he should have gone with Lancelot to retrieve her. Arthur was surprised that magic's call on him as king had not fled his blood this past year. None of this was noble kingly behavior.

He reached for the pitcher of wine and filled his goblet again.

Now, it was nearly midnight. Merlin had come back to chide Arthur for staying behind, which devolved to an all-out shouting match, and (once cooler heads prevailed) the mage explained that Guinevere and Lancelot would be along shortly after.

That had been three hours ago. There was no good reason for them to be delayed this much. Arthur's mind shot to worst-case scenarios. Was she already dead? Had she lost her mind straightaway? Had Lancelot been forced to kill her again?

He took another swig from his cup as the door on the far end of the hall opened.

Merlin came in the room, and even with the whole hall's length between them, Arthur instantly saw the relief splayed across the mage's features.

"Fuck," Arthur murmured into his cup, certain this meant she'd arrived. "Is that it, then?" he asked when Merlin was close enough to not require shouting. "Is she here?"

"She is," Merlin said. "Let's go."

He didn't give Arthur an option to discuss it, just turned on his heel and strode away.

Arthur took a long, slow breath before he stood and followed Merlin, his heart raging against the inside of his chest.

He deliberately stared at the floor as he rounded the corner into the entry hall, but he could see the two of them standing there in his periphery. Lancelot.

And her.

When he could avoid looking at her no longer and tipped his eyes up to meet her gaze, Arthur saw that she was afraid, saw the way his harshness landed. It was easy to keep his face contorted in a scowl because all of this was wrong.

It was made worse because... because there was some... brightness there in her. Some spark shining from her that wasn't there before—or that hadn't been allowed to be there before. What would her life be if she could just have it elsewhere?

Merlin's voice pierced through Arthur's thoughts. "It's not unreasonable that remembering His Majesty will take time."

Arthur turned his sights on the mage, heat racing up his spine. Yes, it would take time, time enough for her to lose all the life in her.

"That's not her," he said.

Not her burden. Not her fate to suffer and . . . the last, a plea: that's not the ailing woman whose fate is doomed.

Please. Please, God, please.

Arthur turned and left.

Lancelot found him in the great hall—with the wine again. The knight ignored the available bench and dragged a chair over, poured himself a goblet of wine, and sat down. Then, elbows on his knees, holding the cup between them, he stared at Arthur.

Arthur hoped Lancelot would tell him about her. Despite all his misgivings, he was curious. He didn't want to own that. He didn't want to have any interest in her, and Lancelot knew that.

"I'm not going to do this again," Arthur said after a long stretch of silence.

Lancelot watched him and let the quiet have another moment before he broke it with a heavy sigh as he leaned back in his chair. "She's very different. Good different."

Arthur bristled. He resented the notion there'd been something deficient in her before. She'd been hurting. But she'd also taken on more than anyone should. And she'd endured more. He'd seen awful deaths in battle, yes, but she'd seen her share of trauma, too. She'd watched her own mother die.

"Well, father says I was there, but I don't remember it. You can't be hurt by something you don't remember," she'd told him. And she'd smiled when she said it, which was the final tell that it was something that made her very sad to say. And he was quite certain she was wrong too. He was quite certain her wounds were so deep she'd convinced herself they didn't exist.

But.

Different. Good different. This time, he couldn't resist the temptation. "How so?"

Lancelot's lips tilted nearly imperceptibly up, and Arthur knew he was pleased that he'd gotten what he hoped for: enough interest from Arthur to continue the conversation. "She likes me, for one." Lancelot's smile broadened.

"Really?" Arthur colored his tone with disbelief and quirked an eyebrow, surprising himself by indulging the levity, but more so that Lancelot's instinct to show up for Guinevere had been a good one. Maybe, in a turn none of them could have guessed, Lancelot had been what she needed all along.

"She does," Lancelot said proudly. "And she'd just left her whole world behind. Everything, Arthur. And she still seemed happy. Not thrilled by the circumstances, obviously. But different from the others. It's not just wishful thinking, I know it. I just . . . I know it."

Arthur's muscles had relaxed. He realized he was no longer clenching his jaw. But this woman being different didn't fix anything. "That's all the more reason I should stay away."

Lancelot sighed. "She's going to need your help, Your Majesty."

"Don't call me that," Arthur said. He'd never gotten used to hearing the formal title from his oldest friend, and it landed heavy, especially now. "I tried to help the others. It ended poorly."

"I know." This, his friend offered more gently. "So maybe you do it different this time. Maybe you tell her."

"Tell her?"

"Yes." Lancelot's eyes lit as he took a long drink, emptying his cup. "Tell her about the others. Tell her all of it."

Everything in Arthur jolted like he'd been knocked sideways. "Are you mad? That's the surest way to damn her. Merlin said—"

"I know what he said. It doesn't mean he's right." He turned the cup in his hands, seeming to study it for a long moment. "She's going to need you."

Arthur raised an eyebrow at him. Lancelot's instincts were unmatched, and Arthur trusted him implicitly—but in this matter, Arthur could not trust himself. "I can't help her."

Lancelot scoffed. "What is she supposed to do? She'll need someone who isn't Merlin. He'll be gone half the time anyway."

"She'll have you. I'll stay as far from her as I can."

Lancelot shook his head as he released a long breath through his nostrils. "It's a mistake, Your Majesty."

"Stop calling me that." Arthur drained his own cup and set it down on the table harder than he meant to. Nearly slammed it, really.

"You're still king, Arthur," Lancelot said softly. "Even when you're feeling ashamed. And when you're three sheets to the wind. You're still my king. You're still her king." He took the pitcher and refilled Arthur's cup and then his own. "If you think staying away will protect her, I'll try it. Nothing else has worked."

He wasn't sure of anything, but Lancelot had gotten her safely here. Lancelot had been a friend to her and—Arthur blinked. "Did you just leave her out there?"

"Yes." Lancelot rolled his eyes. "Shut up. So did you." He wasn't wrong. "Merlin's out there. She's fine. She knows how to hold her own." He gave a lopsided grin, and his eyes glimmered.

"You really like her," Arthur said.

"Very much. And you will too."

Arthur's insides lurched, but he nodded.

"I'm going to bed. You should too." Lancelot took one last swig from his cup before he stood. "You don't sleep enough."

Arthur huffed. "I'm not the one running through the woods before daybreak."

Lancelot grinned, tilting his head to the side. He looked like he swallowed something he'd thought to say and started to leave.

But Arthur couldn't resist. "What?"

Lancelot turned back quickly and sat back down in his chair. "She runs, mate. Brought shoes with her—snuck them in her bag. She laughs really easily." He raised his eyebrows with a chuckle. "And she curses rather a lot."

Arthur smiled at that. "Curses? Well. That's not Guinevere."

"Maybe not." Lancelot clicked his tongue. "Maybe that's a good thing. But I like her, and I trust her."

Arthur liked the sound of all that. And he had a mission: Stay away. Keep this woman alive. Get her back home, so she could live her life. "We've got to get her through six months without . . ."

Without me destroying her.

Lancelot nodded. "And the memories?"

"If Merlin can help her recover them, fine. Otherwise, sod it. This is our mess, not hers. We're on our own." Arthur raised his cup to Lancelot. "And you'll take care of her?"

Lancelot tapped his drink against his king's. "With my life, Arthur."

Arthur had climbed the stairs and entered his chamber without even thinking that she would be there. He'd grown so used to coming to this room alone, and his mind was still foggy from the wine. But as he turned into the room after locking the door, he saw her right away—in the center of his field of vision, seated on the foot of the bed. Fuck. Of course she was there. Where else would she be?

She stood up quickly, her eyes wide and desperate and fingers pressing hard into the book she held. He'd seen expressions so like this one on Guinevere's face, and the panic that rose stole Arthur's breath. All he could manage to do was set his jaw and stare at the wardrobe.

Just get there. Get to the wardrobe. Get clothing. Leave her be.

But when he stepped in her direction, she flinched away. He wanted her to stay away from him—not fear for her bodily safety in his presence. He needed her to know that he she need not fear . . . assault from him.

Fuck. This was awful.

"I'm not going to hurt you." He had to force his vocal cords to function.

He skirted a deliberate and wide path around her. As he dug through the wardrobe for the clothing he'd wear in the morning, he was certain he could feel her eyes on his back as goosebumps rose along his spine. Maybe he imagined that.

He wanted to turn around. He wanted desperately to talk to her, to ask her questions, to see what Lancelot had seen. Feel the assurance that she was living this happier life, but all of that was selfish, and he would not yield to it.

God. There was no way he'd sleep tonight. All right. He'd stop at the desk and grab The Hobbit. Something to read would inevitably help. What better than a grand adventure written for children?

But when he got to the desk, it wasn't there. Maybe he'd left it somewhere, but . . . wait. She'd had a book in her hands, hadn't she?

He turned, eyes darting to the tome. Now that he was looking, he recognized it as The Hobbit. Something warmed in him that it was the book she'd selected, and an alarming jolt of affection rushed through him. Almost instantly, she'd clocked his eyes on the book and offered it to him. A pang rattled in Arthur's gut. She didn't understand.

"They're yours," he said. "Merlin brought them. He thought they might comfort you." Her eyes still shone with fear, but they searched him with curiosity too, that spark breaking through . . . No. Not good. He shifted his gaze to her shoulder. He wanted to stare at her, to know her. Don't do that.

If she came to him, afraid and seeking comfort, he'd want to give it. He'd want to be there for her. He'd want to help her.

And it would all come to the same end. This woman who'd somehow found a way to claim the vibrance that had thwarted Guinevere would die like the rest.

No. He turned to the door to the side chamber. He was leaving. He. Was. Leaving.

But then she said one word. "Arthur?" Her voice, Guinevere's voice, said his name. It disgusted him that he took pleasure in that.

Then she asked the questions he should have thought to answer. Could she drink the water? How would she turn off the light?

What would his mother say about what a cad he'd been?

The least he could do was provide some simple instructions about how she might be comfortable. He didn't look at her. He didn't offer anything extra. He adopted the focused demeaner of negotiating a peace treaty and kept his face carefully blank.

And then he lay in bed, eyes on the ceiling, except when they darted to the crack beneath the door. Her light was still lit.

An hour passed.

It was still lit.

Two hours. Three.

Shit.

Fuck. Maybe Lancelot was right. Maybe this was worse, and he should talk to her. He'd never been this riddled with uncertainty in all his life.

He opened the door as quietly as he could. "Guinevere?" It was barely loud enough to be a whisper.

Silence answered. The panic that she was dead was immediate—irrational, but not—and he rushed to her side. She lay still, lifeless. He knelt, ready to give her a frantic shake, but he made himself wait and watch with his hand poised over her shoulder.

Her chest rose and fell steadily.

Then Arthur realized—she was sleeping on the side he always used to sleep on. The others hadn't done that either. Her fingers still rested in the book, marking her page. Her arms and legs were both curled in close.

She was cold.

Very carefully, he slid the book from beneath her fingers and, not wanting to lose her page, found a scrap of parchment from his desk to tuck into it before he closed it on the table. She was on top of the blankets on the bed, so he went to the chest and drew out another and laid that over her, gingerly pulling it up to her shoulders.

Before he had a moment to think better of it, Arthur reached down and tucked a few stray hairs behind her ear. She did not stir. Her breath did not change. But her furrowed brow smoothed and for one fleeting moment, a soft smile rose on her lips.

Arthur was so stunned that he sunk down on one knee to be at eye level with her sleeping face. It had been so quick, but she had smiled. He was sure of it. And the crease between her brows had not returned.

His lips tugged up at the corners as he watched her because, just now, she did look a little bit . . . happy.

He decided right there, kneeling on the floor at her side: this was what he would do. Arthur would care for her in every quiet, invisible way he could find. He'd watch what brought her delight and silently deliver it. He'd notice what released the tension from her shoulders and shift castle life to bring that peace.

He rose, went to the opposite side of the bed, and lowered the light before he retreated to his room. Though he knew better than to think it anything other than a coincidence, he could not shake the whisper of hope that she had smiled at his touch.

Or perhaps it was merely wishful thinking.

Acknowledgments

This book exists because of a long line of support, care, and magic. I could lay out pages of gratitude, but I'll do my best to rein it in. From the bottom of my heart, thank you—to Mike, who didn't know he taught me how to build the muscle of persistence necessary to write a book, and to Lochlyn, who is the smartest and most creative person I know and who inspires me with stories every single day.

To my family, especially Dad & Deb, Erin & Kyle (and the boys!), and Mom, who watched my starry-eyed delusions and said, "Go!"

To a wide crew of beloved friends: The Twelve and their endless alpha reading, proofing, and encouragement, The MoonBass crew, the Saturday Coffee Club, The Beavers, the staff and community of Peace Church KC, and The Incomparables. To Melissa Reynolds, who taught me how to try, succeed, and fail at scary things. To Larry Ivy, who brought me as an intern on the great adventure that planted the seed for this book.

To Ceva Jill Story & Michael Moore for being my ride or dies.

To the big Guinevere team: the artists who made this book beautiful—Niall Grant, Aftyn Shah, Chaim Holtjer, and Paige Dainty, to Andrew and the Merrick Books community, Mackenzie Walton, Taryn Fagerness, who did the most in getting this book out in the wide world, Julia Whelan, who saw me on the internet, took a chance on my manuscript, and leant Vera her voice, Geof Prysirr, whose artistic precision in audio editing is even more impressive than his grilling prowess (which is saying quite a lot), the Hodderscape team, and finally to Alex Sunshine (the editor with the single greatest name) and the many good folks at Kensington for inviting Vera's story and me into a whole new world of opportunities.

To so many authors who lowered ladders and pulled me up, and last, but certainly not least: to the remarkable book communities of Instagram and TikTok, who gave me the courage to take wild leaps.

Author Bio

Paula Lafferty lives in the Kansas City area with her husband, daughter, and Otto (the sweetest dog there ever was). She received a BFA in Film Production from Chapman University and a Master of Divinity from Saint Paul School of Theology. She has a taste for finding magic in "the ordinary" and a spark for discovering stories at every turn. Telling stories is the thread that runs through Paula's life, and The Once and Future Queen is her debut novel which she originally funded through a hugely successful Kickstarter campaign.

HODDERSCAPE

WANT MORE HODDERSCAPE?
JOIN US!

Sign up to our mailing list to get exclusive early sneak peeks and offers:

Follow us on our social channels:
@hodderscape

Buy our books, find out more, and discover exclusive content:
www.hodderscape.co.uk